BLOOD 20
TALES OF VAMPIRE HORROR

BLOOD 20
TALES OF VAMPIRE HORROR

Tanith Lee

Published in 2015 by Telos Moonrise: Dark Endeavours
(An imprint of Telos Publishing)
5A Church Road, Shortlands, Bromley, Kent BR2 0HP, UK

www.telos.co.uk

Telos Publishing Ltd values feedback. Please e-mail us with any comments
you may have about this book to: feedback@telos.co.uk

Blood 20: Tales of Vampire Horror © 2015 Tanith Lee
Please also see the individual story copyright details at the end of the book.

Cover Art © 2015 Iain Robertson
Cover Design: David J Howe
Internal illustrations: © 2015 Carolyn Edwards

ISBN: 978-1-84583-909-3

The moral right of the author has been asserted.

British Library Cataloguing in Publication Data. A catalogue record for this
book is available from the British Library.

CONTENTS

ON REFLECTION

The patrol had been that way before. They had even once stopped at the well, to drink and to water their horses. This time the well was in a bad state. Part of its stony shell had collapsed into the shaft, fouling the water, leaving the opening wide to the dusts, and making it difficult of access, however desperate the visitor. This well though had always been vulnerable, and besides often missed by travellers – since not a single tree any longer grew there, not even a straggly shrub. Laurus had asked Corbo if he thought the Madmen had vandalised the well purposely. Corbo thought it possible, but unlikely. Even the Madmen would surely stick to that oldest code of the desert peoples: to damage a water-source, whatever the excuse, was a crime beyond forgiveness.

He would remember, after, that a slender golden lizard darted suddenly across the path of his horse. Battle-trained, the animal did not shy. It was an omen, perhaps, but he had missed it.

There was an added reason for that, of course.

They decided against sampling the well water. Instead a couple of the men marked its broken shell in chalk with the large warning shapes of the *Caveat*. It was not, for the column, a major difficulty. They had their water flasks, and besides, the fort and its attendant township were now less than twenty miles off. They should be there by sundown.

It was only as they rode away over the first up-sweep of a hill that Corbo became aware – almost as if, until then, something had hidden it from him – that the seal-ring had vanished from his right hand.

The ring had been his father's, and he valued it. It bore the family crest of the black Crow, bedded in agate.

Marcus Scorpius Corbo trotted his horse aside, and gave the lead of the column to the reliable Laurus. 'I have to go back – one further thing I need to be sure of.'

'Very well, sir.'

'It's not even a mile. I'll be with you again shortly.'

He would, Corbo, later remember too those words, those *ominous* words. *I will be with you. I.*

The gods maybe had tried to show him. But then, the gods also should respect his care of his father's memory and goods. When the Tablet had been written, the Eastern mages said, none could unwrite it.

Corbo rode back down the slope to the wreck of the well.

He saw swiftly now that a smallish animal seemed to have been burrowing about the well. He had not noted this before in the immediate churning up of the sand by the hoofs of the patrol's horses.

Corbo's heart sank. Had the creature, some rat or other desert beast, since come up after the ring, carried it away and down?

He dismounted, and unwillingly and superficially at first began to kick the sand about. Then – a glint of something caught the westering sun. Corbo knelt. He scuffed the dune over, more lightly, with one hand. Something hard lay under the surface.

Next moment he had uncovered some portion of a piece that was unlike anything he had ever, in his life so far, encountered. What was it? Metal? No – nothing so uncomplex. Nor was it so small. Certainly no seal-ring, this. Going more cautiously than ever, he brushed off the grains with his fingers, which were scarred and hardened and numbed by the calluses of his work: a legionary officer of what, by now, was known here in the Exterra as the Crow Battalion.

As he revealed then lifted free his discovery, Corbo was blinded a second by the sun-struck flash it gave. Then it lay there, balanced on his hand, an indecipherable object. It was filthy mostly, some extra disguise, the accretions of sand, damp from the nearness of the well, baking by heat, the mess of things that had decayed across it – the defecations, blood, demises of little animals, insects, and of time itself. But under the muck, in patches, was an extraordinary, never-before-witnessed by the onlooker, glacial yet metallic gleam – ice and steel, and the sword's edge. It was in shape completely and, as seemed, perfectly, round. Like the full moon in a clear sky.

Corbo put down the moon-thing. And then noticed that his seal-ring, obvious as a visual shout, was lying about four arm-lengths off, glinting reproachfully black and gold. Only one blind, surely, would not have seen it until then.

He had an urge to leave the other thing behind. Even to cover it over again. But that was superstitious unwisdom. He had a sense it was worth something, and also a partial idea as of what, incredibly, it might really be.

And so, standing up, the ring safe again on his finger – how had it come off?; it was firm enough that replacing it had taken some work – he stuffed what else he had found in his satchel. Re-fastening the straps, he was already thinking, in an odd mixture of idleness and irresistible lust, of Yeila.

Arida: the fortress, and the straggle of half-born town. Like its name, this place in the low hills above the desert plains, was a country neither fertile nor in any way, other than strategic, valuable. That value nevertheless persisted, and sharply. Among these sparse and shallow water-courses, these stunted groves, the fort kept itself alert.

The name the local Romans had chosen for those desert tribesmen who had recently risen in the south was the *Vecordia* – the Insanity – the 'Madmen'. Their own name for themselves was apparently the Elect of the Gods. They had come at first, it seemed, from nowhere, like a stultifying mist, overwhelming, obscuring, even often vanishing with little trace. Aside, that was, from the mutilated corpses, human and beast, and the burned and hacked masonry ruins left behind. Any not of their own, sworn to their law and their specialised deities, the Madmen would eradicate. While they themselves fought, so the stories had it, without fear, regardless of injury or death. Such as their inimical kind had, inevitably, come and gone, in the past. But now Rome's long-reaching might, her infallible arm, had weakened.

Rome had become remote. Who among her legions, at such far-flung outposts as Arida, did not now know? The Mother of Cities was sinking like a sun. There could, no longer, be any help expected of her. And all over the wide, wild world of the Empire, her orphaned citizens, her armies, once themselves the Elite of the Earth, maintained her rule, and their personal lives, merely as best they could.

The desert's own sun was almost gone too, when the column reached the town of Arida. The last miles to her gates had taken longer than expected. They had encountered a small procession of refugees from elsewhere. Fearful of the Madmen, they had left their village and gathered themselves in toward the fort. Women and children, and carts of belongings, and goats bleating. It was the men who wept. Save one man, more a westerner, Corbo thought him, brown as a nut, and with a look of purpose … They crowded the gate. The patrol cursed quietly, longing for shade and wine.

All this was virtually forgotten now, however, as Corbo stood alone in the presence of his Commander, and made his report of the patrol; things seen, or *not* seen, evidence of the elusive yet concrete enemy. Of which anyway, it turned out now, the Commander already had extra information.

'They have occupied Aquaelis. You saw the refugees? The messenger was just ahead of them. He might almost have crossed your path, and left for you blood-stained hoof prints in the sand. Aquaelis has not been razed, it seems. But most of its occupants, including the Roman garrison, were slaughtered, just a few taken for slaves – most of those blinded, crippled, their tongues cut out, genitals cut off.' Julusarus cursed, controlled himself, and downed his wine. 'We know, don't we, Marcus, that any foul Madmen's nest should be scoured out to its bones, before they can spread their bloody claws any farther. We don't want them in Aquaelis, let alone coming on here. And we Sons of Empire move fast. So, we must move fast. Eh, Marcus?'

'Yes, sir.'

'It's only – *how*, by Pater Martis' fiery Spear? Their numbers are, allegedly, impressive. Their stealth, if not organisation, remarkable. But no. That won't do. We are the Legions. What's left of us. So, we must move, act – we must *win*.'

The fort Commander Julusarus paced back and forth through the bleak stony room. Here and there a sword, a pilum, a saddle, hung on the wall. A lamp, unlit, stood on a table, and the unfull wine flagon. In the three western windows, unglazed and hollow as air, any red sun-blood had all but seeped away, down into Hades' own blue night. A dog or two howled lamentingly in the town below. A bird whirred by a window, crow-black. One more omen, and flying the wrong way; right to left.

'Go get yourself some food, Marcus. Get some rest. You've been on the road some while. We'll meet tomorrow.'

Corbo saluted. As he left the room, Julusarus was swearing again, bellowing for a slave to light the lamp. Probably to fill up the flagon, too.

Corbo ate in the mess, with his men and the others present. The place was alight with chat of the latest Vecordia incursion.

There was a mood of anger, impatience, and doubt. The messenger had relayed information that, conceivably, a full thousand of the Madmen were in Aquaelis. Until then it had been filled by Roman officials, ex-patriots, or affiliated locals who had bloomed into Roman ways, as generally all, or most other peoples did. What needed resistance, after all? You could even keep your own gods, provided you were respectful to those of the incomers. Aside from that, the rule of Roman law was effective, and there were too games and festivals, a theatre perhaps, baths and public latrines, a system for feeding those in need, and elevating those who earned it. But despite this, rebellion, when it flared, would always break in horrid extremis. Remember, some muttered, the mad sorceress-queen Woadica in the Tin Isles, or the fanatics of Hierosolyma. Back then, however, Roma, stronger than lions, had stamped upon dissention with a giant's boot.

Tonight, these frustrated debates and fears and militancies irritated Corbo. Though he concealed his mood, he soon went to the old bathhouse. This building was past its best also, but the decrepit slave boiled him up the decrepit hypocaust enough so he could get clean. None of the rest of the fort, it seemed, often bothered. But then, Corbo meant to see Yeila tonight.

Before that, though, he must go to his own cell and clean the moon.

When he entered the cramped space, he felt a curious kind of pressure, as it seemed on the air, like that of an approaching storm. It must be his sexual desire, building for the evening ahead. He had no qualms she would not welcome him. She was, after all, favoured, whatever her looks or skill, to receive the custom of a Battalion Leader from the fort.

He lit the lamp himself, and sitting down, undid the satchel. The moon-thing from the well slid outward, and he turned it instantly to face the lamplight. And with an oiled and a dry rag, some salt, a splash of wine, he began to clean the face of the object. The dirt started at once to slough off, in chunks, and then in slimes. Beneath, against his hand, a strange, almost malleable smoothness resulted. Corbo, during this procedure, looked at the thing only indirectly. That seemed, although he did not ask himself why, the surest way properly to attend to it. Inside what would have been half an hour, by the ancient water-clock in the mess that no longer functioned, the surface of his find had come clear, gleaming and blazing back the ray of the smoky lamp.

By then Corbo knew exactly what it was he had found. Really, from the first, he had guessed. Yet not believed it. Elsewhere, in the sophisticated Roman provinces, he had seen many mirrors in the homes of the wealthy. They were fashioned of metal, normally bronze, very occasionally silver. They gave a fascinating impression of the person who stood or sat down before them and stared to see their own resemblance. But there was, of course, often great distortion – a flaw in the metal, the wear and tear of a life of burnishing. Old rich women, he had heard, and some old rich men, preferred this kind of an image, slightly fuzzed and gauzed, to the sudden vivid jolt they might observe, say, in a black bowl filled by clean still water. Once or twice, though, Corbo had heard of another type of mirror, in the East, these used mostly by mages or tricksters. Such a mirror had a face of glass, and could reflect with this accordingly the face of man or woman, and so flawlessly it might drive them mad, unless they took care with it, or were, too, extremely young, and beautiful.

Which, it went without saying, and despite her trade, the Romanised Eastern Yeila was.

Now however Corbo himself must glance, if quickly, in the mirror, and check the surface of it, both for its refreshed material and for any flaws.

He took it up, its countenance yet turned away, and fully to the lamp. How the light was strengthened! The room seemed to blaze from torches. As for its shiny carapace, this priceless beetle from the dunes was pure and whole.

He might, therefore, why not, just slide it back into the satchel? No. Before doing that, he had better also be sure of the frame of it.

Corbo lifted the mirror up. Round as the moon, the rim was also smooth and solid, but narrow as a woman's smallest finger. Ivory, he thought, that had turned dark brown with age and wear and ill-use, but had stayed mellifluous to touch as a lovely skin …

Well, but best be certain that the image it relayed, at least, made sense. Could there be some terrible inner fissure, unfelt but monstrously distorting whatever looked in it? That would spoil his gift for Yeila.

He was most reluctant to do this last prudent thing. Since to check it that way, he, Marcus Scorpius Corbo, really must, himself, if only for the fraction of an instant, look into the glowing, lake-like, moon-like orb. The dragon's eye.

Ah. He had, almost unthinkingly, turned it back to him, without quite realising –

And there – *there* – there he was. A man. Not Corbo. Of course, how could it be he? A stranger – a youngish man, still dark, his black hair and olive skin – familiar in fact from visual traffic with the rest of his own body – torso, arms, legs –

No, he could not see himself properly, anyway. The flame of the lamp had slopped, and tilted a little, was smoking worse. The reflection was of a shadow, a shadow of – some man.

Corbo sat still and silent now, transfixed. As if the Gorgon herself had peered out from this magic and impossible glass. Not a total paralysis to stone. Very nearly.

These eyes – are – *mine*.

That mouth – *mine*.

That is the *face* – the *mask* – the *self* I have *lived* within, *behind, aside from*, all this while. Other men I know, by their appearance, as well as the brothers of my youth. But not myself. Never – me.

I, Corbo.

I.

I am *there* –

And then a sensation passed over Marcus Scorpius Corbo, peculiar and unnerving as finding abruptly the floor gave way beneath, and he stared down into an emptiness of unknown distance and otherness.

He felt and saw the blood smear vaguely over his eyes, dimming them, as in that awful time when he had fainted from loss of such blood after the fight at Goria. But the darkening faded, it went away. And now his eyes were open wide, and clear, themselves, as a razor's edge, or the edge of a polished mirror.

He must have blinked. Or had he, like a total fool, slumped asleep, in the manner of some elderly watchman after bread and beer.

At least, he had not dropped the bloody mirror.

Odd – something odd – he was now *no longer* visible in it – or – it had only swerved a little to one side. It reflected instead, again, the lamp, although from a different angle, enhancing its ray into a sun blast.

The mirror was perfection.

All was well.

He must get up now, and seek out his pretty whore. The Lion Star was already high in the east, he could see it through the window-slit, over the walls of Arida.

Corbo rose to his feet. Then everything seemed to shatter, glittering, away. But next everything was once more where it needed to be, the earth firm, the night open. No time to waste. Mirrors were the toys of women, and idiots.

He strode from the room, down through the fort, and out by the Lamb Gate into the darkling town below.

How dark the streets were. Few stars, but for the Lion, no moon, he thought, till later, and she would be thin as a bone.

As a rule, the square below the fort, and the sloping road to and from its walls, were lit by burning brands. Tonight some had gone out, or been missed. While either side of the main path, few lights showed; most of the living premises were to the back, only the occasional tiny window, or signalling lamp in the doorway of a drinking shop. But the general sense he had of the town was of something muffled in a dense black veil.

Not many were ever abroad by night. The odd thief, probably, slinking through the back alleys, a stray dog or hunting cat or two on its own business. The general whores kept sensibly to their own group-houses, with guards on hand.

There was little sound either. It seemed to Corbo the night was pressing close and closer. Yet he moved freely in it, knowing, and able to decipher the way.

When he reached the corner where Yeila had her apartment above a baker's, and he had walked up the brief familiar outer stair, he found her window rather better lighted.

Then he paused, and stood in darkness, looking in, as if into another mirror, this one of pale amber. And there she was, beautiful as some exotic creature not quite mortal: the cloud of her loose black hair with its hint of red-copper, her long-lidded, slightly slanted eyes of a silken fawn shade, in colour most like the shell of some fabulous tortoise ... She was dressed in her finery, with combs and necklaces, bracelets and anklets; and about her in the small, oblong, almost luxurious room, things had been made ready to entertain a valued guest. As he had supposed, she was expecting him. The news would have been brought to her at sunset of his return to Arida.

The lowest, softest lamplight, perfumed no doubt with myrrh and olibanum, eddied in the chamber, like the gentle currents of a calm lake. Her skin, a little tawnier than his, so caressable, so smooth, bathed and depilated, creamed, scented for his hands, his limbs, the two organs of his hunger, mouth and loins. Even stood outside in the night, he felt his body swim and centre against hers, could taste her hair, the ripe berry she would leave for him to eat from her navel.

After watching her a while he noted, neither aggravated or amused, the slight impatience growing in her gestures. She had begun to stray about the room, picking up, tossing back the cushions of dyed Eastern silk into new and less studied patterns.

He was late. Almost moonrise. She must realise, maybe, the business of the fort had delayed him: the Madmen at Aquae.

But Corbo did not shift. He did not go to the side door. Did not even tap on the lattice that fragilely guarded the lower half of the window. He stood outside, in night, and night covered and hid him. If she looked outward – she had, and see, now and then did so again – plainly she did not perceive him there. His eyes had been filled with darkness. He *was* the dark. Invisible. In a minute more, or possibly rather longer – she had lain down by then on a couch, drinking the iced and honeyed wine, having kicked off her sandals with the serpent heads – Corbo had grasped that he would not, after all, be going in to visit her. He would not be giving her the magic mirror, even though he had taken, cleaned and brought it with him for that purpose.

As he turned away, it seemed to him he had grown twice his own not insignificant height. Tall as a house-roof, perhaps, his feet upon the dark, his eyes shining with the dark, darkness upon and within him.

He could see himself for a second, definite as he had seen Yeila in her room. And he was as the mirror had shown him, unknown, a stranger, a *shadow*.

When the man jumped him next, in the alley, Corbo was not startled.

What might have startled him, although he only thought this after, was his total preparedness and consequent reaction.

Corbo was, evidently, a trained soldier. He had been attacked countlessly and in myriad ways. It was not that. It was as if – as if he himself, somehow, enticed the attack. So that in the first flicker of impact, he was already springing about.

Without recourse to a weapon, let alone a verbal challenge, he flung the hefty man back and downward, smashing his head against the nearest flinty wall. Then Corbo, a legionary and officer, knelt on his groaning, palpitating body, and with his own sharp Roman teeth, took out the bastard's throat.

The blood shone black as liquid night, as the River of the Underland. It tasted meat-thick, and salt, and sweet, familiar as wine or milk or oil. He gulped it down and down. And as he drank, every physical apparatus of his body shone within as if with cores of fire. His lungs expanded like the opened wings of an eagle, his ears opened to every littlest sound and whisper, his heart slowed to a strong and marvellous beat. Even his sexual blade unsheathed and rose up to its fullest stamina – yet not as if in actual desire, more as if it flexed itself in a rare, luxurious, undemanding pleasure of power and pride.

When he had finished drinking, and it did not take so long, Corbo was well aware he had emptied his assailant. There was not a drop of blood left in him, and his wilted corpse, dead as anything left sliced upon a battlefield, statically flopped on the stones and earth, with its huge, popping eyes still blindly glaring.

The slim moon was going over now, and cruelly sparkled them, but Corbo, unconcerned, walked quiet and steady on, up the incline to the Lamb Gate of the fort.

Old Sato let him in.

'A peaceful night, sir,' said Sato. 'I reckon we must make the most of such, before the filthy Madmen come.'

And Corbo nodded, and gave him a coin, and went up, in the usual manner, to his pallet and sleep.

In the morning, Sato was apparently also waiting for Corbo below.

Corbo was puzzled by this. What did the old man want?

But the morning itself seemed puzzling, in the oddest fashion. The brightness of the sun, which appeared to flatten out the sky to an opaque pane; the annoying movement of sunbeams; it was as if he had never seen them before, or not properly. At first, mere light stung his eyes. Obviously he had drunk too much last night – except, when had that happened? He had meant to visit Yeila, he recalled, but for some reason had turned back. And there had been, had there not, some sort of altercation with a rough in an alley – which was itself curious enough. Not many men tried to insult or assault soldiers of the Legion, who were so dangerously able to defend themselves, and to hit back. And even in the casual wear of the fort, who did not know how a Roman legionary looked?

Dressed and tidied, Corbo went down to the lower hall where Sato, off duty now, was idling.

'What is it?'

'Leader Corbo, there's a man at the Courtyard Gate. Says he must see you. He gave me quite a nice bribe, so I tell you this.'

Ever-honest Sato! Corbo smiled, and decided to go at once and learn what went on. Certainly he had no appetite for breakfast, felt even rather feverish as he crossed the lower court and the full sun swiped his body. Yet then the discomfort seemed to ebb away as confusingly as it had slammed into him.

By the time he reached the gate-yard all was well with Corbo. Though he was racking his brains as to what he had done – said – got involved in – the previous evening.

The instant he saw the man, who was leaning back in the deep shade of a wall, a fold of his ragged cloak pulled over his head as if to shield him, Corbo remembered.

He stopped dead. The world splintered in pieces and fell. As it had … last night. Through a hailstorm of flying visual shards and sparks he gaped at the attacker who, at moonrise in the alley, he had bested, battered, and drunk dead to the dregs.

Forty days later, inside the oasis of Erum, he and Slinger, rather than stand transfixed in terrified fury and disbelief, would sit eating dates and drinking a little harsh sour wine. The military strategy by then was established and, unusually, everybody of one consenting and eager mind. They were less men on the evening-dawn of battle than hounds, acute and able, and lacking all sentiment. Just starving enough to be looking forward: to nightfall. Just human enough still to revel in their gods-given luck.

All that, however, was to come.

Those first few moments in the courtyard at Arida, Slinger and Corbo were neither comrades nor co-conspirators. Each man stared at the other and his world – quite literally visually in Corbo's case – fell apart. Metamorphosis, as any god, or god's victim, might tell you, was not always the happiest phase of a man's life.

'I – killed you,' Corbo stated, finally. 'Or I was mistaken.'

'No,' grumbled the man, who soon enough would say his name was Slinger. 'You surely did. But you don't, do you, puffed shit of a Roman officer, know how. Or –' he broke off as Corbo, able to see once more, strode over to him and slapped him hard across the face.

Unusually, at such a blow, the man-who-was-Slinger did not drop on the ground. He swayed, righted himself, and said, 'If I don't geta drop of what you took off me last night, I shall puke. And I'll make sure it'll be all across your damned soldier-sandals.'

Corbo stared. 'You want money? You jumped me to rob me. I took care of you. The jail is the place for you –'

'Oh no it's not. And you *know* it's not. *Wake up. I* know what's gone on. Are you, you educated lad, such a slosh-head?'

Corbo could not get his bearings. He stretched out his hand – to render another blow, or only to grab the fellow. But instead Slinger seized his wrist. Lowering his head, he bit deep into Corbo's muscular wrist, before Corbo could even guess – or violently respond.

And another startlement then. Corbo did not resist. He stood there patiently with the stranger, in the shade of the wall. And when one of the sentries called down the wall-walk to him, the man being unable to discern details, and less in unease than mere nosiness, Corbo called back, off-handedly, 'No matter, Gaius. Just fort business.'

A minute after, he pushed Slinger off him, and Slinger withdrew meekly enough, wiping his red mouth on one gruesome sleeve. Corbo looked at the wound of teeth. It was already shut. He suspected the marks he himself had scored in Slinger's throat would leave more enduring evidence.

Had that hurt him? This bite had not hurt Corbo.

'That's better,' mumbled Slinger. 'But you owed me.'

'Very well.' Corbo surrendered. 'What in the Name of Everlasting Jupiter is going on?'

It was insane, all of this. Madder than the antics of the Madmen. How bizarre that, as it transpired, in this at least there were answers.

Slinger's head resembled an egg. The high brown bald smooth dome, and rounded face beneath, blending into the short tough neck, and so to the stocky, muscular body. All of him was tanned, hardened. A scar like a thin faint river-course traced the back of his skull. No leftover from the blow in the alley. But on his throat, as Corbo had predicted, and later beheld, that attack showed as a cicatrice upraised, blue-white and absolute as a piece of tribal scarring.

His race was mixed, and with some Roman, Slinger said. Why disbelieve that? It was true of half the civilised world, what was left of it. And his black eyes, narrow and humorous, had, he declared, eyesight to rival that of Apollo. Hence his former trade: a slinger with the ramshackle armies, also partly indigenous, partly Roman, that straggled now around the periphery of everywhere. There had been also one famous slinger, Slinger told Corbo later, on some other evening: David, who slew a giant with a single stone and so became a king. But Slinger himself was thrown on hard times. He had trekked to Arida, hoping to enlist with the battalions, as a messenger, even as a pot-boy, a scout. No-one had wanted him. And so, belly empty and heart soured, he had turned to crime. And who had he picked to rob? A new-made demon.

'But *your* luck was in, my sir. You had no idea what went on. But *I*, I did and do. You found a mirror, you say, of real glass, sheer and unclouded, and it reflected you! By the God of the Wilderness – that mirror you have is a succubus. In you looked, and saw yourself reflected there. And the mirror in turn saw *you* – and it *ate your soul*! Yes, my friend, so sorry, but your soul is *gone*. It sucked it from you, with your likeness in the glass. Which is why you'll never reflect in any surface ever again. As nor will I, since you despoiled me too of that soul that was mine.'

Corbo had sat by then with his head in his hands. Useless to deny, however crazed and stupid all this sounded, seemed. He knew, he knew that it was the truth. As if he had never realised before that he was a mortal man, and some sage had told him. Save now he was man no more. He was – *this. This.*

They were in a wine shop off the Street of Birds.

Nobody disturbed them.

Corbo, or his rank, was generally recognised, and Slinger – it must be – was therefore assumed to be some useful runner or spy, in deep converse with him.

'One thing,' Slinger added then, sprightly as a vindictive maiden Corbo had insulted. 'Next time you need to fill up with fresh blood – and you will, if only to endure the sunlight – don't drain your prey. Leave them alive, they'll recover, or so the old texts say. Or, if you *do* kill, you must lop off the head, and maybe burn it, and the body, for good measure. No, don't wince, my son. This lesson is for your own good. How many more of *my* type do you want, after all, elegant Leader, trotting after you for a drop of *aqua vitae*?'

Corbo thought, I have gone mad.

He knew he had not.

'How do you know this?' he said to the slinger.

'Stories told to me in childhood. Long ago. As if, prophetically, to prepare me.'

'You're lying.'

'I don't lie unless I have to. Now I don't have to. I've always had an ability to see in *images* – I have an imagination. You, honoured Leader, less so. But now it will come. Don't try to hide from it. *Embrace* it. Look, there's the sun, all shiny as a shield! Have another drink. You've taken enough blood you can do what you want. Even screw a woman. If you like.'

'You know so much,' said Corbo bleakly. 'How shall I die?'

'That … Probably not for centuries. Unless one does to you as you should have to me – burn, decapitate – you're more or less invulnerable. I am. Remember where I bit you for the blood — there's not even a mark, is there? Look.' Slyly Slinger took a thin vile knife from the lining of his belt – no doubt a tool of his robbery trade. Bending forward slightly, to conceal what he did from the general area, Slinger stuck it straight in the side of his neck. It was a stab that might well have killed him. But did not. Unblinking, he slid the knife out; no hint of blood – not even a bruise remained. Some tricky blade then? Corbo did not believe so. A dull yet fiery ache, not physical, thrummed in his gut, his heart and mind. He knew that Slinger was a part of his destiny, as he had been of Slinger's. Slinger had spoken only facts. Nothing was ever without a reason. The gods knew their business. It was not only the evil who were chosen.

As he was about to report again to Julusarus the Commander, one of the runners of the fort brought Corbo a scrap of scented letter. It was actual parchment, if of a rather tattered kind. The writing was ornate and the syntax of not very accurate Latin. But then, by now, at such outposts as Arida, most of the use of the pure tongue of Rome had grown slovenly, slangy, inventive and eccentric, as well as being tangled with native phrases.

> 'His Handmaid Yeila to her lord-master the Battalion Leader
> Marcus Scorpius Corbo:
> 'Why are you not come? Are you of sick? Are you full tired of
> me? Me beg you will reassure I otherwise. Or if I hear not, then
> expect no more shred of I, ever.
> 'In sorrows, Yeila'

He had saved her life by not going in to her. Or robbed her of eternity.

He sighed, a man beset by troubles, and climbed the stone stair to the Commander's room.

The pilum was of course on the wall, the saddle, the dented sword. The frustrated anger was still there also. It hung like a cloud of fizzing flies, ready to sting.

Six Battalion Captains stood in the room with Julusarus, as he outlined in vast and weighty detail the activities of the Vecordia, their seemingly irrevocable possession of Aquaelis. They had hung Roman men, merchants, soldiers, to scorch and die on the outer walls. They had paved the square with dead children. None who was not of their race and faith, chosen of their gods, might live. Even the mules and the dogs they had had away with. Even the birds of the air.

'And in number, mark this now, for here is the final estimate, they exceed seven thousand men. In the past when we stood high and fine, a far smaller number of legionaries could have dealt with them. As few even as three thousand.

This we know from the history of Rome herself. But now we lack such numbers, and even our machines, our catapults and engines of siege. Even our shields are bent from shape. Like that sword there, of my father, old Austus Vario, may he feast in the Undercountry. And what full number of soldiers can we anyway muster, and not leave this arid town of ours unguarded? Why, at top pitch, twelve-hundred men.' Julusarus slammed his wine cup down on the table. The wine spilled, an inadvertent offering to some uncaring deity – Bacchus, Mars, Mercury, Callidus –

The other men in the room murmured, softly growled.

'Nevertheless, sir, we must *go*. It *must* be seen to.'

'And that's precisely it, Fero. Such as we are now can't see to it. Can we? The Madmen will destroy our force, easy as spit, and then come prowling here to wipe this place too off the map. For them there must be a world that contains only them, and their non-human, honourless, bowel-dipped kind.'

Arguments rang like gongs then. Men swore, oaths impossible. Hopefully the gods, who ignored the inadvertent wine, ignored also these.

The room was very hot. As if a storm brewed there in it. It did. But to no effect.

Provisional decisions lay in tottering stacks, and the meeting disbanded.

Julusarus noted that one man had remained in the shadow by the wall with the sword.

'Well, Marcus Corbo. Here we are. We shall have to meet and argue again. Worse than the Senate. What did you want from me?'

'Hear me out, sir.'

'If I must.'

Corbo spoke. Had the water-clock in the mess been working, it would have recorded an equivalent of seven minutes only.

The Commander began in a bored and weary pose, altered to disbelief, and close to mockery. Then to a moment of rage. Then to an utter silence.

'You've lost your bloody mind, soldier.'

'Perhaps. But the risk to our forces *here* will be negligible. You'll lose only, at most, 16, 17 men.'

'Mad. I said. What's got into you? Your pretty whore bitten you and given you the foaming sickness?'

'No, sir.'

'Sleep on it, Marcus. Don't think I don't value your courage and your nerve. Your resolution. This is the stuff on which the spines of our legions were built. But – by Martis, by the Jupitrexium –'

'Sir, I've checked. These men I've selected from my Battalion are unattached to any great obligation. None has living parents, or is married, none has children even, or none he will recognise. Laurus does have a dog, but we can find the dog a kind secondary home. And who knows, maybe Laurus will come back.'

'You're mad. I said. And all this because of this scout or whatever he is

20

from Aquae – what's he called? *Slinger*? And he knows some hidden way into the oasis town? Well. He may be a rogue. A liar, a villain in Madmen pay.'

'No, sir. He and I, we have a bond – blood brothers, sir. It goes – way back. I'd trust him, and he me. I only need now the authority of your agreement, and your seal.'

'Madness.'

'Then, Commander, may such madness as mine rule, until the other alien lunacy is crushed and rinsed from the earth.'

Corbo called the men to him after the sun had set. He did it in an established way, from which each individual would guess, as with certain previous other assemblies, matters must be kept secret. They arrived expectantly, gathering in the gathering dark, motes and men forming a single entity. He spoke to each alone.

'It's a mission that may well mean death, as you understand; that will, I promise, include a sort of death. Can you trust me in this?'

All but one assured him of agreement. The one who hesitated had just taken up with a woman of Arida, and might be going to have with her, so Corbo learned, a child. That seemed fair enough. Corbo dismissed him civilly, blameless, if with a mild iron warning not to speak of the unknown venture to any other.

It would be 16 men then, and Slinger, and Corbo himself. In total 18.

If any of this living dream was real, that would be plenty.

He let them into his cell also one by one, now in the shade of a moonless night that had, by then, absorbed everything it could, only the small yellow star of the oil lamp fluttering.

'You will pledge to this task for the honour of the Empire, and the last fair Glory of Rome?'

'I will.'

'Look down,' he said, 'into the light.'

One by one, they looked.

And yes, the moon, no longer in heaven, lay on the table.

Each man started, stared, gazed – transfixed, *pinned*. Some swore. Some only audibly breathed.

'What – is it?'

'A mirror.'

'I *saw* a mirror before, once – at Hiersol'a – it was silver with gold. I could see myself – unnerved me a minute. But not like this – it's glass. They burn the desert sand, don't, they, to make glass. He's – is he me? I? So clear – but now – where am I? What – what – has happened to me?'

'You are yet yourself,' he said. Truth and lie, like all things. 'You are more yourself now than ever before.'

And reaching across the table, he placed his wrist before the man, each man, one by one. There was a tiny wound, just ready-made, in the vein. A thread of scarlet. 'This has to be a pact of blood.'

Most instantly bent their heads, like thirsty beasts to water. The instinct was very strong, as he recollected. A few delayed for a moment. Laurus was one of these; but then, when he bent his head also to suck up the vital ichor, his teeth ground in Corbo's flesh, more savage than Corbo had expected.

After this, Slinger every time stepped out of the shadows. He told the men, the 16 of the new Blood Crow Battalion, the rules and gambits of survival – sunlight, other sustenance – the partaking of, and leaving of friends, healthy, alive and unaware of quite what had been done. Conversely, the tidy utter slaying of enemies – drained to empty wine-sacks, decapitated, burned to black cinders that made – not glass, as the dusts of the desert could – but lifeless ashes.

That last lesson they would require most of all.

The remainder of the night was filled by hidden and sudden things.

Next day they were out, flinching a little at the first sunlight, but adjusting quite swiftly, as Corbo had – all strong, youngish men, in their prime, able to support their transformation, ready for action as ever. Laurus's dog, guard and companion, had taken up residence, it seemed, with a local butcher. The dog and the butcher were old friends, the dog had patrolled the premises before. The dog would get fat, Laurus concluded sadly.

They readied their horses and their weapons. Provisions were brought to them; water, wine, and – at Corbo's particular order – raw bloody hanks of fresh meat, redder than sunrise or even the red of the legionary cloaks and helmet crests.

Scarlet in the dawn, riding away southward. Bloody Rome on the march.

Fourteen days:

During their initial advance, retracing their earlier returning fortwards steps on the patrol, passing again now even the wrecked well where the mirror had hidden under the sand. Not much unusual presented itself this time. The occasional desert village lay undisturbed, if anxious, as before. Only in one place had the people abruptly fled their settlement, too scared to stay, fearing the Madmen would arrive. The nearly eyeless brown dwellings stood blindly, the lintels of doorways already fallen. The people had poured sand into their own well – again, a form of sacrilege. But then, if they expected the nightmare Vecordia to want the water, why not destroy its source?

Beyond the fifteenth day, more abandoned villages appeared. In one, the leavers had even burned the grove of fruit trees they had cultivated, to deny them to the foe.

Following that, they passed no more inhabited or once-inhabited places. There were sand-blows too, in one of which Corbo's Battalion was caught. After it, they hunted for fresh game. The animal blood was equally welcome with the meat. But their stamina, to a man, was so improved on its already healthy status, they seemed able to withstand most things; ordinary hunger, thirst, the gentle insistent longing for blood, like a vague craving for something sweet …

By the time they reached the oasis of Erum – untouched and opulent – confidence was high. They were an elite. And unlike the Vecordia, a verifiable one. Erum was their justified pre-battle reward.

In the dusk, Corbo oversaw the concealment of a cook-fire and the roasting there of a wild goat.

Then he and Slinger drew aside, as earlier now and then they had, under the tall palms.

Here the water-course burst from the rock, with a soft pattering. From here too, some thirty miles off along the sand plains, it was just possible to make out, side lit by the settling sun, the walls of Aquaelis. You could tell nothing from that.

Or everything. The town still stood. The devils still had it. They were smug and safe, gathering their crazed, merciless, unhuman minds and bodies for a further journeying, slaughter and hell.

Corbo turned his father's seal-ring on his finger absently as he always had. He had sent Yeila a note of regret, with a pretty brooch from the market, of two silver doves, the birds of Venus, upon a blue enamel flower.

Slinger spoke quietly. 'Soon, we'll take the town. Once the full night comes.'

'You know a hidden way in, you've said.'

'Yes, I do. Sheer luck, I heard of it the single day I stayed there, almost a year ago. These things happen. The gods mean them to happen. So I think. Or none of it makes sense.'

'So you still believe in gods, Slinger, even after what's gone on.'

'Yes. What's happened with us is clever and heartless. That'd be the gods. Who else? But I think too – for some reason maybe I owed you my death, Marcus. But you in turn owed me my life.'

'Why?'

'The gods know. They'll tell us one day. Or not.'

Corbo looked about at his chosen men, the 16 he had murdered and given immortality. He felt no remorse. He was a soldier, had always been chasing after the legions since the age of five or six. You used the weapons to hand. And, it was as if he had done it before, somehow, this riotous act, in some previous era. The men were eating the roasted goat, and the sugary dates that grew in the oasis; drinking wine.

He turned the ring again. Stiff and close, grown long since into his flesh, the knuckle, with the years. Yet somehow it had slid from him, leading him back to the wrecked well to search until he found the succubus of mirror in the sand. Yes. Fate – the gods? – had done all this.

The sky lowered itself, turning bronze and lilac. Faint as a sigh, a hint of light haloed the distant walls of Aquaelis. Torches, he decided it must be, to show so far.

The Battalion made polite offerings to Father Jupiter and Brother Mars. And to Chance. The horses would be tethered here, enough water and grazing, shade, safe for this while. The men would lope to the town. They would make good speed, now.

Black silk covered the world in a praetorium tent.

The rhythmic water of the fountain sounded – *Stay – No, you must hurry on – Come back* – bright and loud as music.

Stars in the sky looked near as beads on a ceiling.

Am I yet a human man? Or is that all truly gone from me, with my soul, into the mirror? Some other day or night an hour will come, I know, and I shall die. There will be nothing then left of me to go down into the grey Underland. I shall be a smoke that blows about the sky, one more reason for darkness, one more hollowness against which the stars can flaunt themselves. But not yet. *Not yet.* First there is the *now*.

It was like a snake, the twisting crawl-space of a passage rising up into and through the town wall. It began about a quarter mile from the town, humped under the sand among some stony monument or other, long since smashed down to boulders by the Madmen, who would never tolerate, it seemed, any evidence or honour of gods other than their own. Slinger said he had overheard the story of the secret entrance from a thief who had once utilised it. In the beginning, very likely, it had been an integral part of the town's barricades and defences, perhaps then openly marked as an outpost, with gate and guards. Now it was like climbing and slithering through an intestine – through the *snake-bowel*. Then: an exit. It was only able to be recognised by a slender crack, going up and up and up. A fissure in the wall. From the other, inner town side, no doubt it seemed like nothing more than one extra, insignificant fault in the stone.

Slinger had said he knew what must be done.

He did.

Crouching over the glimmering crack, he felt after something, then *shoved* it very hard.

The wall gave. No, it was a door, of sorts.

The men filed out, able to straighten as they did so, one by one, 16, 18 of them, stepping onto the platform beyond – a wall-walk, unmistakably Roman in construction, solid and lasting. Small hollow towers went up along and all around; watchtowers not, now, seeming in proper use. The torches, or whatever had puffed off that faint previous powder of illumination, were out. They had a curfew here, it seemed, on light.

Against the nearest tower, about 13 feet from him, Corbo began to discern a shape. It had appeared to be part of the masonry. It was not. Like some mechanical apparatus of war, its *head* was turning toward them. He was reminded of a theatre, an actor masked and seeming soulless. *Soulless.* As were they – he and his men?

Wound in black cloth, body and head covered, and face, yet the eyes still gleamed, two wet, white-black slits. The eyes had fixed on him. Out of its unseen, perhaps non-existent mouth, burst a thin and eerie howl. Up flew its robe-sleeved arm – a blade flashed darkest white. The being surged toward them, singing its warbling battle-song, and Corbo ran to meet it. Too late. Slinger was already there. The curved foreign knife sliced downward, passed directly through Slinger's shoulder. Slinger gave off a loud raw noise. It was not the note of agony or death but a sort of utter filthy joy. Next second, unharmed, Slinger had seized the throat of his foe. Blood spurted blacker than the moonless sky, thicket than lust. The body of the Madman, flailing – arms, legs, coverings, as if it had as many appendages as a spider — cascaded over. It was gurgling now, like a half-blocked water-vent. Then all its roiling and uproar ended. Slinger, a leopard, lay over it, drinking deep.

Next instant the entire upper walk erupted into veiled and knife-armed live automata. Corbo's Battalion of Blood made little answering sound as they leaped and thrust among them. Not a single Roman weapon was employed. What requirement for sword or dagger? Their teeth were diamond, were steel and fire. Their throats and guts were wide and clear and empty and hungry. As Corbo slaked his initial thirst, he felt two or three of the curved blades hacked into him, back and ribs. He paid them no heed. He had no need to. And one feast partaken of, insatiable, he rose up, the power in him like a black and singing sunrise. Pleasure and glory – had ever anything matched this ecstasy? He had known battle-fever before – but even that was not like this. In that, you were lost. But in *this* you were All, and *It – You*.

The alien blades fell from him.

Everywhere about, as he sprang and grasped, lifted and met and felled and fed, he saw the others of his band. Eighteen men. They seemed a million.

Curious. A clot of Madmen had now clutched him. Blind and stupid, they could learn nothing, it seemed. He shook them away, easy as large unwieldy pieces of dirt. Then, turning to each assailant as he spun, Corbo sank his teeth into the creature's throat, through veil and sinew and bone. Where he did not immediately drain them – less urgent now, the want of blood – he left them choking and bleeding to death. But he would take no chances. Every one of these monsters should be rendered bloodless soon, and the heads lopped from their bodies. There was after all one of the ugly knives still lodged in his arm. He pulled it out and thrust it, almost playfully – Is this toy *yours?* – straight through the enveloped face of a Madman. Corbo laughed softly with a nearly childish amusement as he wrung the gouts of life from the cleft face, lapping it like milk.

How simple this was. The true order of the Earth.

An orgy, the divine battle-feast, went on and on.

His men were laughing too, sheer happiness. A festival.

Down from the wall, they expanded their remit into the town. Through the streets, across the two squares of Aquaelis, whose fine forum and statues of Jupiter and Juno had been hammered into rubble, around the lanes, the alleys, through doors into shops, apartments in five-storey blocks, or houses lying behind the street. Not a human being was to be found. Only the mechanised Vecordia, these now only creeping out, when discovered some even kneeling and wailing to their selective gods, or only in abstract panic. Whatever their credo, the result the same.

So many black sacks with dead-fish eyes. The town carpeted now with veiled corpses.

No others were left there, it seemed. No Roman or Romanised local. The Madmen had destroyed all those. In certain areas there were evidential remains, pegged out or hung up, or slung in heaps. You saw how they had been made to die. The Roman men and women, the native friends of Rome. Their children. Their animals.

At the very end, whenever that was, the end of that long, intensive night, a few last Madmen were discovered hiding in a drain beneath the stones of a street. They gazed dumbly now at what came in to find them.

The night was blood. Of course, at last, the tell-tale crimson streak must also appear in the east. The sun too had taken her bath in the cornucopia.

How still the town. Yet even so, the few last chores to tend to. They were soldiers. You did not stint, or, as they said in the markets of the Mother of Cities, 'spoil the stew for a pinch of salt.'

Salt was the sword at last. Clean, it struck off the thousands of heads. Out of their coverings the faces sometimes rolled. Mindless and soulless faces. *These*, the succubae. *These*, the walking dead.

As the day rose up on her brief incarnadine wings, the soldiers made their bonfire in the central space of the ruined forum. And as the torsos and limbs and separated heads were burned, stinking as only human flesh truly can when cooked, the Blood Battalion of the Crow and the Mirror toasted their own gods in the last of the wine, and the first bright draughts of Eternity.

One recounting has it, some eight thousand men of the Vecordia were slain at Aquaelis that night. Slain by 18 Roman legionaries, a rogue squadron from Arida.

But such a victory could not be possible.

Even to Romans.

Three days later, a watcher, were there one, could see the smoke yet rising from the immolation in the forum. And this from some miles farther to the south.

Corbo and his men had not turned back toward Arida. They had spared no one of their number as messenger. The news would reach the fort eventually; somehow news always did, the worst, the best.

They had not discussed future plans, he and the Blood Battalion. They had slept a lot, mostly by day, among the dunes, and at the next rough oasis, some ten miles on from the town.

That night, they sat and drank water, ate a little dried meat and fruit. Watched the stars that, in turn, seemed always to be watching them.

'Are they eyes?' Laurus had murmured, just the previous evening.

'Who knows?'

'I miss my bloody dog,' had said Laurus then.

Corbo said, 'You can always go back.'

'Can I?'

'Certainly. Only – if any of us do, we must tread carefully.'

'They won't believe what we did,' said Laurus. 'Sir.'

'Don't call me *sir* now. That's past. My name is Marcus. They'll come to believe it. Better than that, we shall go on and do more. As we know, the Vecordia are everywhere.'

'Yes, that's the only answer, isn't it, s – Marcus.'

That then was their plan. Slightly discussed, a moment here, or there, after sunset and before the uprush of dawn. Despite the blood, they felt the light a little, sometimes. A sort of soreness, a kind of unease. Like the bite of an insect that could never entirely heal, though it would never utterly harm.

Marcus considered, as Laurus lay down to catch some sleep, his head pillowed on part of the old rolled-up blanket his dog had been want to lie on – Laurus had left the other half for the dog. Marcus Corbo thought of Arida, and regretfully of Yeila.

But then, would he ever have trusted himself with her again? The urge to drink her blood would have mounted in him, he suspected, intrinsic component of sex. One night, however abstemious he had tried to be, he would go too far, and then – like Slinger – she would become one of their kind, and attached to him. With Slinger he was comfortable; the company of men and brothers. But women were different fare. Gorgeous. Sometimes too much. No. He did not want to risk that, with Yeila. Left alone she would forget him mostly. Or, when she learned what a hero he had become, she would never leave off vaunting their intimacy.

What they would do, he and the Battalion, was continue their march. Over and across the entire map of the Exterra. They would go to find the other outposts of the enemy. It would not matter, their own low numbers or their apparently slight strength.

No one man of Corbo's band had been lost. Probably they would seldom be depleted. Or ... be added to?

They would live – as long as life.

It did not bear thinking of. Corbo did not, beyond the occasional second, think of it.

Next morning, as they were preparing to move away again southward, relentless on the trail of their predestined prey, a peculiar disturbance became visible over a clutch of high dunes to the north.

They paused to watch, not alarmed, only perplexed.

'It's sheep –'

'No – a child –'

Laurus gave a shout. And then he ran away from them, toward the distance, laughing and calling.

'It's his damned dog!'

So it was.

Across the sands, frothed in a dusty sunlit haze, the dog of Laurus bounded. No spot on Earth was worth the patch of ground beside his master. The dog did not care that Laurus was a vampire, had no soul, sucked the blood of his enemies, and maybe his friends. The dog did not care that Laurus had left him behind – anyone could make a mistake.

Watching them rolling together in the sand, laughing and barking and chirruping, and coughing at the grains, Corbo smiled. So huge the arena of the world, and the deeds that must be done there, and so silly, and now and then so kind, the tiny moments mosaic-laid all around them. A misplaced ring and a sorcerous mirror found, a blow of Fate colossal as the sky, a lost kiss, a question with no answer. Laurus was weeping, without shame, as he carried the huge and sandy, wriggling dog back into their camp. The camp raised a cheer. He said nothing, only looked to Corbo. Corbo patted the dog, who licked his face. 'Better feed him. He'll be missing the butcher.'

He mounted up. How many days lay ahead? How many centuries?

Corbo glanced back once. You could not, now, really tell one horizon from the other. As you could not really tell the past from the future. For the past altered its shape, as most men knew too well, and the future sometimes showed itself with awful accuracy. Corbo thought of a final nightfall, his bones, and with them the mirror, whole, or by then in fragments, lying under the sands, the grasses, the roots of trees as yet unborn. But then instead, Corbo thought of Yeila's eyes, her breasts, her thighs, her hands. He too could always return. He could live. The sun rose higher as they rode. The desert shone like glass.

BITE-ME-NOT
(Or, *Fleur de Fur*)

I

In the tradition of young girls and windows, the young girl looks out of this one. It is difficult to see anything. The panes of the window are heavily leaded, and secured by a lattice of iron. The stained glass of lizard-green and storm-purple is several inches thick. There is no red glass in the window. The colour red is forbidden in the castle. Even the sun, behind the glass, is a storm sun, a green-lizard sun.

The young girl wishes she had a gown of palest pastel rose – the nearest affinity to red that is ever allowed. Already she has long dark beautiful eyes, a long white neck. Her long dark hair is however hidden in a dusty scarf and she wears rags.

She is a scullery maid. As she scours dishes and mops stone floors, she imagines she is a princess floating through the upper corridors, gliding to the dais in the Duke's hall. The Cursed Duke. She is sorry for him. If he had been her father, she would have sympathised with and consoled him. His own daughter is dead, as his wife is dead, but these things, being to do with the Cursing, are never spoken of. Except, sometimes, obliquely.

'*Rohise!*' dim voices cry now, full of dim scolding soon to be actualised.

The scullery maid turns from the window and runs to have her ears boxed and a broom thrust into her hands.

Meanwhile, the Cursed Duke is prowling his chamber, high in the East Turret carved with swans and gargoyles. The room is lined with books, swords, lutes, scrolls, and has two eerie portraits, the larger of which represents his wife, and the smaller his daughter. Both ladies look much the same with their pale, egg-shaped faces, polished eyes, clasped hands. They do not really look like his wife or daughter, nor really remind him of them.

There are no windows at all in the Turret; they were long ago bricked up and covered with hangings. Candles burn steadily. It is always night in the Turret. Save, of course, that by night there are particular sounds all about it, to which the Duke is accustomed, but which he does not care for. By night, like most of his court, the Cursed Duke closes his ears with softened tallow. However, if he sleeps, he dreams, and hears in the dream the beating of wings … Often, the court holds loud revel all night long.

The Duke does not know that Rohise the scullery maid has been thinking of him. Perhaps he does not even know that a scullery maid is capable of thinking at all.

Soon the Duke descends from the Turret and goes down, by various stairs and curving passages, into a large, walled-garden, on the east side of the castle.

It is a very pretty garden, mannered and manicured, which the gardeners keep in perfect order. Over the tops of the high, high walls, where delicate blooms bell the vines, it is just possible to glimpse the tips of sun-baked mountains. But by day the mountains are blue and spiritual to look at, and seem scarcely real. They might only be inked on the sky.

A portion of the Duke's court is wandering about in the garden, playing games or musical instruments, or admiring painted sculptures, or the flora, none of which is red. But the Cursed Duke's court seems vitiated this noon. Nights of revel take their toll.

As the Duke passes down the garden, his courtiers acknowledge him deferentially. He sees them, old and young alike, all doomed as he is, and the weight of his burden increases.

At the furthest, most eastern end of the garden, there is another garden, sunken and rather curious, beyond a wall with an iron door. Only the Duke possesses the key to this door. Now he unlocks it and goes through. His courtiers laugh and play and pretend not to see. He shuts the door behind him.

The sunken garden, which no gardener ever tends, is maintained by other, spontaneous, means. It is small and square, lacking the hedges and the paths of the other, the sundials and statues and little pools. All the sunken garden contains is a broad paved border, and at its centre a small plot of humid earth. Growing in the earth is a slender bush with slender velvet leaves.

The Duke stands and looks at the bush only a short while.

He visits it every day. He has visited it every day for years. He is waiting for the bush to flower. Everyone is waiting for this. Even Rohise, the scullery maid, is waiting, though, being only 16, born in the castle and uneducated, she does not properly understand why.

The light in the little garden is dull and strange, for the whole of it is roofed over by a dome of thick smoky glass.

It makes the atmosphere somewhat depressing, although the bush itself gives off a pleasant smell, rather resembling vanilla.

Something is cut into the stone rim of the earth-plot where the bush grows. The Duke reads it for perhaps the thousandth time. *O, fleur de feu* –

When the Duke returns from the little garden into the large garden, locking the door behind him, no-one seems truly to notice. But their obeisances now are circumspect.

One day, he will perhaps emerge from the sunken garden leaving the door wide, crying out in a great voice. But not yet. Not today.

The ladies bend to the bright fish in the pools, the knights pluck for them blossoms, challenge each other to combat at chess, or wrestling, discuss the menagerie lions; the minstrels sing of unrequited love. The pleasure garden is full of one long and weary sigh.

> *'Oh flurda fur,*
> *'Pourma souffranee –'*

sings Rohise as she scrubs the flags of the pantry floor.

> *'Ned ormey par,*
> *'May say day mwar –'*

'What are you singing, you slut?' someone shouts, and kicks over her bucket.

Rohise does not weep. She tidies her bucket and soaks up the spilled water with her cloths. She does not know what the song means because of which she seems, apparently, to have been chastised. She does not understand the words that somehow, somewhere – perhaps from her own dead mother – she had learned by rote.

In the hour before sunset, the Duke's hall is lit by flambeaux. In the high windows, the casements of oil-blue and lavender glass and glass like storms and lizards, are fastened tight. The huge window by the dais was long ago obliterated, shut up, and a tapestry hung of gold and silver tissue with all the rubies pulled out and emeralds substituted. It describes the subjugation of a fearsome unicorn by a maiden, and huntsmen.

The court drifts in with its clothes of rainbow from which only the colour red is missing.

Music for dancing plays. The lean pale dogs pace about, alert for titbits as dish on dish comes in. Roast birds in all their plumage glitter and die a second time under the eager knives. Pastry castles fall. Pink and amber fruits, and green fruits and black, glow beside the goblets of fine yellow wine.

The Cursed Duke eats with care and attention, not with enjoyment. Only the very young of the castle still eat in that way, and there are not so many of those.

The murky sun slides through the stained glass. The musicians strike up more wildly. The dances become boisterous. Once the day goes out, the hall will ring to *chanson*, to drum and viol and pipe. The dogs will bark, no language will be uttered except in a bellow. The lions will roar from the menagerie. On some nights the cannon are set off from the battlements, which are now all of them roofed in, fired out through narrow mouths just wide enough to accommodate them, the charge crashing away in thunder down the darkness.

By the time the moon comes up and the castle rocks to its own cacophony, exhausted Rohise has fallen fast asleep in her cupboard bed in the attic. For years, from sunset to rise, nothing has woken her. Once, as a child, when she had been especially badly beaten, the pain woke her and she heard a strange silken scratching, somewhere over her head. But she thought it a rat, or a bird. Yes, a bird, for later it seemed to her there were also wings … But she forgot all this half a decade ago. Now she sleeps deeply and dreams of being a princess, forgetting, too, how the Duke's daughter died. Such a terrible death, it is better to forget.

'The sun shall not smite thee by day, neither the moon by night,' intones the priest, eyes rolling, his voice like a bell behind the Duke's shoulder.

'*Ne moi mords pas,*' whispers Rohise in her deep sleep. '*Ne mwar mor par, ne par mor mwar …*'

And under its impenetrable dome, the slender bush has closed its fur leaves also to sleep. O flower of fire, oh *fleur de fur*. Its blooms, though it has not bloomed yet, bear the ancient name *Nona Mordica*. In light parlance they call it Bite-Me-Not. There is a reason for that.

II

He is the Prince of a proud and savage people. The pride they acknowledge, perhaps they do not consider themselves to be savages, or at least believe that savagery is the proper order of things.

Feroluce, that is his name. It is one of the customary names his kind give their lords. It had connotations with diabolic royalty and, too, with a royal flower of long petals curved like scimitars. Also the name might be the partial anagram of another name. The bearer of that name was also winged.

For Feroluce and his people are winged beings. They are more like a nest of dark eagles than anything, mounted high among the rocky pilasters and spinacles of the mountain. Cruel and magnificent, like eagles, the sombre sentries motionless as statuary on the ledge-edges, their sable wings folded about them. They are very alike in appearance (less a race or tribe, more a flock, an unkindness of ravens). Feroluce also, black-winged, black-haired, aquiline of feature, standing on the brink of star-dashed space, his eyes burning through the night like all the eyes along the rocks, depthless red as claret.

They have their own traditions of art and science. They do not make or read books, fashion garments, discuss God or metaphysics or men. Their cries are mostly wordless and always mysterious, flung out like ribbons over the air as they wheel and swoop and hang in wicked cruciform, between the peaks. But they sing, long hours, for whole nights at a time, music that has a language only they know. All their wisdom and theosophy, and all their grasp of beauty, truth or love, is in the singing.

They look unloving enough, and so they are. Pitiless fallen angels. A travelling people, they roam after sustenance. Their sustenance is blood. Finding a castle, they accepted it, every bastion and wall, as their prey. They have preyed on it and tried to prey on it for years. In the beginning, their calls, their songs, could lure victims to the feast. In this way, the tribe or unkindness of Feroluce took the Duke's wife, somnambulist, from a midnight balcony. But the Duke's daughter, the first victim they found 17 years ago, benighted on the mountainside. Her escort and herself they left to the sunrise, marble figures, the life drunk away.

Now the castle is shut, bolted and barred. They are even more attracted by its recalcitrance (a woman who says *No*). They do not intend to go away until the castle falls to them.

By night, they fly like huge black moths round and round the carved turrets, the dull-lit leaded windows, their wings invoking a cloudy tindery wind, pushing thunder against thundery glass.

They sense they are attributed to some sin, reckoned a punishing curse, a penance, and this amuses them at the level whereon they understand it.

They also sense something of the flower, the *Nona Mordica*. Vampires have their own legends.

But tonight Feroluce launches himself into the air, speeds down the sky on the black sails of his wings, calling, a call like laughter or derision. This morning, in the tween-time before the light began and the sun-to-be drove him away to his shadowed eyrie in the mountain-guts, he saw a chink in the armour of the beloved refusing-woman-prey. A window, high in an old neglected tower, a window with a small eyelet that was cracked.

Feroluce soon reaches the eyelet and breathes on it, as if he would melt it. (His breath is sweet. Vampires do not eat raw flesh, only blood, which is a perfect food and digests perfectly, while their teeth are sound of necessity.) The way the glass mists at breath intrigues Feroluce. But presently he taps at the cranky pane, taps, then claws. A piece breaks away, and now he sees how it should be done.

Over the rims and upthrusts of the castle, which is only really another mountain with caves to Feroluce, the rumble of the Duke's revel drones on.

Feroluce pays no heed. He does not need to reason, he merely knows, *that* noise masks *this* – as he smashes in the window. Its panes were all faulted and the lattice rusty. It is, of course, more than that. The magic of Purpose has protected the castle, and, as in all balances, there must be, or come to be, some balancing contradiction, some flaw ...

The people of Feroluce do not notice what he is at. In a way, the dance with their prey has debased to a ritual. They have lived almost two decades on the blood of local mountain beasts, and bird-creatures like themselves brought down on the wing. Patience is not, with them, a virtue. It is a sort of foreplay, and can go on, in pleasure, a long, long while.

Feroluce intrudes himself through the slender window. Muscularly slender himself, and agile, it is no feat. But the wings catch, are a trouble. They follow him because they must, like two separate entities. They have been cut a little on the glass, and bleed.

He stands in a stony small room, shaking bloody feathers from him, snarling, but without sound.

Then he finds the stairway and goes down.

There are dusty landings and neglected chambers. They have no smell of life. But then there comes to be a smell. It is the scent of a nest, a colony of things, wild creatures, in constant proximity. He recognises it. The light of his crimson eyes precedes him, deciphering blackness. And then other eyes, amber, green and gold, spring out like stars all across his path.

Somewhere an old torch is burning out. To the human eye, only mounds and glows would be visible, but to Feroluce, the Prince of the vampires, all is suddenly revealed. There is a great stone area, barred with bronze and iron, and things stride and growl behind the bars, or chatter and flee, or only stare. And there, without bars, though bound by ropes of brass to rings of brass, three brazen beasts.

Feroluce, on the steps of the menagerie, looks into the gaze of the Duke's lions. Feroluce smiles, and the lions roar. One is the king, its mane like war-plumes. Feroluce recognises the king and the king's right to challenge, for this is the lions' domain, their territory.

Feroluce comes down the stair and meets the lion as it leaps the length of its chain. To Feroluce, the chain means nothing, and since he has come close enough, very little either to the lion.

To the vampire Prince the fight is wonderful, exhilarating and meaningful, intellectual even, for it is coloured by nuance, yet powerful as sex.

He holds fast with his talons, his strong limbs wrapping the beast, which is almost stronger than he, just as its limbs wrap him in turn. He sinks his teeth in the lion's shoulder, and in fierce rage and bliss begins to draw out the nourishment. The lion kicks and claws at him in turn. Feroluce feels the gouges like fire along his shoulders, thighs, and hugs the lion more nearly as he throttles and drinks from it, loving it, jealous of it, killing it. Gradually the mighty feline body relaxes, still clinging to him, its cat teeth bedded in one beautiful swan-like wing, forgotten by both.

In a welter of feathers, stripped skin, spilled blood, stray semen, the lion and the angel lie in embrace on the menagerie floor. The lion lifts its head, kisses the assassin, shudders, lets go.

Feroluce glides out from under the magnificent dead-weight of the cat. He stands. And pain assaults him. His lover has severely wounded him.

Across the menagerie floor, the two lionesses are crouched. Beyond them, a man stands gaping in simple terror, behind the guttering torch. He had come to feed the beasts, and seen another feeding, and now is paralysed. He is deaf, the menagerie-keeper, previously an advantage saving him the horror of nocturnal vampire noises.

Feroluce starts towards the human animal swifter than a serpent, and checks. Agony envelops Feroluce, and the stone room spins. Involuntarily, confused, he spreads his wings for flight, there in the confined chamber. But only one wing will open. The other, damaged and partly broken, hangs like a snapped fan. Feroluce cries out, a beautiful singing note of despair and anger. He drops fainting at the menagerie keeper's feet.

The man does not wait for more. He runs away through the castle, screaming invective and prayer, and reaches the Duke's hall, and makes the whole hall listen.

All this while, Feroluce lies in the ocean of almost-death that is sleep or swoon, while the smaller beasts in the cages discuss him, or seem to.

And when he is raised, Feroluce does not wake. Only the great drooping bloody wings quiver and are still. Those who carry him are more than ever revolted and frightened, for they have seldom seen blood. Even the food for the menagerie is cooked almost black. Two years ago, a gardener slashed his palm on a thorn. He was banished from the court for a week.

But Feroluce, the centre of so much attention, does not rouse. Not until the dregs of the night are stealing out through the walls. Then some nervous instinct invests him. The sun is coming and this is an open place – he struggles through unconsciousness and hurt, through the deepest most bladed waters, to awareness.

And finds himself in a huge bronze cage, the cage of some animal appropriated for the occasion. Bars, bars all about him, and not to be got rid of, for he reaches to tear them away and cannot.

Beyond the bars, the Duke's hall, which is only a pointless cold glitter to him in the maze of pain and dying lights. Not an open place, in fact, but too open for his kind. Through the window-spaces of thick glass, muddy sunglare must come in. To Feroluce it will be like swords, acids and burning fire –

Far off he hears wings beat and voices soaring. His people search for him, call and wheel and find nothing.

Feroluce cries cut, a gravel shriek now, the persons in the hall rush back from him, calling on God. But Feroluce does not see. He has tried to answer his own. Now he sinks down again under the coverlet of his broken wings, and the wine-red stars of his eyes go out.

III

'And the Angel of Death,' the priest intones, 'shall surely pass over, but yet like the Shadow, not substance –'

The smashed window in the old turret above the menagerie tower has been sealed with mortar and brick. It is a terrible thing that it was for so long overlooked. A miracle that only one of the creatures found and entered by it. God, the Protector, guarded the Cursed Duke and his court. And the magic that surrounds the castle, that too held fast. For from the possibility of a disaster was born a bloom of great value: now one of the monsters is in their possession. A prize beyond price.

Caged and helpless, the fiend is at their mercy. It is also weak from its battle with the noble lion, which gave its life for the castle's safety (and will be buried with honour in an ornamented grave at the foot of the Ducal family tomb.) Just before the dawn came, the Duke's advisers advised him, and the bronze cage was wheeled away into the darkest area of the hall, close by the dais where once the huge window was but is no more. A barricade of great screens was brought, and set around the cage, and the top of it covered. No sunlight now can drip into the prison to harm the specimen. Only the Duke's ladies and gentlemen steal in around the screens and see, by the light of a candle branch, the demon still lying in its trance of pain and blood loss. The Duke's alchemist sits on a stool nearby, dictating many notes to a nervous apprentice. The alchemist, and the apothecary for that matter, are convinced that the vampire, having drunk the lion almost dry, will recover from its wounds. Even the wings will mend. The Duke's court painter also came. He was ashamed presently, and went away. The beauty of the demon affected him, making him wish to paint it, not as something wonderfully disgusting, but as a kind of superlative man, vital and innocent, or as Lucifer himself, stricken in the sorrow of his colossal Fall. And all that has caused the painter to pity the fallen one, mere artisan that the painter is, so he slunk away. He knows, since the alchemist and the apothecary told him, what is to be done.

Of course much of the castle knows. Though scarcely anyone has slept or sought sleep, the whole place rings with excitement and vivacity. The Duke has decreed, too, that everyone who wishes shall be a witness. So he is having a progress through the castle, seeking every nook and cranny, while, let it be said, his architect takes the opportunity to check no other window-pane has cracked.

From room to room the Duke and his entourage pass, through corridors, along stairs, through dusty attics and musty storerooms he has never seen, or if seen has forgotten. Here and there some retainer is come on. Some elderly women are discovered spinning like spiders up under the eaves, half-blind and complacent. They curtsy to the Duke from a vague recollection of old habit. The Duke tells them the good news; or rather, his messenger, walking before, announces it. The ancient women sigh and whisper, are left, probably forget. Then again, in a narrow courtyard, a simple boy, who looks after a dovecote, is magnificently told. He has a fit from alarm, grasping nothing, and the doves who love and understand him (by not trying to) fly down and cover him with their soft wings as the Duke goes away. The boy comes to under the doves as if in a heap of warm snow, comforted.

It is on one of the dark staircases above the kitchen that the gleaming entourage sweeps round a bend and comes on Rohise the scullery maid, scrubbing. In these days, when there are so few children and young servants, labour is scarce, and the scullerers are not confined to the scullery.

Rohise stands up, pale with shock, and for a wild instant thinks that, for some heinous crime she has committed in ignorance, the Duke has come in person to behead her.

'Hear then, by the Duke's will,' cries the messenger. 'One of Satan's night-demons, which do torment us, has been captured and lies penned in the Duke's hall. At sunrise tomorrow, this thing will be taken to that sacred spot where grows the bush of the Flower of the Fire, and there its foul blood shall be shed. Who then can doubt the bush will blossom, and save us all, by the Grace of God?'

'And the Angel of Death,' intones the priest, on no account to be omitted, 'shall surely –'

'Wait,' says the Duke. He is as white as Rohise. 'Who is this?' he asks. 'Is it a ghost?'

The court stare at Rohise, who nearly sinks in dread, her scrubbing rag in her hand.

Gradually, despite the rag, the rags, the rough hands, the court too begins to see.

'Why, it is a marvel.'

The Duke moves forward. He looks down at Rohise and starts to cry. Rohise thinks he weeps in compassion at the awful sentence he is here to visit on her, and drops back on her knees.

'No, no,' says the Duke tenderly. 'Get up. Rise. You are so like my child, my daughter –'

Then Rohise, who knows few prayers, begins in panic to sing her little song as an orison:

'*O fleur de feu,*
'*Pour ma souffrance –*'

'Ah!' says the Duke. 'Where did you learn that song?'

'From my mother,' says Rohise. And, all instinct now, she sings again:

'*O flurda fur,*
'*Pourma souffrance,*
'*Ned ormey par,*
'*May say day mwar –*'

It is the song of the fire-flower bush, the *Nona Mordica*, called Bite-Me-Not. It begins, and continues: *O flower of fire, For my misery's sake. Do not sleep but aid me; wake!* The Duke's daughter sang it very often. In those days the shrub was not needed, being just a rarity of the castle. Invoked as an amulet, on a mountain road, the rhyme itself had besides proved useless.

The Duke takes the dirty scarf from Rohise's hair. She is very, very like his lost daughter, the same pale smooth oval face, the long white neck and long dark polished eyes, and the long dark hair. (Or is it that she is very, very like the painting?)

The Duke gives instructions and Rohise is borne away.

In a beautiful chamber, the door of which has for 17 years been locked, Rohise is bathed and her hair is washed. Oils and scents are rubbed into her skin. She is dressed in a gown of palest most pastel rose, with a girdle sewn with pearls. Her hair is combed, and on it is set a chaplet of stars and little golden leaves. 'Oh, your poor hands,' say the maids, as they trim her nails. Rohise has realised she is not to be executed. She has realised the Duke has seen her and wants to love her like his dead daughter. Slowly, an uneasy stir of something, not quite happiness, moves through Rohise. Now she will wear her pink gown, now she will sympathise with and console the Duke. Her daze lifts suddenly.

The dream has come true. She dreamed it so often it seems quite normal. The scullery was the thing that never seemed real.

She glides down through the castle and the ladies are astonished by her grace. The carriage of her head under the starry coronet is exquisite. Her voice is quiet and clear and musical, and the foreign tone of her mother, long unremembered, is quite gone from it. Only the roughened hands give her away, but smoothed by unguents, soon they will be soft and white.

'Can it be she is truly the princess returned to flesh?'

'Her life was taken so early – yes, as they believe in the Spice-Lands, by some holy dispensation, she might return.'

'She would be about the age to have been conceived the very night the Duke's daughter d – That is, the very night the bane began –'

Theosophical discussion ensues. Songs are composed.

Rohise sits for a while with her adoptive father in the East Turret, and he tells her about the books and swords and lutes and scrolls, but not about the two portraits. Then they walk out together, in the lovely garden in the sunlight. They sit under a peach tree, and discuss many things, or the Duke discusses them. That Rohise is ignorant and uneducated does not matter at this point. She can always be trained. She has the basic requirements, docility, sweetness. There are many royal maidens in many places who know as little as she.

The Duke falls asleep under the peach tree. Rohise listens to the love-songs her own (her very own) courtiers bring her.

When the monster in the cage is mentioned, she nods as if she knows what they mean. She supposes it is something hideous, a scaring treat to be shown at dinner time, when the sun has gone down.

When the sun moves toward the western line of mountains just visible over the high walls, the court streams into the castle and all the doors are bolted and barred. There is an eagerness tonight in the concourse.

As the light dies out behind the coloured windows that have no red in them, covers and screens are dragged away from a bronze cage. It is wheeled out into the centre of the great hall.

Cannon begin almost at once to blast and bang from the roof-holes. The cannoneers have had strict instructions to keep up the barrage all night without a second's pause.

Drums pound in the hall. The dogs start to bark.

Rohise is not surprised by the noise, for she has often heard it from far up, in her attic, like a sea-wave breaking over and over through the lower house.

She looks at the cage cautiously, wondering what she will see. But she sees only a heap of blackness like ravens, and then a tawny dazzle, torchlight on something like human skin.

'You must not go down to look,' says the Duke protectively, as his court pours about the cage. Someone pokes between the bars with a gemmed cane, trying to rouse the nightmare that lies quiescent there. But Rohise must be spared this.

So the Duke calls his actors, and a slight, pretty play is put on throughout dinner, before the dais, shutting off from the sight of Rohise the rest of the hall, where the barbaric gloating and goading of the court, unchecked, increases.

IV

The Prince Feroluce becomes aware between one second and the next. It is the sound – heard beyond all others – of the wings of his people beating at the stones of the castle. It is the wings that speak to him, more than their wild orchestral voices. Beside these sensations, the anguish of healing and the sadism of humankind are not much.

Feroluce opens his eyes. His human audience, pleased, but afraid and squeamish, back away, and ask each other for the two thousandth time if the cage is quite secure. In the torchlight, the eyes of Feroluce are more black than red. He stares about. He is, though captive, imperious. If he were a lion or a bull, they would admire this 'nobility'. But the fact is, he is too much like a man, which serves to point his supernatural differences unbearably.

Obviously, Feroluce understands the gist of his plight. Enemies have him penned. He is a show for now, but ultimately to be killed – for with the intuition of the raptor he divines everything. He had thought the sunlight would kill him, but that is a distant matter now. And beyond all, the voices and the voices of the wings of his kindred beat the air outside this room-caved mountain of stone.

And so, Feroluce commences to sing, or at least, this is how it seems to the rabid court and all the people gathered in the hall. It seems he sings. It is the great communing call of his kind, the art and science and religion of the winged vampires, his means of telling them, or attempting to tell them, what they must be told before he dies. So the sire of Feroluce sang, and the grandsire, and each of his ancestors. Generally they died in flight, falling angels spun down the gulches and enormous stairs of distant peaks, singing. Feroluce, immured, believes that his cry is somehow audible.

To the crowd in the Duke's hall the song is merely that, a song, but how glorious. The dark silver voice, turning to bronze or gold, whitening in the higher registers There seem to be words, but in some other tongue. This is how the planets sing, surely, or mysterious creatures of the sea.

Everyone is bemused. They listen, astonished.

No-one now remonstrates with Rohise when she rises and steals down from the dais. There is an enchantment that prevents movement and coherent thought. Of all the roomful, only she is drawn forward. So she comes close, unhindered, and between the bars of the cage, she sees the vampire for the first time.

She has no notion what he can be. She imagined it was a monster or a monstrous beast. But it is neither. Rohise, starved for so long of beauty and always dreaming of it, recognises Feroluce inevitably as part of the dream-come-true. She loves him instantly. Because she loves him, she is not afraid of him.

She attends while he goes on and on with his glorious song. He does not see her at all, or any of them. They are only things, like mist, or pain. They have no character or personality or worth; abstracts.

Finally, Feroluce stops singing. Beyond the stone and the thick glass of the siege, the wing-beats, too, eddy into silence.,

Finding itself mesmerised, silent by night, the court comes to with a terrible joint start, shrilling and shouting, bursting, exploding into a compensation of sound. Music flares again. And the cannon in the roof, which had also fallen quiet, resume with a tremendous roar.

Feroluce shuts his eyes and seems to sleep. It is his preparation for death.

Hands grasp Rohise. 'Lady – step back, come away. So close! It may harm you –'

The Duke clasps her in a father's embrace. Rohise, unused to this sort of physical expression, is unmoved. She pats him absently.

'My lord, what will be done?'

'Hush, child. Best you do not know.'

Rohise persists.

The Duke persists in not saying.

But she remembers the words of the herald on the stair, and knows they mean to butcher the winged man. She attends thereafter more carefully to snatches of the bizarre talk about the hall, and learns all she needs. At earliest sunrise, as soon as the enemy retreat from the walls, their captive will be taken to the lovely garden with the peach trees. And so to the sunken garden of the magic bush, the fire-flower. And there they will hang him up in the sun through the dome of smoky glass, which will be slow murder to him, but they will cut him, too, so his blood, the stolen blood of the vampire, runs down to water the roots of the *fleur de feu*. And who can doubt that, from such nourishment, the bush will bloom? The blooms are salvation. Wherever they grow it is a safe place. Whoever wears them is safe from the draining bite of demons. Bite-Me-Not, they call it; vampire-repellent.

Rohise sits the rest of the night on her cushions, with folded hands, resembling the portrait of the princess, which is not like her.

Eventually the sky outside alters. Silence comes down beyond the wall, and so within the wall, and the court lifts its head, a corporate animal scenting day.

At the intimation of sunrise the black plague has lifted and gone away, and might never have been. The Duke, and almost all his castle-full of men, women, children, emerge from the doors. The sky is measureless and bluely grey, with one cherry rift in the east that the court refers to as 'mauve', since dawns and sunsets are never any sort of red here.

They move through the dimly lightening garden as the last stars melt. The cage is dragged in their midst.

They are too tired, too concentrated now, the Duke's people, to continue baiting their captive. They have had all the long night to do that, and to drink and opine, and now their stamina is sharpened for the final act.

Reaching the sunken garden, the Duke unlocks the iron door. There is no room for everyone within, so mostly they must stand outside, crammed in the gate, or teetering on erections of benches that have been placed around, and peering in over the walls, through the glass of the dome. The places in the doorway are the best, of course; no-one else will get so good a view. The servants and lower persons must stand back under the trees and only imagine what goes on. But they are used to that.

Into the sunken garden itself there are allowed to go the alchemist and the apothecary, and the priest, and certain sturdy soldiers attendant on the Duke, and the Duke. And Feroluce in the cage.

The east is all 'mauve' now. The alchemist has prepared sorcerous safeguards that are being put into operation, and the priest, never to be left out, intones prayers. The bulge-thewed soldiers open the cage and seize the monster before it can stir. But drugged smoke has already been wafted into the prison, and besides, the monster has prepared itself for hopeless death and makes no demur.

Feroluce hangs in the arms of his loathing guards, dimly aware the sun is near. But death is nearer, and already one may hear the alchemist's apprentice sharpening the knife an ultimate time.

The leaves of the *Nona Mordica* are trembling, too, at the commencement of the light, and beginning to unfurl. Although this happens every dawn, the court points to it with optimistic cries. Rohise, who has claimed a position in the doorway, watches it too, but only for an instant. Though she has sung of the *fleur de fur* since childhood, she had never known what the song was all about. And in just this way, though she has dreamed of being the Duke's daughter most of her life, such an event was never really comprehended either, and so means very little.

As the guards haul the demon forward to the plot of humid earth where the bush is growing, Rohise darts into the sunken garden, and lightning leaps in her hands. Women scream, and well they might. Rohise has stolen one of the swords from the East Turret, and now she flourishes it, and now she has swung it and a soldier falls, bleeding red, red, red, before them all.

Chaos enters, as in yesterday's play, shaking its tattered sleeves. The men who hold the demon rear back in horror at the dashing blade and the blasphemous gore, and the mad girl in her princess's gown. The Duke makes a pitiful bleating noise, but no-one pays him any attention.

The east glows in and like the liquid on the ground.

Meanwhile, the ironically combined sense of impending day and spilled hot blood have penetrated the stunned brain of the vampire. His eyes open and he sees the girl wielding her sword in a spray of crimson as the last guard lets go. Then the girl has run to Feroluce. Though, or because, her face is insane, it communicates her purpose, as she thrusts the sword's hilt into his hands.

No-one has dared approach either the demon or the girl. Now they look on in horror, and in horror grasp what Feroluce has grasped.

In that moment the vampire springs, and the great swan-like wings are reborn at his back, healed and whole. As the doctors predicted, he has mended perfectly, and prodigiously fast. He takes to the air like an arrow, unhindered, as if gravity does not any more exist. As he does so, the girl grips him about the waist, and slender and light, she is drawn upward too. He does not glance at her. He veers toward the gateway, and tears through it, the sword, his talons, his wings, his very shadow beating men and bricks from his path.

And now he is in the sky above them, a black star that has not been put out. They see the wings flare and beat, and the swirling of a girl's dress and unbound hair, and then the image dives and is gone into the shade under the mountains, as the sun rises.

V

It is fortunate, the mountain shade in the sunrise. Lion's blood and enforced quiescence have worked wonders, but the sun could undo it all – luckily the shadow, deep and cold as a pool, envelops the vampire, and in it there is a cave, deeper and colder. Here he alights and sinks down, sloughing the girl, whom he has almost forgotten. Certainly he fears no harm from her. She is like a pet animal, maybe, like the hunting dogs or wolves or lammergeyers that occasionally the unkindness of vampires have kept by them for a while. That she helped him is all he needs to know. She will help again. So when, stumbling in the blackness, she brings him in her cupped hands water from a cascade at the pool-cave's back, he is not surprised. He drinks the water, which is the only other substance his kind imbibe. Then he smooths her hair absently, as he would pat or stroke the pet she seems to have become. He is not grateful, as he is not suspicious. The complexities of his intellect are reserved for other things. Since he is exhausted he falls asleep, and since Rohise is exhausted she falls asleep beside him, pressed to his warmth in the freezing dark. Like those of Feroluce, as it turns out, her thoughts are simple. She is sorry for distressing the Cursed Duke. But she has no regrets, for she could no more have left Feroluce to die than she could have refused to leave the scullery for the court.

The day, which had only just begun, passes swiftly in sleep.

Feroluce wakes as the sun sets, without seeing anything of it. He unfolds himself and goes to the cave's entrance, which now looks out on a whole sky of stars above a landscape of mountains. The castle is far below, and to the eyes of Rohise as she follows him, invisible. She does not even look for it, for there is something else to be seen.

The great dark shapes of angels are wheeling against the peaks, the stars. And their song begins, up in the starlit spaces. It is a lament, their mourning, pitiless and strong, for Feroluce, who has died in the stone heart of the thing they prey upon.

The tribe of Feroluce do not laugh, but, like a bird or wild beast, they have a kind of equivalent to laughter. This Feroluce now utters, and like a flung lance he launches himself into the air.

Rohise at the cave-mouth, abandoned, forgotten, unnoted even by the mass of vampires, watches the winged man as he flies towards his people. She supposes for a moment that she may be able to climb down the tortuous ways of the mountain, undetected. Where then should she go? She does not spend much time on these ideas. They do not interest or involve her. She watches Feroluce and, because she learned long ago the uselessness of weeping, she does not shed tears, though her heart begins to break.

As Feroluce glides, body held motionless, wings outspread on a down-draught, into the midst of the storm of black wings, the red stars of eyes ignite all about him. The great lament dies. The air is very still.

Feroluce waits then. He waits, for the aura of his people is not as he has always known it. It is as if he had come among emptiness. From the silence, therefore, and from nothing else, he learns it all. In the stone he lay and he sang of his death, as the Prince must, dying. And the ritual was completed, and now there is the threnody, the grief, and thereafter the choosing of a new Prince. And none of this is alterable. He is dead. Dead.

It cannot and will not be changed.

There is a moment of protest, then, from Feroluce. Perhaps his brief sojourn among men has taught him some of their futility. But as the cry leaves him, all about the huge wings are raised like swords. Talons and teeth and eyes burn against the stars. To protest is to be torn in shreds. He is not of their people now. They can attack and slaughter him as they would any other intruding thing. Go, the talons and the teeth and the eyes say to him. *Go far off.*

He is dead. There is nothing left him but to die.

Feroluce retreats. He soars. Bewildered, he feels the power and energy of his strength and the joy of flight, and cannot understand how this is, if he is dead. Yet he *is* dead. He knows it now.

So he closes his eyelids, and his wings. Spear swift he falls. And something shrieks, interrupting the reverie of nihilism. Disturbed, he opens his wings, shudders, turns like a swimmer, finds a ledge against his side and two hands outstretched, holding him by one shoulder, and by his hair.

'No,' says Rohise. (The vampire cloud, wheeling away, have not heard her; she does not think of them.) His eyes stay shut. Holding him, she kisses these eyelids, his forehead, his lips, gently, as she drives her nails into his skin to hold him. The black wings beat, tearing to be free and fall and die. 'No,' says Rohise. 'I love you,' she says. 'My life is your life.' These are the words of the court and of courtly love-songs. No matter, she means them. And though he cannot understand her language or her sentiments, yet her passion, purely that, communicates itself, strong and burning as the passions of his kind, who generally love only one thing, which is scarlet. For a second her intensity fills the void that now contains him. But then he dashes himself away from the ledge, to fall again, to seek death again.

Like a ribbon, clinging to him still, Rohise is drawn from the rock and falls with him.

Afraid, she buries her head against his breast, in the shadow of wings and hair. She no longer asks him to reconsider. This is how it must be. *Love* she thinks again, in the instant before they strike the earth. Then that instant comes, and is gone.

Astonished, she finds herself still alive, still in the air. Touching so close that feathers have been left on the rocks, Feroluce has swerved away, and upward. Now, conversely, they are whirling toward the very stars. The world seems miles below. Perhaps they will fly into space itself. Perhaps he means to break their bones instead on the cold face of the moon.

He does not attempt to dislodge her, he does not attempt anymore to fall and die. But as he flies, he suddenly cries out, terrible lost lunatic cries.

They do not hit the moon. They do not pass through the stars like static rain.

But when the air grows thin and pure there is a peak like a dagger stood in their path. Here, he alights. As Rohise lets go of him, he turns away. He stations himself, sentry-fashion, in the manner of his tribe, at the edge of the pinnacle. But watching for nothing. He had not been able to choose death. His strength and the strong will of another, these have hampered him. His brain has become formless darkness. His eyes glare, seeing nothing.

Rohise, gasping a little in the thin atmosphere, sits at his back, watching for him, in case any harm may come near him.

At last, harm does come. There is a lightening in the east. The frozen, choppy sea of the mountains below and all about, grows visible. It is a marvellous sight, but holds no marvel for Rohise. She averts her eyes from the exquisitely pencilled shapes, looking thin and translucent as paper, the rivers of mist between, the glimmer of nacreous ice. She searches for a blind hole to hide in.

There is a pale yellow wound in the sky when she returns. She grasps Feroluce by the wrist and tugs at him. 'Come,' she says. He looks at her vaguely, as if seeing her from the shore of another country. 'The sun,' she says. 'Quickly.'

The edge of the light runs along his body like a razor. He moves by instinct now, following her down the slippery dagger of the peak, and so eventually into a shallow cave. It is so small it holds him like a coffin. Rohise closes the entrance with her own body. It is the best she can do. She sits facing the sun as it rises, as if prepared to fight. She hates the sun for his sake. Even as the light warms her chilled body, she curses it. Till light and cold and breathlessness fade together.

When she wakes, she looks up into twilight and endless stars, two of which are red. She is lying on the rock by the cave. Feroluce leans over her, and behind Feroluce his quiescent wings fill the sky.

She had never properly understood his nature: vampire. Yet her own nature, which tells her so much, tells her some vital part of herself is needful to him, and that he is danger, and death. But she loves him, and is not afraid. She would have fallen to die with him. To help him by her death does not seem wrong to her. Thus, she lies still, and smiles at him to reassure him she will not struggle. From lassitude, not fear, she closes her eyes. Presently she feels the soft weight of hair brush by her cheek, and then his cool mouth rests against her throat. But nothing more happens. For some while, they continue in this fashion, she yielding, he kneeling over her, his lips on her skin. Then he moves a little away. He sits, regarding her. She, knowing the unknown act has not been completed, sits up in turn. She beckons to him mutely, telling him with her gestures and her expression: *I consent. Whatever is necessary.* But he does not stir. His eyes blaze, but even of these she has no fear. In the end he looks away from her, out across the spaces of the darkness.

He himself does not understand. It is permissible to drink from the body of a pet, the wolf, the eagle. Even to kill the pet, if need demands. Can it be, outlawed from his people, he has lost their composite soul? Therefore, is he soulless now? It does not seem to him he is. Weakened and famished though he is, the vampire is aware of a wild tingling of life. When he stares at the creature that is his food, he finds he sees her differently. He has borne her through the sky, he has avoided death, by some intuitive process, for her sake, and she has led him to safety, guarded him from the blade of the sun. In the beginning it was she who rescued him from the human things that had taken him. She cannot be human, then. Not pet, and not prey. For no, he could not drain her of blood, as he would not seize upon his own kind, even in combat, to drink and feed. He starts to see her as beautiful, not in the way a man beholds a woman, certainly, but as his kind revere the sheen of water in dusk, or flight, or song. There are no words for this. But the life goes on tingling through him. Though he is dead, life.

In the end, the moon does rise, and across the open face of it something wheels by. Feroluce is less swift than was his wont, yet he starts in pursuit, and catches and brings down, killing on the wing, a great night bird. Turning in the air, Feroluce absorbs its liquors. The heat of life now, as well as its assertion, courses through him. He returns to the rock perch, the glorious flaccid bird dangling from his hand. Carefully, he tears the glory of the bird in pieces, plucks the feathers, splits the bones. He wakes the companion (asleep again from weakness) who is not pet or prey, and feeds her morsels of flesh. At first she is unwilling. But her hunger is so enormous and her nature so untamed that she soon she accepts the slivers of raw fowl.

Strengthened by blood, Feroluce lifts Rohise and bears her gliding down the moon-slit quill-backed land of the mountains, until there is a rocky cistern full of cold, old rains. Here they drink together. Pale white primroses grow in the fissures where the black moss drips. Rohise makes a garland and throws it about the head of her beloved when he does not expect it. Bewildered but disdainful, he touches at the wreath of primroses to see if it is likely to threaten or hamper him. When it does not, he leaves it in place.

Long before dawn this time, they have found a crevice. Because it is so cold, he folds his wings about her. She speaks of her love to him, but he does not here, only the murmur of her voice, which is musical and does not displease him. And later, she sings him sleepily the little song of the *fleur de fur*.

VI

There comes a time then, brief, undated, chartless time, when they are together, these two creatures. Not together in any accepted sense, of course, but together in the strange feeling or emotion, instinct or ritual, that can burst to life in an instant or flow to life gradually across half a century, and which men call *love*.

They are not alike. No, not at all. Their differences are legion and should be unpalatable. He is a supernatural thing and she a human thing, he was a lord and she a scullery sloven. He can fly, she cannot fly. And he is male, she female. What other items are required to make them enemies? Yet they are bound, not merely by love; they are bound by all they are, the very stumbling blocks. Bound, too, because they are doomed. Because the stumbling blocks have doomed them; everything has. Each has been exiled out of their own kind. Together, they cannot even communicate with each other, save by looks, touches, sometimes by sounds, and by songs neither understands, but which each comes to value since the other appears to value them, and since they give expression to that other. Nevertheless, the binding of the doom, the greatest binding, grows, as it holds them fast to each other, mightier and stronger.

Although they do not know it, or not fully, it is the awareness of doom that keeps them there, among the platforms and steps up and down, and the inner cups, of the mountains.

Here it is possible to pursue the air-borne hunt, and Feroluce may now and then bring down a bird to sustain them both. But birds are scarce. The richer lower slopes, pastured with goats, wild sheep and men – they lie far off and far down from this place as a deep of the sea. And Feroluce does not conduct her there, nor does Rohise ask that he should, or try to lead the way, or even dream of such a plan.

But yes, birds are scarce, and the pastures far away, and winter is coming. There are only two seasons in these mountains. High summer, which dies, and the High Cold, which already treads over the tips of the air and the rock, numbing the sky, making all brittle, as though the whole landscape might snap in pieces, shatter.

How beautiful it is to wake with the dusk, when the silver webs of night begin to form, frost and ice, on everything. Even the ragged dress – once that of a princess – is tinselled and shining with this magic substance, even the mighty wings – once those of a prince – each feather is drawn glittering with thin rime. And oh, the sky, thick as a daisy-field with the white stars. Up there, when they have fed and have strength, they fly, or, Feroluce flies and Rohise flies in his arms, carried by his wings. Up there in the biting chill like a pane of ghostly vitreous, they have become lovers, true blind lovers, embraced and linked, their bodies a bow, coupling on the wing. By the hour that this first happened the girl had forgotten all she had been, and he had forgotten too that she was anything but the essential mate. Sometimes, borne in this way, by wings and by fire, she cries out as she hangs in the ether. These sounds, transmitted through the flawless silence and amplification of the peaks, scatter over tiny half-buried villages countless miles away, where they are heard in fright and taken for the shrieks_of malign invisible devils, tiny as bats, and armed with the barbed stings of scorpions. There are always misunderstandings.

After a while, the icy prologues and the stunning starry fields of winter nights give way to the main argument of winter.

The liquid of the pool, where the flowers made garlands, has clouded and closed to stone. Even the volatile waterfalls are stilled, broken cascades of glass. The wind tears through the skin and hair to gnaw the bones. To weep with cold earns no compassion of the cold.

There is no means to make fire. Besides, the one who was Rohise is an animal now, or a bird, and beasts and birds do not make fire, save for the phoenix in the Duke's bestiary. Also, the sun is fire, and the sun is a foe. Eschew fire.

There begin the calendar months of hibernation. The demon lovers too must prepare for just such a measureless winter sleep, that gives no hunger, asks no action. There is a deep cave they have lined with feathers and withered grass. But there are no more flying things to feed them. Long, long ago, the last warm frugal feast, long, long ago the last flight, joining, ecstasy and song. So, they turn to their cave, to stasis, to sleep. Which each understands, wordlessly, thoughtlessly, is death.

What else? He might drain her of blood, he could persist some while on that, might even escape the mountains, the doom. Or she herself might leave him, attempt to make her way to the places below, and perhaps she could reach them, even now. Others, lost here, have done so. But neither considers these alternatives. The moment for all that is past. Even the death-lament does not need to be voiced again.

Installed, they curl together in their bloodless, icy nest, murmuring little to each other, but finally still.

Outside, the snow begins to come down. It falls like a curtain. Then the winds take it. Then the night is full of the lashing of whips, and when the sun rises it is white as the snow itself, its flame very distant, giving nothing. The cave mouth is blocked up with snow. In the winter, it seems possible that never again will there be a summer in the world.

Behind the modest door of snow, hidden and secret, sleep is quiet as stars, dense as hardening resin. Feroluce and Rohise turn pure and pale in the amber, in the frigid nest, and the great wings lie like a curious articulated machinery that will not move. And the withered grass and the flowers are crystallised, until the snows shall melt. If ever the snows do melt.

At length, the sun deigns to come closer to the Earth, and the miracle occurs. The snow shifts, crumbles, crashes off the mountains in rage. The waters hurry after the snow, the air is wrung and racked by splittings and splinterings, by rushes and booms. It is half a year, or it might be a hundred years, later.

Open now, the entry to the cave. Nothing emerges. Then, a flutter, a whisper. Something does emerge. One black feather, and caught in it, the petal of a flower, crumbling like dark charcoal and white, drifting away into the voids below. Gone. Vanished. It might never have been.

But there comes another time (half a year, a hundred years) when an adventurous traveller comes down from the mountains to the pocketed villages the other side of them. He is a swarthy cheerful fellow, you would not take him for herbalist or mystic, but he has in a pot a plant he found high up in the staring crags, which might after all contain anything or nothing. And he shows the plant, which is an unusual one, having slender, dark and velvety leaves, and giving off a pleasant smell like vanilla.

'See, the *Nona Mordica*,' he says. 'The Bite-Me-Not. The flower that repels vampires.'

51

Then the villagers tell him an odd story, about a castle in another country, besieged by a huge flock, a menace of winged vampires, and how the Duke waited in vain for the magic bush that was in his garden, the Bite-Me-Not, to flower and save them all.

But it seems there was a curse on this Duke, who on the very night his daughter was lost, had raped a serving woman, as he had raped others before. But this woman conceived. And bearing the fruit, or flower, of this rape, damaged her, so she lived only a year or two after it. The child grew up unknowing, and in the end betrayed her own father by running away to the vampires, leaving the Duke demoralised. And soon after that he went mad, and himself stole out one night, and let the winged fiends into his castle, so all there perished.

'Now if only the bush had flowered in time, as your bush flowers, all would have been well,' the villagers cry.

The traveller smiles. He in turn does not tell them of the heap of peculiar bones, like parts of eagles mingled with those of a woman and a man. Out of the bones, from the heart of them, the bush was rising, but the traveller untangled the roots of it with care; it looks sound enough now in its sturdy pot, all of it twining together. It seems as if two separate plants are growing from a single stem, one with blooms almost black, and one pink-flowered, like a young sunset.

'*Fleur de fur,*' says the traveller, beaming at the marvel, and his luck.

Fleur de feu. Of flower of fire. That fire is not hate or fear, which makes flowers come, not terror or anger or lust. It is love that is the fire of the Bite-Me-Not, love that cannot abandon, love that cannot harm, love that never dies.

THE VAMPIRE LOVER

He is with her tonight.

I know it. What shall I do?

Of course, there is no moral dilemma. Those doubts I had – my halting discussion with the priest left me chastened and horrified. Why then hesitate? Can it be – it must be so – the shadow has stretched out to touch me, too? Then I must hurry. It is no longer the single matter of her life and soul, but also of my own.

Mariamme (my sister) was pale. But this was no problem, for she was always beautiful. To say her hair was gold, as the singers always did, was not strictly true. She was a blonde, as our dead mother had been. When the sun met her hair – either Mariamme's, or our mother's in life – it gleamed more fiery white than gold. She had died, our mother, in trying to bear our father a son. At this time I was 13 years old, but my sister only five. Her grief was more easily expressed than mine, and the sooner forgotten. Her nurses loved her and each gladly became her mother, and she was my father's favourite. He and I, alike in our darkness, were often in accord over things of the mind, but since intellectual women mystified him, he was also uncomfortable with me. I should have been his son, I suppose. But I was a woman, almost thirty years of age now, to Mariamme's pure two-decades-and-one. I sat in the sun-arbour on the terrace of the Stone House, and watched her as she wandered to and fro. She seemed preoccupied, and how listless. Now and then she would indicate a flower to be plucked. 'Yes, that one.' The maid would snip it from the trellis, or perhaps, if she were not quick enough, one of the two or three gallants would break it less tidily. Such young men always provided Mariamme her own court. They were knights of our father's, but he made no objection. Chivalrous love, the woman-worshipped-as-Madonna, it was all the fashion. He had announced no plans to marry her to anyone as yet. She was so lovely, one might imagine he was saving her for some especially expedient match. But he liked her by him, too. For myself, a political marriage had long ago been arranged; actually the second, for I had first married when I was 16, by proxy. The union, to the Lion House, would have been helpful to my father, but the prospective husband (he was 12) died of plague a month later, even as I was on my journey to him. Sent back again, I waited another ten years for my second betrothal. Though unblemished, straight, and healthy – and still a virgin – I was no longer young. My new bridegroom was some twenty years my senior, but, like the first, I had never set eyes on him. He had agreed to me by messenger. We were to wed when he returned from the long northern wars. Provided, of course, he did return. As yet he showed no sign of it. But I too was in no hurry. I would obey, when I must.

'And this?' said my sister, pointing to a smiling rose, with a finger on which three large jewels flashed.

'No, another. That is the thirteenth on the stem –' The gallants laughed, but they were in earnest, too, being superstitious to a man.

'Then this?' And the three jewels flashed again, and then more brightly as Mariamme put her hand to her forehead.

Her knights were alarmed. They supported her. But it was only a momentary weakness. Once she came to sit by me, and had begun to sip the cup of wine one of them poured for her, she was soon merry enough. Yet, she was very pale.

I tried to continue with my reading, but it became more difficult against the chatter, and presently one of the gallants had produced a lyre, and it was to be a singing game. Marking my place in the bestiary, an enormous book I carried with some awkwardness, I said I would leave them. No-one stayed me, I did not expect it, but as I rose, I noticed a strange little mark, to the left side of my sister's throat. Pausing, and at the risk of offending with the interruption, I asked, 'Why, Mariamme, have you been stung?'

'Oh –' she said, and a curious look came over her face. 'No – I think – I scratched myself yesterday evening, when I undid my necklace.'

'But your maids see to your jewellery,' I said. 'They must in future be more careful.'

'No. It was my fault. I was – hasty – Oh, play for me!' she cried suddenly to the gallant with the lyre. 'A happy song, very fast.'

They took great pleasure in her changeableness. Only I found it peculiar. But then, I was not courtly-in-love with Mariamme.

Puzzled, I left them in the peach-leaf shadows of the arbour.

The flowers she had picked, or selected to be picked, were on the high table to grace our dinner, and my father was charmed. Despite this, Mariamme seemed excitable, half uneasy, as if afraid she might annoy him inadvertently – something that never happened; I was the one who did that. I gazed at my sister surreptitiously, but with an increasing sense of some strangeness. It came in a while to take my appetite, as plainly it had already taken Mariamme's. Our father was concerned she did not eat, but she lowered her eyes and turned shy, and I saw him make the decision that this was all due to the 'Moon'. He became gruff, then jovial, to offset the masculine gaff. However, her condition was nothing of the sort. Her sister, sleeping as I did in an adjoining chamber, I knew generally when it was that she bled, her seasons and pulses, as one knows weather in a familiar country.

Much later, I went to her room.

She was knelt at prayer before her icons, in her shift, her hair spangle-veiled by the candles. But when I entered she sprang up as if I had caught her out in some guilty act.

'This is not like you,' she said, 'to come into my room at bedtime. I remember how I used to entreat you to, when we were children and I was so afraid of the dark –'

'The dark never frightens you now.'

'Ah, why should it? Night is as beautiful as day –'

I had noted the lower window stood wide open. The evening was mild, but not airless. I asked her why she had opened the shutters.

'For the scent of the flowers on the creeper,' she said. 'No, you no longer scare me, unkind sister. Do you remember how you used to make me cry with your stories of huge night insects flying in between the sheets – or bats that would perch on me and end all tangled up in my hair –?'

I may have warned her of such things when she was little. All I recalled was her own fear of ghosts. But at this moment an odd thing happened. Like a black paper, as if summoned by her words, a bat did go flitting across the window, and up, out of our sight.

'Well, so you see,' I said. And I went to the shutters and drew them closed.

Mariamme observed me. She said nothing more.

High above her bed, the inner window of glass, lit by the great three-night candle behind it, blazed a sombre rich crimson, and now some draught from the closing shutters caused the light to flutter and cast shadow – as if somehow the bat had after all come in, and hid there, beating its narrow black dragon wings impatiently.

The disturbance of the red light caused me to see another thing that before I had missed. It was a vague trailing mark among the covers of the bed – pale, as if attempts had been made to erase it. But even countered by water and much scrubbing, I thought I recognised the stain of dried blood.

Now I said nothing and went away to my own chamber.

Two thicknesses of wooden doors separated me here from Mariamme, and the little stone annexe between. She seemed removed by miles, by mighty cliffs and forests. I lay awake a long while, and, intuitively, I listened, but all I heard was the faintest rustling of the creeper on the house wall as the night-breeze whispered to it; the hunting cry of a nocturnal bird in the woods.

The lights of my inner window – this a gift of glass our father gave us; it is an important symbol of status and wealth – were cool and customary blue. They trembled lake-like on my bed and soothed me. My outer window was shuttered.

Nothing would get in. This was my last, macabre thought, before I slept.

Next day, about noon, players came to the gates. Our father allowed them in. He was generally indifferent to such shows (as I was), but his household liked them, and Mariamme had adored all spectacle from the time of her childhood – he was in an indulgent mood. They put on their entertainment in the hall after the evening meal, having fed well themselves in the kitchen court. From the gossip, one heard they had been in the neighbourhood some weeks, nor were they strangers to us, having performed in the Mallet House at Mid-Winter, where some of my father's people had travelled to see them: they were reckoned excellent of their kind.

It bored me, I fear, the whole business, but I must not go up to bed or book, my father had brought everyone in for the fun and would be offended. He himself sat stoically, even raising a laugh at some of the idiotic antics. Every actor was masked, naturally, in the tradition, which to me only enhances the preposterousness of the situation. There was a white-masked fool, gymnastic and limber, constantly cart wheeling and bending backwards – our father particularly remarked him, and called him out at one point to throw him some gold – at which we all clapped, the actors prudently included. But the jollity was marred nevertheless.

If he had meant this treat to rejoice Mariamme, our father seemed mysteriously to have failed. She had risen late today. I had not seen her until supper. If she had been out of sorts before, now she was wan and sleepy. Her face looked white as the white mask of the jester. When our father was amused, sometimes she would force a laugh, but otherwise, how drawn she seemed. Her hands shook, so the jewels spurted continuous fire, she trembled all over, and bit her lip. I found I could not take my eyes from her, and what they did on their stage of tables, mostly I missed.

But then there came a scene with death in it, the way these mountebanks invariably show it – a man, black cloaked and cowled, with a crown of staring bones. He entered with a swirl of his mantle, jumping from nowhere it looked, so some of the ladies screamed. My sister, too, started in her skin. Something made me say to her, 'But you have seen them act this before, surely, at Mallet?' And she answered, 'Not death,' and then toppled lightly out of her chair. One of her retinue of knights caught her before she struck the floor.

Our father was enraged with the players, and turned them out of doors immediately. I could have told them, in their sulks, they were lucky to get off without being ordered a whipping.

Mariamme was put to bed. She would not consult the physician, and even the priest was refused. She wept and clung to our father's hand. 'You,' he said to me, 'must stay by her.' Dismayed at her emotion, he left her to me, and for a while I sat by her bedside under the ruby flame of the inner window. I felt myself grown chilled as I sat there. I could not tell what it was.

Finally I said, for she did not sleep, 'Why not undo the ribbon at your throat. Perhaps it makes you uncomfortable. At once, she raised her hand to cover throat and ribbon together. She stared at me with confused, frightened eyes.

'Oh,' she said, 'what do you know? Tell me now.'

'I? What should I know, Mariamme? It is for you to tell me –'

'I can tell nothing. But you are so clever. Do you hate me?'

I flinched at her words. They wounded me.

'I am your sister. How can I hate you, and for what?' (Her eyes now evaded mine.) 'Mariamme,' I said, 'tomorrow, let the physician come and look at you.'

'No,' she said, 'I am not sick. Only –'

'What, Mariamme?'

'Nothing at all,' she said hoarsely. And then, with wild desperation, 'Please go – leave me. How can I sleep when you glare at me all the while? Let me alone!'

I got up. 'Very well.'

She sighed deeply. She was frantic to have me gone, yet did not seem to understand her own vehemence. As she had writhed, the ribbon shifted on her neck. There, where I had seen the small freckle of blood, a thunderous bruise now swelled the white skin. I said nothing of this. Bidding her goodnight, I went out, closing her door, and presently mine. Now I too trembled. My hands were icy. My heart hammered.

In those minutes I already knew it all. But, sceptic that I am naturally inclined to be, I would not surrender to my instincts – or not entirely.

I rarely pray, save from duty. But then I went to my knees and I admit that I required of God a sign. I had some learning, and even in superstition, or those matters I attributed to superstition, I was not uninformed. After a long while, I rose and sought the old volume of supernatural bestiary. There I searched out a particular word, and read again the text and examine again the drawing that lay under the word. Then I laughed at my own imaginings, though my body stayed cold and shivering.

Going to my own shutters, I opened them, slowly and cautiously, and leaned out a short distance.

It was a little beyond midnight, dark travelling toward dawn in its long black hourly wagons, silent each as a grave. My window looked from the same stretch of wall, creeper-wrapped, as Mariamme's. Turning my head I saw how the winged shutters of her room again stood wide. They had been fastened when I was with her. She must have risen and seen to them once I had gone away.

Something then made me rapidly draw back, pulling my own shutters almost to, but without a sound. It seemed to me I dared not breathe, dared not glance – but clearly I must see if something were to be visible – what did I anticipate? Only the thing I had read of in a book I did not believe.

As I had kneeled to pray, so now I knelt again, and putting my face close to the slats of my shutter, stared through them, towards Mariamme's window, so open, so much an invitation.

There was a dearth of light, but suddenly from that very window bloomed a blood-red ghost that dewed every one of the creeper's leaves with blood – It would seem she had renewed the three-night candle behind her inner window of ruby glass, even as I had left that behind my window of blueness to go out. A signal – what else? Heaven help her, as the victim so frequently is, she was in collusion now with the creature that slowly murdered and damned her.

And then my heart froze. Peering between the slats, I made out something, in the creeper, there, easing and gliding like a snake – *up the very wall of the house* –

At the last moment my courage failed me; I covered my eyes as it began to slide in over the threshold of her room.

Needless to say, as I huddled in the half-dark, I *pictured* it all. How she lay, my sister, voiceless, will-less, and waiting, and the black thing came to her and covered her whiteness with its ink. It seemed to me I heard a small stifled cry – and at that I knew she had again been pierced by the hungry fangs of it. There under the blood-coloured window, the vampire that preyed on Mariamme sucked her blood from a cup of pale flesh and gilded hair.

At first, I could not move from sheer horror. Then a sort of lethargy overcame me. Eventually, a stupor –

I wakened – and the sun rose! When I forced myself to look out again, the shutters of the other window were fastened closed. Only a slight tearing in the creeper marked the invader's progress. Obviously, demon of night that he was, he would be long gone before sunrise. I gazed and could not think. My mind was empty of anything. There my sin began. My sin was, of course, this: I did not speak of it.

I did not speak, and quantities of days followed, quantities of nights between, when I knew – days of Mariamme moving listlessly about the house, now drooping and ashen, next volatile as if in a high fever. Always a ribbon or a necklace to conceal the tell-tale bruises at her throat. She kept away from me. I did not seek her. She was to me like one infected by plague; she revolted me, yet I was tortured by the image of her subjugation, the pouring in of darkness, the plundering – worst of all, the submission that the vampire inspires in and exacts from his prey. Every night that she went to her bedchamber, sending out her maids (who sometimes loitered in the anteroom, talking of her pallor and her nervousness), every night then I felt I must run to her door, beat on it or force it open; she locked it when once alone, I was certain. Over and over I rehearsed my plan. The anteroom led into a corridor, barred at its far end by a large door. Outside this, turn by turn, chosen knights of our father's, two by two, stood each a month-long service of guard, and had done so all our lives. We were precious, for our various reasons, my father's daughters. We had only to cry out to bring the pair of champions of that night's watch, fully armed, hurtling to our defence. But I would go to them softly. By the rituals and ordeals of their knighthood itself, they knew that evil existed, and in many forms, to battle with the hosts of God. Generally, I had found them as superstitious as the lowliest peasant, though their phrases in describing the affair were high-flown. Now I might thank all the saints they had kept this innocent wisdom. Once I had told them all I had witnessed, could they prevaricate? From the window of my room, screened by darkness (the candle in the blue window put out) and the creeper's fall, they could behold for themselves that eerie awful progress the monster made up the stone walls of this house. Even to think of it – I had never again been able to bring myself to regard it – filled my veins with show.

Then again, it had occurred to me I should seek the priest of our house.

He was an old man, also learned, and no scoffer at what I had always called 'myths'. Though I was never less than respectful toward him, and steadily attentive to my religious duties, maybe he did not care for me. Mariamme, who lapsed and committed childish sins continually, also burned with an emotive childish devotion to the idea of God, which the priest liked much more than my unfluctuating piety. He had had to set me no proper penance since I was 16, just before my first marriage. He seemed ever on the verge of telling me now that my confessions were a lie; he would have enjoyed doing so. But as I had always told him only the simple facts, he could never catch me out. And though not the favourite, I was still the Lord's daughter.

However, in this, surely in this, he would help me, advise me. If not, I must go elsewhere. The Devil worked upon us – and I did nothing.

Nothing, though I had seen the proofs and could communicate them to others; all those dreadful proofs the bestiary, treating the vampire as a submortal, thus a *beast*, had digressed upon. (And had not the hand of Fate been even in this, that I should have chanced on this very passage and read it, only a few minutes before I saw the mark on my sister's neck?) The book related all. First the shape-changing, to a wolf, or to that other vampire thing, the bat – just as I had seen him, going by the window. Next how, though I myself had closed the way, he manifested from thin air behind the lens of red glass – so they did, no human barrier could keep them out. And oh, the stain of blood, her blood spilled from the wound he had made, on her sheet. And the tiny puncture in her neck that, with his constant use, swelled up and blackened in that terrible bruise she must always conceal. Her weakness, her paleness – sure signs – her fainting at the image of Death, which was a cipher for the vampire. How he entered by night, abandoned her before the sun or the crowing of the cock, leaving her ever more despoiled, until, at length, she would die. And worse than die, die and become one of his own, dead yet possessed, a live corpse with my sister's face, but motivated by the will of a demon.

And knowing all this, *I kept silent*.

Why? It comes hard to me, I partly do not believe it – and partly I do. She was so lovely, and I – well, I was not Mariamme. She had so long been before me, the vision of her brightness, which captivated all as I captivate none. Let me say it out then. I accuse myself of jealousy, of the Sin of Envy. Could it be I would be glad to see her perish, the victim of the Beast? But no – no. How could such a thing be true? She was my sister.

It was this anguish that drove me to the priest tonight. It was before him, having woken him in his bed, that I stumbled through a confession in which I murmured of certain things, hinted at others. At one juncture the old man caught his breath and broke in – 'Your lord father will ask an appalling payment for it – but not from her. He has always loved her. I would rest my own life on that –' Then I saw he had misunderstood me, so I spoke more precisely if perhaps no more succinctly. Abruptly he too blanched, and crossed himself, whispering a snatch of prayer. At this I left him. I fled.

I returned here to my chamber and paced about.

Soon the moon rose. In terror and trouble I put out the candle behind the blue window. I crept to my shutters and opened them only a crack. When the creeper rustled I ran and hid my eyes – Coward!

He climbed, he reached the window and passed inside.

He is with her now, milking her life and purity –

If I have not the wit to go for the knights of our guard, let me go alone and sink my woman's nails in his undead flesh, let me harm him all I can for daring to take her. I have felt his shadow. His shadow has come to me in dreams – a faceless presence – I see now, not my fault – it is his thrall that has corrupted me, made me as compliant as she is – and I shall be his next victim. Yes, he will claim me, too, as his bride of death –

No more. I must act swiftly and at once.

She runs along the corridor, Mariamme's elder sister. She opens the door there at its end and goes out to the two nightly knightly guard, astonishing them. Her story, which she tells with a powerful and controlled hysteria, is more energising than any passion. It turns them from civilised men to embattled warriors. This night is a fortuitous choice – these two knights are founders of Mariamme's inner court. They definitely love her, and grow instantly afraid.

So they go along the corridor, through the anteroom, at a noiseless rush, and flinging themselves against the door of Mariamme's chamber, smash through its one flimsy lock in a few seconds, Then they are in the room, the room of their sacred Madonna, while the dark sister stands in the doorway behind them, still as a post.

The ruby window, bleeding, gives good light. What do they see? What horror, what demoniac extravagance?

Their goddess lies naked, sprawling on the pillows, helpless, with a look of fear beyond any they have ever seen, except perhaps in a deer about to be ripped by the hounds.

At the bed's foot, a man-shaped being, flowing in and out of blackness against the crimson lambency – seeming as if about to dissolve, of which the vampire, as they know, is capable.

Each man stands transfixed, raising against Satan the cross-piece of his sword. *Un*manned.

It takes the other woman, she in the doorway, to cry out: 'No – he will be gone – kill him! Look how he has used Mariamme! And then, more terribly: 'Or give me your swords. Must I do it?'

That shifts them. Both spring, and taking hold of the creature that even now is in its turn springing, pantherish and abnormally agile, toward the window, they bring it down. It screams as their blades go through it, guts and heart – but there is only one sure way with a vampire. Of this they are aware. As one man drags back the head by its hair, the other hacks it off.

Bizarrely, the screaming fails to stop.

No longer the vampire, it is Mariamme who screams. She kneels on the bed, screaming and screaming, her face mindlessly turning its screaming mouth to each of them, one by one.

Suddenly one of the knights falls to his knees before her. He lifts his blood-red sword into the blood-red light, a sort of pledge, dazzled by her nakedness and her defilement. At the gesture, Mariamme's screams die. All at once she is totally dumb, though her look of abject fright remains. And in dumbness and in fright, she steps from the bed, runs to the window and throws herself out of it. Before anything can be done, she is gone into the darkness with a ghastly striking wrenching sound that may only be the tearing of the creeper on the wall.

My father summoned me in the last quarter of the hour before dawn. I had been praying with the old priest, who had been very constrained with me, his fear and distress evident in every mannerism. The whole of the Stone House was wracked, in uproar, weeping and wailing. From far off, any who chanced to hear, would think us doomed.

He was in the chapel, my father, where the two bodies had been taken. The demon's remains, under its black cloak, had been ringed by in-pointing swords, fragments of the Host, branches of thorn hastily lopped and smelling still of their sap. The arms and legs, the torso, the severed head, all were discernible in outline. My sister's poor pitiful corpse was less well-arranged, so shattered was it by its fall. It lay, a heap, wrapped in a red mantle, and already some flowers scattered over it. One hand, still whole and perfect, had been allowed to lie out on the robe's surface. The jewels glimmered on its fingers, but only with the motion of the candles.

I told my father, with a bowed head, of my grief and guilt. I was brief, not wishing to inflame his hurt. I had already cut off all my hair, in token of mourning.

'Look up,' said my father. I obeyed, of course.

'You wish me to tell my story?' I asked.

'I have heard your story from others.' His face was like the house stone, unmarked by any tears. Neither of us had cried at all. I have never found it easy. 'I am only interested, he said, 'in how you, who have never credited such things, came to credit this.'

'I saw the proofs,' I said. 'My shame is, I waited too long. His hold on her was by then too great.'

'These proofs.'

'As I have described. Her pallor and lassitude. The wound on her neck. And the stain in her bed, though faded by much washing. Lastly, when I saw him climb the sheer wall.'

'There is a creeper on the wall. A strong creeper,' said my father. 'Even Mariamme's body, striking there repeatedly till all her little bones were smashed, did not tear it away. Firmly footed, the creeper. And he was very athletic and supple. Did no-one tell you, it was the actor who played the fool – oh, and he played Death, also.'

'In his human form, he was one of the actors?' I said. 'Well, I have heard of such things. Did his fellows never suspect?'

'No. Never. They knew he would go out at night. Some girl, they thought. Which was, too, why he wished to return here. Some high-born girl he wanted, who gave herself to him. A silly thing to do, they always guessed as much. It would seem she was afraid of her father, a man inclined to anger. She was pale with fear every next day, though there was also another cause of that; her paleness, her weakness, her fainting at a sudden public sight of her lover, and the premonition of his death – she was with child.'

I stood transfixed, bemused. I felt as cold as when I recognised the vampire. (Through the deep windows, as if to augment the rest, it was beginning to get light.)

'What are you saying?' I asked him, my father.

'As for the wound in her throat, she caught her skin in the clasp of her necklace, hurrying to remove it so her maids would go, and leave her to the longed-for company of her visitor. And the next night, you see, he kissed the little wound, and his kiss grew impassioned – a type of kiss you know nothing about, since no man has ever kissed you in such a way, nor shall one, I imagine. A bruising kiss. But she hid that from me, too, and all the others. She thought I would be enraged and kill her. *Her*. I would have been enraged. I would have killed him – or perhaps not, if she wanted him, if she had pleaded for him … I could never refuse her anything. When she asked me for the coloured window of glass for you, too, not just for her, a blue window for her red window – she said you would feel the slight otherwise. No, I could refuse her nothing. I loved her. When she begged me not to marry her to this one, or that – I always relented. I let go good matches that way, and fine men. Not like the leavings who would agree to take you – and even they have no stomach for you in the end, they prefer the plague or the war. But even so, she never trusted me, my Mariamme. Some flaw there, I never saw it. Nor, it seems, did I ever see you, my scholarly dark daughter.'

I said, 'Her bed was marked with blood.'

He said, brusquely, 'She was a virgin when he first had her. Even *you* must have heard of Showing the Sheet of the First Night.'

We stood almost idly then, and the sun came in through the windows.

It came to the vampire under his cloak, next across the body of my sister in its red mantle. The shape of limbs, broken or only hacked, did not alter, no stench rose of grave mould and crumbling dust. My father crossed to the sword-ringed corpse. He lifted a corner of the covering. I glimpsed young skin and staring eyes –

'One omission from the itinerary,' said my father. 'Sunlight, which destroys vampires, leaves him untouched.' He let the cover fall again. 'And her. I suppose, if she had not killed herself, you would have found some excuse – a fiendish glint in her eyes, a look of the Devil – you would have had do to *that* work yourself. Her knights would never have been able to take blade to *her*.'

'I was mistaken,' I said. My head rang, as if from a blow. I heard myself say, 'But do you want this blazed abroad? Your younger daughter a whore, lying down under a common mountebank? Better keep to the other tale; it has a nicer flourish. A vampire who raped only her sweet soul, which was then freed by your gallant knights. She died absolved, naturally, and now queens it again, in Heaven.'

'Ah, yes,' murmured my father. 'Now I hear you.'

'Why?' I whispered. 'What did I say?'

It is a dire time we have of it. The Stone House has more than earned the grimness of its name.

All are smitten by sorrow. I, who can never weep, feel it perhaps more than most. I miss the sunshine of Mariamme. There is no-one to take her place. Her special knights have already begun to find excuses to desert us. My father lets them go on their pretexts of campaigns and crusades. He is, I am afraid, somewhat unhinged by bereavement.

Yes, I do fear for his mind. He will not see me, or let me near him. I keep to my room therefore, and read the large old books. It is peaceful, though sometimes I grow unaccountably anxious.

Even, sometimes, I admit, I become fearful to eat any of the food that is sent me, or to drink the wine. For a reason I cannot quite fathom, and that is certainly foolish, I begin to think he may very soon poison me, my father.

WINTER FLOWERS

Pierre was burned at Bethelmai; I helped them light the fire.

Parts of the town were already burning, and under cover of that, and the general sack, we had gone about our own business. There had been no real pay for months and Bethelmai was full of trinkets, particularly in the houses around the church, and there were the cellars of wine and the kitchens that still had chickens and loaves despite five weeks of siege. And there were the plump, cream-fed women. Duke Waif's boys were well occupied. There should have been room enough for anything.

I had found an old narrow house in a byway that the onslaught had either missed or else run over and left behind. Probably not the latter, for though there were signs of upset, broken pots, a few coins scattered from a chest, the hurried household may have made a mess in getting out. Upstairs someone was moving, or maybe only breathing. I climbed the stair and pushed open the door. Into the gloom of the chamber from a slit of window a light ray fell from the smoking town, and lit a pair of brown-amber eyes wide with fright.

'Don't rape me,' she said, and then a fragment of bad Latin, the kind you hear all over a camp before the assault, prayer in pieces. She was obviously a servant, abandoned, only about 14 years old.

'No, I won't do that.'

I went right over and sat beside her on the wooden bed of her deserting master and mistress. I took her hand. Of course I reeked of the fight, metal and blood and smoke, but not of lust. I was only thirsty.

There was a tiny silver ring on her wrist.

'Don't take it,' she said. 'It's all I've got.'

'No, I won't take it.'

I raised her hand to my mouth, and moved the ring up a little, away from the vein. I put my mouth there, and sucked at the flesh, letting my saliva numb her, the way it does. And I crooned in my throat. She became still and soft, and when I bit into the vein she never flinched, only sighed once.

It was some while since I had had blood. That is the way of it. The campaigns are often long and it will be difficult to get anything. The battles make up for this, affording as they usually do so many opportunities.

The nourishment went into me and I could feel it doing me good, better than wine and meat. But I did not take too much, and when I finished I tore her sleeve and bound up the wound. They rarely remember.

She was drowsy, and I kissed her forehead and put some of the coins from the chest downstairs into her hand.

'Stay up here till nightfall. Then go carefully, and you might sneak away.' There was nowhere much for her to fly to, in fact, for the countryside had been shaved bald by Waif's hungry vicious troops. Still, she must take her chance. It is all any of us can do.

Downstairs I worked a touch more damage on the hall, and gathered up the last coins from the chest, the lock of which I smashed with my dagger-hilt for good measure. It now looked for sure as though the soldiers had already been through and there would be nothing remaining to filch.

Outside I went looking for a drink of wine. I felt strong, alert, and clean now, the way we do after living blood. With bright clear eyes I viewed the smouldered roofs, and on the ground the occasional corpse, and many looted objects cast aside. Waif's happy men were throwing down treasures from upper windows and over walls. The mailed soldiers swaggered, drunk, round the streets, toasting the Duke, and now and then some of the captains rode by on their steaming horses, trailing Waif's colours proudly, as if something wonderful had been done. Dim intermittent thuds and crashes, shouts, and the continual high cries of women, thickened the air like the smirch.

Bethelmai was hot from the fires, although outside winter had set in on the plains and hills. Bollo had said it would snow before the week was out and he was seldom wrong. God help them then, all the towns and villages Duke Waif had cracked. Where next? There had been talk of Pax Pontis to the north. That was greater than Bethelmai and might require some months of siege. From somewhere Waif would have to get more cash and further provisions, or his toasting proud army would desert him. So I was thinking, idling along with a wine-skin I had pulled off an addled soldier, not realising that none of this would presently concern me.

It was when I came out into the square before the church that I beheld a secondary commotion was going on, and Pierre was in the midst of it. Waif's men had him by both arms, and all across the distance I could see the scarlet marker, like the kiss of a rose, on his mouth.

Up on the church steps, before the broken gaping door, some of Waif's officers were stood, looking on. But all around the pillaging soldiers scurried, not noticing what happened with Pierre, supposing it possibly some breach of petty discipline peculiarly upheld, as often happens, in the middle of a riot.

Then big-bellied Captain Rotlam came at me, pushing his beaked, scarred and scowling face forward like an angry, oddly-neckless goose.

'You, Maurs. That's your man there. You see, the one my fellows have got.'

'I see, Captain. Yes, he's one of mine.'

'Stinking mercenaries,' said Rotlam. He spat at my boot. No matter. It had had worse on it today, and several times. 'You God-cursed filthy thieves,' he enlarged. 'Taking the Duke's pay –' I wondered what pay he meant – 'skulking – have you even killed anything this morning, aside from your own fleas? Any enemy?'

I said, 'Shall I bring you their severed hands?'

'Eh? Shut your mouth. That bastard there. Your scum. Do you know what we caught him at?'

I knew. Already and quite well I knew, and my heart, which had been high, was growing cold. It had happened before, and when it did, there was not much that could be done. We all understood that. Even Arpad the hothead, and Yens the grumbler, and melancholy, colicky Festus. You must take your chance. All luck runs dry at last, like every river, now or tomorrow or at World's End.

But I said, scowling back, 'What's Pierre done?'

'Pierre is it? Don't you know he's a stinking blasphemous witch?'

I crossed myself. I make my mistakes but am not a fool.

'Yes, God guard us –' Rotlam gestured at his men to bring my one forward, and they dragged Pierre, pulling him off his feet, so by the time they reached us he was kneeling.

His dark eyes moved up to mine above the red mouth. Poor lost Pierre. Dead brother to be. But I had my other brothers to consider, and my own damnable skin.

'Well,' I said roughly, 'what's this? What have you been doing, in God's name?'

'Nothing, Maurs,' said Pierre. He added expertly, and hopelessly, 'There was this boy, he had a gold chain hidden, and when I tried to get it off him, he went for me like a mad dog. I fought him off but I couldn't get my knife – so I bit him. In the neck. It stopped him. Then the Captain's soldiers found us, and for some reason –'

'He was drinking the boy's blood,' broke in the man who had Pierre by the left arm. He shook the arm as if to get it free of the socket, and Pierre yelped. 'Accursed demon shit!' the soldier shouted. He was terrified, all the drink gone to venom.

'He wanted to kill this bastard on the spot,' said the other man, 'but I said, bring him to the Captain.'

'Oh, by God,' I said, sounding amused, amazed, my heart like the snow Bollo had told me was coming.

'By God, can't my fellow defend himself without –'

'He drank the boy's blood,' said the calm soldier stolidly, staring at me. 'If you'd seen, you'd believe. Or have you seen, sometime, and not minded?'

At that Rotlam punched me in the chest. 'Eh? Answer that, Maurs, you bit of muck.'

I straightened up and shrugged. 'These two are drunk out of their wits. What do they know?'

There was some shouting then, and the calmer of the soldiers drew his sword on me and I knocked him flat. Then Rotlam hit me and I had to take it, since he was one of the marvellous Duke's astounding captains. Pierre by this time had lowered his head. When the noise lessened, I heard him murmur, 'Let me go, Maurs. My fault. Who cares? I've had enough.'

'What's the devil say?' roared goose-face Rotlam, hissing and bubbling.

'God hears, not I,' I said. 'I don't know this man well. You'd better get a priest. See what he says.'

So, like Peter before Cockcrow, I gave my friend over to oblivion. And like Peter I sweated chill and was full of darkness.

They made quite a show of it, calling all the troops they could prise from the sack, setting up a sort of court. Examining Pierre. There were three greasy priests, rats who had been busy enough themselves on Bethelmai's carcass until called off. The Duke's bastard looked in upon the 'trial', but did not bother to stay. Bollo and I were asked questions, and Johan, who had been Pierre's companion on various forays, and Festus and Lutgeri, who had been with Pierre getting in over the fallen gates of the town. We all said we did not know Pierre that well, for he had not been with us very long. He had come out of the night to our fire that summer, just before we offered our swords to the Duke. And as we said this rubbish, I watched Pierre slightly nodding to himself. Once, long, long ago, at a similar scene, I had wept, and nearly implicated myself. But the tears dry like the luck and the fucking rivers.

In the end, Pierre was pronounced demon-possessed, a witch. He admitted it, because otherwise they would have broken his fingers, lashed him, done other choice things. They made up a makeshift but efficient pyre, with a pole in the centre that had been a cross-beam of some house. They pushed Pierre up and bound him. He looked at me, and his eyes said *Curse me now*. So we cursed him, and asked the priests for help and penances, and what prayers to say, since we had been all summer and fall in Pierre's deadly company. The priests were sweet. They took our spoils of gold from Bethelmai and instructed us to abstain from wine and women, and meat. To beg from God morning and evening. And such clever methods.

When they set fire to the wood, I ran and flung a torch into the sticks, howling. My men cheered and spat upon Pierre. He looked down at us from beyond the smoke. He was a beautiful boy, seeming not more than twenty, with a face to charm the girls, and, come to that, the Dukes of this Earth. He knew every foul name we called him was a prayer, and every gob of spit a cry for his forgiveness.

In the end he screamed in agony, and forgot us all.

They say the fire is cold. I heard it once – *So cold! So cold!*

It would be easy to abstain from meat after all.

When he was gone and the flames sank and gave way, and they had raked about and made sure that nothing lived in them, they sprinkled the place with holy water.

Soon after, Rotlam the goose told us to get going. We were to have no pay – what pay? – and to take nothing from the town – the priests had had most of it. I argued, since not to do so would seem strange and perhaps suspicious. 'We fought hard and well for Duke Waif.' But Rotlam laughed, and that in a ring of swords.

From the hills above the plain we glanced back, but Bethelmai was still burning, although Pierre had finished.

'May they eat their own flesh and vomit their own guts,' said Arpad.

'They will,' said Lutgeri. 'They all do in the end.'

I thought of the girl with a fawn's amber eyes, and if she would escape the town. To think of Pierre was a more terrible thing I must come to softly. For he was all the others who had died, and he was also all of us. No-one spoke to me as we tramped across the hills, with the smut of Bethelmai upon our hides and the blood of Bethelmai in our bellies, and Pierre's death our banner.

Bollo had been right about the snow. It came like a great grey bird from the heart of the sky. The whiteness fell like petals. So cold. So cold.

'There'll be wolves,' said Gilles.

'So, wolves are nothing,' said Johan stoically.

There are always two schools of thought with wolves. One says they are fiends who will tear you up as you sleep and chew your genitals till you wake shrieking. The other school, which from experience is mine, will tell that wolves seldom attack a moving man, or a sleeping man for that matter. Once, Johan was relieving himself in a winter field and a wolf appeared and stared at him. The eyes of wolves are human, and Johan was costive for three days. But when he shouted at the wolf it fled.

In any case, we did not hear their song, up on the lean white hills. We heard nothing. The world had died. Good riddance.

Once, from a height, we saw a town far off, walls and towers, and when the dark began, that buzz of half-seen light, all the candles, torches, hearths, all the dreams and desires of the hive. Yens said that he thought the town was Musen, but we did not know, and hated it only dimly, like the distance.

After about two days, we began to talk of Pierre. We recalled things he had said and done, how he had been a friend, how he had enraged us. Those of us who recollected the first meeting between us spoke of that. It was true he had come to the campfire in the night, but that was a century ago. He found us by stealth and the magic of our kind. Our brotherhood of blood is old and uncanny, but we are like the wolves. Timid, lonely. Our pack cleaves to itself. We prey only where we can. And we too have human eyes.

In the dark white of the snow, Johan said to me, 'You talked about bringing Rotlam the severed hands of those you killed. Was that unwise? Does it give away something? The Egyptians by the Nilus did that. Suppose you chatter to a scholar.'

'Then I'm done for, Johan. One day.'

Yes, no fool, but I make mistakes, and who does not?

Pierre ...

It was not like he had been my lover, or some son I had never seen. He was myself. And to each of us, he was that.

Lutgeri may be the oldest of us. Sometimes he dreams of painted icons in a hut of logs, and smoke, and a hymn that brought the light.

As we age, we lose the nearer past a little, as any old man does.

For the rest, it is lies. The sun does not smite us, nor the moon by night. Garlic is a fine flavour. Thorns rip but that is all. Iron and silver – we have had both, and lost both. And for the cross of the Christ? Well, He was one of us, or so Pierre once said. Did they not drink blood?

But kill us, we die. Burn us, we are ashes.

Ah, Pierre ...

And so, through the death of Pierre, we wandered, a band of mercenaries without a lord, scavengers on the winter land, wolves, crows. And so, we saw the castle.

Maybe we would have turned to it our shoulders, but the hour was sunset, and in the sunset we saw this place, on a sky as red as blood and threaded with gold like the robe of a priest.

The castle looked black. Not a light, not a glim to be glimpsed.

'Perhaps there is some count or duke there,' said Arpad, 'who wants men to serve him. Wants to take some city in the spring. The rotten old bastard. He'll feed us.'

'And women,' said Festus.

'Gorgeous women, white as the snow, with sweets for tits and cores of roses.' This, Gilles.

We scanned the landscape for a village or town, some settlement to support the castle, and there was none. Under the snow, and the blood of crimson dying sun, nothing moved.

'A ruin,' said Yens. 'Taken, despoiled. Empty.'

'We'll go and see.' Arpad.

'Winter in a ruin. Not for the first.' Johan.

But we sat on the hill, slept by the fire. In the dawn we looked down again, and now the castle was not black but warm, the sun's rays on it over the cloth of the snow.

If we had had his body, we would have buried him here, at this castle, our brother Pierre. But we did not have a mote of black dust.

Lutgeri said, 'Pierre would have liked that place. He'd have waxed lyrical. Remember how well he sang. A troubadour.'

We thought of Pierre under the long thin windows of the castle, singing to some princess of story.

As we descended we found the snow was deep. We were pulled in and hacked our way out. It was another battle. Under the snow, Hades, a Hell of ice.

When we began to get level with the castle, we looked it over again. It was not so large. Some big towers with crenelations, and an inner block, high-roofed and capped by snow, with one slender squinnying tower all its own. Up there, a stab of light went through a window, rose-red, deathly green as a dying thorn.

'By the Christ,' said Johan.

We stopped.

'What's that, by the Mass?'

'Flowers,' said Gilles.

'No.'

There could be no flower in the snowlands.

'Remember –' said Arpad – 'remember what Pierre called it – the battlefield –'

Memory again. We had once come to a place, the plain of a war, in the snow, years back. And on the plain, left to God and the carrion birds, were the dying men, and the blood leaking from their bodies, red on the white. A feast. A horrible and cursed feast we were then too desperate to ignore.

And Pierre had named the sight.

'The blood in the sunlight on the snow,' he said. 'Red roses. Winter flowers.'

'Flowers in winter,' said Arpad now, so low only we could have heard him, and we did.

There was something blooming along the walls of the castle, and it looked like flowers. Winter flowers. Roses.

'There's nothing like that,' said Johan. 'We – *we* are the legend.'

We laughed.

We forced our way on toward the castle.

There is a tradition of Maryam, the Virgin Mother of the Christ: that she has a garden enclosed by high walls. And in the garden it is always summer and the flowers grow.

Had we come to the Garden of Maryam?

As the castle's barriers loomed up over us, we searched walks and towers with our gaze. But there was no sentry. No-one called a challenge. We came up to the doors – and they stood ajar. This was curious and foreboding in itself, but we had seen such things; the bizarre is not always dangerous, just as sometimes, the ordinary is.

They were huge heavy doors too, with valves of iron like black stone. We went in, and there was the castle yard, save it was not. It was this garden.

The snow was on the ground, and on the steps that went to the towers, and to the central place with its tall snowy roof. But out of the snow of the yard, the flowers climbed on their briars up the high walls, up to the very tops, a curtain of dark green and lavish reds, of smoky pinks and peaches too, of murrey and magenta and ivory.

Here and there the snow had even touched the faces of these flowers, but it had not burnt them. It was only like a dusting of white spice. And they had scent. In the cold static air it was rich and heady.

Gilles said, 'Oh God, it's beautiful. Will it poison us?'

'Yes,' said Festus. He wrenched out his knife and made a move toward the rose-vines. Johan caught his arm.

Lutgeri said softly, 'Better not. You might anger … someone.'

'Who?' snapped Festus.

'God, perhaps,' said Lutgeri. 'If He's gone to so much trouble.'

In the middle of the yard was a stone well, ornamented with upright stone birds. I crossed to the well, Johan and Arpad coming with me. Deep down the water was shining green as a Pope's jasper ring, though along the coping speared icicles.

Up on the battlements nothing stirred but a trace of wind, blowing off a spray of snow, and perfume.

'Is it magic?' said Gilles.

'Yes,' said Bollo. 'Like the virgin sleeping in her garden, and only the kiss of God can wake her.'

'I don't like it,' said Yens. 'My guts are changing into snakes.'

'That door is open too,' said Arpad, pointing up at the central building just over from the well. He strode off toward it. 'A nice virgin in a bower. That's no threat to me.'

Festus, knife still drawn, went after him.

Johan said, 'What do you want to do, Maurs?'

'Look and see. Perhaps the inside is good, too.'

Arpad and Festus had gone through the door. Then Arpad gave a shout, and we ran, all of us, getting the blades free as we did so.

As we burst through the door, it became a silly clowns' performance, for bringing up short Johan, Gilles, Lutgeri and I were collided with by Yens and Bollo.

Arpad and Festus were in the midst of the castle hall, just stood there and gazing about. There was something to look at.

I have seen the house-halls of wealthy dukes and counts and other princes of the world, here and otherwhere. But none better, and few so fine. And probably not one like that one.

There were carpets on the walls from the East, wonderful scarlets and saffrons, and high up the walls were carved, and the ceiling, with beasts and birds. And these were very strange, mythical, women things with the tails of fish and serpents, winged horses, lions with three heads, horned bears, birds with the faces of ancient bearded men. Out of the ceiling dropped brazen lamps on long chains, and they were alight, giving to the wide chamber a deep burnished glow broken only by the flutter of a large and burning hearth. The fireplace was fronted with rosy marble that ran off into a floor formed of squares of this rose marble and another that was of russet. A stair ascended between two statues. The figures were taller than a man, one of a woman holding up a gilded shield or mirror before her countenance, and one of king Death, a robed creature with the head of a skull crowned by gold. The windows that ran above the hall had glass in them, and in each pane was a single ruby jewel. The sun had got now behind three of these, and the bloody drops fell down to the room, directly on Death's diadem and robe. We took this sour omen in like vinegar.

Near the hearth, however, was a table set with chairs. The table was also laid with flagons and jars and jugs, with plates and knives, and the light danced on the gold-work. There were roasts on that table, pork and hare, a wide side of beef. And on the plates piled up the plaited pies and loaves, the sweetmeats you see and never taste, the mounded summer fruits like balls of enamel and gold. The fruit was fresh and ripe, the bread and meat were hot, you could smell them.

'What is it?' said Gilles.

'It's the Devil,' said Yens.

Arpad had wandered to the table and stretched out his hands.

'No, fool,' I shouted. 'No.'

Arpad put his hands down by his sides. He blushed.

Bollo said, 'It's so miraculous it might be sound. It might be a gift from on high.'

'But is it?' I said.

Bollo shrugged.

Festus said, 'Well, what do we do?'

'We'll search this hold,' I said, 'and then we'll see if it's fit to banquet in.'

And so we searched the building, the hub of the little castle on the plain of snow, the castle of summer and lit lamps and bright fire and new-cooked food.

It was uniformly splendid. It was beautiful. Everywhere the carvings, that had to do it seemed with every myth and fantasy of the Earth. Wherever there was a window, it was glass, and in many of them was a gem of coloured vitreous, or the delicate pattern of grisaille. Tapestries and carpets on the walls, gleaming with lustre and tints as if sloughed from the loom only yesterday. Above the hall was a library with old, old books and scrolls in Latin and in Greek, and some even in the picture writing of earlier lands. An armoury there was, its door open like all the rest. The weapons were antique and modern, well-cared for, the leather and lacquer oiled and rubbed, the iron shined. Bows of horn, bronze maces, lances notched like the swords from use ...

There were side chambers with sumptuous beds, and carved chests that, when they were easily undone, revealed the clothes of lords folded among herbs, and belts inlaid with gold. In caskets were found the jewelleries of queens and kings, corals and pearls, amethysts like pigeons' blood, brooding garnets, crosses of silver pierced by green beryl, and from the East again armlets of heavy gold, headdresses of golden beads and discs, things the Herods might have looked on, worn.

'Take none of this.'

'No, Maurs,' they said.

Johan said, 'I think it is a spell after all.'

'Yes, a stink of a spell, to entrap us.'

We said we would be better going at once, hunting the lean hills for mice, sleeping in the snow about a pale fire. Yet we were in love with the castle, as if with a beautiful woman. She may mean you no good and yet you hang about her. Perhaps you can charm the bitch, perhaps her heart is fair like her face, and needs only to be persuaded.

From the upper chambers we glared out beyond the castle walls, and the snow was teeming once again. The day was dark now as evening, and how thoughtful the sorcery of the castle was, lighting all its lamps for us, in every room, and on the stairs the torches in their ornamented brackets.

At last we were weary of it, sick of it. Too many sweets and none to be eaten.

Then, we reached a door that did not give.

'What's *this*?'

'It could lead into that tower we spied,' said Johan, 'so I'd guess. With the pretty window.'

Glancing up, I saw, carved in the stone above the door, the words: *Virgo pulchra, claustra recludens.*

'Lovely maiden, undo the bolt,' translated Bollo.

'Does it only mean a girl?' said Yens. 'Isn't it invoking the Mother of God?'

'It's all we need,' said Gilles, 'lovely maidens.'

'No, one other thing,' said Lutgeri.

'Blood,' I said.

There was a silence, under the locked door.

'Perhaps this place will give us that, too,' said Johan. 'Since it offers everything else.'

We examined each other.

Arpad's eyes glittered, and the eyes of Gilles were heavy. Yens frowned and gnawed his lip, Festus had turned away, and Bollo was blank as a worn page in one of the ancient books. Lutgeri and Johan seemed to be thinking, gazing down some tunnel of memory or the mind. And I? I recollected Pierre. And after him, the girl in the house at Bethelmai, who had wanted the impossible to be spared rape, to keep her bracelet.

'We'll go down,' I said.

'The food –' said Arpad, and Yens added, 'I'm hungry enough I'd risk hemlock.'

When we regained the hall, the fire was still as bright, its logs and sticks had not burnt up, and the lamps were glowing. But on the table, quite naturally, the feast had turned a little cold and greasy. We cut off chunks of meat and sliced the fruits and broke off the caps of the crystalline castle. There was no smell or appearance of anything bad, no taste, no evidence. We drew lots, and Arpad and Yens gladly tried the dishes, a mouthful of this and that. We would be likely to save them, if they had not had much. But then they did not sicken, and by the time the occluded sun had passed over to the other windows, we sat square at the table and gorged ourselves like the poor slaves of life we were.

I woke afraid. But that is not so unusual.

There are dreams, unrecalled. There are noises heard in sleep, quite innocent, that remind the floating brain of other times when they were not

I pushed myself up and my head rang slightly from the draughts of precious wine. Then it cleared and I remembered where I had lain down, and why, and that to fear might be quite wise.

Yes, the very image before me was one of alteration and so perhaps of warning.

The lamps had all gone out, and the changeless fire was sunken low, livid hovering lizard tongues on the remnants of the wood like blackened bones. Outside, beyond the enchanted castle, the weather seemed purified. The snow had been vomited out, and the sky was a sheer thin blackish-blue, threadbare with stars. This, through the high up windows of the hall, gave the light the lamps now withheld. The moon must be up.

I scrutinised the vast chamber and saw it all congealed in slabs of lunar ice. The great table ruined by our orgy of hunger. The carvings and the carved cupboards, the carpets hung on the walls with here and there some sequin of pallor, a hand, a unicorn, a skull.

No-one was in the room but I, yet someone had been there. Who? Most of my brotherhood had gone up to slumber in the haughty, luxurious beds of the castle. I had put Johan to watch at the stair-head, and Lutgeri and Festus to stroll the passages in a pair. The hall door we had bolted. And I had rolled myself to sleep before the fire in my cloak, with one of the fancy cushions under my head.

If something had happened, I would have heard a commotion.

But, by the Christ, something had happened. My heart and my soul knew it, if my stupid mind did not.

I got on my feet all the way, and went to the table. The wine had been unvenomous, and I took a drink of it, to steady me.

What had been in the hall with me was a whisper, a gliding sigh. Probably not that which had woken me at all, this cobweb of nothingness, this ghost. No, some deep instinct, clamouring, had reached me finally after a long while. It was as if a bell had been clanging in my blood and I had only just heard it – then, it stopped.

I did not call for the sentries, Lutgeri, Festus, Johan. Surely they should have woken me by now, and Yens and Bollo, to take our turn?

How silent the castle, and the land beyond. Rarely is anything so dumb. The wind calls, and the beasts that roam the night. And in the dwellings of men the rats and vermin move about, the timbers stir, the furniture creaks. Here – not a note. Only I had made a sound, and that not much.

I drew my sword, and my knife for the left hand. Then I climbed the stair, between Death and his Lady, noiseless, seeing.

Johan was not above. That was not like him. If he had gone from his post it was because something had summoned him. And then, certainly, he would have alerted me.

'Johan,' I said, quietly. And he would have heard. But there was no answer, and beyond the windows there, the dark was full.

I went into it, that dark. One learns to use one's eyes, and so sight grudgingly came. I beheld the twisting passageway, and there a door. And there, something lay on the threshold.

For more than three hundred years, I knew him. He did not sleep unless he might. And now, he did not sleep. Across the door of the room Arpad had chosen, Johan lay dead.

This was not new to me. Yet never does it grow stale. To find your friend and brother is a corpse.

I bent over him, one ear, one eye upon the dark, and tried him.

Oh Christ – Oh, he was not a human thing anymore. No, no. He was a sack of emptiness. A rattling sack filled by loose bones. Like the picture of Death, whose cart is stacked by the skeletons of the dead that have a tiny, immodest fragment of skin on them. Like that. Johan. So.

I let go of him, and held down my screaming. I am practiced. And since that night, better.

There were no muscles left in his body, no *flesh*. I had no true light, and yet I *knew*. No *blood*.

In the dark, some demon had come, and sucked him dry. Oh, not as we do. Not like that. You give us sustenance like a maiden at a well, raising the bucket brimmed with water. Like the lord at the dinner, offering us wine. A drink. The drink of life. And with the woman or boy who sucks the smooth sword of our cock, tender and cunning, careful and fierce and honey in the dark, and with the girl who takes in our seed at her other mouth, and grows in the closed garden of her womb a rose: so it goes back to you. *But not like this.*

He had been drained. As the fire does it. Like Pierre. Save that burnt inward, and this, *out*.

No longer Johan.

I turned, and opened Arpad's selected door, and stepped into the chamber.

Moonlight streamed here on the floor and over the bed, in a white mirror from the window, and in its heart a black cicatrice lay from the decaying window jewel the moon could not rouse.

Arpad sprawled half from the majestic bed he had chosen. His head drooped to the floor, and one arm, and when I tried him, Arpad, who had been sparks and pepper, hot iron and strong drink, Arpad was another flaccid sack on the cart of Death.

Then a fear came over me I had never felt. Not once, in all my long life. I have been pent and pinned, they have promised me all sorts of torture, and Hell after, and never once, no never had I felt this fear. It was born in me that night. Shall I ever be free of it?

I left Arpad, and Johan, and walked out along the passage.

In their brackets the kind torches had guttered out. Only the moon slid through the narrow slits, each with that mole of dark on it from its jewel, or else weird shapes from the painting on the flags. And then the corridor turned any way, and the moon had gone behind a wall. White Face they called her, long ago. She is fickle, and not your helpmeet. A betrayer, Dame Moon.

I came on Festus not long after. And then Lutgeri. Festus too was in the bone cart of Death. And I gave Lutgeri a shake, like a rat, but I hated him because he was dead. And then I heard him breathing, rasping and interrupted, like a rusty machine, some windmill, or thing of the old sieges they cannot make anymore.

'Lutgeri – Lutgeri –'

'Hush,' he said. 'Calmly, my boy.'

I held him in my arms.

'If you die, you shit-rat, I'll kill you.'

'I know you will, Maurs. I'll try not to.'

I wept on his shoulder, which had the feel of life and humanity. One whole second. Then I was myself again.

'What did this?'

'How many?' he gasped.

'Arpad. Festus – Johan –'

'Ah,' he said, 'Johan.'

Then he lost consciousness and I squeezed on his neck, against the vein, to haul him back.

'Tell me, Lutgeri.'

'I can't. I don't – something came from the shadow. It was like – no, it was like nothing at all. It didn't croon. And it hurt me. Christ's soul. It's teeth went in my breast – And the blood was ripped from me, Maurs, like my living organs, before I could struggle. And no voice in my throat.'

'How do you survive?' I said. I was numb.

'God knows. Perhaps my old ichor wasn't to its taste, or a little did for more.'

'The others,' I said.

Lutgeri whispered, 'Arpad? Festus – yes. Yens and Gilles – they must be gone if it came to them. Bollo, perhaps – old alligator. He might –'

His head fell back. He had fainted again, but still lived. I crushed my wrist between his teeth. 'Drink it, you swine, you shit-heart. *Drink it.*'

In his stupor, he took a morsel from me.

Then, in my arms, he drew his sword.

'Leave me here, Maurs. I'm ready for it now. If it returns. But you must –'

'Yes.' I got up. I raised him and slung him over my shoulder and took him into the library. Its lamp was out. I fetched down a book and pressed it on his hand. 'When the weight changes, if it grows –'

'I know, Maurs. Then I'm lighter. I have the sword. Go find them. *Go.*'

Bollo had gone to sleep in the armoury. That was, he had told me he would be there, to examine the weapons alone. He had not meant to sleep, and took with him a jar of the wine from the table. He could go days and nights, up to ten, without sleeping. I had seen it. But then, why battle the god of slumber here? I ran, up the stairs, up into the height of the place, to reach Bollo.

When I was near the door, something laid hold of me, and made me pause. I went slowly after that, the drawn sword and knife before me. I crept to the door of the armoury, and it was partly open, as all the doors of the castle seemed to wish to be, but one, the virgin door to the tower.

I eased the armoury door inward. So I saw.

Lovers making love cannot always stop.

There was a window, and the moon was in it, it was an arch of light, with only the dark Mark of Cain upon its forehead from the intercepting jewel. More than enough light to see.

Bollo sat at the table, one of the old books open in front of him from below, and a mace, and a candle that had been burning and that had gone out. Moonlight described the weapon, and the book, a great capital of gilding and indigo, and on it a gem of blackness that, in daylight, would have been red.

The eyes of Bollo were wide, and stiffly, like the cogs of a machine, they crawled in their sockets, till he could look at me. He knew me, he was coherent, but paralysed.

While it bent over him, obscuring him as a cloud will the moon. It was so filmy, so wraith-like, yet so real.

What did I regard? The sight is printed on my mind. I can never forget, yet how to relate?

It was old, ancient as nothing in the castle was, not even the scrolls penned before the Flood. It was like something made of rags and bones, filaments and tendrils, pasted together, strung, like a harp of the air. Moonlight passed through its wrappings, but not through itself, though dimly in it, stones in a frozen river, you saw the elements of its skeleton like the teeth of a comb. It was, or had been, of human shape. But of what gender, God knew. It held Bollo, beneath the arms, and its head, from which a hank of gauzy hair spun out, was bowed upon his chest.

This looked like a deed of repentance. As if it had gone to him and sobbed on his breast. But I knew, for Lutgeri had told me, what it did.

I rammed my sword into its back, up into the spot where the heart is come on.

And it was like thrusting into snow.

But at the blow it left him, it straightened up, and turning like a snake it gazed on me.

Oh it had eyes. The eyes of wolves, our own, are human. But these were not. Like round black beads they shone, harder and more true than all the rest of it. Bits of night, but not this night. No night we will ever see.

And then it gaped its mouth, and its sharp yellow teeth were there, and the swarthy tongue, pointed and too long. It hissed at me, and I fell back.

My sword had come from it as if out of sticky vapour.

I hung before it, not knowing what I must do. And then it seemed to me I should strike that weaving insubstantial head from its shoulders. But as I drew my arm for the stroke, it smeared away. It slid, *rolled* at the wall, moving as the snake does. And the wall parted, to let it by.

Yes, like soft butter the stone gave way, and it slipped through. And then Bollo cried to me, as if he choked, 'Maurs – there – there –'

And in his eyes I saw the deaths of Yens and Gilles. I saw King Death himself, on his fish-white charger, pacing slowly. Then I turned and flung myself through the wall before it closed. After the vampire.

I have done things in battle, many have, crazy things called after 'brave'. But they are the madness of war. And this, this was not like them, for I was afraid going in through

that wall, and yet could not keep back.

It had come to me, this thing, or others of its kind. That had been the sigh, the whisper, in the dark. But I had woken, before its fangs could fasten into me. And why was that? But then, why ask? Each of us knows he alone is immortal, cannot die. And that whoever falls, he will survive it. Death may touch, but then he is gone.

The corridor inside the wall was black as pitch, and yet I could just see, for as I said, I have learned to use my eyes, and besides, what went before me, invisible now in itself, gave off a faint luminescence, like the crests of waves, like fungus, such things.

It progressed quickly, but not as if it went on legs or feet. And the elf-light flowed behind it, and now and then I was close enough a long trailing wisp of its garment, or perhaps *itself*, billowed around a turn of the passage, and I might have plucked at it, but I did not.

How to kill it when I caught it? Would beheading do? We were vulnerable, but I had stabbed it through and it lived. Why then follow? I must. Or Bollo had put it on me that I must.

It went somewhere, evidently. To some lair.

Then the corridor began to branch. Constricted twisting routes led off this way and that, and it chose without hesitation, but now I was lost. We were inside the walls of the castle, in the very veins and arteries of it.

The passage ended at the foot of a sort of chimney. I dropped back, and beheld the aura of the being oozing up a flight of straight and narrow steps, directly up, and its glow abated as it vanished from sight.

The fear I felt was now so awful I could not for a moment or two more move or go after. And yet it was the fear itself, it seemed, that pushed me on.

Presently I eased out, and looking up into the shaft where the stairway went, saw the thing had completed its climb and gone in at a slender archway above. There was a hint of light inside the arch, but not like the other, the phosphorous of the vampire. This was warm.

I ran up the stair without a sound, and sprang into the arch. Within the vault of it, to the left, was another half-open door, and out of this stole the myrrh-soft shine. It was a gentle light, and by that I began to realise what might be there. Even so, when I had slunk to the doorway's edge, I peered around the door, and found I had not been prepared.

I grasped at once what chamber it was. None other than that upper room in the tower to which the lower outer door had refused us admittance. *Lovely girl, undo the bolt.* Up here, no doubt, she had done so, to let her creature in.

But the room was beautiful, like a painting, so neat and pleasant, every little accessory in its place. The slim white maiden's bed with its canopy of ashy rose, the tapestry of rainbow threads on its frame, the tiring table inlaid with different woods, the unguents and wooden combs, the trickle of a precious necklace from a carven box. There were little footstools with embroidered hounds and rabbits and birds, and on one of these, before her, the vampire I had pursued kneeled now, holding up its mealy hands. I learned here there had been others, three of them, who had taken the lives from my men. These vampires were like the first one, flimsy dolls of silver wire and thinnest samite, and crinkled now, folded over in strange shapes, like things that had no bones at all, like stiff clothing discarded.

She had had their message and their gift already; she had emptied them in turn. And now she received the last of our ichor from the final creature, the one knelt in front of her, lifting its hands so she might bow her head and bite the powdery wrists and drink, from that transferring vessel, *our blood.*

I moved into the doorway, and so into the room, and stood there, and looked on as she drained the wine-sack dry.

The ceiling was painted violet, with little golden stars. Under the stained glass window, which was black and moonless, only the brazen lamps to give their dulcet light, a rose bush grew in a pot. The great red blooms were open wide and I could smell their scent, and over that the perfume of the girl.

She had a skin like the snow, and hair like ebony, which fell all round her, with raven glints in it. Her gown was a pale sweet pink, the shade of fresh blood mixed into ice. There were rings on her fingers, gold, emeralds, and as she lifted her head and let her servant go – it folded, discarded, lifeless, like the others – I saw that around her white forehead passed a golden chain fashioned into tiny flowers.

She had a lovely face. All of her was lovely. Not a flaw. There was not even any trace of blood on the petals of her lips, and her eyes were clear and innocent, the colour of dark amber.

'At last you have come to me,' she said. 'I've waited so long.'

'Have you, Lady?'

'Many, many years.'

I believed her. I understood it all and did not need a lesson. Nor did I get one. The castle was her web. Probably it was a ruin, and every tasteful glamorous thing inside mildew and muck. God knew what we had eaten off that banquet table. For the rest, when we were lulled, her emissaries came. They filled themselves from us like jars, then glided back to her and gave up every drop to make her strong and fair. What had she been before? A desiccated insect lying, wheezing and murmuring on her charming bed, which maybe was a stinking gaping grave.

And one she wanted as her lover. Perhaps to continue her race through him, if she was the last of that particular kind. Or maybe only to ease her loneliness. Or to champion her, to take her out into the world beyond the web, where she could become a mighty sorceress, out in the thousand lands where blood runs in rivers.

Yet she looked at me and I loved her. Such adoration. She was the Virgin Queen and the fount of all delicious sin. She was my mother and my child, my sister, my soul.

Her magic was strong enough, and she had fed.

She held out her perfect hand to me, and I went forward.

And the lamplight shone through her amber eyes, and I remembered the girl in the upper room, her little ring of silver on her roughened hand. 'Don't rape me. Don't take my bracelet.' And it came to me as if I heard the words, that the soldiers had found her, or she had stumbled amongst them. They had raped her, they had stolen her solitary treasure, they had thrown her down in the mud among the reeking corpses. So then I saw the corpse of Pierre, his black dust raked over in the dying pyre. I saw the battlefield in the snow, where we had sucked out the life of dying, crying men, the crimson winter roses, since we must. And into us had passed with their life the despair of their death, so the tears froze on our faces with the blood cold against our lips. All that I saw, there in the eyes of the lovely maiden in the tower, and so I saw my brothers she had fed on. Arpad and Yens, Festus and Gilles. Johan. And Lutgeri with the sword, and the book on his hand to remind him to live, and Bollo staring. And I saw myself before her, tall and sombre as a shadow, with the blade in my hand.

God knows, He has ordained it, we prey upon each other. As the lion on the deer, the cat upon the mouse. There is no penance we may do to right this wrong. There is no excuse for that we live by killing, save only that we must. To survive is all. And she, the maiden, like us was vulnerable, for unlike the automata of her slaves, she was a thing of flesh and blood. My sister, as Pierre had been my brother and myself. And, so beautiful –

The dawn was coming up, sluggish, like heavy iron. No colour on the earth. The roses would be burnt papers and the books grey flour, like all the stuff in the upper chamber.

Lutgeri was sharpening his knife, slow. He did not speak to me of the cold grim rooms, the fallen areas and the rotted carpets. But Bollo, who had gone out and broken the thick corded ice of the well, informed me it stank, not fit to drink.

I told them of the girl in the tower. They listened. Before we went to bury our dead in the hard soil beyond the castle, they asked what I had done.

'I loved her, of course,' I said. 'I never loved any woman like that one. It was her spell.'

'So you went to her,' said Bollo, but Lutgeri held up his hand, mildly, as if to caution him.

'I went to her,' I said.

'And then,' Lutgeri said. 'And then.'

'With my sword I struck the head from her body.'

IL BACIO (IL CHIAVE)[1]

Roma, late in her 15th Century after the Lord, packed on the banks of her yellow river, had entered that phase of summer known by some as the *Interiore*. This being a kind of pun – interior place, or – frankly – entrails. It was a fact, Roma, brown and pink and grey and white and beautiful, ripely stank. Before the month was over, there might very possibly be plague.

Once the red cannon-blast of the sunset, however, left the cool garden on the high hill, the dusk began to come with all its tessellated stars, and the only scent was from the grapevines and the dusty flowers, and the last aromas of the cooked chickens now merely bones on a table. Four men had dined. From their garments and their demeanour it was easy to locate their portion, the noble rich, indolent and at play. They had no thought of plague, even though they had disparagingly discussed it an hour before. They were young, the youth of their era – the oldest not more than twenty years – and in the way of the young knew they would live forever, and in the way of their time, as in the way of all times, understood they might die horribly in a month, or a day. And naturally also, since such profound and simple insight is essentially destructive where too often recognised, they knew nothing of the sort.

There had, very properly, been talk of horses, too, and clothing and politics. Now, with the fruit and the fourth or fifth cups of wine, there came

---

[1] The Kiss (The Key)

talk of women, and so, consecutively, of gambling.

'But have no fear, Valore, you shall be excluded.'

'Shall I? A pity.'

'Yes, no doubt. And worse pity to have you more in debt to us than already you are.'

'You owe me two hundred ducats, Valore, since the horserace. Did you forget?'

'No, dearest Stephano. I very much regret it.' Valore della Scorpioni leaned back in his chair and smiled upon them with the utmost confidence. Each at the table was fine-looking in his way, but Valore, a torch among candles, far outshone them and blinded, for good measure, with his light.

His was that unusual and much-admired combination of dark, red hair and pale, amber skin sometimes retained in the frescoes and on the canvasses of masters, a combination later disbelieved as capable only of artificial reproduction. Added to this, a pair of large hazel eyes brought gorgeousness to the patrician face, white teeth blessed it; while all below and beyond the neck showed the excellent results of healthful exercise, good food consumed not in excess, and the arrogant grace evolving upon the rest. In short, a beauty, interesting to either sex, and not less so to himself.

Added to his appearance and aura, however, Valore della Scorpioni had the virtue of an ill name. His family drew its current rank out of an infamous house not unacquainted with the Vatican. As will happen, bad things were said of it, as of its initiator. Untrue as the friends and adorers of Valore knew all such things to be, yet they were not immune to the insidious attraction of all such things. No trace of witchcraft or treachery might be seen to mar the young man, scarcely 18, who sat godlike in their midst. That he, rich as they, owed money everywhere, was nothing new. It pleased them, perhaps excited them, Stephano, Cesco, Andrea, that this creature was in their debt.

'Well,' said Andrea now. 'I, for one, have nothing left to put forward on the dice, save my jewels.'

'And I,' said Valore della Scorpioni, with a flame-quick lightness that alerted them all, 'have only *this*.'

On, the table, then, among the bones, fruit and wine cups, was set an item of black iron at odds with all. A key. Complex and encrusted, its size alone marked it as the means to some portentous entry.

'Jesu, what's this?' Stephano cried. 'The way into your lord father's treasury?'

Valore beamed still, lowering his eyes somewhat, giving them ground.

'It's old,' said Andrea. 'It could unlock a secret route into the catacombs –'

And Cesco, not to be outdone: 'No, it is the door to the Pope's wine-cellar, no less. Is it not, Valore?'

The hazel eyes arose. Valore looked at them.

'It is,' he said, 'the key to a lady's bedchamber.'

They exclaimed, between jeering mirth and credulity. They themselves were unsure of which they favoured. The dark was now complete, and the candles on the table gave the only illumination. Caught by these, Valore's beautiful face had acquired a sinister cast, impenetrable and daunting. So they had seen it before, and at such moments the glamour of evil repute, though disbelieved, seemed not far off.

'Come, now,' Andrea said at length, when the jibes had gone unanswered. 'Whose chamber is it? Some harlot –'

'Not at all,' said Valore. He paused again, and allowed them to hang upon his words. 'Would I offer you such dross in lieu of honest recompense for my debts?'

'Oh, yes,' said Cesco. 'Just so you would.'

'Then,' said Valore, all velvet, 'for shame to sit here with such a wretch. Go home, Cesco, I entreat you. I'd not dishonour you further.' And when Cesco had finished uneasily protesting, Valore picked up the great black key and turned it in his flexible fingers. 'This, sweet friends, fits the lock of one, a lady of high birth. A lady most delectable, who is kindred to me.'

They exhibited mirth again, sobered, and stared at him.

Andrea said, 'Then truly you make sport here. If she is your kin, you would hardly disgrace her so.'

'She's not disgraced. She will not be angry.' In utter silence now they gazed on their god. Valore nodded. 'I see you doubt her charms. But I will show you. This attends the key.' And now there was put on the table a little portrait, ringed by pearls, the whole no bigger than a plum.

One by one, in the yellow candlelight, they took it up and peered at it. And one by one they set it down; and their faces, also oddly-lit, their eyes en-embered, turned strange, unearthly, and lawless.

There was no likelihood the woman in the painting was not kindred of the Scorpion house. Evident in her, as in the young man at the table, was that same unequivocal hair falling about and upon that same succulent skin. The contour of the eyes, and all the features, was so similar to Valore's own that it could have been modelled on him, save for some almost indefinable yet general difference, and a female delicacy absent from the masculine lines of the one who – in the flesh and to the life – sat before them, indisputably a man.

'But,' Stephano murmured eventually, 'she might be your sister.'

'My sisters, as you are aware, Stephano, do not so much resemble me. They are besides raven-haired. Therefore, the lady's not my sister. Not, to forestall you, my cousin, my mother, any sister of my mother's or my sire's, or even, *per Dio*, any forward daughter of my own. Yet she is kin to me. Yet this key is the key to her chamber. Yet she will not turn away whoever of you may win it at the dice. If any win, save I. If not, it is mine, as now mine. I have done.'

The fox-lit faces angled to each other.

'An enigma.'

'If you wish.'

At that moment, one of Andrea Trarra's servants came out into the garden like a ghost. Bending to the master of the feast, the man whispered. Andrea's face underwent a subtle fortuitous alteration. He spoke in assent to the servant, who moved away. Then, turning to the company, he dazzled them with the words:

'A fourth guest has just now arrived.'

There followed a popular demand as to whom this guest might be, formerly unexpected, conceivably unwelcome. Valore did not join in the outcry. He sat, toying with the key, and only stilled his fingers when Andrea announced: 'It is one you know of. Di Giudea.'

'What do you say?' protested Cesco, flushing. 'We must sit at table with a Jew?'

'Not at all,' said Andrea placidly, and with a little soft sneer. 'Being a Jew, as you note, Olivio di Giudea will not eat with anyone, since the way we prepare our meat and wine is contrary to his religion.'

'And even so,' said Stephano, 'it's not at all certain he's a Jew by blood. He has travelled widely in the East, and is perhaps titled for that. No-one, it seems, credits this his real name – I cite "Olivio" – that does not strike the Judean note.'

'I, for one,' said Cesco, 'resent your act, Andrea, bringing the man upon us in this way. Did you invite him?'

'My house was open to him on his return to Roma. He is an alchemist, and a painter of some worth, who has been recognised by the Holy Father himself. Am I to put myself above such social judgements? Besides, I have business with him.'

'To cheat money from your countrymen – ever a Jew's business.'

'Actually to debate the repair of same frescoes in my villa at Ostia. There is no craftsman like Olivio for such things. The man's a genius.'

'He is a Jew,' said Cesco, and he rose magnificently to his feet, bowing in anger to the table. 'Thanks for the pleasant supper, Andrea. I hope to see you again at a more amenable hour.'

With a flurry of snatched mantle he strode from the garden, and passed in the very doorway a tall straight darkness, to which he paid no heed at all.

'I trust,' Andrea said, 'no other will take flight.'

'Why,' said Stephano, 'my nicest whore is a Hebrew. It's nothing to me.'

'And we should recall, perhaps,' added Galore della Scorpioni gently, 'that the Christ Himself –'

'No, no, an Egyptian, I do assure you –'

Someone laughed, a quiet and peculiarly sombre laugh, from the shadow beyond the vines. A man stepped out of the shadow a moment later, and stood before them in the candlelight for their inspection. He was yet smiling faintly, without a trace of bitterness, rage, or shame. It might be true he was of the Judean line, for though he had no mark of what a Roman would deem Semitic, yet he had all the arrogance of the Jew. He carried himself like a prince and looked back at them across a vast distance through the black centres of his eyes. His hair, long and sable, fell below his wide shoulders; he was in all respects of apparel and appurtenance a man of fashion, the swarthy red cloth and snow-white linden hung and moulded on an excellent frame. Nor was there anything vulgar, or even anything simply challenging in his dress. He had not sought to rival the splendours of the aristocracy, rather he seemed uninterested, beyond all such concerns, having perhaps precociously outgrown them, for he appeared not much older than Andrea's twenty years. But there was in Olivio called di Giudea that unforgiveable air of superiority, whether religious or secular, genuine, or false, that had from the time of the Herods – and indeed long before – been the root cause of the hatred toward and the endlessly attempted ruin of the Jewish race.

It was Andrea who was momentarily ill-at-ease, Stephano who donned an almost servile smirk of condescension. Valore della Scorpioni merely watched.

'Good evening to you, 'ser Olivia,' said Andrea. 'Be seated. Is there anything I may offer you?'

'I think not, as you will have explained to your guests.'

The voice of the Judean, if so he was, was firm and clear, and of the same dark flavour as his looks. 'Had I known you entertained these gentlemen, my lord, I should not have intruded.'

'It's nothing, 'ser Olivio. We had just foundered on the serious matter of a dice-game, and you have saved me from it.'

'Not at all.' It was Valore who spoke. 'Escape is impossible.' Valore himself smiled then, into the face of the newcomer, a smile of the most dangerous and luminous seduction imaginable. 'And perhaps your friend will join the game, since Cesco was so suddenly called away. Or do you also, sir, omit to gamble, along with all these other omissions?'

Di Giudea moved around the table and sat calmly down in Cesco's emptied place. Another servant had come during the interchange, with more wine. As the jar approached, not glancing at it, the man placed one hand over the vacant cup.

'I gamble,' he said quietly, returning the golden regard, seemingly quite resistant to it. 'Who can say he lives, and does not?'

Stephano grunted. 'But your laws do not bar you from the dice?'

'Which laws are these?'

'The laws of your god.'

The Jew seemed partly amused, but with great courtesy he replied, 'The god to whom you refer, my lord, is I believe the father of your own.'

There was a small clatter. Valore had tossed the dice on to the table, and now held up the iron key before them all.

'We are playing for this,' he said, 'and this.' And he reached for the portrait of the girl, shifting it till it lay directly in front of di Giudea. 'The first gives access to the second.'

Stephano swore by the Antichrist. Even Andrea Trarra was provoked and protested.

'The play is open to all your guests,' said Valore. 'This gentleman is rich? I will accept his bond. And you, sir, do you understand what is offered?'

'Such games were current in this city in the time of the Caesars,' di Giudea said, without a hint of excitement or alarm.'

'And even then,' Valore softly remarked, 'my forebears had their booted feet upon the necks of yours.'

Di Giudea looked from the portrait back to its owner. The foreigner's face was grave. 'There,' he said, 'is your booted foot. And here, my neck. Should you try to bring them closer, you might find some inconvenience.'

Valore said smoothly, 'Am I threatened? Do you know me, sir, or my family?'

'The banner of the Scorpion,' said the Jew, with a most insulting politeness, 'is widely recognised.'

'Scorpions,' said Valore, 'sting.'

'And when surrounded by fire,' the Jew appended mercilessly, 'sting also themselves to death.'

Valore gazed under long lids. 'Where is the fire?'

'It's well known, though all its other faculties are acute, the power of observation is, in the scorpion, very poor.'

Valore widened his eyes, and now offered no riposte. Andrea and Stephano, who had sat transfixed, broke into a surge of motion. They had been stones a second before, and all the life of the table concentrated at its further end.

'Come,' Stephano almost shouted. 'If we are to play, let's do it.'

'No, no,' said Andrea. 'I shall abstain. 'Ser Olivio –'

'He plays,' said Valore. 'Do you not?'

Andrea wriggled like a boy. Olivio de Giudea was immobile, save for the hand that took up the pair of dice.

'I have,' he said, 'examined your frescoes, my lord Andrea. I regret they are beyond my help, or anyone's.'

Andrea's face fall heavily.

Presently, the dice also fell.

The game, now common, next subject to certain innovations of a pattern more complex and more irritant, grew dependently more heated. The dice rang, chattered, scattered, and gave up their fortunes. The wine ran as the dice ran, in every cup save that adjacent to the chair of the Judean. Stephano waxed drunken and argumentative, Andrea Trarra, as was his way, became withdrawn. On Valore, the wine and the game made no decided impression, though he lost consistently; and it came upon them all, perhaps even upon the sombre and dispassionate intellect of the Jew, that Valore meant this night to lose and to do nothing else. Only the frenzy of the dice went on and on, and then finally and suddenly stopped, as if tired out.

It was almost midnight. The city lay below and about the garden, nearly black as nothingness, touched only here and there by lights of watch or revelry. There was no breeze at all; and far away a bell was ringing, sonorous and dreadful in the silence.

Valore offered the key. Andrea turned from it with a grimace, and Stephano with a curse.

'Well, sir. My noble familiars reject their prize. I must spew ducats for them, it seems. But you, I owe you more now than all the rest. Do you accept the key, and allow its promise to cancel my debt? Or will you be my usurer?'

Olivia de Giudea extended that same strong graceful hand that had sealed off the wine cup and plucked up the dice.

'I will accept the key.'

Stephano rounded on him , striking at his arm.

'You forget yourself. *Per Dio!* If he speaks the truth, a lady's honour is at stake – and to be yours, you damned infidel dog!'

The Jew laughed, as once before in the shadow beyond the candlelight, mild and cruel, unhuman as the bell.

It was Valore who leaned across the table, caught Stephano's shirt in his grip and shook the assemblage, linen and man. And Valore's eyes that spat fire, and Valore's lips that said: 'You would not take it. If he will, he shall.'

And Stephano fell back, grudging and shivering.

Valore got to his feet and gestured to the alien who, rising up, was noticed as some inches the taller.

'I am your guide,' Valore said. 'Think me the gods' messenger, and follow.' He put away the portrait in his doublet, and – catching up his mantle – turned without another word to leave Andrea's garden. It was di Giudea who bowed and murmured a farewell. Neither of the remaining men answered him. Only their eyes went after, and lost their quarry as the low-burning candles guttered on their spikes. While in the heart of the city the bell died, and the melancholy of the ebbing night sank down upon the earth.

It appeared the lordly Valore had not brought with him any attendant, and that di Giudea had been of like mind. No torch walked before them, therefore; they traversed the scrambling streets like shadows in that black hour of new-born morning. A leaden moisture seemed to have fallen from the sky, dank but hardly cold, and the stench of the narrower thoroughfares might have disgusted even men well-used to it. Both, however, in the customary manner, were armed, and went unmolested by any mortal thing. So they turned at length onto broader streets, and thus toward a pile of masonry, unlit, its sentinel flambeaux out, that nevertheless proclaimed itself by the escutcheon over its gate as the palace now in the possession of the Scorpioni.

Having gone by the gate, they sought a subsidiary entrance and there passed through into an aisle of fragrant bushes. Another garden, spread under the walls of the palace, lacking form in the moonlessness.

'Keep close, or you may stumble,' Valore said with the solicitousness of a perfect host: the first words he had uttered since their setting out. Di Giudea did not, even now, reply. Yet, moving a few steps behind Valore across the unfamiliar land, it seemed his own sense of sight was more acute than that of the scorpion he had mentioned.

Suddenly, under a lingering, extending tree, Valore paused. The second shadow paused also, saying nothing.

'You do not anxiously question me,' Valore said, 'on where we are going, how soon we shall arrive, if I mean to dupe you, if you are to be set on by my kinsmen – are such things inconsequent to you, Olivio of Judea? Or can it be you trust me?'

After a moment, the other answered him succinctly. 'Your family have left Roma to avoid the heat. A few servants only remain. As to our destination, already I behold it.'

'*Sanguigno,*' swore Valore softly. 'Do you so?'

Some hundred paces away, amid a tangle of myrtles, a paler darkness rose from black foliage to black sky. To one who knew, its shape was evident, for memory filled in what the eyes mislaid. Yet it transpired the foreigner, too, had some knowledge, not only of the departure of the household, but of its environs and architecture left behind.

What stood in the myrtle grove of the Scorpioni garden, long untended, a haunted, eerie place even by day, was an old mausoleum. Such an edifice was not bizarre. In the tradition of the city, many a powerful house retained its dead. The age of the tomb, however, implied it had preceded the advent of the noble bastardy that lifted the Scorpioni to possession of this ground – or, more strange, that the sepulchre had been brought with them from some other spot, a brooding heirloom.

'Come on, then, good follower,' said Valore, and led the way over the steep roots of trees, among the sweet-scented myrtles, and so right up to a door bound with black ironwork. A great lock hung there like a spider. It was but too obvious that the mysterious key belonged to this, and to this alone.

The foreigner did not baulk. He came on, as requested, and stood with Valore, whose fire and gold were gone to soot and silver in the dark.

'A lady's bedchamber,' said di Giudea, from which it appeared he had divined rather more of the conversation at Andrea's table than supposed.

Valore was not inclined to debate on this. 'So it is. A woman lies sleeping within, as you shall witness, have you but the courage to employ the key. A being as beautiful as her picture, and my kin, as I have said. Not will she deny you entry to the room, or think herself dishonoured. You will be fascinated, I assure you. It is a marvel of my family, not frequently revealed to strangers.'

'Which you yourself,' said Olivio de Giudea, 'have never ventured to inspect.'

'Ah! You have me, messer Jew. But then, I happened upon the key only yesterday. Why deny some friend, also, a chance to see the wonder, which is surely most wonderful if as the parchment describes it.'

Di Giudea raised the key and pierced the heavy lock. The awful spider did not resist him, its mechanism grated and surrendered at the insistence of that strong hand. His composure hung about him yet; it was Valore's breath that quickened.

The door swung wide, its iron thorns outstretched to tear the leaves from the myrtles. Beyond, a fearful opening gaped, black past blackness, repellent to any who had ever dreamed of death.

Valore leaned to the earth, arose, and there came the scrape of kindled flame. Candles had been left lying in readiness, and now burst into flower. Colour struck against the void of the mausoleum's mouth, and did it no great harm.

'Take this light. You may hereafter lead the way, *caro*. It is not far.'

Di Giudea's eyes, polished by the candle as he received it, seemed without depth or soul; he in his turn had now absorbed a wicked semblance from the slanted glow. It was a season for such things. He did not move.

'Afraid to enter?' Valore mocked, himself brightly gilded again on the night. 'Follow me still, then.' And with this, walked directly into the slot of the tomb.

It was quite true, he had not previously entered this place. Nor was it fear that had kept him out, though a kind of fear was mingled in his thoughts with other swirlings of diverse sort. Neither pure nor simple were the desires of Valore della Scorpioni, and to some extent, even as he revelled in himself, he remained to himself a mystery. What he asked of this adventure he could not precisely have confessed, but that the advent of the infamous magnetic Jew had quickened everything, of that he was in no doubt.

So, he came into the tomb of which the brown parchment had, in its concise Latin, informed him.

It was a spot immediately conjurable, dressed stone of the antique mode, the light barely dispelling the gloom, yet falling out from his hand upon a slab, and so impelling the young man to advance, to search, to find the curious miracle the paper had foretold.

'Ah, by the Mass. *Ipssisima verba*.'

And thus Olivio di Giudea came on him an instant later, his words still whispering in the breathless air and the candlelight richening as it was doubled on the stone and the face of what lay on that stone.

She was as the portrait had given her, the hair like rose mahogany shining its rays on the unloving pillow, the creamy skin defiled only by the gauzy webs that had clustered too upon her gown of topaz silk, now fragile as a web itself, and all its golden sequins tarnished into green. Her face, her throat, her breast, the long-stemmed fingers sheared of rings – these marked her as a girl not more than 19 years of age, a woman at the fullness and bloom of her nubility. There was about her, too, that indefinable ghastliness associated with recent death. It would have seemed, but for the decay of her garments, that she had been brought here only yesterday. Yet, from her dress, the gathering cobwebs, it had been considerably longer.

'You see,' Valore said, very low, 'she is as I promised you. Beautiful and rare. Laid out upon her couch. Not chiding, but quiescent. To be enjoyed.'

'And you would wake her with a kiss?'

Valore shuddered. 'Perhaps. My reverie is not lawful as I look at her. No holy musings come to me. Her flesh is wholesome, lovely. I would ask her if she went to her bed a virgin. Alas, unpardonable sin.'

'You have lain with your sisters. What's one sin more?'

Valore turned to study his companion, but that face had become a shadow upon shadows.

'*Caro*, she is too old to tempt me, after all. Let me tell you what the parchment said of her. Aurena della Scorpioni, for that was her name, unknown in the days of our modesty, lived unwed in her father's house until that year the Eastern Plague fell upon Roma as upon all the world. And before the merciful, if dilatory, angel stood upon the Castel San Angelo to sheathe his dripping sword, shut up in that house, Aurena took the fever of the peste and life passed from her. Having no mark upon her, it was said she had died the needle-death – for they believed, *caro*, that certain Jews had gone about scratching the citizens with poisoned needles ... And the year of her death is graven there, beneath her feet. You see the candle shine upon it?'

Di Giudea did not speak, but that he had noted the carving was quite likely. It revealed clearly enough that the pestilence to which the younger man referred was that that would come to be known uniquely as the Death, or the Black Death, and that Aurena della Scorpioni, lying like a fresh-cut rose, had died and been interned almost a century and a half before.

Valore leaned now to the dead girl, close enough for sure to have embraced her. And to her very lips he said, 'And are we to believe it?'

The Jew had set his candle in a little niche in the wall, where once maybe a sacred image had been placed, now vanished. As the young man flirted with the corpse, bending close, his long hair mingling with hers and of the self-same shade as hers, di Giudea stood in silence, his tall straight figure partly shrouded in the dark, his arms folded. There was about him a curious air of patience, that and some inexorable and powerful quality having no name. The tomb, with its pledge of death, the miracle that lay there, if miracle it was and not some alchemical trick, each seemed to have left him undisturbed. The younger man sparkled on the dark like a jewel; the Judean was, in some extraordinary way, an emissary and partner of that dark. So that, looking up once more, Valore very nearly started, and might be forgiven for it, as if he had glimpsed the figure of Death himself.

But, 'Well,' said Valore then, regaining himself in a moment, 'what shall we do? Shall we withdraw? I for one am loath to desert her. How long she has endured alone here, unvisited save by beetles, unwooed save by worms. If I could wake her, as you postulate, with a loving kiss – shall I try it, noble pagan? Will you act my brother at this wedding, stay and kiss her, too …

Olivia di Giudea did not respond, standing on, the shadows like black wings against his back. And Valore offered him again that glorious smile, and put down his beautiful face toward the beautiful face of the dead. The lips met, one pair eager with heat, one passive and cool. Valore della Scorpioni hissed his kindred with great insistence, his mouth fastened on hers as if never to be lifted, his fingers straying, clasping, the smooth flesh of her throat, the loose knot of her fingers on her breast.

The Jew watched him.

Valore raised his head, staring now only at the woman. 'Divine madonna,' he exclaimed, 'beloved, can I not warm you? I must court you further, then –' And now he half lay against the body, taking it in his arms, his eyes blazing like gold coins –

And for the third occasion of that darkness, the Jew laughed.

Valore acknowledged this only by the merest sound, his lips active, his hands at work, his pulses louder in his ears than any laughter.

But in another instant, de Giudea left his post by the wall, breaking the shadows in pieces and striding to the slab. Here he set a grip like iron on the young man's shoulder and prised him from his employment. With a slitted gaze, now, breathing as if in a race, Valore looked at him perforce, and found him laughing still, mainly the two eyes glittering like black stones with laughter.

'Your kisses after all, I fear, leave her but too cold,' said the Judean.

'Oh, you will do better? Do it. I shall observe you closely and take instruction.'

'First,' said di Giudea, holding him yet in that awesome iron grip, 'I will tell you this much. You rightly suppose she is not dead. She only sleeps. Should she rouse, will you run away?'

'I? I have seen many things done, and stayed to see others. Things even you may never have looked on.'

'That I doubt. I am older than you, and much-travelled.'

Valore attempted to dislodge the iron vice, and failed. He relaxed, trembling with excitement, anger, a whole host of emotions that charged him with some delicious sense of imminence. Even the punishing hand that held him was, in that moment, not displeasing.

'Do as you wish, and all you wish,' said Valore hoarsely. 'And you will find me here, obedient.'

The Jew showed his white teeth and with a casual violence quite unlooked-for, flung the young man from him and simultaneously from the couch. Valore rolled on the floor and came to rest against the worn stones of one wall. Dazed, he lay there, and from that vantage saw the tall figure of the Judean stoop as he himself had done toward the slab. 'You will learn now,' the voice said above him, 'which kiss it is that wakens.' But there was no meeting of the lips. Instead the dark head bent, black hair fell upon white skin, yellow silk. It was the throat di Giudea kissed, and that only for a space of seconds. Then the dark head was lifted, strong and slowly as some preying beast's from a kill, and there, a mark, a blush left behind on the skin, the silk.

Valore ordered himself. He came to his feet and stole back across the tomb, and so beheld, with an elated astonishment, how his shadowy companion milked the broken vessel of the throat with his fingers, smearing them, then pressed these fingers to the lips of the dead. Which quietly, and apparently of their own accord, parted to receive them.

'Take,' said di Giudea, the one word a sound like smoke. And the parted lips widened and there came a savage glint of teeth. So Valore had seen a dog maul the hand of its master! Yet the Judean was impassive as this terrible thing occurred, still as the night, until he spoke again, a second word: 'Enough.' And the mouth slackened, and he drew his fingers away, bloody and appalling, seeming bitten through. The sight of all this sent Valore reeling. He fell against the couch again, full finally of a sensation that prompted him to hilarity or screaming, he was not sure which.

'What now?' he cried. 'What now?' Swaying over her, his Aurena, supported by one hand against the slab, the other fixed on the Jew's wrist. But the question required no answer. Fed by that elixir of blood the Jew had given her, her own and his, the being that lay before them both began, unconscionably, to awaken. The signs off it were swift, and lacking all complexity. The parted lips drew a breath, the eyelids tensed, and unfurled. Two eyes looked out into the world, upon the vault, upon the form of Valore. She had seemed in all else very like him, but those eyes of hers were not his eyes. They were like burnished jets; the eyes, in fact, of Olivia di Giudea.

'She is more beautiful than truth,' Valore remarked, staring down at her. 'Is it a part of your spell, O Magio, to set your own demoniac optics in her head?' But then he began to murmur to her, caressing her face, smiling on her, and she, as if lessoned in such gestures by him, smiled in return.

It was a joy to Valore, a joy founded upon exquisite fear, to feel her hands steal to his waist and seek to pull him to her. His hold on the other man he relinquished, and taking hold instead once more of her, he sank down.

The Jew spoke quietly at his back.

'It would seem, locked in her father's house against the coming of the plague, she could not find escape, nor would she prey on her kindred. But she has been hungry a great while and forgotten all such nepotism.'

His face buried in Aurena's breast, Valore muttered. It was a name, the name of one who, a legend and a sorcerer, cursed by the Christ to an eternal wandering until Doomsday, when and if it should ever come, was also a Jew; and this persona he awarded Olivio di Giudea now. 'Ahasuere.'

Di Giudea stood at the door of the tomb, looking upon blackness and a faint threat of greyness in the east, where all the stars went out, and from which all the plagues of the world had come – sickness, sorcery and religion.

'Ahasuerus? But if I am he, and immortal,' the Judean replied, 'there must be some reason for it, and some means. Say then, perhaps, my presence at your side tonight also had some reason and some means. You will come to understand, there are other kindred than those of the flesh. And only one race that may safely spurn all the rest.'

Valore did not hear this. There was a roaring like a river in his ears, a burning that ran from his neck into his heart. As he lay in her arms, Valore knew it was his blood now she drank. And first it was an intolerable ecstasy, so he clung to her, but soon it passed into a wonderful and spiritual state wherein he floated, free of all heaviness. But at length this too was changed, and he was invaded by a dreadful languor and an iciness and a raging thirst and a searing agony of the limbs and nerves, so that he would have pulled himself away from her. However, by then it was too late, and helplessly he sprawled upon her till she had drained him.

An emptied wine-skin he lay then, void and dry. The doorway was long-empty also of any other companion, and the door rightly shut against the impending dawn.

Aurena della Scorpioni reclined beneath the coverlet of her victim, her head flung back, her eyes enlarged, her lips curved, smiling still.

Beyond the tomb, the garden and the wall, the city was wakening also, throwing off its stygian sleep.

By noon, some would have asked aloud for Valore, the Scorpion's child, and found him not. It was the same with the clever Judean; he and all his arts and skills and sciences vanished with and in like manner to the darkness. From those who had supped at Andrea's table and remained, uneasy fancies sprang. As days went by thereafter without clue, there began to be a certain hideous curiosity concerning corpses dredged from the yellow river. But twenty days later the veiled person of plague entered the *Interiore*, and thence the forums, and the markets, and the churches, and the proliferation of the dead ended such speculation.

It was not until the winter came to cleanse the ancient thoroughfares with blades that Andrea Trarra, going one evening into his garden to inspect the frost-crippled vines, was shocked to find a figure there before him.

After a moment, recovering somewhat, Andrea stepped briskly forward.

'Valore – where in God's name –?'

'Ah,' said Valore, his face deadly white in the dusk, but beautiful and charming as ever, 'I have countless secrets. Do you, for example, remember when we diced for this?' And held up before the other a great key of iron, now no blacker than the centres of his eyes.

BLOOD CHESS

Winter and the Sorian Approach

A crumbling stone staircase leads down the mountain-hill from the castle. About a mile above the valley, there is a walled terrace, and here the gigantic chessboard is laid out. It is old and faded, the black squares grey, the blood-red squares a lifeless pink. As she crosses the chessboard, each square taking a full three steps, Ismira glances down at it, at the cracks in its paving where wild flowers push up in spring, and where, now winter is approaching, they die.

She is not a vampire, but the people in the valley are afraid of her, thinking she must be. Her brother is the vampire. In the valley they call him the Sorian. He comes from the land of Soriath, over the mountains, so the name is not inappropriate – but really they are trying to distance him in the only way they can. They are aware of his true name, which is Yane, and never use it.

Ismira knows her brother will return during the night. By going down to the village, she is also warning them.

There is an afternoon frost. When she reaches the village street, the tall trees by the well are clouded with cold. Icicles thin as needles spike the roofs. Already the ball of the sun is rolling off the sky. Before, she would often come here in full daylight, striving to convince them she was only herself, had no fear of sunlight, and did not require blood. But when she saw this did no good, she did not do it anymore.

All the doors are shut and the street and alleys empty. Somewhere a dog howls and is struck – she hears the blow – to silence it.

Ismira stops in the centre of the street, by the well. In her long black garments, her long black hair curling down like a fleece to her shoulder-blades, she is only what they must expect.

As she stands waiting, the sun too runs away, afraid she will see its redness and desire its blood.

Yane, the Sorian, once said to her, in one of his intermittent fevers: 'The sun – give me the sun to drink – it's *full* as a wineskin –'

After a time of merely standing there, Ismira sees a door is being eased open in the side of the big house, the one with the carvings that pretend to the decoration of the castle on the mountain-hill. Something is thrust out. It drops and lies motionless on the street.

Ismira goes over to this object, which turns out to be a young woman of about 16, clothed in white, and with her fair hair washed and braided. She is not unconscious, as sometimes they are. She stares up at Ismira from the dirt.

'Don't make me, lady – Let me go –'

'I can't. Get up and come with me.'

Shaking and temporally past tears, the girl does so. She will probably walk meekly behind Ismira all the way back up the mountain. Now and then, one of them will dash off, and never be seen by Ismira again. She suspects the village pursues and murders them.

Ismira herself has done what she must. She has procured the sacrifice for her brother's needs, and also warned the village by her presence, that he is imminent.

The sky burns crimson.

Ismira and the sacrifice plod doggedly up the terrible, ruinous stair.

'Look,' says Ismira, encouragingly, as the epic bulk of the castle looms over them, touched with ruby by the falling sun they have, through climbing, managed to keep sight of. Now the girl starts to cry.

Ismira hardens her heart, at which act she has, over the 15 years since her tenth birthday, become adept.

Why attempt reassurance? These ones the village selects by unlucky lot. Each of them knows what will happen.

They pass the chessboard. The weeping girl takes no notice of it. All the flowers have been abruptly frost-bitten to death, and above, in the castle garden, scarcely any leaves remain on the tangled trees, and those that do are like silver daggers.

The Return of Yane

The girl's name is Thental. She sits crying on and on.

Once it begins to be very dark, Ismira walks about the castle, the rooms, passages and annexes, lighting a few lamps and enormous candles. She wonders if the girl would be more comfortable in the great hall. But the kitchen, with its huge fire, will be much warmer.

Coming back into the kitchen, there is Thental, still crying.

Ismira has given her white bread and an apple, and wine for courage, none of which has Thental tried.

How dismal it all is, Ismira thinks, lighting another candle on the branch above the hearth. She hopes Yane will soon arrive.

As if reading her mind, Thental checks her sobs.

'Does he fly here, on his bat wings?' she asks.

Ismira senses an unpleasant pettiness in the question. Thental knows she is being given to a monster, the monster must therefore live up to his legends.

'No, in fact he'll ride across the pass.'

'Some demon will have told you he's near.'

'Also no. Common sense, and memory. Snow will soon fall and close all the passes. It's always on this night Yane comes back. Have none of you realised?'

The girl shudders. Her head darts up and her shining hair, loosened by now, flutters candlelit round her head like a bridal veil.

'Is that a clatter of wings?'

Ismira says nothing. She can hear it too, and quite obviously the noise is that of hoofs clattering into the yard outside.

Yane will stable his horse in the stall Ismira has prepared, before he enters the kitchen; they have no servants, of course. But the girl springs up and falls now on her knees, tightly shutting her eyes, and praying.

Ismira feels sorry for her, but also it is all so tiresome, this. '*Shush!*' she exclaims sharply, and Thental becomes quiet as the grave.

It will be useless to try to reason with her. Ismira, long since, additionally gave that up with the sacrifices who accompany her to the castle, their names written helpfully on little scraps of book paper and wrapped round their wrists.

They pose there then, in stasis, Ismira seated on the wooden chair, Thental kneeling abject on the stone-flagged floor.

Outside now a sound of boots, then the door is pushed wide. Yane strides in out of the night, bringing the night in with him, cold and mysterious, across cloak and hair.

Ismira sees, as so often, Thental stare, then avert her gaze.

Yane is very handsome. His blue-black hair falls to his waist, he is tall and straight, his body hard and fined from constant journeys, his large dark eyes full of a luminous introspection fatal to most women.

Ismira gets up. She takes him a cup of wine.

Yane thanks her. He drinks the wine. Then he glances at the girl kneeling on the floor, staring at him between fingers she has clamped over her eyes.

'Is she for me?'

'Who else?'

'Dear God,' says Yane. He sighs, perhaps an affectation. He walks across and sits in the wooden chair, and looks at Thental. Thental does not look back, but nor does she cry any more. 'Well,' says Yane, 'good evening. Isn't the floor rather hard on your knees?'

Thental blinks. She puts down her hands.

'Don't kill me,' she says quietly. 'Don't damn my soul.'

'I'm not interested in your soul. Keep it.'

Thental grunts. She lowers her head, desolate now.

Yane stands up, frowning with irritation and tiredness.

Ismira has drawn a bath for him, across the passage, with extra water heating on the fire there. He goes out to this, and Ismira moves around the kitchen, seeing to the supper, constantly detouring past Thental kneeling on the floor.

An Evening at Home

When Yane enters again he is more relaxed, wrapped in a dressing-robe of scarlet, black and gold. He goes to Thental at once and lifts her off the floor, and sits her at the table in a chair adjacent to his own.

She is evidently exhausted by her fright, far worse than Yane from his travels. He takes advantage of that, feeding her scraps of meat and cheese, and making her sip the wine. Her head droops onto his shoulder. He kisses her hair absently.

Ismira watches all this from the other end of the table. It has ceased to offend, puzzle or upset her.

She thinks back to the day the horsemen came to her father's house in another country, not this one, and not Soriath either. That was the day of her tenth birthday. While her proud father sat in talk with the riders, Ismira's chilly mother took her aside. 'Listen to me, Ismira. Today you're to go away to another place. We've never treated you as we do our other children, and this is because, you must now understand, you're no child of ours at all. You are the cuckoo's egg left to hatch in this house. We bore it because we must, and we've done you no harm. You've been raised nobly, as our true children have, although without our love. Under the circumstances, you'll agree, you could hardly expect any.' Astounded, shocked beyond reason, Ismira stood listening. Her mother – who was not – told her she was the child of an ancient and corrupt family who exerted much power in this region and else-where. The Scaratha, they were called. Due to their way of living, which was that of vampires, blood-drinkers and creatures of darkness and horror, they kept no children of their own in their domiciles before the age of ten. At that age they would send for and claim them, whether the vampire strain was prevalent or not. 'You have been closely observed, more for our sakes than yours,' said Ismira's unmother, with great distaste. 'You show no symptoms of any of that. Even so, you are a fiend, the child of fiends. It's made me sick to have you in this house. I have seldom touched you and won't now. Get out and go to your own, you foul abomination.'

'What are you brooding on, Ismi?' asks Yane from along the table. The girl from the village has fallen asleep against him, soothed by his glamorous kindness and the Eastern incense he has rubbed into his hair.

'The past,' says Ismira.

'Oh, that. Don't think of that. Let me tell you what I saw on my way here – something better than the Eastern markets, for all their glitter and show. Better even than the moon-and-star night over the City of Rome.'

'What?' inquires Ismira. She knows what he will say.

'I saw the sun.'

'Which will make you ill. It always does.'

'Yes, it always does, but this was three days ago. And you see, I'm cool and well. Perhaps I'm growing used to the sun, or it to me.'

'The wineskin full of blood,' says Ismira. She becomes angry with him, because in his fevers she must nurse him, and she hates the chore, and also is infuriated to see him suffer so stupidly by his own lack of control. He is addicted to the sun, she sometimes thinks, worse than blood.

But Yane boasts, 'I crept out of my deep hiding cave, and I beheld a sunrise in the mountains. The sky was redder than any blood. I'm cool and hale, Ismi. Can't you see? Perhaps, in a day or so, I can try again.'

'The sun isn't for you.'

'But you can see it every day! Don't you know how jealous I am of you, Ismi?'

She too frowns. She considers how Yane rides about the world, journeying to lands she has never, will never, see. How she remains at home, tending the castle, alone, save for the winter months when Yane comes back, often flaming with sun-fever, crazy and devilish, and girls must be collected from the village, one every thirty days, for Yane's pleasure.

I'm his skivvy, Ismira thinks. And *he* is *jealous*?

In her childhood, once only, she saw one of the Scaratha kin brought to the castle after the sun had caught him, not for a few minutes at sunrise or set, but at the height of noon. He had burned alive and screaming for many hours before he died.

This is why they value those of their kind who are not vampiric. They take them in and load them with codes of honour and high dreams of loyalty, and make them into useful servants of the house.

Ismira can hear Yane talking endlessly, in raptures about the sun. She pretends – she is quite clever at pretence – that she attends to him. She loves him, admires him, but resents him. They may have two hundred years more like this, for, left to themselves, the Scaratha are all long-lived. The rest of the castle inhabitants perished in a war with other Scaratha ten years ago. But other castles and fortresses exist still well-stocked with their kind. Sometimes Yane promises to take her visiting. He never does, and doubtless never will.

She considers leaving him and going off on her own. Wherever she went – on foot, alone, unsafe ways for a woman, even – *especially* – a Scaratha woman to travel – she would in the end fetch up with the Scaratha. She would have no other place to go. And then her life would be the same as it is here, save with more to do, more persons to love, admire and tend – the higher echelons of the practising vampires.

Now Yane is speaking to Thental, the flower-like sacrifice.

'Time for bed, sweetheart.'

There was something too he had put in the wine. The girl stirs and smiles at him, sleepy and adoring, ready as a summer peach on the vine.

He half carries this now-willing and pliable companion – perhaps she thinks this is her wedding-night? – away along the passage, and up the steps of a tower to the bedroom Yane has there. Ismira has put fresh embroidered sheets on the bed, sprinkled lavender and other herbs. Scented lamps burn, and the window is heavily shuttered against sunrise, and locked – Ismira keeps the key.

Up there Yane the Sorian will make love to the girl, exquisitely, and also he will drink her blood, with passionate discretion. It will do her no harm whatsoever. He is wholesome, his teeth clean and flawless. Even the marks on her throat will fade when, after seven or so nights, he turns her out of bed, with enough money and jewels to make her rich beyond her most avaricious dreams. He will also escort her – by night – along the valley. That is Yane's gallantry. He knows about women travelling on their own, particularly with wealth about them. He will make sure she reaches some sort of safety, for the Scaratha are careful with the goods they handle. After a certain point, however, once he has discharged his duty to her, or his payment for her services, Yane will leave the girl. If something happens to Thental then – or has happened in the past to any of the countless others – that will not be Yane's fault.

Ismira tidies the table. She hauls a pitcher of cold water and adds it to a wooden tub of hot, and rinses the platters and knives. The precious cups of emerald crystal, rimmed and stemmed with gold, she replaces on the stone top of the hearth, among the candles, vases of dead flowers, iron keys, onions, and other things.

Outside the wind is rising. It howls like the dog in the village they had struck to make it silent. Who will strike the wind?

The villages naturally believe all who are brought here die, drained like bottles. Or else they are turned into undead devils, and subsequently roam the countryside, preying on the sheep, or small unguarded children, which in fact lammergeyers or starving wolves have picked off. One day perhaps the village may rebel against the castle. But probably they will not, for Scaratha power, though so isolate and scattered, is yet omnipresent and much dreaded.

Ismira blows out the kitchen candles. She takes one with her, and goes about the castle again, replenishing the lights. Later, when her brother has had tonight's fill of the girl, he will ramble through the passages, enter the great hall, take down old swords, and musical instruments to play. The castle is a rare treat for Yane – how not, when he is hardly ever here.

As she retires to her room beyond the kitchen, Ismira hopes the sun will not have made him ill, and that he has enjoyed Thental. But when she falls asleep, Ismira dreams of herself riding his horse away and away, her own black hair and cloak rippling in the race of their speed. Dimly in the distance she thinks she sees the acres of a sea, the domes of the East, the moonlit columns of Rome. *I am Ismira* she sings in her sleep, *nor was I born in Soriath* –

The Chess-Game

It was how the Scaratha taught their young the rules of existence – that is, the *vampiric*, more-valued young, although the others, the lesser, but so-useful breed, they were allowed to stand by and watch. In this way Ismira had been part of the audience at the chess-games, played out on the huge board halfway down the mountain-hill.

They commenced at dusk, often not concluding until midnight, all by torchlight – and in the village below, no doubt the people covered their heads in fear. This was before the war among the Scaratha had wiped away all but two of the castle's indigenous population.

Scaratha chess was not like humanly employed chess, of course. There were no pawns, for humanity was all made up of pawns, as far as the Scaratha were concerned. Here, the Scarathu hunted each *other* over the squares, which then were kept vivid with paint. A knight might take a queen, a queen a priest, as they pleased. Physical figures performed these actions. Deliberately, always, the *wrong* moves were educated into the Scaratha young, so they should learn to break all the other rules of the world.

Only at the very end would the victors fasten on their conquered own. This was not like a war. None died. They milked their victims, in mutual delight, of blood. Tokens, *love* tokens, which still meant someone had won. Blood to the Scaratha was not a food, but a covenant. From human things they took it as of right, from their own they took it as the sigil of conquest. And life was all a game, like chess.

The spilled blood had dripped, during these playings, through the paint into the chessboard, then coloured red for blood and black for night. Because of the nourishment of those libations, when finally allowed by neglect, flowers came to break cracks in the squares. The flowers were very strong, tougher from being kept down, from fighting back. Only harsh frost could kill them now, and in the spring others would come, rising from death as gods and vampires allegedly did.

How Fair the Day

Waking early as always, Ismira gets up. She sets about the business of the morning, equably, quietly. She anticipates nothing of it, but it has a surprise for her after all.

She is in the great hall, clearing up the mess of spent candles and replacing them with fresh, when Thental steals in like a slim white ray around the door.

Sometimes these girls do venture down, while Yane lies sleeping in the dark. Then, by now besotted with the vampire from Soriath, they talk on and on of his virtues to Ismira.

It is her task too, to give them food and drink, to keep them healthy, bathed and appealing, for her brother.

When she turns to Thental, however, Ismira is briefly bemused. It seems to her the girl has impudently put on Yane's dressing-robe of chessboard red and black, edged with gold.

But no. The gold is Thental's dishevelled hair, and the white her own skin, some of it. The red and black, which are thick on her naked body, are rich red blood and skeins of black hair that seems to have been torn out at the roots.

Thental lifts her head and smiles at Ismira.

'How fair the day! I've done what I came for. Just as I swore I would, I did it. I never forgot, never. I can cry always just thinking of her. I told them, this time, let it be me, I'll go. And so they let me. See this? My little dagger, razor sharp. The hilt's silver; that helps with killing a demon-thing. I bartered for it off a pedlar. He fucked me for it. Sensible trade, worth every jolt.' Thental raises the dagger high. If it was ever silver, now it is not. It is blood-red, like most of the rest of her. 'What a lot he had in him,' Thental remarks of this blood, conversational, moving nearer. 'Some of it after all was mine. What he drank from me last night. I stabbed him through as he slept. Then I hacked off his head – quite a job I had of that, but I managed. It's how you must do it with that kind – *your* kind – I'll do it for you –' She runs headlong at Ismira. Ismira, Scaratha though not vampire, kills the girl instantly with one swift sidelong blow that breaks her neck.

Then Ismira stands there, staring at the wreckage, thinking about the other wreckage that will be all that is left of Yane in the tower.

Presently, Ismira sits down.

She considers graves, digging them, which is easy. She has dug a couple, if some years ago. She thinks of her glorious brother, she thinks of the human heritage she has never had, the vampire Scaratha heritage she has also, being second rate, never had.

Yane's horse is in the stable. The snows have not yet begun. The sun, for Ismira, provides no difficulty – though later, she can always make believe it does ...

Ismira goes over to Thental, the fragile white flower that grew strong enough to crack the paving of the chessboard, but that the frost of Ismira's hand then finished. Human flowers do not recover from that, nor vampire flowers, so Ismira has discovered.

Ismira dips her finger in the still-wet blood Thental has thoughtfully brought with her, Yane's blood. Ismira licks the finger. It means nothing to her, nothing at all. But, as with the sun of this fair day, she can always *pretend.*

THE ISLE IS FULL OF NOISES

'… and if you gaze into the abyss, the abyss gazes also into you.'
Nietzsche

I

It is an island here, now.

At the clearest moments of the day – usually late in the morning, occasionally after noon, and at night when the lights come on – a distant coastline is sometimes discernible. This coast is the higher area of the city, that part that still remains intact above water.

The city was flooded a decade ago. The Sound possessed it. The facts had been predicted some while, and various things were done in readiness, mostly comprising a mass desertion.

They say the lower levels of those buildings that now form the island will begin to give way in five years. But they were saying that too five years back.

Also there are the sunsets. (Something stirred up in the atmosphere apparently, by the influx of water, some generation of heat or cold or vapour.) They start, or appear to do so, the sunsets, about three o'clock in the afternoon, and continue until the sun actually goes under the horizon, which in summer can be as late as 7.45.

For hours the roof terraces, towerettes and glass-lofts of the island catch a deepening blood-and-copper light, turning to new bronze, raw amber, cubes of hot pink ice.

Yse lives on West Ridge, in a glass-loft. She has, like most of the island residents, only one level, but there's plenty of space. (Below, if anyone remembers, lies a great warehouse, with fish, even sometimes barracuda, gliding between the girders.)

Beyond her glass west wall, a freak tree has rooted in the terrace. Now nine years old, it towers up over the loft, and the surrounding towers and lofts, while its serpentine branches dip down into the water. Trees are unusual here. This tree, which Yse calls Snake (for the branches) seems unfazed by the salt content of the water. It may be a sort of willow, a willow crossed with a snake.

Sometimes Yse watches fish glimmering through the tree's long hair, that floats just under the surface. This appeals to her, as the whole notion of the island does. Then one morning she comes out and finds, caught in the coils of her snake-willow, a piano.

Best to describe Yse, at this point, which is not easy.

She might well have said herself (being a writer by trade but also by desire) that she doesn't want you to be disappointed, that you should hold onto the idea that what you get at first, here, may not be what is to be offered later.

Then again, there is a disparity between what Yse seems to be, or is, and what Yse *also seems* to be, or *is*.

Her name, however, as she has often had to explain, is pronounced to rhyme with *please* – more correctly, *pleeze: eeze*. Is it French? Or some sport from Latin-Spanish? God knows.

Yse is in her middle years, not tall, rather heavy, dumpy. Her fair, greying hair is too fine, and so she cuts it very short. Yse is also slender, taller, and her long hair (still fair, still greying) hangs in thick silken hanks down her back. One constant, grey eyes.

She keeps only a single mirror, in the bathroom above the wash basin. Looking in it is always a surprise for Yse: Who on earth is that? But she never lingers, soon she is away from it and back to herself. And in this way too, she deals with Per Laszd, the lover she has never had.

Yse has brought the coffee-pot and some peaches onto the terrace. It is a fine morning, and she is considering walking along the bridgeway to the boat-stop, and going over to the cafés on East Heights. There are always things on at the cafés: psychic fairs, art shows, theatre. And she needs some more lamp oil.

Having placed the coffee and fruit, Yse looks up and sees the piano.

'*Oh,*' says Yse, aloud.

She is very, very startled, and there are good reasons for this, beyond the obvious oddity itself.

She goes to the edge of the terrace and leans over, where the tree leans over, and looks at the snake arms that hold the piano fast, tilted only slightly, and fringed by rippling leaves.

The piano is old, huge, a type of pianoforte, its two lids fast shut, concealing both the keys and its inner parts.

Water swirls round it idly. It is intensely black, scarcely marked by its swim.

And has it been swimming? Probably it was jettisoned from some apartment on the mainland (the upper city.) Then, stretching out its three strong legs, it set off savagely for the island, determined not to go down.

Yse has reasons, too, for thinking in this way.

She reaches out, but cannot quite touch the piano.

There are tides about the island, variable, sometimes rough. If she leaves the piano where it is, the evening tide may be a rough one, and lift it away, and she will lose it.

She *knows* it must have swum here.

Yse goes to the table and sits, drinking coffee, looking at the piano. As she does this a breeze comes in off the Sound, and stirs her phantom long heavy soft hair, so it brushes her face and neck and the sides of her arms. And the piano makes a faint twanging, she thinks perhaps it does, up through its shut lids that are like closed eyes and lips together.

'What makes a vampire seductive?' Yse asks Lucius, at the Café Blonde. 'I mean, irresistible?'

'His beauty,' says Lucius. He laughs, showing his teeth. 'I knew a vampire, once. No, make that twice. I met him twice.'

'Yes?' asks Yse cautiously. Lucius has met them all, ghosts, demons, angels. She partly believes it to be so, yet knows he mixes lies with the truths; a kind of test, or trap, for the listener. 'Well, what happened?'

'We walk, talk, drink, make love. He bites me. Here, see?' Lucius moves aside his long locks (luxurious, but greying, as are her own). On his coal-dark neck, no longer young, but strong as a column, an old scar.

'You told me once before,' says Yse, 'a shark did that.'

'To reassure you. But it was a vampire.'

'What did you do?'

'I say to him, *Watch out, monsieur.*'

'And then?'

'He watched out. Next night, I met him again. He had yellow eyes, like a cat.'

'He was undead?'

'The undeadest thing I ever laid.'

He laughs. Yse laughs, thoughtfully. 'A piano's caught in my terrace tree.'

'*Oh* yeah,' says Lucius, the perhaps arch liar.

'You don't believe me.'

'What is your thing about vampires?'

'I'm writing about a vampire.'

'Let me read your book.'

'Someday. But Lucius – it isn't their charisma. Not their beauty that makes them irresistible –'

'No?'

'Think what they must be like ... skin in rags, dead but walking. Stinking of the grave –'

'They use their *hudja-magica* to take all that away.'

'It's how they make *us* feel.'

'Yeah, Yse. You got it.'

'What they can do to *us*.'

'Dance all night,' says Lucius, reminiscent. He watches a handsome youth across the café, juggling mirrors that flash unnervingly, his skin the colour of an island twilight.

'Lucius, will you help me shift the piano into my loft?'

'Sure thing.'

'Not tomorrow, or next month. I mean, could we do it today, before sunset starts?'

'I love you, Yse. Because of you, I shall go to Heaven.'

'Thanks.'

'Shit piano,' he says. 'I could have slept in my boat. I could have paddled over to Venezule. I could have watched the thought of Venus rise through the grey brain of the sky. Piano, huh, piano. Who shall I bring to help me? That boy, he looks strong, look at those mirrors go.'

The beast had swum to shore, to the beach, through the pale, transparent urges of the waves, when the star Venus was in the brain-grey sky. But not here.

There.

In the dark before star-rise and dawn, more than two centuries ago. First the rifts, the lilts of the dark sea, and in them these mysterious thrusts and pushes, the limbs like those of some huge swimmer, part man and part lion and part crab – but also, a manta ray.

Then, the lid breaks for a second through the fans of water, under the dawn star's piercing steel. Wet as black mirror, the closed lid of the piano, as it strives, on three powerful beast-legs, for the beach.

This Island is an island of sands, then of trees, the sombre sullen palms that sweep the shore. Inland, heights, vegetation, plantations, some of coffee and sugar and rubber, and one of imported kayar. An invented island, a composite.

Does it crawl onto the sand, the legs still moving, crouching low like a beast? Does it rest on the sand, under the sway of the palm trees, as a sun rises?

The Island has a name, like the house that is up there, unseen, on the inner heights. Bleumaneer.

(Notes: Gregers Vonderjan brought his wife to Bleumaneer in the last days of his wealth ...)

The piano crouched stilly at the edge of the beach, the sea retreating from it, and the dark of night falling away ...

It's sunset.

Lucius, in the bloody light, with two men from the Café Blonde (neither the juggler), juggles the black piano from the possessive tentacles of the snake-willow.

With a rattle, a shattering of sounds (like slung cutlery), it fetches up on the terrace. The men stand perplexed, looking at it. Yse watches from her glass wall.

'Broke the cock thing.'

'No way to move it. Shoulda tooka crane.'

They prowl about the piano, while the red light blooms across its shade.

Lucius tries delicately to raise the lid from the keys. The lid does not move. The other two, they wrench at the other lid, the piano's top (pate, shell). This too is fastened stuck. (Yse had made half a move, as if to stop them. Then her arm fell lax.)

'Damn ol' thing. What she wan' this ol' thing for?'

They back away. One makes a kicking movement. Lucius shakes his head; his long locks jangle across the flaming sky.

'*Do* you want this, girl?' Lucius asks Yse by her glass.

'Yes.' Shortly. 'I said I did.'

''S all broke up. Won't play you none,' sings the light-eyed man, Carr, who wants to kick the piano, even now his loose leg pawing in its jeans.

Trails of water slip away from the piano, over the terrace, like chains.

Yse opens her wide glass doors. The men carry the piano in, and set it on her bare wooden floor.

Yse brings them, now docile as their maid, white rum, while Lucius shares out the bills.

'Hurt my back,' whinges Carr the kicker.

'Piano,' says Lucius, drinking, 'pian-o – O pain!'

He says to her at the doors (as the men scramble back into their boat), 'That vampire I danced with. Where he bit me. Still feel him there, biting me, some nights. Like a piece of broken bottle in my neck. I followed him, did I say to you? I followed him and saw him climb in under his grave just before the sun came up. A marble marker up on top. It shifted easy as breath, settled back like a sigh. But he was beautiful, that boy with yellow eyes. Made me feel like a king, with him. Young as a lion, with him. *Old* as him, too. A thousand years in a skin of smoothest suede.'

Yse nods.

She watches Lucius away into the sunset, of which three hours are still left.

Yse scatters two bags of porous litter-chips, which are used all over the island, to absorb the spillages and seepages of the Sound, to mop up the wet that slowly showers from the piano. She does not touch it. Except with her right hand, for a second, flat on the top of it.

The wood feels ancient and hollow, and she thinks it hasn't, perhaps, a metal frame.

As the redness folds over deeper and deeper, Yse light the oil lamp on her work-table, and sits there, looking forty feet across the loft, at the piano on the sunset. Under her right hand now, the pages she has already written, in her fast untidy scrawl.

Piano-o. O pain.

Shush, says the Sound-tide, flooding the city, pulsing through the walls, struts and girders below.

Yse thinks distinctly, suddenly – it is always this way – about Per Laszd. But then another man's memory taps at her mind.

Yse picks up her pen, almost absently. She writes:

'Like those hallucinations that sometimes come at the edge of sleep, so that you wake, thinking two or three words have been spoken close to your ear, or that a tall figure stands in the corner ... like this, the image now and then appears before him.

'Then he sees her, the woman, sitting on the rock, her white dress and her ivory-coloured hair, hard-gleaming in a post-storm sunlight. Impossible to tell her age. A desiccated young girl, or unlined old woman. And the transparent sea lapping in across the sand ...

'But he has said, the Island is quite deserted now.'

II: Antoinelle's Courtship

Gregers Vonderjan brought his wife to Bleumaneer in the last days of his wealth.

In this way, she knew nothing about them, the grave losses to come, but then they had been married only a few months She knew little enough about him, either.

Antoinelle was raised among staunch and secretive people. Until she was 14, she had thought herself ugly, and after that, beautiful. A sunset revelation had put her right, the westering glow pouring in sideways to paint the face in her mirror, on its slim, long throat. She found too she had shoulders, and cheekbones. Hands, whose tendons flexed in fans. With the knowledge of beauty, Antoinelle began to hope for something. Armed with her beauty she began to fall madly in love – with young officers in the army, with figures encountered in dreams.

One evening at a parochial ball, the two situations became confused.

The glamorous young man led Antoinelle out into a summer garden. It was a garden of Europe, with tall dense trees of twisted trunks, foliage massed on a lilac northern sky.

Antoinelle gave herself. That is, not only was she prepared to give of herself sexually, but to give herself up to this male person, of whom she knew no more than that he was beautiful.

Some scruple – solely for himself, the possible consequences – made him check at last.

'No – no –' she cried softly, as he forcibly released her and stood back, angrily panting.

The beautiful young man concluded (officially to himself) that Antoinelle was 'loose', and therefore valueless. She was not rich enough to marry, and besides, he despised her family.

Presently he had told his brother officers all about this girl, and her 'looseness'.

'She would have done anything,' he said.

'She's a whore,' said another, and smiled.

Fastidiously, Antoinelle's lover remarked, 'No, worse than a whore. A whore does it honestly, for money. It's her work. This one simply does it.'

Antoinelle's reputation was soon in tatters, which blew about that little town of trees and societal pillars, like the torn flag of a destroyed regiment.

She was sent in disgrace to her aunt's house in the country.

No-one spoke to Antoinelle in that house. Literally, no-one. The aunt would not, and she had instructed her servants, who were afraid of her. Even the maid who attended Antoinelle would not speak, in the privacy of the evening chamber, preparing the girl for the silent evening supper below, or the lump-three-mattressed bed.

The aunt's rather unpleasant lap-dog, when Antoinelle had attempted, unwatched, to feed it a marzipan fruit, had only turned its rat-like head away. (At everyone else, save the aunt, it growled.)

Antoinelle, when alone, sobbed. At first in shame – her family had already seen to that, very ably, in the town. Next in frustrated rage. At last out of sheer despair.

She was like a lunatic in a cruel, cool asylum. They fed her, made her observe all the proper rituals. She had shelter and a place to sleep, and people to relieve some of her physical wants. There were even books in the library, and a garden to walk in on sunny days. But language – *sound* – they took away from her. And language is one of the six senses. It was as bad perhaps as blindfolding her. Additionally, they did not even speak to each other, beyond the absolute minimum, when she was by – coarse-aproned girls on the stair stifled their giggles, and passed with mask faces. And in much the same way, too, Antoinelle was not permitted to play the aunt's piano.

Three months of this, hard, polished months, like stone mirrors that reflected nothing.

Antoinelle grew thinner, more pale. Her young eyes had hollows under them. She was like a nun.

The name of the aunt who did all this was Clemence – which means, of course, clemency – mild, merciful. (And the name of the young man in the town who had almost fucked Antoinelle, forced himself not to for his own sake, and then fucked instead her reputation, which was to say, her *life* ... His name was Justus.)

On a morning early in the fourth month, a new thing happened.

Antoinelle opened her eyes, and saw the aunt sailing into her room. And the aunt, glittering with rings like knives, *spoke* to Antoinelle.

'Very well, there's been enough of all this. Yes, yes. You may get up quickly and come down to breakfast. Patice will see to your dress and hair. Make sure you look your best.'

Antoinelle lay there, on her back in the horrible bed, staring like the dead newly awakened.

'Come along,' said Aunt Clemence, holding the awful little dog untidily scrunched, 'make haste now. What a child.' As if Antoinelle were the strange creature, the curiosity.

While, as the aunt swept out, the dog craned back and chattered its dirty teeth at Antoinelle.

And then, the third wonder, Patice was chattering, breaking like a happy stream at thaw, and shaking out a dress.

Antoinelle got up, and let Patice see to her, all the paraphernalia of the toilette, finishing with a light pollen of powder, even a fingertip of rouge for the matt pale lips, making them moist and rosy.

'Why?' asked Antoinelle at last, in a whisper.

'There is a visitor,' chattered Patice, brimming with joy.

Antoinelle took two steps, then caught her breath and dropped as if dead on the carpet.

But Patice was also brisk; she brought Antoinelle round, crushing a vicious clove of lemon oil under her nostrils, slapping the young face lightly. Exactly as one would expect in this efficiently cruel lunatic asylum.

Presently Antoinelle drifted down the stairs, lightheaded, rose-lipped and shadow-eyed. She had never looked more lovely or known it less.

The breakfast was a ghastly provincial show-off thing. There were dishes and dishes, hot and cold, of kidneys, eggs, of cheeses and hams, hot breads in napkins, brioches, and chocolate. (It was a wonder Antoinelle was not sick at once.) All this set on crisp linen with flashing silver, and the fine china normally kept in a cupboard.

The servants flurried round in their awful, stupid (second-hand) joy. The aunt sat in her chair and Antoinelle in hers, and the man in his, across the round table.

Antoinelle had been afraid it was going to be Justus. She did not know why he would be there – to castigate her again, to apologise – either way, such a boiling of fear – or something – had gone through Antoinelle that she had fainted.

But it was not Justus. This was someone she did not know.

He had stood up as she came into the room. The morning was clear and well-lit, and Antoinelle had seen, with a dreary sagging of relief, that he was old. Quite old. She went on thinking this as he took her hand in his large one and shook it as if carelessly playing with something, very delicately. But his hand was manicured, the nails clean and white-edged. There was one ring, with a dull colourless stone in it.

Antoinelle still thought he was quite old, perhaps not so old as she *had* thought.

When they were seated, and the servants had doled out to them some food and drink, and gone away, Antoinelle came to herself rather more.

His hair was not grey but a mass of silvery blond. A lot of hair, very thick, shining, which fell, as was the fashion then, just to his shoulders. He was thick-set, not slender, but seemed immensely strong. One saw this in ordinary, apparently unrelated things – for example the niceness with which he helped himself now from the coffee-pot. Indeed, the dangerous playfulness of his handshake with a woman; he could easily crush the hands of his fellow men.

Perhaps he was not an old man, really. In his forties (which would be the contemporary age of fifty-five or -six.) He was losing his figure, as many human beings do at that age, becoming either too big or too thin. But if his middle had spread, he was yet a presence, sprawled there in his immaculately white ruffled shirt, the broad-cut coat, his feet in boots of Spanish leather propped under the table. And to his face, not much really had happened. The forehead was both wide and high, scarcely lined, the nose aquiline as a bird's beak, scarcely thickened, the chin undoubted and jutting, the mouth narrow and well-shaped. His eyes, set in the slightest ruching of skin, were large, a cold clear blue. He might actually be only just forty (that is, fifty). A fraction less.

Antoinelle was not to know that, in his youth, the heads of women had turned for Gregers Vonderjan like tulips before a gale. Or that, frankly, now and then they still did so.

The talk, what was that about all this while? Obsequious pleasantries from the aunt, odd anecdotes he gave, to do with ships, land, slaves and money. Antoinelle had been so long without hearing the speech of others, she had become nearly word-deaf, so that most of what he said had no meaning for her, and what the aunt said even less.

Finally the aunt remembered an urgent errand, and left them.

They sat, with the sun blazing through the windows. Then Vonderjan looked right at her, at Antoinelle, and suddenly her face, her whole body, was suffused by a savage burning blush.

'Did she tell you why I called here?' he asked, almost indifferently.

Antoinelle, her eyes lowered, murmured childishly, thoughtlessly, 'No – she – she hasn't been speaking to me –'

'Hasn't she? Why not? Oh,' he said, 'that little business in the town.'

Antoinelle, to her shock, began to cry. This should have horrified her – she had lost control – the worst sin, as her family had convinced her, they thought.

He knew, this man. He knew. She was ashamed, and yet unable to stop crying, or to get up and leave the room.

She heard his chair pushed back, and then he was standing over her. To her slightness, he seemed vast and overpowering. He was clean, and smelled of French soap, of tobacco, and of some other nuance of masculinity, which Antoinelle at once intuitively liked. She had scented it before.

'Well, you won't mind leaving her, then,' he said, and he lifted her up out of her chair, and there she was in his grip, her head drooping back, staring almost mindlessly into his large, handsome face. It was easy to let go. She did so. She had in fact learnt nothing, been taught nothing by the whips and stings of her wicked relations. 'I called here to ask you,' he said, 'to be my wife.'

'But ...' faintly, 'I don't know you.'

'There's nothing to know. Here I am. Exactly what you see. Will that do?'

'But ...' more faintly still, 'why would you want me?'

'You're just what I want. And I thought you would be.'

'But,' nearly inaudible, 'I was – disgraced.'

'We'll see about that. And the old she-cunt won't talk to you, you say?'

Antoinelle, innocently not even knowing this important word (which anyway he spoke in a foreign argot), only shivered. 'No. Not till today.'

'Now she does because I've bid for you. You'd better come with me. Did the other one, the soldier-boy, have you? It doesn't matter, but tell me now.'

Antoinelle threw herself on the stranger's chest – she had not been told, or heard his name. 'No – no –' she cried, just as she had when Justus pushed her off.

'I must go slowly with you then,' said this man. But nevertheless, he moved her about, and leaning over, kissed her.

Vonderjan was an expert lover. Besides, he had a peculiar quality, which had stood him, and stands those like him, in very good stead. With what he wanted in the sexual way, provided they were not unwilling to begin with, he could spontaneously communicate some telepathic echo of his needs, making them theirs. This Antoinelle felt at once, as his warm lips moved on hers, his hot tongue pierced her mouth, and the finger of the hand that did not hold her tight, fire-feathered her breasts.

In seconds her ready flames burst up. Businesslike, Vonderjan at once sat down, and holding her on his lap, placed his hand, making nothing of her dress, to crush her centre in an inexorable rhythmic grasp, until she came in gasping spasms against him, wept, and wilted there in his arms, his property.

When the inclement aunt returned with a servant, having left, she felt, sufficient time for Vonderjan to ask, and Antoinelle sensibly to acquiesce, she found her niece tear- stained and dead white in a chair, and Vonderjan drinking his coffee, and smoking a cigar, letting the ash fall as it wished onto the table linen.

'Well then,' said the aunt, uncertainly.

Vonderjan cast her one look, as if amused by something about her.

'Am I to presume – may I – is everything –?'

Vonderjan took another puff and a gout of charred stuff hit the cloth, before he mashed out the burning butt of the cigar on a china plate.

'Antoinelle,' exclaimed the aunt, 'what have you to say?'

Vonderjan spoke, not to the aunt, but to his betrothed. 'Get up, Anna. You're going with me now.' Then, looking at the servant (a look the woman said after was like that of a basilisk), 'Out, you, and put some things together; all the lady will need for the drive. I'll supply the rest. Be quick.'

Scarlet, the aunt shouted, 'Now sir, this isn't how to go on.'

Vonderjan drew Antoinelle up, by his hand on her elbow. *He* had control of her now, and she need bother with nothing. She turned her drooping head, like a tired flower, looking only at his boots.

The aunt was ranting. Vonderjan, with Antoinelle in one arm, went up to her. Though she was not a small woman, nor slight like her niece, he dwarfed her, made of her a pygmy.

'Sir – there is her father to be approached – you must have a care –'

Then she stopped speaking. She stopped because, like Antoinelle, she had been given no choice. Gregers Vonderjan had clapped his hand over her mouth, and rather more than that. He held her by the bones and flesh of her face, unable to pull away, beating at him with her hands, making noises but unable to do more, and soon breathing with difficulty.

While he kept her like this, he did not bother to look at her, his broad body only disturbed vaguely by her flailing, weak blows. He had turned again to Antoinelle, and asked her if there was anything she wished particularly to bring away from the house.

Antoinelle did not have the courage to glance at her struggling and apoplectic aunt. She shook her head against his shoulder, and after a little shake of his own (at the aunt's face) he let the woman go. He and the girl walked out of the room and out of the house, to his carriage, leaving the aunt to progress from her partial asphyxia to hysterics.

He had got them married in three days by pulling such strings as money generally will. The ceremony did not take place in the town, but all the town heard of it. Afterwards Vonderjan went back there, without his wife, to throw a lavish dinner party, limited to the male gender, which no person invited dared not attend, including the bride's father, who was trying to smile off, as does the death's-head, the state it has been put into.

At this dinner too was Justus. He sat with a number of his friends, all of them astonished to be there. But like the rest, they had not been able, or prepared, to evade the occasion.

Vonderjan treated them all alike, with courtesy. The food was of a high standard – a cook had been brought from the city – and there were extravagant wines, with all of which Gregers Vonderjan was evidently familiar. The men got drunk; that is, all the men but for Vonderjan, who was an established drinker, and consumed several bottles of wine, also brandy and schnapps, without much effect.

At last Vonderjan said he would be going. To the bowing and fawning of his wife's relatives he paid no attention. It was Justus he took aside, near the door, with two of his friends. The young men were all in full uniform, smart as polish, only their bright hair tousled, and faces flushed by liquor.

'You mustn't think my wife holds any rancour against you,' Vonderjan announced, not loudly, but in a penetrating tone. Justus was too drunk to catch himself up, and only idiotically nodded. 'She said, I should wish you a speedy end to your trouble.'

'What trouble's that?' asked Justus, still idiotically.

'He has no troubles,' added the first of his brother officers, 'since you took that girl off his hands.'

The other officer (the most sober, which was not saying much – or perhaps the most drunk, drunk enough to have gained the virtue of distance) said, 'Shut your trap, you fool. Herr Vonderjan doesn't want to hear that silly kind of talk.'

Vonderjan was grave. 'It's nothing to me. But I'm sorry for your Justus, naturally. I shouldn't, as no man would, like to be in his shoes.'

'What shoes are they?' Justus belatedly frowned.

'I can recommend to you,' said Vonderjan, 'an excellent doctor in the city.' They say he is discreet.'

'*What?*'

'What is he saying –?'

'The disease, I believe they say, is often curable, in its earliest stages.'

Justus drew himself up. He was almost the height of Vonderjan, but like a reed beside him. All that room, and waiters on the stair besides, were listening. 'I am not – I have no – *disease* –'

Vonderjan shrugged. 'That's your argument, I understand. You should leave it off perhaps, and seek medical advice, certainly before you consider again any courtship. Not all women are as soft-hearted as my Anna.'

'What – what?'

'Not plain enough? From what you showed her she knew you had it, and refused you. Of course, you had another story.'

As Vonderjan walked through the door, the two brother officers were one silent and one bellowing. Vonderjan half turned, negligently. 'If you don't think so, examine his prick for yourselves.'

Vonderjan did not tell Antoinelle any of this, but a week later, in the city, she did read in a paper that Justus had mysteriously been disgraced, and had then fled the town after a duel.

Perhaps she thought it curious.

But if so, only for a moment. She had been absorbed almost entirely by the stranger, her strong husband.

On the first night, still calling her Anna, up against a great velvet bed, he had undone her clothes and next her body, taking her apart down to the clockwork of her desires.

Her cry of pain at his entry turned almost at once into a wavering shriek of ecstasy. She was what he had wanted all along, and he what she had needed. By morning the bed was stained with her virginal blood, and by the blood from bites she had given him, not knowing she did so.

Even when, a few weeks after, Vonderjan's luck began to turn like a sail, he bore her with him on his broad wings. He said nothing of his luck. He was too occupied wringing from her again and again the music of her lusts, forcing her arching body to contortions, paroxysms, screams, torturing her to willing death in blind red afternoons, in candlelit darkness, so that by daybreak she could scarcely move, would lie there in a stupor in the bed, unable to rise, awaiting him like an invalid or a corpse, and hungry always for more.

III

Lucius paddles his boat to the jetty, lets it idle there, looking up.

Another property of the flood-vapour, the stars by night are vast, great liquid splashes of silver, ormolu.

The light in Yse's loft burns contrastingly low.

That sweet smell he noticed yesterday still comes wafting down, like thin veiling, on the breeze. Like night-blooming jasmine, perhaps a little sharper, almost like oleanders.

She must have put in some plant. But up on her terrace only the snake tree is visible, hooping over into the water.

Lucius smokes half a roach slowly.

Far away the shoreline glimmers, where some of the stars have fallen off the sky.

'What you doing, Yse, Yse-do-as-she-please?'

Once he thought he saw her moving, a moth-shadow crossing through the stunned light, but maybe she is asleep, or writing.

It would be simple enough to tie up and climb the short wet stair to the terrace, to knock on her glass doors. (How are you, Yse? Are you fine?) He had done that last night. The blinds were all down, the light low, as now. But through the side of the transparent loft he had beheld the other shadow stood there on her floor. The piano from the sea. No-one answered.

That flower she's planted, it is sweet as candy. He's never known her do a thing like that. Her plants always died; killed, she said, by the electrical vibrations of her psyche when she worked.

Somewhere out on the Sound a boat hoots mournfully.

Lucius unships his paddles, and wends his craft away along the alleys of water, toward the cafés and the bigger lights.

Whenever she writes about Per Laszd, which, over 27 years, she has done a lot, the same feeling assails her: slight guilt. Only slight, of course, for he will never know. He is a man who never reads anything that has nothing to do with what he does. That was made clear in the beginning. She met him only twice, but has seen him, quite often, then and since, in newspapers, in news footage, and on network TV. She has been able therefore to watch him change, from an acidly, really too-beautiful young man, through his thirties and forties (when some of the silk of his beauty frayed, to reveal something leaner and more interesting, stronger and more attractive) to a latening middle age, where he has gained weight but lost none of his masculine grace, nor his mane of hair that – only perhaps due to artifice – has no grey in it.

She was in love with him, obviously, at the beginning. But it has changed, and become something else. He was never interested in her, even when she was young, slim and appealing. She was not, she supposed, his 'type'.

In addition, she rather admired what he did, and how he did it, with an actor's panache and tricks.

People who caught her fancy she had always tended to put into her work. Inevitably Per Laszd was one of these. Sometimes he appeared as a remote figure, on the edge of the action of other lives. Sometimes he took the centre of the stage, acting out invented existences, with his perceived actor's skills.

She had, she found though, a tendency to punish him in these roles. He must endure hardships and misfortunes, and often, in her work, he was dead by the end, and rarely of old age.

Her guilt, naturally, had something to do with this – was she truly punishing him, not godlike, as with other characters, but from a petty personal annoyance that he had never noticed her, let alone had sex with her, or a single real conversation? (When she had met him, it had both times been in a crowd. He had spoken generally, politely including her, no more than that. She was aware he had been arrogant enough, if he had wanted to, to have demandingly singled her out.)

But really she felt guilty at the liberties she took of necessity, with him, on paper. How else could she write about him? It was absurd to do otherwise. But describing his conjectured nakedness, both physical and intellectual, even spiritual (even supposedly 'in character'), her own temerity occasionally dismayed Yse. How dared she? But then, how dare ever to write anything, even about a being wholly invented.

A mental shrug. *Alors* ... well, well. And yet ...

Making him Gregers Vonderjan, she felt, was perhaps her worst infringement. Now she depicted him (honestly) burly with weight and on-drawing age, although always hastening to add the caveat of his handsomeness, his power. Per himself, as she had seen, was capable of being majestic, yet also mercurial. She tried to be fair, to be at her most fair, when examining him most microscopically, or when condemning him to the worst fates. (But, now and then, did the pen slip?)

Had he ever sensed those several dreadful falls, those calumnies, those *deaths*? Of course not. Well, well. There, there. And yet ...

How wonderful that vine smells tonight, Yse thinks, sitting up in the lamp-dusk. Some neighbour must have planted it. What a penetrating scent, so clean and fresh yet sweet.

It was noticeable last night, too. Yse wonders what the flowers are, that let out this aroma. And in the end, she stands up, leaving the pen to lie there, across Vonderjan and Antoinelle.

Near her glass doors, Yse thinks the vine must be directly facing her, over the narrow waterway under the terrace, for here its perfume is strongest.

But when she raises the blinds and opens the doors, the scent at once grows less. Somehow it has collected instead in the room. She gazes out at the other lofts, at a tower of shaped glass looking like ice in a tray. Are the hidden gardens there?

The stars are impressive tonight. And she can see the hem of the star-spangled upper city.

A faint sound comes.

Yse knows it's not outside, but in her loft, just like the scent.

She turns. Looks at the black piano.

Since yesterday (when it was brought in), she hasn't paid it that much attention. (Has she?) She had initially stared at it, tried three or four times to raise its lids – without success. She had thought of rubbing it down, once the litter-chips absorbed the leaking water. But then she had not done this. Had not touched it very much.

Coming to the doors, she has circled wide of the piano.

Did a note sound, just now, under the forward lid? How odd, the two forelegs braced there, and the final leg at its end, more as if it balanced on a tail of some sort.

Probably the keys and hammers and strings inside are settling after the wet, to the warmth of her room.

She leaves one door open, which is not perhaps sensible. Rats have been known to climb the stair and gaze in at her under the night blinds, with their calm clever eyes. Sometimes the criminal population of the island can be heard along the waterways, or out on the Sound, shouts and smashing bottles, cans thrown at brickwork or impervious, multi-glazed windows.

But the night's still as the stars.

Yse goes by the piano, and through the perfume, and back to her desk, where Per Laszd lies helplessly awaiting her on the page.

IV: Bleumaneer

Jeanjacques came to the Island in the stormy season. He was a mix of black and white, and found both peoples perplexing, as he found himself.

The slave-trade was by then defused, as much, perhaps, as it would ever be. He knew there were no slaves left on the Island; that is, only freed slaves remained. (His black half lived with frenzied anger, as his white half clove to sloth. Between the two halves, he was a split soul.)

There had been sparks on the rigging of the ship, and all night a velour sky fraught with pink lightning. When they reached the bay next morning, it looked nearly colourless, the sombre palms were nearly grey, and the sky cindery, and the sea only transparent, the beaches white.

The haughty black master spoke in French.

'They call that place Blue View.'

'Why's that?'

'Oh, it was for some vogue of wearing blue, before heads began to roll in Paris.'

Jeanjacques said, 'What's he like?'

'Vonderjan? A falling man.'

'How do you mean?'

'Have you seen a man fall? The instant before he hits the ground, before he's hurt – the moment when he thinks he is still flying.'

'He's lost his money, they were saying at Sugarbar.'

'They say so.'

'And his wife's a girl, almost a child.'

'Two years he's been with her on his Island.'

'What's she like?'

'White.'

'What else?'

'To me, nothing. I can't tell them apart.'

There had been a small port, but now little was there, except a rotted hulk, some huts and the ruins of a customs house, thatched with palm, in which birds lived.

For a day he climbed with the escorting party, up into the interior of the Island. Inside the forest it was grey-green-black, and the trees gave off sweat, pearling the banana leaves and plantains. Then they walked through the wild fields of cane, and the coffee trees. Dark figures still worked there, and tending the kayar. But they did this for themselves. What had been owned had become the garden of those who remained, to do with as they wanted.

The black master had elaborated, telling Jeanjacques how Vonderjan had at first sent for niceties for his house, for china and Venetian glass, cases of books and wine. Even a piano had been ordered for his child-wife, although this, it seemed, had never arrived.

The Island was large and overgrown, but there was nothing, they said, very dangerous on it.

Bleumaneer, Blue View, the house for which the Island had come to be called, appeared on the next morning, down a dusty track hedged by rhododendrons of prehistoric girth.

It was white-walled, with several open courts, balconies. Orange trees grew along a columned gallery, and there was a Spanish fountain (dry) on the paved space before the steps. But it was a medley of all kinds of style.

'Make an itinerary and let me see it. We'll talk it over, what can be sold.'

Jeanjacques thought that Vonderjan reminded him most of a lion, but a lion crossed with a golden bull. Then again, there was a wolf-like element, cunning and lithe, which slipped through the grasslands of their talk.

Vonderjan did not treat Jeanjacques as what he was, a valuer's clerk. Nor was there any resentment or chagrin. Vonderjan seemed indifferent to the fix he was in. Did he even care that such and such would be sorted out and taken from him? That glowing canvas in the salon, for example, or the rose-mahogany cabinets, and all for a third of their value, or less, paid in banknotes that probably would not last out another year. Here was a man, surely, playing at life, at living. Convinced of it and of his fate, certainly, but only as the actor is, within his part.

Jeanjacques drank cloudy orjat, tasting its bitter orange-flowers. Vonderjan drank nothing, was sufficient, even in this, to himself.

'Well. What do you think?'

'I'll work on, and work tonight, present you with a summary in the morning.'

'Why waste the night?' said Vonderjan.

'I must be ready to leave in another week, sir, when the ship returns.'

'Another few months,' said Vonderjan, consideringly, 'and maybe no ship will come here. Suppose you missed your boat?'

He seemed to be watching Jeanjacques through a telescope, closely, yet far, far away. He might have been drunk, but there was no smell of alcohol to him. Some drug of the Island, perhaps?

Jeanjacques said, 'I'd have to swim for it.'

A man came up from the yard below. He was a white servant, shabby but respectable. He spoke to Vonderjan in some European gabble.

'My horse is sick,' said Vonderjan to Jeanjacques. 'I think I shall have to shoot it. I've lost most of them here. Some insect, which bites.'

'I'm sorry.'

'Yes.' Then, light-heartedly, 'But none of us escape, do we.'

Later, in the slow heat of the afternoon, Jeanjacques heard the shot crack out, and shuddered. It was more than the plight of the unfortunate horse. Something seemed to have hunted Vonderjan to his Island and now picked off from him all the scales of his world, his money, his horses, his possessions.

The clerk worked at his tally until the sun began to wester about four in the evening. Then he went up to wash and dress, because Vonderjan had said he should dine in the salon, with his family. Jeanjacques had no idea what he would find. He was curious, a little, about the young wife – she must by now be 17 or 18. Had there been any children? It was always likely, but then again, likely too they had not survived.

At five, the sky was like brass, the palms that lined the edges of all vistas like blackened brass columns, bent out of shape, with brazen leaves that rattled against each other when any breath blew up from the bay. From the roof of the house it was possible also to make out a cove, and the sea. But it looked much more than a day's journey off. Unless you jumped and the wind blew you.

Another storm mumbled over the Island as Jeanjacques entered the salon. The long windows stood wide, and the dying light flickered fitfully like the disturbed candles.

No-one took much notice of the clerk, and Vonderjan behaved as if Jeanjacques had been there a year, some acquaintance with no particular purpose in the house, neither welcome nor un.

The 'family', Jeanjacques saw, consisted of Vonderjan, his wife, a housekeeper and a young black woman, apparently Vrouw Vonderjan's companion.

She was slender and fine, the black woman, and sat there as if a slave-trade had never existed, either to crucify or enrage her. Her dress was of excellent muslin, ladyishly low-cut for the evening, and she had ruby ear-drops. (She spoke at least three languages that Jeanjacques heard, including the patois of the Island, or house, which she exchanged now and then with the old housekeeper.)

But Vonderjan's wife was another matter altogether.

The moment he looked at her, Jeanjacque's blood seemed to shift slightly, all along his bones. And at the base of his skull, where his hair was neatly tied back by a ribbon, the roots stretched themselves, prickling.

She was not at all pretty, but violently beautiful, in a way far too large for the long room, or for any room, whether spacious or enormous. So pale she was, she made her black attendant seem like a shadow cast by a flame. Satiny coils and trickles of hair fell all round her in a deluge of gilded rain. Thunder was the colour of her eyes, a dark that was not dark, some shade that could not be described visually but only in other ways. All of her was a little like that. To touch her limpid skin would be like tasting ice-cream. To catch her fragrance like small bells heard inside the ears in fever.

When her dress brushed by him as she first crossed the room, Jeanjacques inadvertently recoiled inside his skin. He was feeling, although he did not know it, exactly as Justus had felt in the northern garden. Though Justus had not known it, either. But what terrified these two men was the very thing that drew other men, especially such men as Gregers Vonderjan. So much was plain.

The dinner was over, and the women got up to withdraw. As she passed by his chair, Vonderjan, who had scarcely spoken to her throughout the meal (or to anyone) lightly took hold of his wife's hand. And she looked down at once into his eyes.

Such a look it was. Oh God, Jeanjacques experienced now all his muscles go to liquid, and sinking, and his belly sinking down into his bowels, which themselves turned over heavily as a serpent. But his penis rose very quickly, and pushed hard as a rod against his thigh.

For it was a look of such explicit sex, trembling so colossally it had grown still, and out of such an agony of suspense, that he was well aware these two lived in a constant of the condition, and would need only to press together the length of their bodies to ignite like matches in a galvanic convulsion.

He had seen once or twice similar looks, perhaps. Among couples kept strictly, on their marriage night. But no, not even then.

They said nothing to each other. Needed nothing to say. It had been said.

The girl and her black companion passed from the room, and after them the housekeeper, carrying a branch of the candles, whose flames flattened as she went through the doors onto the terrace. (Notes: This will happen again later.)

Out there, the night was now very black. Everything beyond the house had vanished in it, but for the vague differential between the sky and the tops of the forest below. There were no stars to be seen, and thunder still moved restlessly. The life went from Jeanjacques' genitals as if it might never come back.

'Brandy,' said Vonderjan, passing the decanter. 'What do you think of her?'

'Of whom, sir?'

'My Anna.' (Playful; who else?)

Jeanjacques visualised, in a sudden unexpected flash, certain objects used as amulets, and crossing himself in church,

'An exquisite lady, sir.'

'Yes,' said Vonderjan. He had drunk a lot during dinner, but in an easy way. It was evidently habit, not need. Now he said again, 'Yes.'

Jeanjacques wondered what would be next. But of course nothing was to be next. Vonderjan finished his cigar and drank down his glass. He rose, and nodded to Jeanjacques.

'*Bon nuit.*'

How could he even have forced himself to linger so long? Vonderjan demonstrably must be a human of vast self-control.

Jeanjacques imagined the blond man going up the stairs of the house to the wide upper storey. An open window, drifted with a gauze curtain, hot, airless night. Jeanjacques imagined Antoinelle, called Anna, lying on her back in the bed, its nets pushed careless away, for what bit Vonderjan's horses to death naturally could not essay his wife.

'No, I shan't have a good night,' Jeanjacques said to Vonderjan in his head. He went to his room, and sharpened his pen for work.

In the darkness, he heard her. He was sure that he had. It was almost four in the morning by his pocket watch, and the sun would rise in less than an hour.

Waveringly she screamed, like an animal caught in a trap. Three times, the second time the loudest.

The whole of the inside of the house shook and throbbed and scorched from it.

Jeanjacques found he must get up, and standing by the window, handle himself roughly until, in less than 13 seconds, his semen exploded on to the tiled floor.

Feeling then slightly nauseous, and dreary, he slunk to bed and slept gravely, like a stone.

Antoinelle sat at her toilette mirror, part of a fine set of silver-gilt her husband had given her. She was watching herself as Nanetta combed and brushed her hair.

It was late afternoon, the heat of the day lying down but not subsiding.

Antoinelle was in her chemise; soon she would dress for the evening dinner.

Nanetta stopped brushing. Her hands lay on the air like a black slender butterfly separated in two. She seemed to be listening.

'More,' said Antoinelle.

'Yes.'

The brush began again.

Antoinelle often did not rise until noon, frequently later. She would eat a little fruit, drink coffee, get up and wander about in flimsy undergarments. Now and then she would read a novel, or Nanetta would read one to her. Or they would play cards, sitting at the table on the balcony, among the pots of flowers.

Nanetta had never seen Antoinelle do very much, and had never seen her agitated or even irritable.

She lived for night.

He, on the other hand, still got up mostly at sunrise, and no later than the hour after. His man, Stronn, would shave him. Vonderjan would breakfast downstairs in the courtyard, eating meat and bread, drinking black tea. Afterwards he might go over the accounts with the secretary. Sometimes the whole of the big house heard him shouting (except for his wife, who was generally still asleep). He regularly rode (two horses survived) round parts of the Island, and was gone until late afternoon, talking to the men and women in the fields, sitting to drink with them, rum and palm liquor, in the shade of plantains. He might return about the time Antoinelle was washing herself, powdering her arms and face, and putting on a dress for dinner.

A bird trilled in a cage, hopped a few steps and flew up to its perch to trill again.

The scent of dust and sweating trees came from the long windows, stagnant yet energising in the thickening yellow light.

Nanetta half turned her head. Again she had heard something far away. She did not know what it was.

'Shall I wear the emerald necklace tonight?' asked Antoinelle, sleepily. 'What do you think?'

Nanetta was used to this. To finding an answer. 'With the white dress? Yes, that would be effective.'

'Put up my hair. Use the tortoiseshell combs.'

Nanetta obeyed deftly.

The satiny bright hair was no pleasure to touch, too electric, stickily clinging to the fingers – full of each night's approaching storm. There would be no rain, not yet.

Antoinelle watched as the black woman transformed her. Antoinelle liked this, having only to be, letting someone else put her together in this way. She had forgotten by now, but never liked, independence. She wanted only enjoyment, to be made and remade, although in a manner that pleased her, and that, after all, demonstrated her power over others.

When she thought about Vonderjan, her husband, her loins cinched involuntarily, and a frisson ran through her, a shiver of heat. So she rationed her thoughts of him. During their meals together, she would hardly look at him, hardly speak, concentrating on the food, on the light of the candles reflecting in things, hypnotising herself and prolonging, unendurably, her famine, until at last she was able to return into the bed, cool by then, with clean sheets on it, and wait, giving herself up to darkness and to fire.

How could she live in any other way?

Whatever had happened to her? Had the insensate cruelty of her relations pulped her down into a sponge that was ultimately receptive only to this? Or was this her true condition, which had always been trying to assert itself, and which, once connected to a suitable partner, did so, evolving also all the time, spreading itself higher and lower and in all directions, like some amoeba?

She must have heard stories of him, his previous wife, and of a black mistress or two he had had here. But Antoinelle was not remotely jealous. She had no interest in what he did when not with her, when not about to be, or actually in her bed with her. As if all other facets, both of his existence and her own, had now absolutely no meaning at all.

About the hour Antoinelle sat by the mirror, and Vonderjan, who had not gone out that day, was bathing, smoking one of the cigars as the steam curled round him, Jeanjacques stood among a wilderness of cane fields beyond the house.

That cane was a type of grass that tended always to amaze him, these huge stripes of straddling stalks, rising five feet or more above his head. He felt himself to be a child lost in a luridly unnatural wood, and besides, when a black figure passed across the view, moving from one subaqueous tunnel to another, they now supernaturally only glanced at him, cat-like, from the sides of their eyes.

Jeanjacques had gone out walking, having deposited his itinerary and notes with Vonderjan in a morning room. The clerk took narrow tracks across the Island, stood on high places from which (as from the roof) coves and inlets of the sea might be glimpsed.

The people of the Island had been faultlessly friendly and courteous, until he began to try to question them. Then they changed. He assumed at first they only hated his white skin, as had others he had met, who had refused to believe in his mixed blood. In that case, he could not blame them much for the hatred. Then he understood he had not assumed this at all. They were disturbed by something, afraid of something, and he knew it.

Were they afraid of her – of the white girl in the house? Was it that? And why were they afraid? Why was he himself afraid? Because afraid of her he was. Oh yes, he was terrified.

At midday he came to a group of hut-houses, patchily colour-washed and with palm-leaf roofs, and people were sat about there in the shade, drinking, and one man was splitting rosy gourds with a machete, so Jeanjacques thought of a guillotine a moment, the red juice spraying out and the *thunk* of the blade going through. (He had heard they had split imported melons in Marseilles, to test the machine. But he was a boy when he heard this tale, and perhaps it was not true.)

Jeanjacques stood there, looking on. Then a black woman got up, fat and not young, but comely, and brought him half a gourd, for him to try the dripping flesh.

He took it, thanking her.

'How is it going, Mother?' he asked her, partly in French, but also with two words of the patois, which he had begun to recognise. To no particular effect.

'It goes how it go, monsieur.'

'You still take a share of your crop to the big house? She gave him the sidelong look. 'But you're free people, now.'

One of the men called to her sharply. He was a tall black leopard, young and gorgeous as a carving from chocolate. The woman went away at once, and Jeanjacques heard again that phrase he had heard twice before that day. It was muttered somewhere at his back. He turned quickly, and there they sat, blacker in shade, eating from the flesh of the gourds, and drinking from a bottle passed around. Not looking at him, not at all.

'What did you say?'

A man glanced up. 'It's nothing, monsieur.'

'Something came from the sea, you said?'

'No, monsieur. Only a storm coming.'

'It's the stormy season. Wasn't there something else?'

They shook their heads. They looked helpful, and sorry they could not assist, and their eyes were painted glass.

Something has come from the sea.

They had said it too, at the other place, further down, when a child had brought him rum in a tin mug.

What could come from the sea? Only weather, or men. Or the woman. She had come from there.

They were afraid, and even if he had doubted his ears or his judgement, the way they would not say it straight out, that was enough to tell him he had not imagined this.

Just then a breeze passed through the forest below, and then across the broad leaves above, shaking them. And the light changed a second, then back, like the blinking of the eye of God.

They stirred, the people. It was as if they saw the wind, and the shape it had was fearful to them, yet known. Respected.

As he was walking back by another of the tracks, he found a dead chicken laid on a banana leaf at the margin of a field. A proprietary offering? Nothing else had touched it; even a line of ants detoured out onto the track, to give it room.

Jeanjacques walked into the cane fields and went on there for a while. And now and then other human things moved through, looking sidelong at him.

Then, when he paused among the tall stalks, he heard them whispering, whispering, the stalks of cane, or else the voices of the people. Had they followed him? Were they aggressive? They had every right to be, of course, even with his kind. Even so, he did not want to be beaten, or to die.

He had invested such an amount of his life and wits in avoiding such things.

But no-one approached. The whispers came and went.

Now he was here, and he had made out, from the edge of this field, Vonderjan's house with its fringe of palms and rhododendrons (Blue View) above him on the hill, only about half an hour away.

In a full hour, the sun would dip. He would go to his room and there would be water for washing, and his other clothes laid out for the dinner.

The whispering began again, suddenly, very close, so Jeanjacques spun about, horrified.

But no-one was there, nothing was there.

Only the breeze, that the black people could see, moved round among the stalks of the cane, that was itself like an Egyptian temple, its columns meant to be a forest of green papyrus.

'It's black,' the voices whispered. 'Black.'

'Like a black man,' Jeanjacques said hoarsely.

'Black like black.'

Again, God blinked his eyelid of sky. A figure seemed to be stood between the shafts of green cane. It said, 'Not black like men. So black we

132

filled with terror of it. Black like black of night is black.'

'Black like black.'

'Something from the sea.'

Jeanjacques felt himself dropping, and then he was on his knees, and his forehead was pressed to the powdery plant-drained soil.

He had not hurt himself. When he looked up, no-one was in the field that he could see.

He got to his feet slowly. He trembled, and then the trembling, like the whispers, went away.

The storm rumbled over the Island. It sounded tonight like dogs barking, then baying in the distance. Every so often, for no apparent reason, the flames of the candles flattened, as if a hand had been laid on them.

There was a main dish of pork, stewed with spices. Someone had mentioned there were pigs on the Island, although the clerk had seen none, perhaps no longer wild, or introduced and never wild.

The black girl, who was called Nanetta, had put up her hair elaborately, and so had the white one, Vonderjan's wife. Round her slim pillar of throat were five large green stars in a necklace like a golden cake-decoration.

Vonderjan had told Jeanjacques that no jewellery was to be valued. But here at least was something that might have seen him straight for a while. Until his ship came in. But perhaps it never would again. Gregers Vonderjan had been lucky always, until the past couple of years.

A gust of wind, which seemed to do nothing else outside, abruptly blew wide the doors to the terrace.

Vonderjan himself got up, went by his servants, and shut both doors. That was, started to shut them. Instead he was stood there now, gazing out across the Island.

In the sky, the dogs bayed.

His heavy bulky frame seemed vast enough to withstand any night. His magnificent mane of hair, without any evident grey, gleamed like gold in the candlelight. Vonderjan was so strong, so nonchalant.

But he stood there a long while, as if something had attracted his attention.

It was Nanetta who asked, 'Monsieur – what is the matter?'

Vonderjan half turned and looked at her, almost mockingly, his brows raised.

'Matter? Nothing.'

She has it too, Jeanjacques thought. He said, 'The blacks were saying, something has come from the sea.'

Then he glanced at Nanetta. For a moment he saw two rings of white stand clear around the pupil and iris of her eyes. But she looked down, and nothing else gave her away.

Vonderjan shut the doors. He swaggered back to the table. (He did not look at his wife, nor she at him. They kept themselves intact, Jeanjacques thought, during proximity, only by such a method. The clerk wondered, if he were to find Antoinelle alone, and stand over her, murmuring Vonderjan's name, over and over, whether she would fall back, unable to resist, and come, without further provocation and in front of him. And at the thought, the hard rod tapped again impatiently on his thigh.)

'From the sea, you say. What?'

'I don't know, sir. But they were whispering it. Perhaps mademoiselle knows?' He indicated Nanetta graciously, as if giving her a wanted opening.

She was silent.

'I don't think,' said Vonderjan, 'that she does.'

'No, monsieur,' she said. She seemed cool. Her eyes were kept down.

Oddly – Jeanjacques thought – it was Antoinelle who suddenly sprang up, pushing back her chair, so it scraped on the tiles.

'It's so hot,' she said.

And then she stood there, as if incapable of doing anything else, of refining any desire or solution from her own words.

Vonderjan did not look at her, but he went slowly back and undid the doors. 'Walk with me on the terrace, Anna.'

And he extended his arm.

The white woman glided across the salon as if on runners. She seemed weightless – *blown*. And the white snake of her little narrow hand crawled round his arm and out on to the sleeve, to rest there. Husband and wife stepped out into the rumbling night.

Jeanjacques sat back and stared across the table at Nanetta.

'They're most devoted,' he said. 'One doesn't often see it, after the first months. Especially where the ages are so different. What is he, thirty, thirty-two years her senior?'

Nanetta raised her eyes and now gazed at him impenetrably, with the tiniest, most fleeting smile.

He would get nothing out of her. She was a lady's maid, and he a jumped-up clerk, but both of them had remained slaves. They were calcined, ruined, defensive, and armoured.

Along the terrace he could see that Vonderjan and the woman were pressed close by the house, where a lush flowering vine only partly might hide them. Her skirts were already pushed askew, her head thrown sideways, mouth open and eyes shut. He was taking her against the wall, thrusting and heaving into her.

Jeanjacques looked quickly away, and began to whistle, afraid of hearing her cries of climax.

But now the black girl exclaimed, 'Don't whistle, don't do that, monsieur!'

'Why? Why not?'

She only shook her head, but again her eyes – the black centres were silver-ringed. So Jeanjacques got up and walked out of the salon into Vonderjan's library across the passage, where now the mundane papers concerning things to be sold lay on a table.

But it has come, it has come through the sea, before star-rise and dawn, through the rifts and fans of the transparent water, sliding and swimming like a crab.

It has crawled onto the sand, crouching low, like a beast, and perhaps mistaken for some animal.

A moon (is it a different moon each night; who would know?) sinking, and Venus in the east.

Crawling into the tangle of the trees, with the palms and parrot trees reflecting in the dulled mirror of its lid, its carapace. Dragging the hind limb like a tail, pulling itself by the front legs, like a wounded boar.

Through the forest, with only the crystal of Venus to shatter through the heavy leaves of sweating bronze.

Bleumaneer, La Vue Bleu, Blue Fashion, Blue View, seeing through a blue eye to a black shape, which moves from shadow to shadow, place to place. But always nearer.

Something is in the forest.

Nothing dangerous. How can it hurt you?

V

Yse is buying food in the open air market at Bley. Lucius has seen her, and now stands watching her, not going over.

She has filled her first bag with vegetables and fruit, and in the second she puts a fish and some cheese, olive oil and bread.

Lucius crosses through the crowd, by the place where the black girl called Rosalba is cooking red snapper on her skillet, and the old poet paints his words in coloured sand.

As Yse walks into a liquor store, Lucius follows.

'You're looking good, Yse.'

She turns, gazing at him – not startled, more as if she doesn't remember him. Then she does. 'Thank you. I feel good today.'

'And strong. But not this strong. Give me the vegetables to carry, Yse.'

'Okay. That's kind.'

'What have you done to your hair?'

Yse thinks about this one. 'Oh. Someone put in some extra hair for me. You know how they do, they hot-wax the strands onto your own.'

'It looks fine.'

She buys a box of wine bottles.

'You're having a party?' Lucius says.

'No, Lucius. I don't throw parties. You know that.'

'I know that.'

'Just getting in my stores. I'm working. Then I needn't go out again for a while, just stay put and write.'

'You've lost some weight,' Lucius says. 'Looks like about 25 pounds.'

Now she laughs. 'No. I wish. But you know I do sometimes, when I work. Adrenaline.'

He totes the wine and the vegetables, and they stroll over to the bar on the quay, to which fresh fish are being brought in from the Sound. (The bar is at the top of what was, once, the Aquatic Museum. There are still old cases of bullet-and-robber-proof glass, with fossils in them, little ancient dragons of the deeps, only three feet long, and coelacanths with needle teeth.)

Lucius orders coffee and rum, but Yse only wants a mineral water. Is she dieting? He has never known her to do this. She has said, dieting became useless after her forty- third year.

Her hair hangs long, to her waist, blonde, with whiter blonde and silver in it. He can't see any of the wax-ends of the extensions, or any grey either. Slimmer, her face, hands and shoulders have fined right down. Her skin is excellent, luminous and pale. Her eyes are crystalline, and outlined by soft black pencil he has never seen her use before.

She says sharply, 'For a man who likes men, you surely know how to look a woman over, Lucius.'

'None better.'

'Well don't.'

'I'm admiring you, Yse.'

'Well, still don't. You're embarrassing me. I'm not used to it anymore. If I ever was.'

There is, he saw an hour ago – all across the market – a small white surgical dressing on the left side of her neck. Now she absently touches it, and pulls her finger away like her own mother would do. They say you can always tell a woman's age from her hands. Yse's hands look today like those of a woman of 35.

'Something bite you, Yse?'

'An insect. It itches.'

'I came by in the boat,' he says, drinking his coffee, leaving the rum to stand in the glass. 'I heard you playing that piano.'

'You must have heard someone else somewhere. I can't play. I used to improvise, years ago. But then I had to sell my piano back then. This one ... I haven't been able to get the damn lid up. I'm frightened to force it in case everything breaks.'

'Do you want me to try?'

'Thanks – but maybe not. You know, I don't think the keys can be intact. How can they be? And there might be rats in it.'

'Does it smell of rats?'

'Oddly, it smells of flowers. Jasmine, or something. Mostly at night, really. A wonderful smell. Perhaps something's growing inside it.'

'In the dark.'

'Night-blooming Passia,' Yse says, as if quoting.

'And you write about that piano,' says Lucius.

'Did I tell you? Good guess then. But it's not about a piano. Not really. About an Island.'

'Where is this island?'

'Here.' Yse sets her finger on a large notebook that she has already put on the table. (Often she will carry her work about with her, like a talisman. This isn't new.)

But Lucius examines the blank cover of the book as if scanning a map. 'Where else?' he says.

Now Yse taps her forehead. (*In my mind.*) But somehow he has the impression she has also tapped her left ear, directly above the bite – as if the Island was in there too. *Heard* inside her ear. Or else, heard, felt – inside the *bite.*

'Let me read it,' he says, *not* opening the note-book.

'You can't.'

'Why not?'

'My awful handwriting. No-one can, until I type it through the machine and there's a disc.'

'You write so bad to hide it,' he says.

'Probably.'

'What's your story really about?'

'I told you. And Island. And a vampire.'

'And it bit you in the neck.'

Again, she laughs. '*You're* the one a vampire bit, Lucius. Or has it gone back to being a shark that bit you?'

'All kinds have bit me. I bite them, too.'

She's finished her water. The exciting odour of cooking spiced fish drifts into the bar, and Lucius is hungry. But Yse is getting up.

'I'll carry your bag to the boat-stop.

'Thanks, Lucius.'

'I can bring them to your loft.'

'No, that's fine.'

'What did you say about a vampire?' he asks her as they wait above the sparkling water for the water-bus. 'Not what they are, what they do to you – what they make you feel?'

'I've known you over five years, Lucius –'

'Six and a half years.'

'Six and a half then. I've never known you very interested in my books.'

The breeze blows off the Sound, flattening Yse's shirt to her body. Her waist is about five inches smaller, her breasts formed, and her whole shape has changed from that of a small barrel to a curvy egg-timer. Woman-shape. Young woman-shape.

He thinks, uneasily, will she begin to menstruate again, the hormones flowing back like the flood of the Sound tides through the towers and lofts of the island? Can he scent, through her cleanly-showered soap and shampoo smell, the hint of fresh blood?

'Not interested, Yse. Just being nosy.'

'All right. The book is about, among others, a girl, who is called Antoinelle. She's empty, or been made empty, because what she wants is refused her – so she's like a soft, flaccid, open bag, and she wants and wants. And the soft wanting emptiness pulls him – the man – inside. She drains him of volition, and of his good luck. But he doesn't care. He also wants this. Went out looking for it. He explains that in the next section, I think ...'

'So she's your vampire.'

'No. But she makes a vampire possible. She's like a blueprint – like compost, for the plant to grow in. And the heat there, and the decline, that lovely word *desuetude*. And empty spaces that need to be continually *filled*. Nature abhors a vacuum. Darkness abhors it too, and rushes in. Why else do you think it gets dark when the sun goes down?'

'Night,' he says flatly.

'Of course not,' she smiles. 'Nothing so ordinary. It's the black of outer space rushing to fill the empty gap the daylight filled. Why else do they call it space?'

She's clever. Playing with her words, with quotations and vocal things like that.

Lucius can see the tired old rusty boat chugging across the water.

(Yse starts to talk about the planet Vulcan, which was discovered once, twice, a hundred or a hundred and fifty years ago, and both times found to be a hoax.)

The bus-boat is at the quay. Lucius helps Yse get her food and wine into the boat. He watches as it goes off around this drowned isle we have here, but she forgets to wave.

In fact, Yse has been distracted by another thought. She found a seashell lying on her terrace yesterday. This will sometimes happen, if an especially high tide has flowed in. She's thinking about the seashell, and the idea has come to her that, if she put it to her left ear, instead of hearing the sound of the sea (which is the rhythm of her own blood, moving) she might hear a piano playing.

Which is how she might put this into the story.

By the time the bus-boat reaches West Ridge, sunset is approaching. When she has hauled the bags and wine to the doors of her loft, she stands a moment, looking. The snake-willow seems carved from vitreous. The alley of water is molten. But that's by now commonplace.

Even out here, before she opens her doors, she can catch the faint overture of perfume from the plant that may – must – be growing in the piano.

She dreamed last night she followed Per Laszd for miles, trudging till her feet ached, through endless lanes of shopping mall, on the mainland. He would not stop, or turn, and periodically he disappeared. For some hours too she saw him in conversation with a slender, dark-haired woman. When he vanished yet again, Yse approached her. 'Is he your lover?' '*No*,' chuckled the incredulous woman. '*Mine? No.*' In the end Yse had gone on again, seen him ahead of her, and at last given up, turned her back, walked away briskly, not wanting him to know she had pursued him such a distance. Then only did she feel his hands thrill lightly on her shoulders –

At the shiver of memory, Yse shakes herself.

She's pleased to have lost weight, but not so surprised. She hasn't been eating much, and change is always feasible. The extensions cost a lot of money. Washing her hair is now a nuisance, and probably she will have them taken out before too long.

However, seeing her face in the mirror above the wash basin, she paused this morning, recognising herself, if only for a moment.

A red gauze cloud drifts from the mainland.

Yse undoes her glass doors, and in the shadow, there that other shadow stands on its three legs. It might be anything but what it is, as might we all.

VI: Her Piano

On the terrace below the gallery of orange trees, above the dry fountain, Gregers Vonderjan stood checking his gun.

Jeanjacques halted. He felt for a moment irrationally afraid – as opposed to the other fears he had felt here.

But the gun, plainly, was not for him.

It was just after six in the morning. Dawn had happened not long ago, the light was transparent as a window-pane.

'Another,' said Vonderjan enigmatically. (Jeanjacques had noticed before, the powerful and self-absorbed were often obscure, thinking everyone must already know their business, which of course shook the world.)

'... Your horses.'

'My horses. Only two now, and one on its last legs. Come with me if you like, if you're not squeamish.'

I am, extremely, Jeanjacques thought, but he went with Vonderjan nevertheless, slavishly.

Vonderjan strode down steps, around corners, through a grove of trees. They reached the stables. It was vacant, no-one about but for a single man, some groom.

Inside the stall, two horses were together, one lying down. The other, strangely uninvolved, stood aloof. This upright one was white as some strange pearly fish-animal, its eyes almost blue, Jeanjacques thought, but perhaps that was a trick of the pure light. The other horse, the prone one, half lifted its head, heavily.

Vonderjan went to this horse. The groom did not speak. Vonderjan kneeled down.

'Ah, poor soldier –' Then he spoke in another tongue, his birth-language, probably. As he murmured, he stroked the streaked mane away from the horse's eyes, tenderly, like a father, caressed it till the weary eyes shut, then shot it, quickly through the skull. The legs kicked once, strengthlessly, a reflex. It had been almost gone already.

Jeanjacques went out and leaned on the mounting-block. He expected he would vomit, but did not.

Vonderjan presently also came out, wiping his hands, like Pilot.

'Damn this thing, death,' he said. The anger was wholesome, *whole*. For a moment a real man, a human being, stood solidly by Jeanjacques, and Jeanjacques wanted to turn and fling his arms about this creature, to keep it with him. But then it vanished, as before.

The strong handsome face was bland – or was it *blind*?

'None of us escapes death.'

That cliché once more, masking the *horror* – but what was the horror? And was the use of the cliché only acceptance of the harsh world, precisely what Vonderjan must have set himself to learn?

'Come to the house. Have a brandy,' said Vonderjan.

They went back, not the way they had come, but using another flight of stairs. Behind them the groom was clearing the beautiful dead horse like debris or garbage. Jeanjacques refused to look over his shoulder.

Vonderjan's study had no light until great storm-shutters were undone. It must face, like the terrace, toward the sea.

The brandy was hot.

'All my life,' said Vonderjan, sitting down on his own writing-table, suddenly unsolid, his eyes wide and unseeing, 'I've had to deal with fucking death. You get sick of it. Sick to death of it.'

'Yes.'

'I know you saw some things in France.'

'I did.'

'How do we live with it, eh? Oh, you're a young man. But when you get past forty, Christ, you feel it, breathing on the back of your neck. Every death you've seen. And I've seen plenty. My mother, and my wife. I mean, my first wife, Uteka. A beautiful woman, when I met her. Big, if you know I mean. White skin and raven hair, red-gold eyes. A Viking woman.'

Jeanjacques was mesmerised, despite everything. He had never heard Vonderjan expatiate like this, not even in imagination.

They drank more brandy.

Vonderjan said, 'She died in my arms.'

'I'm sorry –'

'Yes. I wish I could have shot her, like the horses, to stop her suffering. But it was in Copenhagen, one summer. Her people everywhere. One thing, she hated sex.'

Jeanjacques was shocked despite himself.

'I found other women for that,' said Vonderjan, as if, indifferently, to explain.

The bottle was nearly empty. Vonderjan opened a cupboard and took out another bottle, and a slab of dry, apparently stale bread on a plate. He ripped off pieces of the bread and ate them.

It was like a curious Communion, bread and wine, flesh, blood. (He offered none of the bread to Jeanjacques.)

'I wanted,' Vonderjan said, perhaps two hours later, as they sat in the hard stuffed chairs, the light no longer window-pane pure, 'a woman who'd take that, from me. Who'd want me pushed and poured into her, like the sea, like they say a mermaid wants that. A woman who'd take. I heard of one. I went straight to her. It was true.'

'Don't all women –' Jeanjacques faltered, drunk and heart racing, 'take –?'

'No. They give. Give, give, give. They give too bloody much.'

Vonderjan was not drunk, and they had consumed two bottles of brandy, and Vonderjan most of it.

'But she's – she's taken – she's had your luck –' Jeanjacques blurted.

'Luck. I never wanted my luck.'

'But you –'

'Wake up. I had it, but who else did? Not Uteka, my wife. Not my wretched mother. I hate cruelty,' Vonderjan said quietly. 'And we note, this world's very cruel. We should punish the world if we could. We should punish God if we could. Put Him on a cross? Yes. Be damned to this fucking God.'

The clerk found he was on the ship, coming to the Island, but he knew he did not want to be on the Island. Yet of course, it was now too late to turn back. Something followed through the water. It was black and shining. A shark, maybe.

When Jeanjacques came to, the day was nearly gone and evening was coming. His head banged and his heart galloped. The dead horse had possessed it. He wandered out of the study (now empty but for himself) and heard the terrible sound of a woman, sick-moaning in her death-throes: Uteka's ghost. But then a sharp cry came; it was the other one, Vonderjan's second wife, dying in his arms.

As she put up her hair, Nanetta was thinking of whispers. She heard them in the room, echoes of all the other whispers in the house below.

Black – it's black – not black like a man is black … black as black is black …

Beyond the fringe of palms, the edge of the forest trees stirred, as if something quite large were prowling about there. Nothing else moved.

She drove a gold hairpin through her coiffure.

He was with her, along the corridor. It had sometimes happened he would walk up here, in the afternoons. Not for a year, however.

A bird began to shriek its strange stupid warning at the forest's edge, the notes of which sounded like *'J'ai des lits! J'ai des lits!'*

Nanetta had dreamed this afternoon, falling asleep in that chair near the window, that she was walking in the forest, barefoot, as she had done when a child. Through the trees behind her something crept, shadowing her. It was noiseless, and the forest also became utterly still with tension and fear. She had not dared look back, but sometimes, from the rim of her eye, she glimpsed a dark, pencil-straight shape, that might only have been the ebony trunk of a young tree.

Then, pushing through the leaves and ropes of a wild fig, she saw it, in front of her not at her back, and woke, flinging herself forward with a choking gasp, so that she almost fell out of the chair.

It was black, smooth. Perhaps, in the form of a man. Or was it a beast? Were there eyes? Or a mouth?

In the house, a voice whispered, 'Something is in the forest.'

A shutter banged without wind.

And outside, the bird screamed *I have beds! I have beds!*

The salon: it was sunset and thin wine light was on the rich man's china, and the Venice glass, what was left of it.

Vonderjan considered the table, idly, smoking, for the meal had been served and consumed early. He had slept off his brandy in twenty minutes on Anna's bed, then woken and had her a third time, before they separated.

She had lain there on the sheet, her pale arms firm and damask with the soft nap of youth.

'I can't get up. I can't stand up.'

'Don't get up. Stay where you are,' he said. 'They can bring you something on a tray.'

'Bread,' she said. 'I want soft warm bread, and some soup. And a glass of wine.'

'Stay there,' he agreed again. 'I'll soon be back.'

'Come back quickly,' she said. And she held out the slender, strong white arms, all the rest of her flung there and limp as a broken snake.

So he went back and slid his hand gently into her, teasing her, and she writhed on the point of his fingers, the way a doll would, should you put your hand up its skirt.

'Is that so nice? Are you sure you like it?'

'Don't stop.'

Vonderjan had thought he meant only to tantalise, perhaps to fulfil, but in the end he unbuttoned himself, the buttons he had only just done up, and put himself into her again, finishing both of them with swift hard thrusts.

So, she had not been in to dine. And he sat here, ready for her again, quite ready. But he was used to that. He had, after all, stored all that, during his years with Uteka, who, so womanly in other ways, had loved to be held and petted like a child, and nothing more. Vonderjan had partly unavoidably felt that the disease that invaded her body had somehow been given entrance to it because of this omitting vacancy, which she had not been able to allow him to fill – as night rushed to engulf the sky once vacated by a sun.

This evening the clerk looked very sallow, and had not eaten much. (Vonderjan had forgotten the effect brandy could have.) The black woman was definitely frightened. There was a type of magic going on, some ancient fear-ritual that unknown forces had stirred up among the people on the Island. It did not interest Vonderjan very much; nothing much did, now.

He spoke to the clerk, congratulating him on the efficiency of his lists and his evaluation, and the arrangements that had been postulated, when next the ship came to the Island.

Jeanjacques rallied. He said, 'The one thing I couldn't locate, sir, was a piano.'

'Piano?' Puzzled, Vonderjan looked at him.

'I had understood you to say your wife – that she had a piano –'

'Oh, I ordered one for her years ago. It never arrived. It was stolen, I suppose, or lost overboard, and they never admitted to it. Yes, I recall it now, a pianoforte. But the heat here would soon have ruined it anyway.'

The candles abruptly flickered, for no reason. The light was going, night rushing in.

Suddenly something, a huge impenetrable shadow, ran by the window.

The woman, Nanetta, screamed. The housekeeper sat with her eyes almost starting out of her head. Jeanjacques cursed. *'What was that?'*

As it had run by, fleet, leaping, a mouth gaped a hundred teeth – like the mouth of a shark breaking from the ocean. Or had they mistaken that?

Did it have eyes, the great black animal that had run by the window?

Surely it had eyes –?

Vonderjan had stood up, and now he pulled a stick from a vase against the wall – as another man might pick up an umbrella, or a poker – and he was opening wide the doors, so the women shrank together and away.

The light of day was gone. The sky was blushing to black. Nothing was there.

Vonderjan called peremptorily into the darkness. To Jeanjacques the call sounded meaningless, gibberish, something like *Hooh! Hoouah!* Vonderjan was not afraid, possibly not even disconcerted or intrigued.

Nothing moved. Then, below, lights broke out on the open space, a servant shouted shrilly in the patois.

Vonderjan shouted down, saying it was nothing. 'Go back inside.' He turned and looked at the two women and the man in the salon. 'Some animal.' He banged the doors shut.

'It – looked like a lion,' Jeanjacques stammered. But no. It had been like a shark, a fish, that bounded on two or three legs, and stooping low.

The servants must have seen it too. Alarmed and alerted, they were still disturbed, and generally calling out now. Another woman screamed, and then there was the crash of glass.

'Fools,' said Vonderjan, without any expression or contempt. He nodded at the housekeeper. 'Go and tell them I say it's all right.'

The woman dithered, then scurried away – by the house door; avoiding the terrace. Nanetta too had stood up, and her eyes had their silver rings. They, more even than the thing that ran across the window, terrified Jeanjacques.

'What was it? Was it a wild pig?' asked the clerk, aware he sounded like a scared child.

'A pig. What pig? No. Where could it go?'

'Has it climbed up the wall?' Jeanjacques rasped.

The black woman began to speak the patois in a singsong, and the hair crawled on Jeanjacques' scalp.

'Tell her to stop it, can't you.'

'Be quiet, Nanetta,' said Vonderjan.

She was silent.

They stood there.

Outside the closed windows, in the closed dark, the disturbed noises below were dying off.

Had it had eyes? Where had it gone to?

Jeanjacques remembered a story of Paris, how the guillotine would leave its station by night and patrol the streets, searching for yet more blood. And during a siege of antique Rome, a giant phantom wolf had stalked the seven hills, tearing out the throats of citizens. These things were not real, even though they had been witnessed and attested, even though evidence and bodies were left in their wake. And, although unreal, yet they existed. They grew, such things, out of the material of the rational world, as maggots appeared spontaneously in a corpse, or fungus formed on damp.

The black woman had been keeping quiet. Now she made a tiny sound.

They turned their heads.

Beyond the windows – dark blotted dark, night on night.

'It's there.'

A second time Vonderjan flung open the doors, and light flooded, by some trick of reflection in their glass, out across the place beyond.

It crouches by the wall, where yester eve the man carnally had his wife, where a creeper grows, partly rent away by their movements.

'In God's sight,' Vonderjan says, startled finally, but not afraid.

He walks out, straight out, and they see the beast by the wall does not move, either to attack him or to flee.

Jeanjacques can smell roses, honeysuckle. The wine glass drops out of his hand.

Antoinelle dreams, now.

She is back in the house of her aunt, where no-one would allow her to speak, or to play the piano. But she has slunk down in the dead of night, into the sitting-room, and rebelliously lifted the piano's lid.

A wonderful sweet smell comes up from the keys, sand she strokes them a moment, soundlessly. The feel … like skin. The skin of a man, over muscle, young, hard, smooth. Is it Justus she feels? (She knows this is very childish. Even her sexuality, although perhaps she does not know this, has the wanton ravening quality of the child's single-minded demands.)

There is a shell the inclement aunt keeps on top of the piano, along with some small framed miniatures of ugly relatives.

Antoinelle lifts the shell, and puts it to her ear, listens to hear the sound of the sea. But instead, she hears a piano playing, softly and far off.

The music, Antoinelle thinks, is a piece by Rameau, for the harpsichord, transposed.

She looks at the keys. She has not touched them, or not enough to make them sound.

Rameau's music dies away.

Antoinelle finds she is playing four single notes on the keys, she does not know why, and neither the notes, nor the word they spell, mean anything to her.

And then, even in the piano-dream, she is aware her husband, Gregers Vonderjan, is in the bed with her, lying behind her, although in her dream she is standing upright.

They would not let her speak or play the piano – they would not let her have what she must have, or make the sounds that she must make …

Now *she* is a piano.

He fingers her keys, gentle, next a little rough, next sensual, next with the crepitation of a feather. And, at each caress, she sounds, Antoinelle, who is a piano, a different note.

His hands are over her breasts. (In the dream too, she realises, she has come into the room naked.) His fingers are on her naked breasts, fondling and describing, itching the buds at their centres. Antoinelle is being played. She gives off, note by note and chord by chord, her music.

Still cupping, circling her breasts with his hungry hands, somehow his scalding tongue is on her spine. He is licking up and up the keys of her vertebrae, through her silk- thin skin.

Standing upright, he is pressed behind her. While lying in the bed, he has rolled her over, crushing her breasts into his hands beneath her, lying on her back, his weight keeping her pinned, breathless.

And now he is entering her body, his penis like a tower on fire.

She spreads, opens, melts, dissolves for him. No matter how large, and he is now enormous, she will make way, then grip fierce and terrible upon him, her toothless springy lower mouth biting and cramming itself full of him, as if never to let go.

They are swimming strongly together for the shore.

How piercing the pleasure at her core, all through her now, the hammers hitting with a golden quake on every nerve string.

And then, like a beast (a cat? a lion?) he has caught her by the throat, one side of her neck.

As with the other entry, at her sex, her body gives way to allow him room. And, as at the very first, her virgin's cry of pain changes almost at once into a wail of delight.

Antoinelle begins to come (to enter, to arrive).

Huge thick rollers of deliciousness, purple and crimson, dark and blazing, tumble rhythmically as dense waves upward, from her spine's base to the windowed dome of her skull.

Glorious starvation couples with feasting, itching with rubbing, constricting, bursting, with implosion, the architecture of her pelvis rocks, punches, roaring and spinning in eating movements and swallowing gulps –

If only this sensation might last and last.

It lasts. It lasts.

Antoinelle is burning bright. She is changing into stars. Her stars explode and shatter. There are greater stars she can make. She is going to make them. She does so. And greater. Still she is coming, entering, arriving.

She has screamed. She has screamed until she no longer has any breath. Now she screams silently. Her nails gouge the bed-sheets. She feels the blood of her virginity falling drop by drop. She is the shell and her blood her sounding sea, and the sea is rising up and another mouth, the mouth of night, is taking it all, and she is made of silver for the night that devours her, and this will never end.

And then she screams again, a terrible divine scream, dredged independently up from the depths of her concerto of ecstasy. And vaguely, as she flies crucified on the wings of the storm, she knows the body upon her body (its teeth in her throat) is not the body of Vonderjan, and that the fire-filled hands upon her breasts, the flaming stem within her, are black, not as black is black, but black as outer space, which she is filling now with her millions of wheeling, howling stars.

VII

The bird that cries *Shadily! Shadily!* flies over the Island above the boiling afternoon lofts, and is gone, back to the upper city mainland, where there are more trees, more shade.

In the branches of the snake-willow, a wind-chime tinkles, once.

Yse's terrace is full of people, sitting and standing with bottles, glasses, cans, and laughing. Yse has thrown a party. Someone, drunk, is dog-paddling in the alley of water.

Lucius, in his violet shirt, looks at the people. Sometimes Yse appears. She's slim and ash-pale, with long, shining hair, about 25. Closer, 35, maybe.

'Good party, Yse. Why you throw a party?'

'I had to throw something. Throw a plate, or myself away. Or something.'

Carr and the fat man, they've got the two lids up off the piano by now. It won't play, everyone knew it wouldn't. Half the notes will not sound. Instead, a music centre, straddled between the piano's legs, rigged via Yse's generator, uncoils the blues.

And this in turn has made the refrigerator temperamental. Twice people have gone to neighbours to get ice. And in turn these neighbours have been invited to the party.

A new batch of lobsters bake on the griddle. Green grapes and yellow pineapples are pulled apart.

'I was bored,' she says. 'I couldn't get on with it, that vampire story.'

'Let me read it.'

'You won't decipher my handwriting.'

'Some. Enough.'

'You think so? All right. But don't make criticisms, don't tell me what to do, Lucius, all right?'

'Deal. How would *I* know?'

He sits in the shady corner (*Shadily!* the bird cried mockingly (*J'ai des lits!*) from Yse's roof), and now he reads.

He can read her handwriting; it's easier than she thinks.

Sunset spreads an awning.

Some of the guests go home, or go elsewhere, but still crowds sit along the wall, or on the steps, and in the loft people are dancing now to a rock band on the music centre.

'Hey this piano don't play!' accusingly calls Big Eye, a late learner.

Lucius takes a polite puff of a joint someone passes, and passes it on. He sits thinking.

Sunset darkens, claret colour, and now the music centre plays Mozart.

Yse sits down by Lucius on the wall.

'Tell me, Yse, how does he get all his energy, this rich guy. He's forty, you say, but you say that was like fifty, then. And he's big, heavy. And he porks this Anna three, four times a night, and then goes on back for more.'

'Oh that. Vonderjan and Antoinelle. It's to do with obsession. They're obsessive. When you have a kink for something, you can do more, go on and on. Straight sex is never like that. It's the perversity – so-called perversity. That revs it up.'

'Strong guy, though.'

'Yes.'

'Too strong for you?'

'Too strong for me.'

Lucius knew nothing about Yse's 'obsession' with Per Laszd. But by now he knows there is something. There has never been a man in Yse's life that Lucius has had to explain to that he, Lucius, is her friend only. Come to that, not any women in her life, either. But he has come across her work, read a little of it – never much – seen this image before, this big blond man. And the sex, for always, unlike the life of Yse, her books are full of it.

Lucius says suddenly, 'You liked him but you never got to have him, this feller.'

She nods. As the light softens, she's not a day over thirty, even from two feet away.

'No. But I'm used to that.'

'What is it then? You have a bone to pick with him for him getting old?'

'The real living man you mean? He's not old. About fifty-five, I suppose. He looks pretty wonderful to me still.'

'You see him?' Lucius is surprised.

'I see him on TV. And he looks great. But he was – well, fabulous when he was younger. I mean actually like a man out of a fable, a myth.'

She's forgotten, he thinks, that she never confided like this in Lucius. Still though, she keeps back the name.

Lucius doesn't ask for the name.

A name no longer matters, if it ever did.

'You never want to try another guy?'

'Who? Who's offering?' And she is angry, he sees it. Obviously, he is no use to her that way. But then, did she make a friendship with Lucius for just that reason?

'You look good, Yse.'

'Thank you.' Cold. Better let her be. For a moment.

A heavenly, unearthly scent is stealing over the evening air.

Lucius has never seen the plant someone must have put in to produce this scent. Nothing grows on the terrace but for the snake-willow, and tonight people, lobster, pineapple, empty bottles.

'This'll be a mess to get straight,' he says.

'Are you volunteering?'

'Just condoling, Yse.'

The sunset totally fades. Stars light up. It's so clear, you can see the Abacus Tower, like a Christmas tree, on the mainland.

'What colour are his eyes, Yse?'

'... Eyes? Blue. It's in the story.'

'No, girl, the other one.'

'Which –? Oh, *that* one. The vampire. I don't know. Your vampire had yellow eyes, you said.'

'I said, he made me feel like a king. But the sex was good, then it was over. Not as you describe it, extended play. '

'I did ask you not to criticise my work.'

'No way. It's sexy. But tell me his eye colour?'

'Black, maybe. Or even white. The vampire is like the piano.'

'Yeah. I don't see that. Yse, why is it a piano?'

'It could have been anything. The characters are the hotbed, and the vampire grows out of that. It just happens to form as a piano – a sort of piano. Like dropping a glass of wine, like a cloud – the stain, the cloud, just happen to take on a shape, randomly, that seems to resemble some familiar thing.'

'Or is it because you can play it?'

'Yes, that too.'

'And it's an animal.'

'And a man. Or male. A male body.'

'Black as black is black. Not skin-black.'

'Blacker. As black as black can be.'

He says quietly, '*La Danse aux Vampires*.'

A glass breaks in the loft and wine spills on the wooden floor – shapelessly? Yse doesn't bat an eyelash.

'You used to fuss about your things.'

'They're only things.'

'We're all only things, Yse. What about the horses?'

'You mean Vonderjan's horses. This is turning into a real interrogation. All right. The last one, the white one like a fish, escapes, and gallops about the Island.'

'You don't seem stuck, Yse. You seem to know plenty enough to go on.'

'Perhaps I'm tired of going on.'

'Looked in the mirror?'

'What do you mean?'

'Look in the mirror, Yse.'

'Oh that. It's not real. It won't last.'

'I never saw a woman could do that before, get 15 years younger in a month. Grow her hair fifty times as thick and twenty times longer. Lose forty pounds without trying, and nothing *loose*. How do *feel*, Yse?'

'All right.'

'But do you feel good?'

'I feel all right.'

'It's how they make you feel, Yse. You said it. They're not beautiful, they don't smell like flowers or the sea. They come out of the grave, out of beds of earth, out of the cess-pit shit at the bottom of your soul's id. It's how they make you feel, what they can do to change you. *Hudja-magica*. Not them. What they can do to *you*.'

'You are crazy, Lucius. There've been some funny smokes on offer up here tonight.'

He gets up.

'Yse, did I say, the one I followed, when he went into his grave under the headstone, he said to me, *You come in with me, Luce. Don't mind the dark. I make sure you never notice it.*'

'And you said no.'

'I took to my hot heels and ran for my fucking life.'

'Then you didn't love him, Lucius.'

'I loved my fucking life.'

She smiles, the white girl at his side. Hair and skin so ivory pale, white dress and shimmering eyes, and who in hell is she?

'Take care, Yse.'

'Night, Lucius. Sweet dreams.'

The spilled wine on the floor has spilled a random shape that looks like a screwed-up sock.

Her loft is empty. They have all gone.

She lights the lamp on her desk, puts out the others, sits, looking at the piano from the Sound, forty feet away, its hind lid and its fore lid now raised, eyes and mouth.

Then she gets up and goes to the piano, and taps out on the keys four notes.

Each one sounds.

D, then E, then A. And then again D.

It would be *mort* in French, *dood* in Dutch, *tod* in German. Danish, Czech, she isn't sure … but it would not work.

I saw in the mirror.

PianO. O, pain.

But, it doesn't hurt.

VIII: Danse Macabre

A wind blew from the sea, and waxy petals fell from the vine, scattering the lid of the piano as it stood there, by the house wall.

None of them spoke.

Jeanjacques felt the dry parched cinnamon breath of Nanetta scorching on his neck, as she waited behind him. And in front of him was Vonderjan, examining the thing on the terrace.

'How did it get up here?' Jeanjacques asked, stupidly. He knew he was being stupid. The piano was supernatural. It had run up here.

'Someone carried it. How else?' replied Vonderjan.

Did he believe this? Yes, it seemed so.

Just then a stifled cry occurred above, detached itself and floated over them. For a moment none of them reacted to it; they had heard it so many times and in so many forms.

But abruptly Vonderjan's blond head went up, his eyes wide. He turned and strode away, half running. Reaching a stair that went to the gallery above, he bounded up it.

It was the noise his wife made, of course. But she made it when he was with her (inside her). And he had been here –

Neither Nanetta nor Jeanjacques went after Gregers Vonderjan, and neither of them went any nearer the piano.

'Could someone have carried it up here?' Jeanjacques asked the black woman, in French.

'Of course.' But as she said this, she vehemently shook her head.

They moved away from the piano.

The wind came again, and petals fell again across the blackness of its carapace.

Jeanjacques courteously allowed the woman to precede him into the salon, then shut both doors quietly.

'What is it?'

She looked up at him sleepily, deceitfully.

'You called out.'

'Did I? I was asleep. A dream ...'

'Now I'm here,' he said.

'No,' she said, moving a little way from him. 'I'm so sleepy. Later.'

Vonderjan stood back from the bed. He gave a short laugh, at the absurdity of this. In the two years of their sexual marriage, she had never before said anything similar to him. (And he heard Uteka murmur sadly, 'Please forgive me, Gregers. Please don't be angry.')

'Very well.'

Then Antoinelle turned and he saw the mark on her neck, glowing lushly scarlet as a flower or fruit, in the low lamplight.

'Something's bitten you.' He was alarmed. He thought at once of the horses dying. 'Let me see.'

'Bitten me? Oh, yes. And I scratched at it in my sleep, yes, I remember.'

'Is that why you called out, Anna?'

She was amused and secretive.

Picking up the lamp, he bent over her, staring at the place.

A little thread, like fire, still trickled from the wound, which was itself very small. There was the slightest bruising. It did not really look like a bite, more as if she had been stabbed on purpose by a hat-pin.

Where he had let her put him off sexually, he would not let her do so now. He went out and came back, to mop up the little wound with alcohol.

'Now you've made it sting. It didn't before.'

'You said it itched you.'

'Yes, but it didn't worry me.'

'I'll close the window.'

'Why? It's hot, so hot –'

'To keep out these things that bite.'

He noted her watching him. It was true she was mostly still asleep, yet despite this, and the air of deception and concealment that so oddly clung to her, for a moment he saw, in her eyes, that he was old.

When her husband had gone, Antoinelle lay on her front, her head turned, so the blood continued for a while to soak into her pillow.

She had dreamed the sort of dream she had sometimes dreamed before Vonderjan came into her life. Yet this had been much more intense. If she slept, would the dream return? But she slept quickly, and the dream did not happen.

Two hours later, when Vonderjan came back to her bed, he could not at first wake her. Then, although she seemed to welcome him, for the first time he was unable to satisfy her.

She writhed and wriggled beneath him, then petulantly flung herself back. 'Oh finish then. I can't. I don't want to.'

But he withdrew gently, and coaxed her. 'What's wrong, Anna? Aren't you well tonight?'

'Wrong? I want what you usually give me.'

'Then let me give it to you.'

'No. I'm too tired.'

He tried to feel her forehead. She seemed too warm. Again, he had the thought of the horses, and he was uneasy. But she pulled away from him. 'Oh, let me sleep, I must sleep.'

Before returning here, he had gone down and questioned his servants. He had asked them if they had brought the piano up onto the terrace, and where they had found it.

They were afraid, he could see that plainly. Afraid of unknown magic and the things they beheld in the leaves and on the wind, which he, Vonderjan, could not see and had never believed in. They were also afraid of a shadowy beast, which apparently they too had witnessed, and which he thought he had seen. And naturally, they were afraid of the piano, because it was out of its correct situation, because (and he already knew this perfectly well) they believed it had stolen by itself out of the forest, and run up on the terrace, and *was* the beast they had seen.

At midnight, he went back down, unable to sleep, with a lamp and a bottle, and pushed up both the lids of the piano with ease.

Petals showered away. And a wonderful perfume exploded from the inside of the instrument, and with it a dim cloud of dust, so he stepped off.

As the film cleared, Vonderjan began to see that something lay inside the piano. The greater hind lid had shut it in against the piano's viscera of dulcimer hammers and brass-wire strings.

When all the film had smoked away, Vonderjan once more went close and

153

held the lamp above the piano, leaning down to look, as he had with his wife's bitten throat.

An embalmed mummy was curled up tight in the piano.

That is, a twisted knotted thing, blackened as if by fire, lay folded round there in a preserved and tarry skin, tough as any bitumen, out of which, here and there, the dull white star of a partial bone poked through.

This was not large enough, he thought, to be the remains of a normal adult. Yet the bones, so far as he could tell, were not those of a child, nor of an animal.

Yet, it was most like the burnt and twisted carcass of a beast.

He released and pushed down again upon the lid. He held the lid flat, as if it might lunge up and open again. Glancing at the keys, before he closed them away too, he saw a drop of vivid red, like a pearl of blood from his wife's neck, but it was only a single red petal from the vine.

Soft and loud. In his sleep, the clerk kept hearing these words. They troubled him, so he shifted and turned, almost woke, sank back uneasily. *Soft and loud –* which was what *Pianoforte* meant ...

Jeanjacques' mother, who had been accustomed to thrash him, struck him round the head. A loud blow, but she was soft with grown men, yielding, pliant. And with him, too when grown, she would come to be soft and subserviently polite. But he never forgot the strap, and when she lay dying, he had gone nowhere near her. (His white half, from his father, had also made sure he went nowhere near his sire.)

Nanetta lay under a black, heavily-furred animal, a great cat that kneaded her back and buttocks, purring. At first she was terrified, then she began to like it. Then she knew she would die.

Notes: The black keys are the black magic. The white keys are the white magic. (Both are evil.) Anything black, or white, must respond.

Even if half-black, half-white.

Notes: The living white horse has escaped. It gallops across the Island. It reaches the sea and finds the fans of the waves snorting at them, and canters through the surf along the beaches, fish-white, and the sun begins to rise.

Gregers Vonderjan dreams he is looking down at his dead wife (Uteka) in the rain, as he did in Copenhagen that year she died But in the dream she is not in a coffin, she is uncovered, and the soil is being thrown onto her vulnerable face. And he is sorry, because for all his wealth and personal magnitude, and power, he could not stop this happening to her. When the Island sunrise wakes him at Bleumaneer, the sorrow does not abate. He wishes now she had lived, and was here with him. (Nanetta would have eased him elsewhere, as she had often done in the past. Nanetta had been kind, and warm-blooded enough.) (Why speak of her as if she too were dead?)

Although awake, he does not want to move. He cannot be bothered with it, the eternal and repetitive affair of getting up, shaving and dressing, breakfasting, looking at the accounts, the lists the clerk has made, his possessions, which will shortly be gone.

How has he arrived at this? He had seemed always on a threshold. There is no time left now. The threshold is that of the exit. It is all over, or soon will be.

Almost all of them had left. The black servants and the white, from the kitchen and the lower rooms. The white housekeeper, despite her years and her pernickety adherences to the house. Vonderjan's groom – he had let the last horse out, too, perhaps taken it with him.

Even the bird had been let out of its cage in Antoinelle's boudoir, and had flown off.

Stronn stayed, Vonderjan's man. His craggy indifferent face said, *So, have they left?*

And the young black woman, Nanetta, she was still there, sat with Antoinelle on the balcony, playing cards among the Spanish flowers, her silver and ruby earrings glittering.

'Why?' said Jeanjacques. But he knew.

'They're superstitious,' Vonderjan, dismissive. 'This sort of business has happened before.'

It was four in the afternoon. Mornings here were separate. They came in slices, divided off by sleep. Or else, one slept through them.

'Is that – is the piano still on the terrace? Did someone take it?' said Jeanjacques, giving away the fact he had been to look, and seen the piano was no longer there. Had he dreamed it?

'Some of them will have moved it,' said Vonderjan. He paced across the library. The windows stood open. The windows here were open so often, anything might easily get in.

The Island sweated, and the sky was golden lead.

'Who would move it?' persisted Jeanjacques.

Vonderjan shrugged. He said, 'It wasn't any longer worth anything. It had been in the sea. It must have washed up on the beach. Don't worry about it.'

Jeanjacques thought, if he listened carefully, he could hear beaded piano notes, dripping in narrow streams through the house. He had heard them this morning, as he lay in bed, awake, somehow unable to get up. (There had seemed no point in getting up. Whatever would happen would happen, and he might as well lie and wait for it.) However, a lifetime of frantic early arisings, of hiding in country barns and thatch, and up chimneys, a lifetime of running away, slowly curdled his guts and pushed him off the mattress. But by then it was past noon.

'Do they come back?'

'What? What did you say?' asked Vonderjan.

'Your servants. You said, they'd made off before. Presumably they returned.'

'Yes. Perhaps.'

Birds called raucously (but wordlessly) in the forest, and then grew silent.

'There was something inside that piano,' said Vonderjan. 'A curiosity. I should have seen to it last night, when I found it.'

'What – what was it?'

'A body. Oh, don't blanch. Here, drink this. Some freakish thing. A monkey, I'd say. I don't know how it got there, but they'll have been frightened by it.'

'But it smelled so sweet. Like roses –'

'Yes, it smelled of flowers. That's a funny thing. Sometimes the dead do smell like that. Just before the smell changes.'

'I never heard of that.'

'No. It surprised me years ago, when I encountered it myself.'

Something fell through the sky – an hour. And now it was sunset.

Nanetta had put on an apron and cooked food in the kitchen. Antoinelle had not done anything to assist her, although in her childhood she had been taught how to make soups and bake bread, out of a sort of bourgeois pettiness.

In fact, Antoinelle had not even properly dressed herself. Tonight she came to the meal, which the black woman had meticulously set out, in a dressing-robe, tied about her waist by a brightly-coloured scarf. The neckline drooped, showing off her long neck and the tops of her round young breasts, and the flimsy improper thing she wore beneath. Her hair was also undressed, loose, gleaming and rushing about her with a water-wet sheen.

Stronn too came in tonight, to join them, sitting far down the table, and with a gun across his lap.

'What's that for?' Vonderjan asked him.

'The blacks are saying there's some beast about on the Island. It fell off a boat and swam ashore.'

'You believe them?'

'It's possible, *mijnheer*, isn't it. I knew of a dog that was thrown from a ship at Port-au-Roi and reached Venice.'

'Did you indeed.'

Vonderjan looked smart, as always. The pallid topaz shone in his ring, his shirt was laundered and starched.

The main dish they had consisted of fish, with a kind of ragout, with pieces of vegetable, and rice.

Nanetta had lit the candles, or some of them. Some repeatedly went out. Vonderjan remarked this was due to something in the atmosphere. The air had a thick, heavy saltiness, and for once there was no rumbling of thunder, and constellations showed, massed above the heights, once the light had gone, each star framed in a peculiar greenish circle.

After Vonderjan's exchange with the man, Stronn, none of them spoke.

Without the storm, there seemed no sound at all, except that now and then, Jeanjacques heard thin little rills of musical notes.

At last he said, 'What is that I can hear?'

Vonderjan was smoking one of his cigars. 'What?'

It came again. Was it only in the clerk's head? He did not think so, for the black girl could plainly hear it too. And oddly, when Vonderjan did not say anything else, it was she who said to Jeanjacques, 'They hang things on the trees – to honour gods – wind gods, the gods of darkness.'

Jeanjacques said, 'But it sounds like a piano.'

No-one answered. Another candle sighed and died.

And then Antoinelle – *laughed*.

It was a horrible, terrible laugh. Rilling and tinkling like the bells hung on the trees of the Island, or like the high notes of any piano. She did it for no apparent reason, and did not refer to it once she had finished. She should have done, she should have begged their pardon, as if she had belched raucously.

Vonderjan got up. He went to the doors and opened them on the terrace and the night.

Where the piano had rested itself against the wall, there was nothing, only shadow and the disarrangement of the vine, all its flower-cups broken and shed.

'Do you want some air, Anna?'

Antoinelle rose. She was demure now. She crossed to Vonderjan, and they moved out on to the terrace. But their walking together was unlike that compulsive, gliding inevitability of the earlier time. And, once out in the darkness, they *only* walked, loitering up and down.

She is mad, Jeanjacques thought. This was what he had seen in her face. That she was insane, unhinged and dangerous, her loveliness like vitriol thrown into the eyes of anyone who looked at her.

Stronn poured himself a brandy. He did not seem unnerved, or particularly *en garde*, despite the gun he had lugged in.

But Nanetta stood up. Unhooking the ruby ear-drops from her earlobes, she placed them beside her plate. As she went across the salon to the inner door, Jeanjacques noted her feet, which had been shod in city shoes, were now bare. They looked incongruous, those dark velvet paws with their nails of tawny coral, extending long and narrow from under her light gown; they looked lawless, in a way nothing of the rest of her did.

When she had gone out, Jeanjacques said to Stronn, 'Why is she barefoot?'

'Savages.'

Old rage slapped the inside of the clerk's mind, like his mother's hand. Though miles off, he must react. 'Oh,' he said sullenly, 'barbaric, do you mean? You think them barbarians, though they've been freed.'

Stronn said, 'Unchained is what I mean. Wild like the forest. That's what it means, that word, savage – forest.'

Stronn reached across the table and helped himself from Vonderjan's box of cigars.

On the terrace, the husband and wife walked up and down. The doors stayed wide open.

Trees rustled below, and were still.

Jeanjacques too got up and followed the black woman out, and beyond the room he found her, still in the passage.

She was stood on her bare feet, listening, with the silver rings in her eyes.

'*What can you hear?*'

'You hear it too.'

'Why are your feet bare?'

'So I can go back. So I can run away.'

Jeanjacques seized her wrist and they stood staring at each other in a mutual fear, of which each one made up some tiny element, but which otherwise surrounded them.

'What –' he said.

'Her pillow's red with blood,' said Nanetta. 'Did you see the hole in her neck?'

'No.'

'No. It closes up like a flower – a flower that eats flies. But she bled. And from her other place. White bed was red bed with her blood.'

He felt sick, but he kept hold of the wand of her wrist.

'There *is* something.'

'You know it too.'

Across the end of the passageway, then, where there was no light, something heavy and rapid, and yet slow, passed by. It was all darkness, but a fleer of pallor slid across its teeth. And the head of it one moment turned, and, without eyes, as it had before, it gazed at them.

The black girl sagged against the wall, and Jeanjacques leaned against and into her. Both panted harshly. They might have been copulating, as Vonderjan had with his wife.

Then the passage was free. They felt the passage draw in a breath.

'Was in my room,' the girl muttered. 'Was in my room that is too small anything so big get through the door. I wake, I see it there.'

'But it left you alone.'

'It not want me. Want *her*.'

'The white bitch.'

'Want her, have her. Eat her alive. Run to the forest,' said Nanetta, in the patois, but now he understood her, 'run to the forest.' But neither of them moved.

'No, no, please, Gregers. Don't be angry.'

The voice is not from the past. Not Uteka's. It comes from a future now become the present.

'You said you have your courses. When did that prevent you before? I've told you, I don't mind it.'

'No. Not this time.'

He lets her go. Lets go of her.

She did not seem anxious, asking him not to be angry. He is not angry. Rebuffed, Vonderjan is, to his own amazement, almost relieved.

'Draw the curtains round your bed, Anna. And shut your window.'

'Yes, Gregers.'

He looks, and sees her for the first time tonight, how she is dressed, or not dressed.

'Why did you come down like that?'

'I was hot ... does it matter?'

'A whore in the brothel would put on something like that.' The crudeness of his language startles him. (Justus?) He checks. 'I'm sorry, Anna. You meant nothing. But don't dress like that in front of the others.'

'Nanetta, do you mean?'

'I mean, of course, Stronn. And the Frenchman.'

Her neck, drooping, is the neck of a lily drenched by rain. He cannot see the mark of the bite.

'I've displeased you.'

Antoinelle can remember her subservient mother (the mother who later threw her out to her aunt's house) fawning in this way on her father. (Who also threw her out.)

But Vonderjan seems uninterested now. He stands looking instead down the corridor.

Then he takes a step. Then he halts and says, 'Go along to your room, Anna. Shut the door.'

'Yes, Gregers.'

In all their time together, they have never spoken in this way, in such platitudes, ciphers. Those things used freely by others.

He thinks he has seen something at the turn of the corridor. But when he goes to that junction, nothing is there And then he thinks, of course, what be there?

By then her door is shut.

Alone, he walks to his own rooms, and goes in. *could*

The Island is alive tonight. Full of stirrings and displacements.

He takes up a bottle of Hollands, and pours a triple measure.

Beyond the window, the green-ringed eyes of the stars stare down at Bleumaneer, as if afraid.

When she was a child, a little girl, Antoinelle had sometimes longed to go to bed, in order to be alone with her fantasies, which (then) were perhaps 'ingenuous'. Or perhaps not.

She had lain curled up, pretending to sleep, imagining that she had found a fairy creature in the garden of her parents' house.

The fairy was always in some difficulty, and she must rescue it – perhaps from drowning in the bird bath, where sparrows had attacked it. Bearing it indoors, she would care for it, washing it in a tea-cup, powdering it lightly with scented dust stolen from her mother's box, dressing it in bits of lace, tied at the waist with strands of brightly coloured embroidery silk. Since it was seen naked in the tea-cup, it revealed it was neither male nor female, lacking both breasts and penis (she did not grossly investigate it further) although otherwise it appeared a full-grown specimen of its kind. But then, at that time, Antoinelle had never seen either the genital apparatus of a man or the mammalia of an adult woman.

The fairy, kept in secret, was dependent totally upon Antoinelle. She would feed it on crumbs of cake and fruit. It drank from her chocolate in the morning. It would sleep on her pillow. She caressed it, with always a mounting sense of urgency, not knowing where the caresses could lead – and indeed they never led to anything. Its wings she did not touch. (She had been told, the wings of moths and butterflies were fragile.)

Beyond Antoinelle's life, all Europe had been at war with itself. Invasion, battle, death, these swept by the carefully closed doors of her parents' house, and by Antoinelle entirely. Through a combination of conspiracy and luck, she learned nothing of it, but no doubt those who protected her so assiduously reinforced the walls of Antoinelle's self-involvement. Such lids were shut down on her; what else was she to do but make music with herself – *play* with herself ...

Sometimes in her fantasies, Antoinelle and the fairy quarrelled. Afterwards they would be reconciled, and the fairy would hover, kissing Antoinelle on the lips. Sometimes the fairy got inside her nightdress, tickling her all over until she thought she would die. Sometimes she tickled the fairy in turn with a goose-feather, reducing it to spasms identifiable (probably) only as hysteria.

It never flew away.

Yet, as her own body ripened and formed, Antoinelle began to lose interest in the fairy. Instead, she had strange waking dreams of a flesh-and-blood soldier she had once glimpsed under the window, who, in her picturings, had to save her – not from any of the wild armies then at large – but from an escaped bear ... and later came the prototypes of Justus, who kissed her until she swooned.

Now Antoinelle had gone back to her clandestine youth. Alone in the room, its door shut, she blew out the lamp. She threw wide her window. Standing in the darkness, she pulled off her garments and tossed them down.

The heat of the night was like damp velvet. The tips of her breasts rose like tight buds that wished to open.

Her husband was old. She was young. She felt her youngness, and remembered her childhood with an inappropriate nostalgia.

Vonderjan had thought something might get in at the window. She sensed this might be true.

Antoinelle imagined that something climbed slowly up the creeper.

She began to tremble, and went and lay down on her bed.

She lay on her back, her hands lying lightly over her breasts, her legs a little apart.

Perhaps after all Vonderjan might ignore her denials and come in. She would let him. Yes, after all, she had stopped menstruating. She would not mind his being here. He liked so much to do things to her, to render her helpless, gasping and abandoned, his hands on her making her into his instrument, making her utter sounds, noises, making her come over and over. And she too liked this best. She liked to do nothing, simply to be made to respond, and so give way. In some other life she might have become the ideal fanatic, falling before the Godhead in fits whose real, spurious nature only the most sceptical could ever suspect. Conversely, partnered with a more selfish and less accomplished lover, with an ignorant Justus, for example, she might have been forced to do more, learned more, liked less. But that now was hypothetical.

A breeze whispered at the window. (What does it say?)

That dream she had had. What had that been? Was it her husband? No, it had been a man with black skin. But she had seen no-one so black. A blackness without any translucence, with no blood inside it.

Antoinelle drifted, in a sort of trance.

She had wandered into a huge room with a wooden floor. The only thing in it was a piano. The air was full of a rapturous smell, like blossom, something that bloomed yet burned.

She ran her fingers over the piano. The notes sounded clearly, but each was a voice. A genderless yet sexual voice, crying out as she touched it – now softly, excitedly, now harsh and demanding and desperate.

She was lying on the beach below the Island. The sea was coming in, wave by wave – glissandi – each one the ripples of the wire harp-strings under the piano lid, or keys rippling as fingers scattered touches across them.

Antoinelle had drained Gregers Vonderjan of all he might give her. She had sucked him dry of everything but his blood. It was his own fault, exalting in his power over her, wanting to make her a doll that would dance on his fingers' end, penis's end, *power's* end.

Her eyes opened, and, against the glass windows, she saw the piano standing, its lids lifted, its keys gleaming like appetite, black and white.

Should she get up and play music on it? The keys would feel like skin.

Then she knew that if she only lay still, the piano would come to *her*. She was *its* instrument, as she had been Vonderjan's.

The curtain blew. The piano shifted, and moved, but as it did so, its shape altered. Now it was not only a piano, but an animal.

(Notes: Pianimal.)

It was a beast. And then it melted and stood up, and the form it had taken now was that of a man.

Stronn walked around the courtyard, around its corners, past the dry Spanish fountain. Tonight the husks of flowers scratched in the bowl, and sounded like water. Or else nocturnal lizards darted about there.

There was only one light he could see in Gregers Vonderjan's big house, the few candles left undoused in the salon.

The orange trees on the gallery smelled bitter-sweet.

Stronn did not want to go to bed. He was wide awake. In the old days, he might have had a game of cards with some of the blacks, or even with Vonderjan. But those times had ceased to be.

He had thought he heard the white horse earlier, its shod hoofs going along the track between the rhododendrons. But now there was no sign of it. Doubtless one of the people of the Island would catch the horse and keep it.

As for the other animal, the one said to have escaped from a passing ship, Stronn did not really think it existed, or if it did, it would be something of no great importance.

Now and then he heard the tinkling noise of hudja bells the people had hung on the banana trees. Then a fragment like piano music, but it was the bells again. Some nights the sea breathed as loudly up here as in the bay. Or a shout from one of the huts two miles off might seem just over a wall.

He could hear the vrouw, certainly. But he was used to hearing that. Her squeaks and yowls, fetching off as Vonderjan shafted her. But she was a slut. The way she had come in tonight proved it, in her bedclothes. And she had never given the meester a son, not even tried to give him a child, like the missus (Uteka) had that time, only she had lost it, but she was never very healthy.

A low thin wind blew along the cane fields, and Stronn could smell the coffee trees and the hairy odour of kayar.

He went out of the yard, carrying his gun, thinking he was still looking for the white horse.

A statue of black obsidian might look like this, polished like this.

The faint luminescence of night, with its storm choked within it, is behind the figure. Starlight describes the outline of it; but only as it turns, moving toward her, do details of its forward surface catch any illumination.

Yet too, all the while, adapting to the camouflage of its environment, it grows subtly more human, that is, more recognisable.

For not entirely – remotely – human is it.

Does she comprehend?

From the head, a black pelt of hair waterfalls away around it, folding down its back like a cloak –

The wide flat pectorals are coined each side three times. It is six-nippled, like a panther.

Its legs move, columnar, heavily muscled and immensely vital, capable of great leaps and astonishing bounds, but walking, they give it the grace of a dancer.

At first there seems to be nothing at its groin, just as it seems to have no features set into its face … except that the light had slid, once, twice, on the long rows of perfect teeth.

But now it is at the bed's foot, and out of the dark it has evolved, or made itself whole.

A man's face.

The face of a handsome Justus, and of a Vonderjan in his stellar youth. A face of improbable mythic beauty, and opening in it, like two vents revealing the inner burning core of it, eyes of grey ice, which each blaze like the planet

Venus.

She can see now, it has four upper arms. They too are strong and muscular, also beautiful, like the dancer's legs.

The penis is large and upright, without a sheath, the black lotus bulb on a thick black stem. No change of shade. (No light, no inner blood.) Only the mercury-flame inside it, which only the eyes show.

Several of the side teeth, up and down, are pointed sharply. The tongue is black. The inside of the mouth is black. And the four black shapely hands, with their twenty long, flexible fingers, have palms that are black as the death of light.

It bends toward Antoinelle. It has the smell of night and of the Island, and of the sea. And also the scent of hothouse flowers, that came out of the piano. And a carnivorous smell, like fresh meat.

It stands there, looking at her, as she lies on the bed.

And on the floor, emerging from the pelt that falls from its head, the long black tail strokes softly now this way, now that way.

Then the first pair of hands stretch over onto the bed, and after them the second pair, and fluidly it lifts itself and pours itself forward up the sheet, and up over the body of the girl, looking down at her as it does so, from its water-pale eyes. And its smooth body rasps on her legs, as it advances, and the big hard firm organ knocks on her thighs, hot as the body is cool.

He walked behind her, obedient and terrified. The Island frightened him, but it was more than that. Nanetta was now like his mother, (when she was young and slim, dominant and brutal.) Once she turned, glaring at him, with the eyes of a lynx. '*Hush.*' 'But I –' he started to say, and she shook her head again, raging at him without words.

She trod so noiselessly on her bare feet, which were the indigo colour of the sky in its darkness. And he blundered, try as he would.

The forest held them in its tentacles. The top-heavy plantains loomed, their blades of black-bronze sometimes quivering. Tree limbs like enormous plaited snakes rolled upwards. Occasionally, mystically, he thought, he heard the sea.

She was taking him to her people, who grasped what menaced them, its value if not its actual being, and could keep them safe.

Barefoot and stripped of her jewels, she was attempting to go back into the knowingness of her innocence and her beginnings. But he had always been over-aware and a fool.

They came into a glade of wild tamarinds. Could it be called that – a *glade*? It was an aperture among the trees, but only because trees had been cut down. There was an altar, very low, with frangipani flowers, scented like confectionary, and something killed that had been picked clean. The hudja bells chimed from a nearby bough, the first he had seen. They sounded like the sistra of ancient Egypt, as the cane field had recalled to him the notion of a temple.

Nanetta bowed to the altar and went on, and he found he had crossed himself, just as he had done when a boy in church.

It made him feel better, doing that, as if he had quickly thrown up and got rid of some poison in his heart.

Vau l'eau, Vonderjan thought. Which meant, going downstream, to wrack and ruin.

He could not sleep, and turned on his side to stare out through the window. The stars were so unnaturally clear. Bleumaneer was in the eye of the storm, the aperture at its centre. When this passed, weather would resume, the ever-threatening presence of tempest.

He thought of the white horse, galloping about the Island, down its long stairways of hills and rock and forest, to the shore.

Half asleep, despite his insomnia, there was now a split second when he saw the keys of a piano, descending like the levels of many black and white terraces.

Then he was fully awake again.

Vonderjan got up. He reached for the bottle of schnapps, and found it was empty.

Perhaps he should go to her bed. She might have changed her mind. No, he did not want her tonight. He did not want anything, except to be left in peace.

It seemed to him that after all he would be glad to be rid of every bit of it. His wealth, his manipulative powers. To live here alone, as the house fell gradually apart, without servants, or any authority or commitments. And without Anna.

Had he been glad when Uteka eventually died? Yes, she had suffered so. And he had never known her. She was like a book he had meant to read, had begun to read several times, only to put it aside, unable to remember those pages he had already laboriously gone through.

With Anna it was easy, but then, she was not a book at all. She was a demon he had himself invented (Vonderjan did not realise this, that even for a moment, he thought in this way), an oasis, after Uteka's sexual desert, and so, like any fantasy, she could be sloughed at once. He had masturbated over her long enough, this too-young girl, with her serpentine body (apple-tree and tempting snake together) and her idealised pleas always for more.

Now he wanted to leave the banquet table. To get up and go away and sleep and grow old, without such distractions.

He thought he could hear her, though. Hear her fast starved feeding breathing, and for once, this did not arouse him. And in any case it might not be Anna, but only the gasping of the sea, hurling herself far away, on the rocks and beaches of the Island.

It – he – paints her lips with its long and slender tongue, which is black. Then it paints the inside of her mouth. The tongue is very narrow, sensitive, incites her gums, making her want to yawn, except that is not what she needs to do – but she stretches her body irresistibly.

The first set of hands settles on her breasts.

The second set of hands on her rib-cage.

Something flicks, flicks, between her thighs … not the staff of the penis, but something more like a second tongue.

Antoinelle's legs open and her head falls back. She makes a sound, but it is a bestial grunting that almost offends her, yet there is no room in her body or mind for that.

'No –' she tries to say.

The no means yes, in the case of Antoinelle. It is addressed not to her partner but to normal life, anything that may intrude, and warns *Don't interrupt*.

The black tongue wends, waking nerves of taste and smell in the roof of her mouth. She scents lakoum, pepper, ambergris and myrrh.

The lower tongue, which may be some extra weapon of the tail, licks at a point of flame it has discovered, fixing a triangle with the fire-points of her breasts.

He – it – slips into her, forces into her, bulging and huge as thunder.

And the tail grasps her, muscular as any of its limbs, and, thick as the phallus, also penetrates her.

The thing holds Antoinelle as she detonates about it, faints and cascades into darkness.

Not until she begins to revive does it do more.

The terror is, she comes to already primed, more than eager, her body spangled with frantic need, as if the first cataclysm were only – foreplay.

And now the creature moves, riding her and making her ride, and they gallop down the night, and Antoinelle grins and shrieks, clinging to its obsidian form, her hands slipping, gripping. And as the second detonation begins, its face leaves her face, her mouth, and grows itself faceless and *only* mouth. And the mouth half rings her throat, a crescent moon, and the many side teeth pierce her, both the veins of her neck.

A necklace of emeralds was nothing to this.

Antoinelle drops from one precipice to another. She screams, and her screams crash through the house called Blue View, like sheets of blue glass breaking.

It holds her. As her consciousness again goes out, it holds her very tight.

And somewhere in the limbo where she swirls, fire on oil, guttering but not quenched, Antoinelle is raucously laughing with triumph at finding this other one, not her parasite, but her twin. Able to devour her as she devours, able to eat her alive as she has eaten or tried to eat others alive. But where Antoinelle has bled them out, this only drinks. It wastes nothing, not even Antoinelle.

More – more – She can never have enough.

Then it tickles her with flame so she thrashes and yelps. Its fangs fastened in her, it bears her on, fastened in turn to it.

She is arched like a bridge, carrying the travelling shadow on her body. Pinned together, in eclipse, these dancers.

More –

It gives her more. And indescribably yet more.

If she were any longer human, she would be split and eviscerated, and her spine snapped along its centre three times.

Her hands have fast hold of it. Which – it or she – is the more tenacious? Where it travels, so will she.

But for all the *more*, there is no more *thought*. If ever there was thought.

When she was 14, she saw all this, in her prophetic mirror, saw what she was made for and must have.

Perhaps many thousands of us are only that, victim or predator, interchangeable.

Seen from above: Antoinelle is scarcely visible. Just the edges of her flailing feet, her contorted forehead and glistening strands of hair. And her clutching claws. (Shockingly, she makes the sounds of a pig, grunting, snorting.)

The rest of her is covered by darkness, by something most like a manta ray out of the sea, or some black amoeba.

Then she is growling and grunting so loudly, on and on, that the looking-glass breaks on her toilette table as if unable to stand the sound, while out in the night forest birds shrill and fly away.

More – always more. *Don't stop –* Never stop.

There is no need to stop. It has killed her, she is dead, she is re-alive and death is lost on her, she is all she has ever wished to be – nothing.

'Dearest … are you awake?'

He lifts his head from his arm. He has slept.

'What is it?' *Who are you?* Has she ever called him *dear* before?

'Here I am,' she says, whoever she is. But she is his Anna.

He does not want her. Never wanted her.

He thinks she is wearing the emerald necklace, something burning about her throat. She is white as bone. And her dark eyes – have paled to Venus eyes, watching him.

'I'm sorry,' he says. 'Perhaps later.'

'I know.'

Vonderjan falls asleep again quickly, lying on his back. Then Antoinelle slides up on top of him. She is not heavy, but he is; it impedes his breathing, her little weight.

Finally she puts her face to his, her mouth over his.

She smothers him mostly with her face, closing off his nostrils with the pressure of her cheek, and one narrow hand, and her mouth sidelong to his, and her breasts on his heart.

He does not wake again. At last his body spasms sluggishly, like the last death-throe of orgasm. Nothing else.

After his breathing has ended, still she lies there, Venus-eyed, and the dawn begins to come. Antoinelle casts a black, black shadow. Like all shadows, it is attached to her. Attached very closely.

Is this her shadow, or is she the white shadow of *it*?

IX

Having sat for ten minutes, no longer writing, holding her pen upright, Yse sighs, and drops it, like something unpleasant, dank or sticky.

The story's erotographic motif, at first stimulating, has become, as it must, repulsive. Disgusting her – also as it should.

And the murder of Vonderjan, presented deliberately almost as an afterthought, (stifled under the slight white pillar of his succubus wife).

Aloud, Yse says almost angrily, 'Now surely I've used him up. All up. All over. Per Laszd, I can't do another thing with you or to you. But then, you've used me up too, yes you did, you have, even though you've never been near me. Mutual annihilation. That Yse is over with.'

Then Yse rises, leaving the manuscript, and goes to make tea. But her generator, since the party (when the music machine had been hooked into it by that madman, Carr) is skittish. The stove won't work. She leaves it, and pours instead a warm soda from the now improperly-working fridge.

It is night-time, or morning, about 3.50 am.

Yse switches on her small TV, which works on a solar battery and obliges.

And there, on the first of the 15 mainland (upper city) channels, is he – is Per Laszd. Not in his persona of dead trampled Gregers Vonderjan, but that of his own dangerous self.

She stands on the floor, dumbfounded, yet not, not really. Of course, who else would come before her at this hour?

He looks well, healthy and tanned. He's even shed some weight.

It seems to be a talk show, something normally Yse would avoid – they bore her. And the revelation of those she sometimes admires as over-ordinary or distasteful, disillusions and frustrates her.

But him she has always watched, on a screen, across a room when able, or in her own head. Him, she knows. He could not disillusion her, or put her off.

And tonight, there is something new. The talk has veered round to the other three guests – to whom she pays no attention – and so to music. And now the TV show's host is asking Per Laszd to use the piano, that grande piano over there.

Per Laszd gets up and walks over to this studio piano, looking, Yse thinks, faintly irritated, because obviously this has been sprung on him and is not what he is about, or at least not publicly, but he will do it from a good showman's common sense.

He plays well, some melody Yse knows, a popular song she can't place. He improvises, his large hands and strong fingers jumping sure and finely-trained about the keyboard. Just the one short piece, concluded with a sarcastic flourish, after which he stands up again. The audience, delighted by any novelty, applauds madly, while the host and other guests are all calling *encore*! (More! More! Again – don't stop –) But Laszd is not manipulable, not truly. Gracious yet immovable, he returns to his seat. And after that a pretty girl with an unimportant voice comes on to sing, and then the show is done.

Yse finds herself enraged. She switches off the set, and slams down the tepid soda. She paces this end of her loft. While by the doors, forty feet away, the piano dredged from the Sound still stands, balanced on its forefeet and its phallic tail, hung in shade and shadow. It has been here more than a month. It's nearly invisible.

So why this now? This TV stunt put on by Fate? Why show her this, now? As if to congratulate her, giving her a horrible mean little failed-runner's-up patronising non-prize. Per Laszd can play the piano.

Damn Per Laszd.

She is sick of him. Perhaps in every sense. But of course, she still wants him. Always will.

And what now?

She will never sleep. It's too late or early to go out.

She circles back to her writing, looks at it, sits, touches the page. But why bother to write any more?

Vonderjan was like the enchanter Prospero, in Shakespeare's *Tempest*, shut up there on his sorcerous Island, infested with sprites and elementals. Prospero too kept close a strange young woman, who in the magician's case had been his own daughter. But then arrived a shipwrecked prince out of the sea, to take the responsibility off Prospero's hands.

(Per's hands on the piano keys. Playing them. A wonderful amateur, all so facile, no trouble at all. He is married, and has been for 12 years. Yse has always known this.)

Far out on the Sound, a boat moos eerily.

Though she has frequently heard such a thing, Yse starts.

Be not afeard: the isle is full of noises,
Sounds and sweet airs, that give delight, and hurt not.

She can no longer smell the perfume, like night-blooming vines. When did that stop? (Don't stop.)

Melted into air, into thin air …

X: Passover

They had roped the hut-house round, outside and in, with their amulets and charms. There were coloured feathers and dried grasses, cogs of wood rough-carved, bones and sprinkles of salt and rum, and of blood, as in the Communion. When they reached the door, she on her bare, navy-blue feet, Jeanjacques felt all the forest press at their backs. And inside the hut, the silver-ringed eyes, staring in affright like the staring stars. But presently her people let her in, and let him in as well, without argument. And he thought of the houses of the Chosen in Egypt, their lintels marked by blood, to show the Angel of Death he must pass by.

He, as she did, sat down on the earth floor. (He noted the earth floor, and the contrasting wooden bed, with its elaborate posts. And the two shrines, one to the Virgin, and one to another female deity.)

Nothing was said beyond a scurry of whispered words in the patois. There were thirty other people crammed in the house, with a crèche of chickens and two goats. Fear smelled thick and hot, but there was something else, some vital possibility of courage and cohesion. They clung together soul to soul, their bodies only barely brushing, and Jeanjacques was glad to be in their midst, and when the fat woman came and gave him a gourd of liquor, he shed tears, and she patted his head, calming him a little, like a dog hiding under its mistress's chair.

In the end he must have slept. He saw someone looking at him, the pale icy eyes blue as murder.

Waking with a start, he found everyone and thing in the hut tense and compressed, listening, as something circled round outside. Then it snorted and blew against the wall of the hut-house, and all the interior stars of eyes flashed with their terror. And Jeanjacques felt his heart clamp onto the side of his body, as if afraid to fall.

Even so, he knew what it was, and when all at once it retreated and galloped away on its shod hoofs, he said quietly, 'His horse.'

But no-one answered him, or took any notice of what he had said, and Jeanjacques discovered himself thinking, *After all, it might take that form, a white horse. Or she might be riding on the white horse.*

He began to ponder the way he must go in the morning, descending toward the bay. He should reach the sea well in advance of nightfall. The ship would come back, today or tomorrow. Soon. And there were the old buildings, on the beach, where he could make a shelter. He could even jump into the sea and swim out. There was a little reef, and rocks.

It had come from the sea, and would avoid going back to the sea, surely, at least for some while.

He knew it was not interested in him, knew that almost certainly it would not approach him with any purpose. But he could not bear to *see* it. That was the thing. And it seemed to him the people of the Island, and in the hut, even the chickens, the goats, and elsewhere the birds and fauna, felt as he did. They did not want to *see* it, even glimpse it. If the fabric of this world were torn open in one place on a black gaping hole of infinite darkness, you hid your eyes, you went far away.

After that, he started to notice bundles of possessions stacked up in corners. He realised not he alone would be going down the Island to the sea.

Dreaming again, he beheld animals swimming in waves away from shore, and birds flying away, as if from a zone of earthquake, or the presage of some volcanic eruption.

Nanetta nudged him. 'Will you take me to St Paul's Island?'

'Yes.'

'I have a sister there.'

He had been here on a clerk's errand. He thought, ridiculously, *Now I won't be paid.* And he was glad at this wince of anxious annoyance. Its normalcy and reason.

XI

Per Laszd played Bach very well, with just the right detached, solemn cheerfulness.

It was what she would have expected him to play. Something like this. Less so the snatch of a popular tune he had offered the talk show audience so flippantly. (But a piano does what you want, makes the sounds you make it give – even true, she thinks, should you make a mistake – for then that is what it gives you. Your mistake.)

As Yse raised her eyes, she saw across the dim sphere of her loft, still wrapped in the last flimsy paper of night, a lamp stood glowing by the piano, both of whose lids were raised. Her stomach jolted and the pain of shock rushed through her body.

'*Lucius –?*'

He was the only other who held a key to her loft. She trusted Lucius, who anyway had never used the key, except once, when she was gone for a week, to enter and water her (dying) plants, and fill her (then operable) refrigerator with croissants, mangoes and white wine.

And Lucius didn't play the piano. He had told her, once. His *amouretta*, as he called it, was the drum.

Besides, the piano player had not reacted when she called, not ceased his performance. Not until he brought the twinkling phrases to their finish.

Then the large hands stepped back off the keys, he pushed away the chair he must have carried there, and stood up.

The raised carapace of the piano's hind lid still obscured him, all but that flame of light that veered across the shining pallor of his hair.

Yse had got to her feet. She felt incredibly young, light as thin air. The thick silk of her hair brushed round her face, her shoulders, and she pulled in her flat stomach and raised her head on its long throat. She was frightened by the excitement in herself, and excited by the fear. She wasn't dreaming. She had always known, when she *dreamed* of him.

And there was no warning voice, because long ago she had left all such redundant noises behind.

Per Laszd walked around the piano. 'Hallo, Yse,' he said.

She said nothing. Perhaps could not speak. There seemed no point. She had said so much.

But, 'Here I am,' he said.

There he was.

There was no doubt at all. The low lamp flung up against him. He wore the loose dark suit he had put on for the TV programme, as if he had come straight here from the studio. He dwarfed everything in the loft.

'Why?' she said, after all.

She too was entitled to be flippant, surely.

'Why? Don't you know? You brought me here.' He smiled, 'Don't you love me anymore?'

He was wooing her.

She glanced around her, made herself see everything as she had left it, the washed plate and glass by the sink, the soda can on the table, her manuscript lying there, and the pen. Beyond an angle of a wall, a corridor to other rooms.

And below the floor, barracuda swimming through the girders of a flooded building.

But the thin air sparkled as if full of champagne.

'Well, Yse,' he said again, 'here I am.'

'But you are not *you*.'

'You don't say. Can you be certain? How am I different?'

'You're what I've made, and conjured up.'

'I thought it was,' he said, in his dry amused voice she had never forgotten, 'more personal than that.'

'*He* is somewhere miles off. In another country.'

'This is another country,' he said, 'to me.'

She liked it, this breathless fencing with him. Liked his persuading her. *Don't stop.*

The piano had not been able to open – or be opened – until he – or she – was ready. (Foreplay.) And out of the piano, came her demon. What was he? *What?*

She didn't care. If it were not him, yet it was, him.

So she said, archly, 'And your wife?'

'As you see, she had another engagement.'

'With you, *there*. Wherever you are.'

'Let me tell you,' he said, 'why I've called here.'

There was no break in the transmission of this scene; she saw him walk away from the piano, start across the floor, and she did the same. Then they were near the window-doors.

He was stood over her. He was vast, overpowering, beautiful. More beautiful, now she could see the strands of his hair, the pores of his skin, a hundred tiniest imperfections – and the whole exquisite manufacture of a human thing, so close. And she was rational enough to analyse all this, and his beauty, and his power over her; or pedantic enough. He smelled wonderful to her as well, more than his clean fitness and his masculinity, or any expensive cosmetic he had used (for her?) It was the scent discernible only by a lover, caused by her chemistry, not his. Unless she had made him want her, too.

But of course he wanted her. She could see it in his eyes, their blue view bent only on her.

If he might have seemed old to an Antoinelle of barely 16, to Yse this man was simply her peer. And yet too he was like his younger self, clad again in that searing charisma that had later lessened, or changed its course.

He took her hand, picked it up. Toyed with her hand as Vonderjan had done with the hand of the girl Yse had permitted to destroy him.

'I'm here for you,' he said.

'But I don't know you.'

'Backwards,' he said. 'You've made it your business. You've bid for me,' he said, 'and you've got me.'

'No,' she said, 'no, no I haven't.'

'Let me show you.'

She had known of that almost occult quality. With what he wanted in the sexual way, he could communicate some telepathic echo of his desires. As his mouth covered and clasped hers, this delirium was what she felt, combining with her own.

She had always known his kisses would be like this, the ground flying off from her feet, swept up and held only by him in the midst of a spinning void, where she became part of him and wanted nothing else, where she became what she had always wanted ... nothing.

To be nothing, borne by this flooding sea, no thought, no anchor, and no chains.

So Antoinelle, as her vampire penetrated, drank, emptied, reformed her.

So Yse, in her vampire's arms.

It's how they make us feel.

'No,' she murmurs, sinking deeper and deeper into his body, drowning as the island will, one day (five years, twenty).

None of us escape, do we?

Dawn is often very short and ineffectual here, as if to recompense the dark for those long sunsets we have.

Lucius, bringing his boat in to West Ridge from a night's fishing and drinking out in the Sound, sees a light still burning up there, bright as the quick green dawn. All Yse's blinds are up, showing the glass loft, translucent, like a jewel. Over the terrace the snake tree hangs its hair in the water, and ribbons of apple-green light tremble through its coils.

Yse is there, just inside the wall of glass above the terrace, stood with a tall heavy-set man, whose hair is almost white.

He's kissing her, on and on, and then they draw apart, and still she holds on to him, her head tilted back like a serpent's, bonelessly, staring up into his face.

From down in the channel between the lofts and towerettes, Lucius can't make out the features of her lover. But then neither can he make out Yse's facial features, only the tilt of her neck and the lush satin hair hanging down her back.

Lucius sits in the boat, not paddling now, watching. His eyes are still and opaque.

'What you doing, girl?'

He knows perfectly well.

And then they turn back, the two of them, further into the loft where the light still burns, although the light of dawn has gone, leaving only a salty stormy dusk.

They will hardly make themselves separate from each other. They are together again and again, as if growing into one another.

Lucius sees the piano, or that which had been a piano, has vanished from the loft. And after that he sees how the light of the guttering lamp hits suddenly up, like a striking cobra. And in the ray of the lamp, striking, the bulky figure of the man, with his black clothes and blond hair, becomes transparent as the glass sheets of the doors. It is possible to see directly, too, through him, clothes, hair, body, directly through to Yse, as she stands there, still holding on to what is now actually invisible, drawing it on, in, away, just before the lamp goes out and a shadow fills the room like night.

As he is paddling away along the channel, Lucius thinks he hears a remote crash, out of time, like glass smashing in many pieces, but yesterday, or tomorrow.

Things break.

Just about sunset, the police come to find Lucius. They understand he has a key to the loft of a woman called Yse (which they pronounce *Jizz*).

When they get to the loft, Lucius is aware they did not need the key, since the glass doors have both been blown outwards and down into the water-alley below. Huge shards and fragments decorate the terrace, and some are caught in the snake-willow like stars.

A bored detective stands about, drinking coffee someone has made him on Yse's reluctant stove. (The refrigerator has shut off, and is leaking a lake on the floor.)

Lucius appears dismayed but innocuous. He goes about looking for something, which the other searchers, having dismissed him, are too involved to mark.

There is no sign of Yse. The whole loft is vacant. There is no sign either of any disturbance, beyond the damaged doors which, they say to Lucius and each other, were smashed outwards but not by an explosive.

'What are you looking for?' the detective asks Lucius, suddenly grasping what Lucius is at.

'Huh?'

'She have something of yours?'

Lucius sees the detective is waking up. 'No. Her book. She was writing.'

'Oh, yeah? What kind of thing was that?'

Lucius explains, and the detective loses interest again. He says they have seen nothing like that.

And Lucius doesn't find her manuscript, which he would have anticipated, anyway, seeing instantly on her work-table. He does find a note – they say it is a note, a letter of some sort, although addressed to no-one. It's in her bed area, on the rug, which has been floated under the bed by escaped refrigerator fluid.

'Why go on writing?' asks the note, or letter, of the no-one it has not addressed. 'All your life waiting, and having to invent another life, or other lives, to make up for not having a life. Is that what God's problem is?'

Hearing this read at him, Lucius's dead eyes reveal for a second they are not dead, only covered by a protective film. They all miss this.

The detective flatly reads the note out, like a kid bad at reading, embarrassed and standing up in class. Where his feet are planted is the stain from the party, which, to Lucius's for-a-moment-not-dead eyes, has the shape of a swimming, three-legged fish.

'And she says, "I want more."'

'I want the terror and the passion, the power and the glory – not this low-key crap played only with one *hand*. Let me point out to someone, Yse is an anagram of Yes. *I'll drown my book.*'

'I guess,' says the detective, 'she didn't sell.'

They let Lucius go with some kind of veiled threat he knows is offered only to make themselves feel safe.

He takes the water-bus over to the Café Blonde, and as the sunset ends and night becomes, tells one or two what he saw, as he has not told the cops from the tideless upper city.

Lucius has met them all. Angels, demons.

'As the light went through him, he wasn't there. He's like glass.'

Carr says, slyly (inappropriately – or with deadly perception?), 'No vampire gonna reflect in a glass.'

XII: Carried Away

When the ship came, they took the people out, rowing them in groups, in the two boats. The man Stronn had also appeared, looking dazed, and the old housekeeper, and others. No questions were asked of them. The ship took the livestock, too.

Jeanjacques was glad they were so amenable, the black haughty master wanting conscientiously to assist his own, and so helping the rest.

All the time they had sheltered in the rickety customs buildings of the old port, a storm banged round the coast. This kept other things away, it must have done. They saw nothing but the feathers of palm boughs blown through the air and crashing trunks that toppled in the high surf, which was grey as smashed glass.

In the metallic after-storm morning, Jeanjacques walked down the beach, the last to leave, waiting for the last boat, confident.

Activity went on at the sea's edge, sailors rolling a barrel, Nanetta standing straight under a yellow sunshade, a fine lady, barefoot but proud. (She had shown him the jewels she had after all brought with her, squeezed in her sash; not the ruby earrings, but a golden hairpin, and the emerald necklace that had belonged to Vonderjan's vrouw.)

He never thought, now, to see anything, Jeanjacques, so clever, so accomplished at survival.

But he saw it.

Where the forest came down onto the beach, and caves opened under the limestone, and then rocks reared up, white rocks and black, with the curiously quiescent waves glimmering in and out around them.

There had been nothing. He would have sworn to that. As if the reality of the coarse storm had scoured all such stuff away.

And then, there she was, sitting on the rock.

She shone in a way that, perhaps one and a quarter centuries after, could have been described as radioactively.

Jeanjacques did not know that word. He decided that she gleamed. Her hard pale skin and mass of pale hair, gleaming.

She looked old. Yet she looked too young. She was not human-looking, nor animal.

Her legs were spread wide in the skirt of her white dress. So loose was the gown at her bosom, that he could see much of her breasts. She was doing nothing at all, only sitting there, alone, and she grinned at him, all her white teeth, so even, and her black eyes like slits in the world.

But she cast a black shadow, and gradually the shadow was embracing her. And he saw her turning over into it like the moon into an eclipse. If she had any blood left in her, if she had ever been Antoinelle – these things he ignored. But her grinning and her eyes and the shadow and her turning inside out within the shadow – from these things he ran away.

He ran to the line of breakers, where the barrels were being rolled into a boat. To Nanetta's sunflower sunshade.

And he seemed to burst through a sort of curtain, and his muscles gave way. He fell nearby, and she glanced at him, the black woman, and shrank away.

'It's all right –' he cried. He thought she must not see what he had seen, and that they might leave him here. 'I missed my footing,' he whined, 'that's all.'

And when the boat went out, they let him go with it.

The great sails shouldered up into the sky. The master looked Jeanjacques over, before moving his gaze after Nanetta. (Stronn had avoided them. The other whites, and the housekeeper, had hidden themselves somewhere below, like stowaways.)

'How did you find him, that Dutchman?' the master asked idly.

'As you said. Vonderjan was falling.'

'What was the other trouble here? They act like it was a plague, but that's not so.' (Malignly Jeanjacques noted the master too was excluded from the empathy of the Island people.) 'No,' the master went on, bombastically, 'if you sick, I'd never take you on, none of you.'

Jeanjacques felt a little better. 'The Island's gone bad,' he muttered. He would look, though, only up into the sails. They were another sort of white to the white thing he had seen on the rock. As the master was another sort of black.

'Gone bad? they do. Land does go bad. Like men.'

Are they setting sail? Every grain of sand on the beach behind is rising up. Every mote of light, buzzing –

Oh God – *Pater noster* – *libera me* –

The ship strode from the bay. She carved her path into the deep sea, and through his inner ear, Jeanjacques hears the small bells singing. Yet that is little enough, to carry away from such a place.

XIII

Seven months after, he heard the story, and some of the newspapers had it too. A piano had been washed up off the Sound, on the beach at the Abacus Tower. And inside the lid, when they hacked it open, a woman's body was curled up, tiny, and hard as iron. She was Caucasian, middle-aged, rather heavy when alive, now not heavy at all, since there was no blood, and not a single whole bone, left inside her.

Sharks, they said.

Sharks are clever. They can get inside a closed piano and out again. And they bite.

As for the piano, it was missing – vandals had destroyed it, burned it, taken it off.

Sometimes strangers ask Lucius where Yse went to. He has nothing to tell them. ('She disappears?' they ask him again. And Lucius once more says nothing.)

And in that way, resembling her last book, Yse disappeared, disappears, is disappearing. Which can happen, in any tense you like.

'Like those hallucinations that sometimes come at the edge of sleep, so that you wake, thinking two or three words have been spoken close to your ear, or that a tall figure stands in the corner … like this, the image now and then appears before him.

'Then Jeanjacques sees her, the woman, sat on the rock, her white dress and ivory-coloured hair, hard-gleaming in a post-storm sunlight. Impossible to tell her age. A desiccated young girl, or unlined old woman. And the transparent sea lapping in across the sand …

'But he has said, the Island is quite deserted now.'

178

ISRABEL

For John Kaiine, who showed me her image more clearly than any mirror could.

Israbel ran through the streets of Paris. The cobbles were slick with filth and wet, the city was made of thick grey rain. Israbel was 16 – probably, who could be quite sure? Her mother was long dead, her father always unknown. Somewhere behind her waited a man with his belt drawn off, like a sword to smite her with. Israbel ran.

The narrow streets were mostly empty now, for night was coming. A fellow with a torch went by to light the lamps along the front of some tavern. Wet cats, thin as strings, shot across the alleys, or slunk over the roofs above.

When Israbel turned a corner into the Place du Coeur, she did not know where she was, but in the deepening dusk one further cat came slinking out to cross her path. This cat was not like the others. It was very big, the size, she was afterwards to believe, of a horse. Though the light was gone, some peculiar sheen on the darkness showed her the faint dapplings along its back, its neck, which was longer than that of any ordinary feline, and the narrow ruff about its head. Its eyes were luminous, and grey as the death of the light. It stopped.

She too, the running girl, had halted.

She thought, confusedly, *It's escaped from the great circus up at Montmartre.*

Israbel had heard of a circus, that it had many curiosities, including both people and beasts of weird appearance and characteristics.

She was not afraid of the cat. That is, not more afraid of it than of the darkness, the sadist she had escaped, the world, everything. And so, she did not, now, run away, only stood watching it, as it stood also watching her.

A hundred years later when Israbel, still 16, rich, lovely, and, in her own way, dangerous, came occasionally to explain about the great cat, she would always add, 'Its pelt was so soft and warm, so smooth and plush, like the double velvets of Venice. Like my hair, you say? Well, perhaps very like that. But truly, its pelt was much better than my hair.'

'She is the woman I intend to be my wife.'

Plinta stared, a moment. He thought, *Your wife?* And then, *She looks like an insect. Oh, a beautiful insect – some sort of exquisite beetle, with gilded black wings.*

'Really?' he said.

'You don't approve.'

Plinta shivered – but unseen: inside his mind.

'Does it matter to you that I approve?'

'Well, no.'

By then, the woman – the *creature* – was approaching them, slipping between the candlelit marbles of the salon.

Dumiere held out his hands. She paused, smiling, and took neither.

'Good evening, my love,' said Dumiere. 'May I present my friend, Monsieur Plinta, the painter.'

She looked at Plinta.

Her eyes were like a flash of blackness seen through blue smoke.

Yes, she was beautiful. A perfect, sculpted face, large dark eyes – blue? – black? – whose lids were just barely touched with kohl, a long aquiline nose (perhaps she was a Jewess?), a wonderful mouth, not large – yet full, and capable of lengthening its shape – blushed either with rouge or uncommon good health.

She was not young. That is, she was about 25 or so, Plinta thought. Not that, physically, she seemed much older than 16. Yet her eyes knew things. Perhaps her clear and unlined eyes were even older – thirty, forty – *fifty*?

Plinta, the artist, now realised why he had thought of her pictorially and specifically as a beetle. Her black dress wrapped her closely, thrusting up a velvet glimpse of breasts, holding her corseted waist like two tight ebony hands ringed with gold. Her hair, too, which she wore partly loose, was quilled and rayed with gold – wings.

He thought, distinctly, *She is a vampire.*

'Madame,' he said, and bowed.

'Oh, but, Monsieur,' she said, 'I'm not married.'

'Not yet,' agreed Dumière. Now he reached out and took hold of her, like the tight hands of her dress on her waist. 'Come on, let's dance.'

As he led her away, she glanced back once, and directly into Plinta's eyes.

What was her name? Had Dumière not told him?

The next evening, as Plinta, who had just left his bed, lay on the sofa reading the morning's journals and drinking bitter coffee, his shambling servant Colas showed Israbel into the studio.

Plinta did not get up. Then he thought he had better, to be rude was too obvious. So he rose. But, when he did that, she laughed at him.

She said, 'I saw last night, Monsieur Plinta, you'd penetrated my disguise.'

Today she wore very dark blue-green, with a lemon plume in her hat. She was still like a beautiful beetle. Or maybe a lizard –

'Disguise? I didn't know you'd worn fancy-dress, madame.'

'Oh yes, of course. Always. But you saw right through to me, didn't you? As if I were – naked.'

Plinta felt at once an unmistakable and vivid surge of lust. Positioned high in his own brain, he looked down at the lust, tingling and flaring about in his body, and said, cautiously, 'I don't know what you mean, madame.'

'I'm not "madame". I have only one name. Israbel. Under that name I sometimes sing and act at the Opèra.'

'Very well,' he said. 'Please sit down.'

She too, he sensed, saw right through him. She knew what he felt, still felt. She knew, too, he was still in command of himself.

Israbel seated herself. She drew off the plumed hat, and her hair fell all around her, down to her waist. There were no longer golden quills and spangles in it, yet it glittered with strange gilding.

'I want you,' she said, 'to paint my portrait.'

'You honour me. Alas, I'm very busy.'

'No, you are not. You haven't had a commission, nor any paid work, for 18 months. You mustn't forget, I know Dumière, who knows you.'

'Dumière doesn't know everything about me, I'm afraid.'

'No. You're a secretive man. But your painting is interesting. Wouldn't you like me to sit for you?'

'Frankly, Madame Israbel –'

'You wouldn't,' she finished for him.

The door opened. In blundered Colas with more wood for the stove, for it was a chilly evening. Israbel watched Colas, then she turned her eyes back to Plinta. And, annoyed, he realised he had been hungry for their return to him, sulky in the split second of her looking away.

Colas banged the stove door shut again and lumbered out. Like two interrupted lovers, they resumed their murmured conversation.

'Dumière may have told you, monsieur, I'm well-off. I can pay you handsomely for your portrait of myself.'

'Why do you want such a portrait?'

She said, without hesitation, 'I'd like to look at it. I'd like to see myself in it.'

And, before he could quite stop himself, if he had even meant to stop himself, Plinta added, 'That being because a portrait is the only way you ever could see yourself. Am I correct, madame? You don't reflect in mirrors.'

Israbel smiled once more. It was difficult to take your gaze away from her mouth – unless you looked into her eyes; and then you could only look at those ....

'I note you understand my predicament, monsieur,' she said, as if they had spoken of something dull.

Plinta decided not to reply.

Israbel got up, and as she did so, even clothed in her fashionable Parisian dress, something fell from her like a seventh veil.

'Others are fooled, of course,' she remarked. 'It's commonly thought no-one can make out a vampire in a mirror. But naturally anyone can see us reflected there – save only we, ourselves.'

'Then you have kindred?' said Plinta, between wonder and alarm.

'Perhaps – but I've met none of them. No, no, I'm quite alone. I speak of them only in the historical and mythic sense. I belong, you understand, monsieur, to an ancient sisterhood, brotherhood, packed with persons. Except I've never met any of them.'

'Then how did you become what you are?' Plinta asked, inevitably.

'If I tell you that, will you paint me? Will you give me my mirror, Monsieur Plinta?'

He turned his back and walked off to the window.

Stood by the frozen glass, he gazed down at the icy, barely lit streets running toward the River Seine; the bell-clanging local church; then, to the sky like black lead. But talking to her was a game he seemed unable to give up playing.

'Why do you want to see yourself, madame? Anyone else's face can tell you how beautiful you are.'

'Not yours,' she said.

Plinta lurched inside his skin. In utter silence, she had drawn physically close to him. Her narrow hand was on his shoulder. Almost as tall as he, she leaned to his ear: 'I'll tell you my story anyway,' she murmured, 'perhaps ...'

Plinta did not move. He wondered if she would sink her teeth, or some other blood-letting implement, into his neck. But he felt only her perfumed warmth, and then a coldness, and turning, he saw she was once more seated far off across the studio, her feet stretched out to the stove, drinking coffee like an ordinary human woman.

She did not appear at the Opèra very often. When she did, she always took some small cameo part, usually limited to a single appearance lasting maybe five minutes, during which she sang an aria by Handel, Rameau, or Voulé. Her voice was good, if not especially brilliant, but nevertheless, a great hush would grip the theatre while she voiced her lines and sang her music. She was always rapturously applauded, and flowers rained on the stage.

She was said to have slept with some of the richer or more notorious patrons – bankers, poets, that sort. None of them had ever seemed any the worse for it. That is, none of them mysteriously died or otherwise disappeared. None of them, perhaps, more to the point, metamorphosed in any way. They merely went on with their own earthbound lives, long after they parted from her.

Men did become infatuated, of course. One had drowned himself, Plinta thought. Plinta had never paid her name much attention, nor even seen her, until Dumière became in turn obsessed by her.

Dumière took Plinta to dinner at the Café d'Orleans. Here they ate oysters and various roasted meats and drank wine and liqueurs. Dumière spoke mostly – solely – of Israbel. Plinta, to his own consternation, listened with interest and completely failed to be bored. He had already agreed with Israbel to paint her. There had seemed to be nothing else he could do. He did not tell Dumière, however, as if this were a guilty secret. He sensed Dumière would call him out over it to a dawn duel in the Bois, and perhaps shoot him dead in jealousy.

Dumière was not really Plinta's friend. Dumière used him as a sort of social musical instrument, a piano perhaps, coming up to him and playing him with enthusiasm for a few hours now and then, even in public, in restaurants and salons, then forgetting him again entirely for months – years – on end.

Plinta watched Dumière all through the dinner. Even over the crystallised fruits, brandy and cigars, Dumière seemed the same as ever: handsome, spoiled and charming.

Finally, when they were drunk enough, Plinta said to him, 'Have you had her yet?'

'*Had* her?'

'The kiss that is more than a kiss.'

'Why, Plinta! What do you think? Aren't I irresistible? Isn't she?'

'You have, then.'

'You prude! Do you want me to describe it?' Amused in victory, Dumière glowed above the glowing cigar. 'Well? I will if you like.'

Plinta thought he *would* like; that was, his *body* would have liked to hear every detail. Conversely, his clever appraising mind was also highly curious.

'No, thank you.'

'I'll tell you this, Plinta, she isn't like any other woman I've ever known.'

'Doesn't the new lover always think that?'

'No, of course he doesn't. How absurd. We *pretend* we do, but we don't.'

'Then –' cautious still, Plinta leaned back – 'then how is she *different*? Is she perverse?'

'No such luck. Not that anything like that is necessary with her. Oh, her skin's soft and smooth, her hair's a marvel, she has a special scent she wears – like spice – her body is lithe as a snake's. It isn't any of that.'

'And *do* you mean to marry her?' asked Plinta, as Dumière fell silent, hypnotised by absorbing thoughts of Israbel.

'I might. I wouldn't mind it. Just to keep her to myself.'

'Do you think you could?'

'Yes. I'd put her in a cage. Like a panther. She only lets me visit her at night. She's nocturnal, like most panthers.'

'A *cage* –?' Despite himself, Plinta was shocked, mostly at Dumière's suddenly active imagination.

'Oh, I mean a house, man, a big, glorious house – but I'd have the only key. I'd keep her there. Do you know,' he added abruptly, 'the strangest thing is when she looks into a mirror. I bought her one, you see, a gorgeous thing from Italy, silvered glass, gilt cupids – she stood in front of it nearly half an hour. Staring in at her reflection. She had such a puzzled look – a *sad* look – as if she were searching for something she couldn't find – I wonder what …?'

Her soul, Plinta thought.

Worse than Dumière's invented cage-house, a door slammed in Plinta's heart then, trapping him inside with Israbel.

Israbel told Plinta at once she wished to pose for him in the nude.

This, rather than excite, made cool sense to him. After all, if she wanted to see *herself* – which no mirror could now ever show her – she wanted to see her flesh, *not* her *clothes* – she need only look into her wardrobe to behold those.

When she came out naked to the lamplight from behind the studio screen, he noted, unsurprised, her body was beautiful. But Plinta had seen the beautiful unclad bodies of women – and men – often in his trade.

What moved him was Israbel herself. Her gestures, expressions. Even the sound of her voice. For she would talk to him as he began his sketches.

Her voice was pleasant, restful. It was elusive, too. Neither young nor old, barely even feminine. A slightly tarnished silver voice, to vie with the gold glints in her eyes and hair.

He found her easy to capture on paper, and presently on canvas. Even her colours were simple – cream and black, with highlights of turquoise, navy and warmer tones, like shining metals. But her red mouth burned for him.

What would it be like – not to kiss – but to be bitten by the teeth of that burning mouth?

Plinta recalled that awareness he had had before, of the casting of a seventh veil – less the provocative act of a dancing Salome, it had been as if Israbel *cast a skin*.

She had not yet, despite her pledge, told him the tale of how she became what he knew she was, a vampire, who lived on the blood of others. But, for that matter, he did not know when or how she took blood. She had never approached him in any way, either in seduction or attack. Naturally, she would want the portrait completed to her satisfaction first. However, one day he would finish.

He actually considered, twice, following her when she left the studio, to see her method of predation. Yet he never did.

What would he do if she suddenly turned her attentions on him? Would he allow her his blood? Would he be able to prevent her?

He was not afraid of Israbel. He was not in love with her. But obsessed he was. Intellectually and artistically at least as much as physically and in his emotions.

A winter dusk brought her early, while a thick sun fall bubbled behind the church like sweet apricot preserves.

The painting was almost done, and he permitted her, when she asked, to see it. She had never asked before.

She stood a long while staring at it, just as Dumière – whom, now, Plinta had not seen for two months – had described with the costly cupid mirror. For one awful second, Plinta thought perhaps she could not see herself in the painted picture, *either* – it was a very exact likeness.

Then she said, 'Oh, thank God. There I am again. Oh, yes. Thank God.'

'Do you know, can you guess,' she whispered presently, when he had sat her down, wrapped her furs about her, given her cognac, 'what it's like – *never again to see your own self?* Oh, there are whole peoples, I know, who never have mirrors and so never look into them – but even so – they may see a reflection in some surface. And here in this city – a polished table-top – window – a pool. Think of me, I was so young. Gazing instead at my hands – my feet – my *shadow* – because my shadow I still have – trying to remember myself from that. I pulled my hair across my eyes, too, and looked at my hair. But myself – my face, my eyes, my mouth – forever gone. All of you could see them, *all of you* – all save I myself. And they were *mine*.'

'The penalty for everything else you've gained,' he said. Was this harsh? No, only a fact.

'True,' she said. 'Nevertheless, I have outwitted the penalty, or I *shall* do so. With the help of Plinta the Painter. Do you know, Plinta, the oddest thing – I'd only seen myself four or five times in any case, before I lost the ability to view my own reflection. In my – shall I even say *home*? – in the slum where I was born, there were few mirrors. Despite that, as I've said – once in a window-pane, and once a table polished with my hand – and once in a pool of rainwater in a gutter, and once in the side of a bottle – but once a man gave me a piece of looking-glass. I looked, and truly saw myself, and he said, *Now you do as I say, or I'll cut that face you see across with my razor.* I did what he said. He still took off his belt to beat me. I hadn't pleased him, you understand. That was when I ran. This, Plinta, was about a hundred, a hundred and seven years ago. It was in the era just before the Revolution. Paris was raw and smarting, not yet seething – I didn't notice. The city was like a model made of wet newspaper. Unreal. And I must only escape. So, I escaped, as you see.'

He said, 'You became what you are now.'

Then she told him.

The great cat in the Place du Coeur had approached her so suddenly and so swiftly, seeming to move as if on wheels, that Israbel had had no time to think, or to decide after all once more to run away. Next second, its body touched hers.

The body of the cat was warm, she said, as a hearth, or a summer stone, and its pelt was smooth, velvet-soft, yet prickling with electric life. The instant they were in contact, a vast soothing, in fact a feeling of *content*, flooded Israbel. 'It was like the first time I ever tasted good brandy.'

The Place du Coeur was now, she said, long felled, its yards and hovels squashed and built over. Alleys attenuated from it however, then and still, creeping toward the Ile de la Cité.

Israbel remembered only this, walking very fast with the great leopard, whose neck was long and who was as tall as a horse, both it and she unseen and incredibly unnoted, through shadows and night. Here and there bleary lights shone in the rain. Sometimes loud displays of inebriation, rage or merriment flowed round the edges of their progress. For everything like that seemed divided by their passage, like a river, which they swam together, she and the cat, effortlessly. They came eventually out onto the open spaces before the Cathedral.

Notre Dame, Our Lady of Paris, was that night herself lit to gold and smoky red. In her windows, dark blue fires and rubies. Far above, her demonic gargoyles craned, peering over and down at the city, their wings locked until midnight should strike in some other dimension and let them loose.

But the leopard drew Israbel away down a sort of slope, and into a cavern under the street. She could not say exactly how it drew her. It was as if she had become invisibly connected to its skin, the vibrant *spirit* of its short, dense fur, which led her along like a benevolent leash.

'What did I think or feel? I was only happy. I felt quite safe, going down into the dark. If instead it had somehow drawn me up the very heights of the Cathedral, I couldn't have been afraid.'

In the cavern – no, she had sometimes, in later years, looked for this spot by Notre Dame, never found it, nor any entrance to it – was the leopard's lair. The stone floor was dry and thick with straw and rushes and scraps of material. The air was warm yet clean, faintly tinged with the incense of Notre Dame, freshened by little cracks and other apertures. She smelled the river, too, wholesome as the rest.

She lay down against the cat, which held her between its great muscled forelegs, the paws resting around her, without a hint of talons. It breathed into her face. And its breath was healthy and clean, and smelled only a little salty.

'Some of those I tell this story ask if the cat then ravished me, as lions can be trained to do with human women. Yet no such thing happened at all. Oh, it wasn't like that. It was as if I lay again, a child, in the arms of my mother or a father who loved me tenderly. I never felt so secure, nor have I ever after. So I slept, my head on one of the huge arms, against the breast of dappled fur, to the rhythmic hymn of its breathing.'

Israbel paused. This hiatus went on and on.

Plinta said finally, 'And then?'

She sighed. 'I woke up. It was twilight. I felt well and strong, as if I'd eaten a nourishing meal and drunk a little wine. And as if I'd bathed in hot scented water – that was how I now smelled. I wasn't under the city anymore. I was on a backstreet against a wall, out of sight, where it must have taken me when it was done. I might have dreamed everything, but for knowing I was glad it wasn't daytime, and for the sense of well-being, of *vitality* – neither of which has ever left me since. Even so, I started to cry. I ran about, trying to find the way back down to my beloved friend – for yes, the great cat had become my only friend and all the family I had. Of course, I detected no way and not a single clue. I never saw my leopard again. Presently, instead, my own – no, *human* – kind discovered me. And so I learned my powers over them, what I could do and gain. What I had become.'

'A vampire.'

'An immortal thing. Naturally limited to the night, but otherwise able to exist as she wishes. And fed – *cherished* – by mortal blood.'

Plinta roused himself. He felt cold and sleepy, inert and depressed, all the opposites of what she had described her own feelings to be.

'But how had – this cat – taken your blood – how had it refashioned you?'

'Do you really wish to know?'

'Yes –'

Israbel lowered her eyes of black turquoise. 'The pelt,' she said simply, in a sad, low voice, 'the beautiful fur of it – every fibre leached every atom of my blood away, and filled me in return with the ichor of the vampire race.'

'Its *fur*!'

Plinta surged up. He strode up and down the studio, rubbing circulation back into numbed arms and hands, stopping only to shovel more wood into the stove. The room seemed hot – yet he was freezing.

When he happened to glance at the clock, he was astounded. Two hours had passed since Israbel had first arrived. The moment he looked at her now, she too got up. She had not taken off any but her outer garments, the furs. It seemed she did not, tonight, mean to pose for her portrait.

Certainly she did not, for she said then, 'Monsieur, your picture of me is all I could ever hope for. You've given me a very special gift. Now I shall pay you.'

'It isn't finished!' Plinta exclaimed. He himself heard the panic in his tone. It was not only the unfinished painting that troubled him. It seemed their commerce, hers and his, was at an end.

But Israbel only nodded gravely. 'Not quite finished, I agree. But that's as it should be – as it *must* be, don't you think. For neither am I, monsieur, *finished*. Nor, perhaps, can I ever be. The picture has reached the very stage I myself am at. Like me, it must remain there, or how can I see myself in it?'

Plinta stood still. He stared at Israbel, memorising her, her grace, elegance and otherness.

'And so,' she said gently, 'let me settle my account with you.'

'I don't know,' he said, 'what this picture can be worth.'

'Everything.'

'Do I ask everything of you, then?'

'You know that I'm rich.'

'Don't pay me,' he said, 'in money.'

'Then how?'

As she questioned him like that, Plinta saw in her a total fatal innocence. It had nothing to do with naiveté or foolishness. *I must never lose her*. Aloud he said, 'Show me.'

'Ah.'

188

'Show me how – *pelt* – can take blood – *how you feed yourself.*'

The crudeness of the words he had used, and his desire to find out, both appalled him. He was humiliated by himself, and trembling, but even so would not deny what he had said.

She answered, 'If you wish. But – I'm hungry, Plinta, Monsieur Plinta the Painter. If it's to be you –'

'*Me.* Who *else!*'

'Then, I shan't hold back. You must become as I am. Do you want such a thing?'

Plinta thought about it. But he had been thinking of it constantly, behind a screen of debate, arguing with himself that, in fact, it was not possible. But it was.

'Madame Israbel, I have so much to learn of my trade. That alone would need immortality. I'd like the time. I don't subscribe to the idea that, being always myself, I must become less. I think one must be able to *evolve* – even in the same continuing body. Yes, I'd give up the daylight. But I too am already partly nocturnal. I sleep through a day, rise at sunset. But more than that – I want to *know* –'

Israbel turned her head. This was as if she listened, obediently, to some angel at her right shoulder, who now told her what she must do. It seemed she knew the angel of old. Its advice was always sound.

Before, he had seen a seventh veil fall from her.

Now Israbel touched the bodice of her dress, and the yellow silk parted and dropped, like a veil, and all else with it. As before, she stood in front of him naked. Her hair, loose and gleaming, framed her face, neck and upper body.

Plinta felt a stab of sexual appetite so intense it hurt him. Then he grasped it was not sexual at all.

She came to him as her kind did, as the great cat had come to her – sudden and swift, gliding as if over burnished ice.

And as she came, her hair, her *hair*, lifted up on her head in two wide, black-flaming wings, glittering with tines and prisms of diamond, topaz and gold, and as it fastened on him, and her flesh met his own clothed body, he felt the touch of her, hair, skin, her eyes, her lips. Oh, not like mother or father. This was like the meeting of mortal man with god.

Plinta seemed to lie that night high up on the roofs of the Cathedral, among the army of gargoyles that, as a white moon rose, flew back and forth, scratching their claws on the parapets, their eyes full of misty smoulderings.

Here, Israbel took his blood, not biting, but through her skin and her hair, the soft persuasive caresses ebbing and swelling like a symphony.

He understood that, in the future, he too must take sustenance in this way. But *her* hair, so long and thick, had become two wings, like those of some giant Egyptian hawk. She too, he saw, as he lay quiet between the delicious bouts of her feeding, flew off the roof, into the sky and stars. Sometimes she even gripped the gargoyles, held them, while both they and she soared across the moon, her hair coiling them, their tails wrapped around her. Did she take blood also from their carved stone, replacing it with immortal vampiric essences? Of course, how else were they able to fly?

Near dawn she closed his eyes with her lips, a kind of kiss.

'Sleep now. Be at peace. Asleep, the sun can't harm you. Tomorrow night you will be changed.'

'Then tomorrow, where shall I meet you?' he said. But Plinta discovered he could not, now she had shut them, open his eyes, and she did not reply, and had drawn away. A colossal slumberousness stole over him. He sank into it, not minding.

In the dream then, a sleep, which itself held a dream. In this second trance, he saw Israbel after all, her face framed now by the velvet and silk curtains of a stage. Wings flew out from her skull. Her eyes were highly reflective – like a pair of looking-glasses. Otherwise, her face had no features at all. It was a faceless face, a perfect, blind face, of fabric stretched taut on bone.

Colas found him the next evening. Plinta lay stiff and marble cold, and looking bloodless as marble, there on the studio rug, splashed by the dregs of a sunset.

Colas gave a yowl. Howling and yelping like a wolf, he rolled Plinta about the floor, and when neighbours rushed up the stairs, wailed that Plinta had died, was dead, and now Colas would be slung out on the street – Colas's only actual concern.

'No, you dolt. Look, he's waking up. *Dead? Plinta?* Only drunk –'

Plinta woke. He stretched, and Colas, who genuinely had seen him minutes before dead as the deadest corpse, backed away gibbering.

But Plinta himself felt wonderful, like a prince who is in love and has, besides, dined on a banquet. He threw a boot at Colas, and Colas, at last reassured his patron was the same as ever, tramped off to fetch the coffee.

Already the marvellous dream – of the Cathedral, the gargoyles, the vampire, and her attentions – was fading. Of the dream-within- the-dream did anything remain? Maybe not. But Plinta soon noticed Israbel had taken her portrait away with her. Why not, when she had bought it, and at an excellent price. Next time he saw it, the picture, he would be again with her.

One last splinter of dream-memory did linger, however. He had asked her where he should meet her, Israbel his sister, now, in blood. But he had been stupid to ask, for he had not needed to. Tonight, as much of Paris knew, Israbel was due to act and sing her glimmering five minutes at the Opèra.

Plinta threw his mirror into the cupboard before he left the studio. Now a vampire, he could never again see himself reflected, and had duly proved as much with one or two contemptuous glares at the glass. Others, though, *would* see him in mirrors and not suspect, just as Israbel had explained.

Would she be glad, at last, of his company? They were brethren, and she had admitted she had discovered no kindred, just as never again had she located the supernatural cat.

Two moods possessed Plinta as he walked the glacial streets of Paris, moving toward the golden ornament of the theatre. One was an elation not unmixed with eager fear. The other was a deep melancholy, a sort of shadow. The first state he comprehended. The second puzzled him. Was he in mourning then for his purely *human* life, now ended? What did that matter? Nothing, not at all. But no, it was not that.

He stood in the light-spiked dark, and thought, *Perhaps immortality is only formed, for us, from those countless days we may never now experience. A life of nights, doubled.*

All things are paid for. Even Israbel had paid for the painting he had made of her.

Plinta took a box at the theatre, a rare extravagance. He soon glimpsed Dumière across the auditorium in a box of his own, with other friends. Dumière saluted Plinta, pleased to see him at a distance. But how jealous Dumière would be, if only he knew. Had he offered Israbel marriage? Israbel and Plinta were married, in more than religion or legality.

One flesh –

Where shall I feed? Plinta thought, as the curtain rose on some spectacular unimportance. *She will show me. She will be my teacher.* Then he sat back, watching the acts of the play through half-closed eyes, and all about the theatre rustled and murmured, whistled and called, alienly alive. He imagined it was like being in the zoological gardens. He had never felt a part of them, the human race, and now was not.

To great clapping and calls, Israbel came out in the fifth act, as the programme stipulated, to perform her part and sing her aria, which that night was by Rameau.

Plinta sat forward. His eyes widened. His heart, or some more profound mechanism, slammed high into his chest, then leapt away, down into a chasm. Tears rolled, helpless to save themselves, from his eyes.

If he had been able, in those minutes, like the Biblical Samson, he would have risen, grabbed vast pillars of the Opèra temple, and brought it crashing down.

Samson had lost all. Plinta too had lost.

Now he could never know, he who must learn *everything* – whether or not he had loved her. Instead he would be, like the rest of his kind, bereft, and quite unique.

On the stage Israbel sang, and the audience hung in wild suspense until the last note, then bellowed its applause and flung its flowers. And across the theatre, Dumière sprang up and raced, fever-flushed from his box, to seek her in the dressing rooms.

But Plinta stayed where he was, still as when Colas had found him and thought him, rightly, dead. Only the mobile tears ran on from Plinta's eyes.

For she had warned him, had she not? Even his mirror, in its own cruelly amusing way, had done so. Certainly his inner dream of facelessness. No vampire could see itself in reflection – only human things could see it there. But that was not only in mirrors. No vampire could see any vampire – themselves or another – either in a mirror, or anywhere in the whole crystal globe of the heartless, lonely, reflective world. On the stage, Israbel was taking her bow. Plinta alone did not applaud. To him she was now entirely inaudible and invisible, just as he was now entirely inaudible and invisible to Israbel, and to all their kind.

REMEMBER ME

From an explanation of origin by John Kaiine.

I

His first memory: darkness, fear, and the smell of water – then two dots of flame, a shape – something that snaked toward him – and ordinary fear changing to whitest terror.

He was three years old, maybe just four. He would never be sure of that. Before the first memory was a nothingness, like death, except he had obviously been alive. And anyway, beyond true death lay another life. He would come to know that, quite soon.

Years after, he realised he must that evening have been stealing from the market stalls, mostly things dropped on the ground. He was hungry, and he had lived like that, stealing, or begging. But there were other thieves and beggars in the grey little town below the mountains, and they had no compassion for any small weak dwarf-thing called a child. So they set on him, and then, getting the taste for it, chased him. He would have run down past the squat cathedral, along roughly cobbled alleys, toward the river, and there crawled in at one of the flood drains that ran away under the town. His adult pursuers were too big to get in, or else he had already lost them and only been too afraid to know he had. Certainly they never followed.

In the flood drain he lay until dusk closed the shutters of the sky

193

against the world. Perhaps he slept, exhausted, there on the shelf just above the water. Rats sometimes swam by below, but none of them troubled him. Later, too, he would think he could just recall the rats. Did he believe the red-eyed thing that was suddenly sliding toward him was itself a rat – a great rat, a king of their kind, come after all to tear him into pieces?

He had no name, and nameless and alone, he waited, the child, whimpering, for the last cruelty and the final blows.

'Whaar tiss thiss?'

So it sounded to him – language he knew, but sibilant and also guttural – an accent. Till then, he had heard only one accent, that of the townspeople.

The voice spoke again. The same words. Now the child knew what they meant.

'What is this?'

He found he had shut his eyes. He opened them, and looked, because surely even a rat king could not speak any human tongue.

A man's face, close to his, very pale, the skin extraordinarily clear and fine, so *pure*. It might have been carved from whitest ivory, and was hard like that, too, with strong narrow bones. It reminded him of the face of one of the saints, probably seen, though not properly remembered, in some religious procession. The eyes were dark. And the voice ... that was dark, too.

'You are a child,' said the voice, deciding.

He could say nothing. He stared. In his brief life, everything had been anyway quite strange, and often senseless. Unkind also. And so when the man stroked back his hair, with a hand that was the perfect companion to the pale, carved, saintly face, the child did not struggle or try to run away.

'What are you doing here, child? You crawled in and lost your bearings, did you? You're too young. Unripe fruit. Only scavengers and weaklings, or those themselves childlike, take your kind before they are grown. Come, I'll lead you up out of this place.'

The saint who had entered the flood drain like a serpent, and whose eyes of shining scarlet were now black as ink, swept the child into his arms. The saint had a curious, not unpleasant smell, like a plant recently pulled from soil, the moist earth still scattered on its leaves. His breath had been wholesome when he spoke, for, as the child would come to learn, he had flawless teeth and lived on a flawless nourishment. Any corruption eventually smelled on such breath had more to do with the rot of the soul.

But what happened next was bizarre enough. At the time the child could not grasp it, it was like those events that happen in dreams.

Afterwards, he would be used to it, and to many similar actions. He would think them all usual, indeed, *enviable*.

There was a kind of rush – a sort of flight, inside the drain. Either the stones gushed back, or the man arrowed forward, the child borne with him. Then wet and darkness opened in an O of brilliant lesser dark. The sky was there, streamered with windblown stars. There was a scent of coming storm. Underfoot, the muddy bank of the river, and close by, one of the ugly little humped bridges, and not so far away, the few leering narrow lamps of humankind.

'There then. Here you are. Go back to your kin, little child. Go back and grow up. Twelve or so years, that will do. Then maybe we shall meet again.'

Turning, the man, in a swagger of black garments, left the child, there on the ground.

The child stood rooted to the mud.

He saw above him the sky, and nearer the miserly lamp-stars on the banks of the river; he smelled the stink of *people*, and heard the murmur of their heartless minds. From the cathedral, midnight struck.

Then a shadow flicked somewhere under the bridge. Probably it was nothing, only a stray dog perhaps, as desolate and desperate as he, but it woke up again the child's terror.

And with a noiseless cry, he came unrooted from the mud and ran after the tall figure that walked so incredibly swiftly away from him.

'Papa!' cried the child, aloud then. 'Papa! Don't leave me –' Where in God's name – yes, God's – had he learned that name *papa*? He never knew. It simply rose in his mouth as the tears rose in his eyes.

But the stranger paused, a hundred yards away along the bank. Then, turning, he came back – and was there beside the child, impossibly, at once. Down from the tower of more than a man's height, he gazed at the boy stood crying before him. Perhaps the man was bemused – or *a*mused. It could not have happened often, this.

'Why call me back? What do you want?'

'Papa,' said the child.

'I'm not your papa. I doubt you have one. What is the matter with you? Go away.'

But neither of them moved. And presently the man leaned down and picked up the child again, raised him high up in arms like steel, looked at him with eyes like ink.

'What shall I do with you?'

The child flung his own arms round the neck of this saint. He seemed to have been born, the child, in those moments. New-born, of *course* his first cry had been *Father! Father!*

The saint laughed. Amused, then.

'I am named Schesparn. Don't call me *papa*. Say my name.'
The child said the name.
'Come then. You shall go with me.'

That night-morning, they went east of the town. The mountains, which then encircled and shut the boy's universe, were as ever immense and craggy, and now blue-veined with starlight. At first he thought they would fly right over them – for of course, they travelled in the air. But Schesparn only went a little way, some twenty miles, maybe. They moved by a form of levitation, or merely juxtaposition, one place to another. There was no changing of shape, not then, for Schesparn carried the child in his arm, and *needed* an arm, to do so.

The estate lay along a lizard-tail coil of the river, deep among pines and then the lighter woods of birch and ash. The house was a mansion of ornamented, decaying stonework. Vast windows glared like beautiful outraged eyes, all glass gone, only the iron lattices or webs of leading still in them. Not a single light showed.

The storm came in those minutes, catching them up, and the old house too. Clouds like huge masonry figures lurched low overhead, cracked with lightnings. Then the storm had passed. Only a white fluttering was left behind in the sky.

Although they had travelled quickly, summer dawn was not so distant. In at one of the wide casements Schesparn bore his charge, and dropped him gently on a floor like watery agate.

Rather than disturb, the lack of lighting encouraged the child. He had only ever been taken into the lighted areas of mankind for some type of punishment. Although he did not remember in after years, the moment of the eyes in the drain being his first adhesive memory, at three or four, no doubt he did recall that lit rooms meant nothing good for him. He liked this domestic darkness therefore, instinctively. He liked the darkness and pallor of Schesparn, the only person who had ever shown him care or any interest.

Then some of the others came.

First was a woman. Her name was Stina, he would learn shortly. She glided forward over the dry watery floor, and she was pale as Schesparn, dark of eye as he was – and, like him, for a second her eyes flashed red. Her mouth was red, too. By the lightning flicker, with innocent acuity, the child saw both the real colour and what it must be, for it ran down her white chin, over the pearly column of her neck, in at the bodice of her gown. But out of her mouth slipped a long tongue, and took the colour away from her face, yes, even off her chin. A white hand attended to the rest, and then she licked the hand, with eager grace.

After Stina, three others entered. They were all men. Every one of them had a likeness to the others, despite some differences of build, hair colour or eyes. The woman too was like this. They might all have been of one family. They *were*.

'Is *that* for us?' one of the men asked Schesparn.

'No. Unripe.'

'True. But perhaps, *sweet* – I've never tried lamb or veal.'

They laughed.

Fearless now, the child also liked their laughter. He laughed too.

And then Stina said, 'How brave he is! Look, how trusting. Come here, little boy, come to Stina. Let her see you close.'

'Go then,' said Schesparn. 'She won't harm you. Not yet.'

But the child had been peeled of fear, at long last. So he went directly to Stina, who crouched down, and looked deep into his eyes. And when she smiled, her teeth were clean and her breath had only a warmth on it, as if she had just eaten a little roast beef and drunk a little wine.

'You are a nice child, I think. Not pretty. But look at your forehead and your skull. A head for intelligence. Oh I had to leave a boy like you, he was my darling – so long ago …'

She took his hand. He gave it.

The man who had asked if the child was 'for' them also walked over. He had dark red hair. He said, 'What's his name?'

Schesparn said, 'I think he has none.'

'I will *christen* you then,' said the other man, whose own name, the child would learn, was Mihaly. 'I will call you Dracul – Dragon.'

Pleased, the child looked at him. Never ever had there been such benign interest, such involvement, from others.

These others sighed and whispered. Some more had come in. They were like ghosts made flesh – never, *never* the other way about. And then, their leader entered.

His name was Tadeusz, for so they addressed him, respectfully and at once. He was older in his looks, his hair grey streaked thickly with white. Yet his physique was like that of a robust man of 25. They all, male and female, older or younger, had firm and perfect faces and bodies, which the child – 'Dracul' – would come to see through the years, both costumed and bare.

Tadeusz looked in turn down at the child. After an age, he spoke. 'You do not know where you are, where you have come. But one day you will be one of us. I choose you, for Schesparn has chosen you. Those we love and keep we never choose lightly. Be aware, we are not kind, as you think us, little boy, little Dragon. We are so different from anything you know, so changed from what we ourselves once were, that we can hardly be expected to abide by the codes of men. But *you* shall be safe among us.' He raised his head. He was like a great wolf, striped with ice, yellow-eyed.

The others nodded. All of them were there by then, all the family that lived in that house. 'Now I will give you your first lesson. You must learn, my dear,' said Tadeusz quietly to the child now called Dracul, 'to sleep by day. Soon the sun will rise. Though some of us may bear it, it is never easy, and some of us it would sear away. Therefore, by day, we slumber. Learn to love instead the night, little child. Night is day to us. And now to you, also.'

The child minded none of that. His life had had no patterns. Now it did. He looked adoringly up at Tadeusz. Father first, then mother. Now grandfather, the patriarch and ruler of the house. How the boy had come by such instant physical categorisation, he could not ever know, as even then he had no memory left of a beginning. But certainly Dracul knew, at last he had come home.

He was used only to sleeping without comfort, and on hard surfaces. So to find somewhere to curl up in the carved, pillared and otherwise generally empty mansion, was simple. Besides, he knew that here, no-one would hurt him. That was a luxury.

Why had he been at once so sure? They had mesmerised with their hypnotic eyes and touches. They had, their kind, great power over his. Just as they could control wild beasts, they could, largely, control savage humanity.

But also – he believed them. Especially Tadeusz, the Old Wolf.

Probably, as he was to think, the child, two decades after that night, had *actual* wolves adopted him and shown him some kindness, he would, like other feral children of whom he later heard, have trusted them, become one of their own.

Sunlight streamed in across the floors, cut little shafts between the columns behind whose bases he had elected to place himself. He woke now and then. But he had slept through days before, having nothing else to do.

As for his name, he prized it, turning it over and over in his mind, even asleep, like a precious jewel. He did not yet, although they had, apply the name to himself. He merely considered it his *possession*. It was the first.

When the sun set, he woke and was thirsty. But he had already found a large room, a hall or court, where a fountain played into a basin. He went and drank the water, which tasted dusty. Leaves had blown in at windows and the open roof, perhaps only last autumn. Some lay in the basin. Frugal with always starving, and having eaten, the day before, a piece of cheese rind and a rotted plum, he did not think of seeking food.

The crimson sky darkened. He knew they would soon arrive, come back from wherever it was they had gone to. He knew infallibly, and maybe they had told him, sunset was dawn to them.

Schesparn and Stina came first. They brought another woman, young, with ash-blonde hair, who was called Medestha. Stina said to Medestha, as they were coming in, 'You understand, *this* one is not for the usual purpose?' And the blonde head nodded. The two women washed the child's face at the basin, and combed his hair. Then they played games with him, having brought a hoop, a ball, and three little bats. Soon the red-haired Mihaly came in, and he had a dead rabbit, which he skinned, then handed to the child a small portion, raw and dripping. 'We do not cook our food, Dracul. Be like us. It's much healthier for you.'

The child – Dracul – took the meat. It was like nothing he had ever known – rich and succulent, savoury and sweet together. He sank in his teeth, and they watched him, the blood running down his chin. It did him, the raw fresh flesh, the blood, great good.

II

Dracul learned them, his companions, like a book. First their faces and names, next their ways, swiftly their magician-like talents and abilities.

He knew, having been instructed by them inside that second day-night, what they *were* – Streghoi – Nosferatu – Oupyrae – Varcolaci – Vampires. The Undead.

Did that mean anything at all? Had he ever heard them spoken of among the haunts of men? Not knowingly, ever. And why was that? Because no men, nor women either, had ever spent any time with this boy, save to ill-treat and chase him with stones. He was as alien to his own race as were his hosts at the mansion – though, like them, he too had been human once.

Now, naturally he altered. Loving them, enthralled, petted, protectively taken on 'excursions,' he aped their manners, longed to be as they were. All that, even despite seeing, after the shortest while, examples of their more terrible – and grosser – acts. But how could it not be so with him? What had humans, also terrible and gross, shown him, or offered? This demonic wolf pack was his family now. And they had promised, from the first, one day he should be one of them. Just as initiation, the rite of passage, was held out before all valued and aspiring males. As was quite normal, he feared it, did not properly grasp what must occur, yet *longed* to be ready and to be made like the rest of his new tribe.

After the first, Dracul seldom went out diurnally. He was trained inside a week to sleep day long and wake at sun fall. His skin paled and grew clear almost as theirs, from the 'healthy' diet of bloody raw meat and juicy fruits – for orchards raved about the upper edges of the forest, pomegranates and peach trees, and higher up the stony sides of the land, orange trees lit bright with moon-washed globes. His night vision strengthened. He saw as he had never done – a snake like black silver in the silvered black of grass – a tiny flaw inside an emerald ring, shaped like a milky hand.

He saw too, shown without reservation, their acts of miracle and magic. How they might *disintegrate* to pass through some obstacle, like snow or mist, how they might raise themselves into the air, or drift across a sky in human, or in other, form. He saw them *change shape*, to bats – wolves – and puzzled as to how it occurred, as if their bodies parted like curtains to let the other creature out. He asked Sraga tenderly if it hurt her to change herself in this way. And Sraga laughed. 'It itches,' she whispered in his ear. 'Then one *scratches*.'

'How can she explain?' said Faliborv. 'You will come to know.'

'Will I do it right, when my time comes?' worried the anxious child. 'How will I know *how*?'

'Your body will be refined and wonderful by then, like ours. Your body will know how, by itself. It's simple to us to do these things, simple as breathing. We are immortal. We are gods, Dracul.'

They were gods. For sure, they were the gods of Dracul. And cruel as gods, uncompassionate, avidly noncompunctious and amoral.

They preyed on all the villages and towns scattered, flea-like, through the tree-furred landscape, and up the flanks of the mountain crags.

Sometimes they took Dracul with them. He rode the winds with one, or two or three of them. Arpaz took the child most often, as if on a hunting trip, and showed him first a narrow house against the wall of a church. The church was beautiless, vegetable in aspect, yet it fascinated Arpaz, as such buildings sometimes did the vampires.

'Do you smell the incense, Dracul?'

'No.'

'That sweet smoky smell – sickening – yet irresistible …?'

'No, Arpaz.'

'One day you will smell it. Nothing is finer than to *take*, right beside one of these shells of their God, who does so little to protect them.' But, passing by the church on the way to the narrow house, Arpaz, gliding like a shadow through shadows, ducked his head aside as if at a blow, where the old crucifix of ancient wood angled from a tree. Arpaz would not look at the God, though he spoke of him with scorn. Nor would he pass any closer to the church than the house.

In the house, a woman was. She was young and fair-haired, and she slept.

Arpaz drifted to the window, the boy somehow borne with him.

The girl on the bed stirred, uneasy, flinging one arm, brown from summer daylight sun, across her face.

Arpaz purred to her then like a great cat, sat there in the window embrasure, purred and hissed and slipped over like velvet into the room, and covered the girl up against the night like her blanket. There was no real movement, not like the struggling plunging scenes of human sexual activity Dracul must sometimes have glimpsed, in horrified disbelief. The girl sighed, and her long plait of hair slid over and along the floor, and then a little vermilion thread dripped down into it. That was all. They went five nights in a row. Once Stina joined them, once Cesaire. The last night there were two big rough men waiting in the room, but Arpaz stood below purring in the dark, having sensed them, and going up, the men too were tranced to a coma-like sleep. Then Arpaz choked. He sneezed and hawked and spat on the floor, backing away. 'Dracul, darling,' he moaned, leaning at the wall as if he might faint, frightening the boy, 'do you see there, those stinking bulbs and flowers – gar-gar-garlic. Move them away, throw them out on the street for me – ' Dracul rushed to help Arpaz. Once the allergy-causing flowers were gone, Arpaz recovered himself. He stared, his eyes burning like red-green coals, at the unconscious maiden. 'You shall pay for that,' he said, and going to her casually, tore out her throat with his clean white teeth.

Schesparn also took Dracul 'hunting.' He had a penchant for caves, tunnels – doubtless why the child had first met him in a flood drain. Travelling this way, rather than having any real sense of forward momentum, Dracul seemed to see the stones instead melt off them in a maelstrom. In towns, emerging from under the earth, Schesparn bent over drunks in alleys, or sleeping guardsmen even, in their barracks, three together, while the boy stood watching in admiring astonishment. Schesparn required the blood of men for his sustenance. Mostly, however, the vampires had a preference for victims of the gender opposite to their own.

Dracul was privy to the suborning, by handsome Cesaire, of a female goat herder on the hills. Cesaire enjoyed the seduction, it appeared, as much as the conquest, and drew the procedure out, meeting the girl twice under the stars before finally overwhelming her. As she sank into his arms, the arch of her white neck offered to him like a slice of moonlight, Cesaire remarked, lingeringly, 'How I adore the reek of goat on her. How earthly she is. How utterly human.'

Chenek and Faliborv were more violent. They would often work together, waylaying young women straying home too late from some mortal tryst or other fleshly business. They felled these prey animals with harsh blows, or leapt down on their backs from trees like panthers, pinning the women to the ground, stifling the screams only fitfully, allowing legs to kick: a form of rape.

Béla hunted always alone. Mihaly was the same. But these were the two who hunted beasts also, sometimes for themselves, and always for the child. In the end, as he grew older, they taught Dracul the ways of ordinary hunting for survival. Though they could, like all their kind, call and draw wild beasts to them, they took a keen interest in the ordinary hunter's skills they had, presumably, possessed in their prevampiric existence.

Nevertheless, lessoned to hunt, Dracul was still envious of that knack of drawing deer, wild pig, and birds of any kind, by the inexplicable charismatic spells of vampire magic. It was Tadeusz himself who drew the wolves to the mansion on certain nights of the full moon. Huge packs would stand, a grey-black tide of pelt, crystalled with eyes, singing their eerie, breaking hymns at the sky. Then Tadeusz, the old leader, would walk among them, stroking their heads, so they whined with pleasure and bowed to him like favoured human courtiers.

The pursuit of human blood, in the case of Tadeusz, the boy, even as years passed, never saw.

Dracul was nine before Stina permitted him to accompany her. Of course physically virtually unaging, she was beautiful, a girl still, and hand in hand they walked on a dusk riverbank, until a dark young man came striding from the fields over the hill.

'Oh come to me, my dear,' called Stina, 'come to me. Here I am. Come and kiss me, beloved.'

The young man turned, and his eyes clouded and brightened, both at once. As he went into Stina's embrace, Dracul felt within himself a new and distinctive urge. It was sexual, but he did not realise that. He thought, with pride and some relief, he too was now coming to desire the drinking of blood. But he was patient and modest. He kept the awakening to himself because he had yet to become a god.

Long before that, in the first year he was with them, Tadeusz had decreed certain matters must occur in Dracul's life.

He called Schesparn and Dracul, and the three of them went to a library high in a square stone tower.

'Since you are, in some manner, his guardian, Schesparn, you may teach him the rules of our life, our needs and codes.' A look passed between them. It was the compact of something, but Dracul did not know what. As he grew older, he came to see, he thought, that Schesparn would be the one to change him, alter him into the being of a vampire. The process stayed always mysterious to Dracul. For although it involved some of the acts of blood he saw the others perform on humans, there was more to it, naturally. Many of those the vampires fully drained did change, rising from graves and deathbeds, becoming a *sort* of vampire – thing – but it was a moron, a kind of automaton, mindlessly lusting for blood, filthy and stinking, with matted hair and the claws of a lion. The soul seemed gone, so much was plain, and the ghastly machine easily trapped. Usually the native village, or other community, settled these zombies swiftly.

In the making of a true vampire, where soul and flesh fused to create an immortal of barely imaginable powers, other rites must additionally be carried out. It was done only for those they loved and wished to keep by them, and seldom done lightly.

Why had the vampires decided to rear the child for this signal honour? Some sentimental thing perhaps, both in Schesparn, and most of the tribe … Stina missing her lost son, Mihaly wanting a boy to teach hunting – human foibles somehow remaining in the luminous material of vampiric life.

Yet Tadeusz, the leader? More gentle, more *implacable* than any other of the band, he had not accepted Dracul, nor allowed him to keep such a name, out of special fondness.

As it seemed to Dracul – a parade of years later, and no *longer* Dracul – Tadeusz had noted something in the randomly rescued and worthless child, some quality of steel, of *self-will*. But at the start of it all, the boy had not known even that he had a self, let alone any will at all.

In the library, nevertheless, it was Tadeusz who began to forge the child from clay to iron and bronze.

'*I* will teach you books, Dracul. If you can read, you may learn anything. See, here – ' His white hand swept across the dark air of the room, describing the cranky ebony shelves, piled high with masked, secret blocks: books, to one who could not yet read. Dust was thick there, and the webs of spiders. Beetles had eaten a way in at certain tomes. Despite that, there was enough. More than enough.

Tadeusz taught the child to read. He did it hurtlessly, and by a method of hypnotism, Dracul presently thought. For one moment he stared at a page covered by an unknown alchemy of symbols – *next* moment he had begun to decipher them. Words – sentences – mental landscapes having no borders.

Nor was it only a single language that Tadeusz lavished on the child. Latin and the purest Greek he gave him, High German, Russian and French. English too, an outlandish teeming tongue, made apparently from an amalgam of all others. 'Be advised,' said Tadeusz to the child, 'sometimes, when you speak to a man in a language that is his, and not your own, it is wise to make a few little slips. If that time is also fraught or dangerous, you may wish to speak gauchely and clownishly, too. For that way he will in turn say and reveal things to you he might not otherwise attempt. And you will likely, if you must, catch him out. Or, if you may rely on him, that you will learn also. The wise are often best served by appearing imperfect, nor too clever. The higher you ascend in one region, the better to frolic and seem ignorant elsewhere.'

Dracul relished these lessons. But he loved *all* the lessons, including the killing of animals for his food, Cesaire's and Stina's seductions, Medestha's childish wiles upon other children scarcely older than Dracul had been himself.

Dracul had been a land burning up with drought. And now the drinkable rain fell on and on. Cascading water for thirst. One day – blood.

He did not confide in Tadeusz, not dreams, nor questions, beyond those of the student. Dracul loved and respected Tadeusz, half feared him, in the way it is possible to fear someone also loved and respected and trusted – fearlessly.

But he loved them all. They were his kin. And he, was theirs.

Twenty years on from then, or was it thirty – forty – a *hundred* – he had driven her mad, literally mad, the human woman he had taken to himself. With *his* nightmares, *his* regrets, *his* rages, anguish – his *erudition*. His *strength*. With all that remained of love, respect, and fearless fear.

From his seventh year, Dracul slept by day, as they did, in a grave.

He had been shown the scrolled stone boxes, filled with earth, containing always elements of their indigenous soil. At sunrise, the lids were lowered, either that or the bed of stone lay in some vault, far down, where daylight never penetrated.

The sun was wasps and scorpions to the vampire kind. It could burn them, tear them. If very vital they might endure it, but never for long. Some would perish in less than a minute should the light fall on them. It was like acid.

One day-night, then, when he was seven, he lay down with Sraga in her box. This had been done to accustom him to such a resting place, before he should have to do it alone. She smiled, and put her arms about him, and slept instantly, as if her life had ended. Sleepless an hour, Dracul stayed looking at her.

Without doubt, they slept – *like the dead.* You could not rouse them. They were helpless at such couchings. Initially, Dracul did not like to believe this, and surely they never said as much. But it was obvious enough.

When he was 12, Dracul had it proved to him, anyway. The event was, at that time, the worst incident of his life.

The vampires spread their activities over a wide area. Travelling in air or mist, running as wolves or flying as bats, they maintained so colossal a territory, they usually eluded too much specific attention.

But Cesaire had fixed on a particular family, and these lived in the nearest village of all. First he had the daughters, all four of them. Then the mother, who was still young and good-looking. All five pushed up from the graveyard with earth in their nails and blood between their fangs, and were put down by the village priest, an irate old man, part crazed, and full of energy.

Following that, the brother of the sisters set out after Cesaire. No-one else would go with him. They were too afraid, even the yowling, hammering priest. But the younger man, a sturdy woodcutter, got through the forest and the birches, and climbed up from the river, the mountains above like silver in the morning light.

The crumbling mansion and wild estate were known of a little. The woodcutter found his way. He got into the house by climbing the face of the carven stones – rather as a vampire might have done it – and stepped through one of the casementless windows, to spring down in the hall.

All was deathly silent, the 12 occupants asleep. The priest had tutored the woodcutter well, and besides, this man had witnessed the curtailment of the zombie second lives of his mother and his four siblings. He had stakes with him of sharpened ash wood, his axe, haft good as any hammer, and a cavalry sword that had lain in the church for a century, rusty but serviceable. Round his neck hung an aromatic garland of garlic, and his mother's silver cross, which she had thrown off for the vampire.

It seemed he knew not only Cesaire was in the mansion. He thought he might get one or two more, if they were present – he had brought five stakes, the same number as his familial dead. He knew that a vampire slept by day. What he did not know was that one of the vampire tribe was not yet vampiric, and slept by day only from choice and habit.

Dracul woke from his human slumber, hearing a noise in the house that normally, from dawn till sunset, was silent. He believed some big animal had got in, and decided, for once, to get up and hunt it, since it had been foolish enough to attract his notice. But the light was so shrill in his streaming eyes, for some while he could barely see. In that condition he almost came to reckon it would be better to leave the animal alone. After all, what harm could it do? Dracul's kin were safe under stone lids or behind vault doors. For the furnishings of the mansion, a handful of antique chairs, cabinets, beds, they were very few, and anyway eaten by moths and damp.

Then though, he heard a sound deep down, down where the vaults were, under the house. And it was the note of something metallic striking, and next of a door opening. Only one animal could undo such a door.

Dracul ran down the stairways of the house toward the vault, and coming into the blessed dimness, could see again. He had been very quiet, having peerless teachers in that as in so much else. The thickset man bending over Cesaire's grave box had not heard anything beyond his own racing heart.

For Dracul, he himself was transfixed. Yes, he had beheld other people – mortals – frequently, when he was in company with his kindred. But *never* any human thing in a position of power over a vampire.

Dracul stood leaden, unmoving. As if helpless in a stupor, he watched the woodcutter heft one of the ash stakes. There was no lid to this box. They were in the vault. Only the light the villager had made, three small wavering candles, illumined Cesaire, lying there handsomely cataleptic in undead sleep. Dracul could have made him out by now, in any event, with no light but that of his own night vision.

But the woodcutter lifted the ash stake high. Although Dracul had heard the *modus operandi* described, *en passant*, by the vampires, who effected no dread, he had never *witnessed* it. This time his mind was slower than his eyes, his body slower yet.

The plunge of the stake, even that, though it horrified Dracul, did not quite bring all his faculties together. Cesaire's scream of fury and agony did so. Dracul bounded forward. Then everything was there at once. He saw Cesaire's wide-open *knowing* eyes, locked like rigid jewels in his immobilised face. *Saw* Cesaire's body already spasming, the hands ripping at empty air. *Heard* the smash of the axe haft coming down as the pointed shaft was hammered home, right through the heart.

A spout of blood burst from Cesaire's chiselled mouth. His eyes grew cloudy – just like the eyes of certain victims of the vampires, when the love-spell-trance enveloped them. Then his eyes went blank. He was – no longer there.

The woodcutter still had not noticed another running up to him. He swung the cavalry sword and lopped off Cesaire's fine head. It lay there on the pillow of earth, marble pale, absurd in its charm and loathsomeness. Then one of the remaining four ash stakes thumped into the woodcutter, back to chest. He half turned, gaping, and saw, judging by his look, a sort of imp – a monster – before the world fell over into darkness. No vampire, the stake had not even needed to pierce his heart, only his intestines. He was humanly dead in minutes.

Dracul did not look at that. He was lying in the grave-bed by then, with Cesaire, holding the dead vampire in his arms, weeping, howling.

He knew it was no use to try to wake the others. By day, once they slept, it was almost impossible to do so. Only Tadeusz, he had gathered from their talk, had sometimes been awake by day. But Dracul had never learned where the leader lay down to sleep. In that insane hour, Dracul vowed he must find out. For of them all, surely Tadeusz might yet have saved Cesaire. Yet Dracul knew also from the talk, the lessons, that these two reductive strokes, the heart-stake, the decapitation, as with sunlight and burning in fire, were the only deaths a vampire must avoid. They were final.

When the others appeared at sundown, looking for Cesaire and for the boy, they found Dracul, there in the vault. Cesaire lay smooth, his head replaced against his body, face wiped clean of blood, eyes closed.

The woodcutter, Dracul had hacked in pieces, employing the man's own axe. As a last statement, Dracul had stuffed his mouth with garlic, and stabbed the silver cross into one of his eyes.

The event of Cesaire's execution was in fact another lesson. When it happened, Dracul did not understand this. Or if he thought it valid instruction, then of another meaning completely. Grieving for Cesaire he found, to his vague surprise, a novel estrangement from the others. For they, after the first shouts of calamity and distress, did not seem to suffer much. Nor Sraga, either, whom Cesaire had made his own and personally altered to the vampire condition, only two or three decades earlier. Tears had run down her face. They were tinged with blood, like palest rubies. But it lasted only moments.

As this – what was it? – *indifference* – was borne in on the boy, he became deeply offended. Somewhere in his unremembered past, he must have seen human funerals, and more recently observed the laments of persons who had lost relatives, lovers or friends to the vampires. Human beings had this quality. Those they cared for that died, they mourned. Yet the Nosferatu, it transpired, were with their own kind also heartless, callous. Rather as they left the butchered woodcutter to rot and rats on the vault floor, they cast Cesaire out of doors, into the sun, and let it burn him up. Like emptying a pail of slops.

Dracul took his problem to Tadeusz.

The boy was taller now, tall and thin, hard and strong. He confronted the old wolf leader of the pack, courteous and overawed as always, by Tadeusz, but with scorched affront.

'Didn't they love him?'

'Yes. Cesaire was ours.'

'Then why – *that*? Why do none of you –?'

'It is a fate any of us may share. Yet, too, we have no vast fear of death, for it is nearly forever avoidable among us. Humankind demonstrates hysteria at human death, but this is a form of panic, for each of them knows he too, today, tomorrow, or in fifty years, must experience the same extinction.'

'You tell me it's cowardice then, not sorrow.'

'To a degree.'

'What then do *I* feel? You promise me immortality, yet I still mourn Cesaire.'

'You are yet human, little Dragon. Listen. Mihaly named you after a very great and mysterious member of our universal family. It was his joke, perhaps, though affectionate enough. And you may grow to reap the name. That one you are named for was a great warrior, and a noble and intellectual scholar, a rare combination. At his changing, he became less and also far more than he had ever been. Yet, even in his human state, before vampiric prowess came to him, it is said he had no fear of death, and both gave his enemies to it, and faced it out himself, laughing. Laughter is king, Dracul. Misery is only negation. Laugh, Dracul, and loudly, in the face of fear and death, or desolation. Give the dead no tears of yours. They, none of them, nor yet Cesaire, can use them. Nor yet can you.'

Dracul – named for some legendary warrior-scholar of the vampire horde – went out and roamed the midnight woods, laughing, *yelling* with laughter, till his throat bled. In the hour before dawn he returned to Tadeusz and knelt at his feet. 'You were right.'

But then he asked Tadeusz where he lay through the daylight hours. Because, if ever this occurred again, Dracul would run to the place and rouse Tadeusz, who might then intervene.

'Ah, Dracul. If it is only the stake, then sometimes it is possible to save us. But the severing of the spinal cord – head from body – after that, it is finished. But I will show you my bed. If you need me, I will try to wake.'

It stood behind a secret wall in the library. It was dark as pitch in there, and smelled of moist earth and green plants, and some other tindery scent, like a cedar scorched by lightning. Maybe that was the odour of Tadeusz or his slumber, for it was always there, in that cubby behind the books. Dracul knew, for he went there twice, by day, about a month after Cesaire's slaughter, and looked for Tadeusz, and found him lying asleep, and the scent was more rich. The leader slept with his eyes open, like a golden snake. Yet *he* was not behind them. Since vampires did not die, did they perhaps instead die in some temporary manner while they slept? For it was obvious, they went far off. To bring them back took the trumpet of sun fall, or the throes of personalised true death. Dracul, seeing the patriarch, the grandfather and king of his adopted life, did not believe he could be woken after all, only by a human boy, however frantic the demand.

III

Until he was 18, or 19, they waited.

That was a proper age for him to alter to their condition, they told him, when – as after his fourteenth year he did – he grew urgently impatient to be as they were. Once changed, he would age very little, and very slowly. He must accordingly reach manhood, before the ordinary process was stopped.

The day-eve of his birthday – that was, where Tadeusz had fixed his birthday, for he himself did not know it, no more than if he was 18 or 19 – Dracul could not sleep. He prowled the hills, looking at everything with sun-inflamed, sore eyes, for the very last. Five, six, or seven nights were needed for his transformation. After that, he would probably never see the sunlit earth again. He thought he was not sorry. He was eager for godhead, and a magician's powers.

That night they had a breakfast feast, in which Dracul joined. Fresh human blood had been collected in a large crock. Next, goblets of tarnished silver were filled with it. Everyone drank deep, Dracul with the rest. Accustomed to the raw bloody meats they had reared him on, he did not mind the blood, was only a little disappointed that it did not yet thrill him. In the past, sometimes, one or two of them had awarded him a sip of blood, smeared on their fingers from a victim. He had been like a child given as a treat a sip of alcohol. He had failed to see much in it. Which had not yet been rectified, but soon, now, would.

Tadeusz spoke some words. Excited and nervous, Dracul barely heard them. Then Schesparn came and led Dracul into one of the smaller stone chambers.

There was an old bed there, its canopy long eaten away and posts fallen. Mice rustled in the depths of the couch, but Dracul had no fear of mice or rats. Presently he would be able, if he wished, to command them. He lay down.

Schesparn sat by Dracul, and stroked back his hair.

'So it is to be now, my friend. Are you content?'

Dracul nodded. He was alight with expectancy, already running before he had assayed a single step.

Schesparn murmured, the purring chant that soothed and controlled. Dracul tried to sink into it, to allow it to do its work. But he had seen this done, listened to it, so often – partially he had become *immune*. Nevertheless, he turned his head, offering the vantage of his neck, the vein there, to be milked.

Perhaps he, or could it be Schesparn himself, misjudged? They knew each other too well. Trusted too much. Or perhaps it was not that at all, could never be only that. The sharp teeth, like great needles, pierced inward in one snapping bite. And at once on the pain, from which Dracul had not flinched, came an awful drawing, a tugging of darkness, and the young man felt his very psyche come loose inside him, and begin to unravel up through the two wounds in his throat. He had anticipated much, something wonderful – *spiritual* – even, he later thought, *sexual*, for he believed he had seen versions of both transports happen in the vampire's victims, yes, even sometimes those Chenek and Faliborv had forced. There were neither now for Dracul. It was only horrible – *disgusting* – and it filled him, he who had looked for anything but fear – with sheer primal terror. For it was death itself he felt fastened there upon him. Not a friend and mentor, not his rescuer, his 'Papa,' nor even his brother or lover. *Death*, stinking of corruption and the repulsive muck of a grave.

So Dracul fought. He did it without thinking. It was spontaneous. But Schesparn, far gone already in his own trance, the ecstasy of drinking living blood, struck Dracul randomly a solitary blow, that had behind it, naturally, incredible strength.

Disabled then, swimming in unspeakable swirlings of pain and miasma and horror, Dracul lay, till Schesparn was done with him. And after that, the others came, like ghosts. One by one each of them sucked out a little more of his life. Tadeusz the leader, first, a moment only. Mihaly, Béla, the hunters, slower. Medestha with a childish little murmur of enjoyment, Faliborv rough, biting him again, Chenek strangely mild, perhaps bored. Last, Sraga, then Stina, Dracul's too-young mother. They had done this because they honoured and cared for him. It was a ritual act, not greed or sadism – but in the nightmare, he no longer knew that. And even when Stina … The feeling and sense was of death, still, of a reeking mouldy corpse, its breath raucous with foulness. And once she too was finished, her cold stony hand on his forehead, 'It's done for this night. Sleep now.'

And into sleep, as into death, he tumbled – screaming, but in silence, dying but yet alive.

Dracul woke at noon. The sunlight pouring in beyond the columns that guarded his box, cut through his eyes like knives. He writhed from the earth bed and threw up on the floor. Then he wept. He kneeled snivelling on the flagstones. Shivering, he dragged himself to the dim hall where the fountain played, and drank the water on and on, a river of it, unable to get enough, until once more he vomited. Then out into the sunlight he staggered, the sun right overhead like a boiling spear, its razor-beak in his brain.

Five or six more nights. He must be brave, and patient. The prize would come to him. Had he really never grasped he must suffer to achieve his longed-for goal? But he knew, Dracul, he *knew*, it was not the suffering, not even the dying that he feared.

How had this happened? He loved them. They him. Yet – *instinct* – or less even than that. *Humanness.* He was human, perhaps more so than most. It was his humanness. It would not let him go, he who had thought of himself, since the age of three or four, as the kindred of vampires, and a student-god.

Push it down. Hold himself in fetters of steel, and allow the process of god-making to take place. Even then, half lying on a tree, whimpering from sun, nearly blinded, Dracul knew he could not.

Yet he tried. That night he tried, and when Schesparn came to him again, Dracul saw the face hover above him, and it was not that of Schesparn, nor any saint, but of a fiend. And Dracul shouted aloud. 'Hush,' said Schesparn, 'be still.' And he sang the purring chant, and now it did not work at all, and despite the fetters of steel Dracul had attempted to put on himself, again he lashed out, and the cuffing paw of the undead smashed him down into oblivion. Much that was Dracul did die then, though it was not yet any fleshly death. It was his love that died, and sympathy, and belief. Later there would come to be what he thought a greater and better belief, one that resided not in men or monsters, but in a single God, brilliant and distant as another sun. For with everything else this young man had learned, he had learned that the Devil existed. And if that were so, God also must exist. One had only to claim Him, and reach out.

When Dracul woke the second day, again at noon, he rushed into the sunlight and let it sear him till he fainted. If the steel had not been able to hold him quiet, still it was there. He had lost his faith and his name. Who was he? A *man* – a *man* of flesh and *blood*.

He knew them too well. Recognised all their charms and spells and tricks – had even gained some of their knack for himself, not noticing, beside the vastness of their talents, that his abilities, now, were something remarkable in a mere human. Oh, he had been well taught.

That afternoon, he walked again among the trees. As if bidding farewell to some beloved, he began to mourn for the loss of day, even though it hurt his eyes, for the greenness of the leaves against sunshine, the colours of fruits in solar light.

Long before sun fall, which had been dawn, he had found an ultimate solution. Deranged as he suddenly was, he thought he heard them laughing, his tormentors, as they slept in their tombs, musing on how they would drain him dry. No, it had been only their game, to keep him, like a favourite calf, letting him grow to his fullest deliciousness, before seeking him with cleavers. Make him their own? Never. He would become what all the other human things had become that he had seen. A mindless automaton, addicted to blood, less than a beast, and, since probably the soul did stay trapped within, damned for all eternity.

In after years, when he had another identity, had *become* another – that was, as he thought, become *himself* – he brooded and wrestled over and with his past, both his time of living among Satan's creatures and his action finally on that last day. Reasoning it through, in ghastly dreams and waking nightmares, he came to see that he had had no choice. For he had only been englamorised, could never have loved them – must in fact have *hated* them, and their vile deeds, yet been unable to see it, like treasure stored in darkness, until they attacked him. Beyond that day, of course, he must *always*, therefore, hate them. Hate them best of all the world, both natural and supernormal. And when he had reasoned it all out, this ranting mental hell, which by then would have driven his wife to madness, it would in turn have driven him, at last, quite sane. But all that was in the future. All that was yet to come.

As the sun westered over the mountains, he went into the house. He found what he needed very easily. The legs of the ruinous old chairs were simply enough refashioned, for though leeched of so much blood, he was fit and tough and not at all near death – they had told him, it would be a formula of seven nights. There were even some ready-prepared weapons, carelessly left lying about, from the previous drama years before. Not to mention a rusty sword.

One by one, he went to them, the young man who had been Dracul. One by one he eased up the lids of the boxes, or stole into the shadows of the vaults where they lay. It was always the same. It did not shock him, the outcry, the eyes, the blood, the severed head. He had seen it before with Cesaire, after all. *He* had at this time no compunction. It was a dirty job that, as with the emptying of night-soil, must be done to make existence a cleaner place.

He visited Tadeusz last of all. Schesparn had been the first, and Stina the second, Mihaly the third. When Undracul drove in the final stake, the open wolf eyes of Tadeusz closed instead. Out of the ancient lips issued, not a shriek, but a breath, carrying two words.

It was this curse of Tadeusz's that would haunt the man who killed him, long, long after he had become that other studious, secretive self, who was called Van Helsing. Those two words would also catapult him onward, into freedom, into hell and out of hell, toward a future that was all to do with explaining and tidying the past. '*Remember me,*' Tadeusz breathed as his life went out of him. Van Helsing's own life became then itself a tomb, the words carved in its granite. He had murdered 11 helpless beings who had perhaps, probably, loved him. If it was not to be his fault, it must be theirs – they and their kind. *Remember me.* Van Helsing, who had learned every lesson perfectly, would never forget.

NIGHT VISITOR

Something scratched at her window. What was it?

A fearsome sound, like long claws scraping over the glass, and then little random thuds. Some creature was beating on the pane, wanting to come in –

She thought, *Imagination. The branch of a tree that I forgot could whip against the window in a strong wind.* But there was no wind.

Anna rose and went to the window.

She stared, and saw – not a branch, not a bat or a night bird – but a tiny vampire, perfect in every detail, small as a child's doll, his black cloak crimson-lined, furling around him, his hungry teeth glittering.

Anna flung open the window with a wild cry.

'Dracul – my beloved – who has made you into a miniature – who has *done* this to you – I will *kill* them –'

THE THIRD HORSEMAN

The hunchback kicked open the door. Uncouth, and grinning his large blunt teeth, he announced: 'Your dinner, Count. I have brought your dinner.'

The man in the carved chair rose to his feet. He looked through the twilight at the pale figure of the girl the hunchback was ushering into the room.

'Don't be a fool, Ygore.'

The hunchback, half resentfully scowling and half intimidated, slunk into shadow by the stair. The girl came forward alone, and the door thudded shut.

'An idiot,' she remarked. 'How he must irritate you. I suppose you keep him ... for the obvious reason.'

'I promised him something of the sort. And he is useful, since I have the primitive leanings of my ancestry: a desire to accommodate my guests.'

'I see. I noticed the bruises on his neck. He's strong. I suppose it can go on some while.'

'Not indefinitely.'

'Nothing,' she answered, 'can do that.'

She drifted to the seat he offered her, and sank lightly into it. He remembered her. He remembered most, perhaps all of them. In the twilight she looked more ghostly than she needed to, her long, smoke-blonde hair, her blonde dress, her slender, bone-pale face and hands, and throat. She still affected a masking device. In her case a ribbon of wine-red velvet. It was an irrelevant affectation now. He was a dark counterpoint to her pallor, or he believed he must be. The incredibly bleached skin was the same in both, of course. He could see it in his own white hand, reaching out to perch little moths of fire on the candle branch.

But he found it easier to recognise her face than he would have done to recognise his own. An aberration common to them all.

'Forgive me,' he said, 'I forget your name.'

'Berenice.'

A strange melancholy pang went through him, the inchoate vignette of a rambling house, a midnight lawn, trees and stars, excitement, sorrow, bitter-sweet; everything faded by time.

He said, 'Yes, I recall now. And you've come to recite to me how it is, and to curse me probably.'

'No,' she said. In her eyes were the same faded emotions his brain and heart had conjured for him. 'Never that. But to speak the truth. If you will listen. You comprehend, your servant was mistaken?'

'Naturally. I've said, I recall our season together.'

'I'm sorry that I can bring you nothing.'

Their glances, which had met, slipped from each other. 'Don't regret that,' he said. 'To stave off the inevitable is always a futile dream. As you'll have seen from the others.'

'Others … yes. The far side of the mountains there was a village. They had found a child, four years old. They'd torn it to pieces, mutilated it beyond hope of resurrection. As my carriage drove past, I think they must have supposed I too – your servant's joke – was *useable*. They had killed all their horses – so they chased me on foot for several miles. I don't know how, they were so weak. One man almost caught up to me – his chalk-white face, the red eyes – but he fell. There were many villages like that, others burned to the ground. Animals butchered beyond butchery, or else wandering, or lying on their sides in ditches, black tongued … the cities were far worse.'

'Speak about the cities.'

'You wish it? Very well. I stayed one night in Paris, another in Prague, in Bucharest – In the stillness of the night, after the sun has set, a sound begins to go up. At first I didn't understand what it was. Then … I understood. A huge screaming, an enormous cry, of agony and despair. Then there are the wine-cellars. Red wine. They drink it and vomit. They resort to anything of a red colour. Vinegar even. Or paint. Sometimes they attack each other. There was a square; the moon was high and white. A hundred, or two hundred lay there. I imagined they were dead. Just before the dawn began to come, a handful of them stirred and started to crawl away. The rest – I saw a man and a girl in the fields of ruined crops beyond the old city wall. His mouth was at her throat, and she held his wrist to her lips. They made no movement. Shall I go on? There were great bonfires burning not six miles from here. I avoided the place. We raced by and the red glare filled the carriage and I heard bells ringing. There was a rumour Prague had burned, like one of those bonfires, and Belgrade; Moscow is blowing with the ashes of those who died in the sunlight, willingly.'

'And westward?' he said quietly.

'Everywhere the same. All Europe, America. Eastwards: Asia, Australia. All continents. All climes. It spread too far. And this came after.'

'Yes,' he said. He murmured something she did not hear. She did not ask what it was, but her sad intelligent eyes came to his face again, a question. 'I was considering the whales,' he said. 'How it was believed they would be hunted out, so great was our need for what we might get from them. And so eventually there would be no whales to hunt. And what then? But you,' he said, 'how did you manage to travel so far?'

'It's simple. There was a young girl I had found. I kept – hid – her in my apartment. And then, when I accepted how things were, I was extra careful. She was very sweet and innocent. Very loyal. I had to leave her at Bucharest. I saw to it myself. I cried when I sealed her in the box. It was in a private vault – she was safe enough, that way. But. She has nothing to come back to. I felt I should have stayed with her. She was so young. But she insisted, at the very last, that I go on. My driver deserted me a mile from the city. After that, I drove the horses myself.'

'And why did you?'

'Why?'

'Why did you go on? Why have you sought me now, if not to curse me?'

She looked down, at her hands. The candleshine glowed through them, gentle, revealing the shapes of bones, but no rosiness of blood. Beyond, the room was black now. In the window, framed by velvet drapes irrelevant as thought, the bleak nightscape was featureless, real only in unreality.

'You were the first,' she said. 'You re-made me in your image – father, lover, god – who could I run to but you, when the world was crumbling? There must be very many who would have run to you, if they could.'

In her eyes, cast up like wreckage on an ocean he seemed to see reflected the nights of her past that had involved him, that had formed this moment, and all brief future moments between them. The night he had seen her. The night he had – what word? – wooed, perhaps – wooed her. The night when she had sought him, drifting then as now, like a blanched paper doll over the lawn. She had sunk into his arms beneath the tall black tree. As the leaves rustled, she had sighed. He had lifted the blonde hair back from her throat, kissed her, kissed her and drunk from her crystal brim the ruby liquor of her blood. She had come to him three nights, for she was young and vital. The exquisite experience they had shared, that continually he had shared, that she would afterwards share with others, was mystical and beyond description. Yes, beyond description, which could only liken it to gluttony, to sex, to lust, or to some arcane religion … Unique, the ecstasy of the vampire, the sharing, the given gift of eternal life. Of course she died, on the fourth night. He did not see her daylight burial, but he saw her rise, resurrected from the stone tomb, drifting to him again over the sable grass, going out to hunt, to share, to take her gift of blood and joy and everlasting life to others, who, in their turn, would become as she. As he.

He was the Fountainhead. And, unlike the cistern, which contained, the fountain overflowed. Overflowed into godlike creation of sons and daughters, sprung not from his loins, but from his psyche. How could he have known, have reasoned it out? How could he, or any of his 'children', his disciples, have predicted that one became two. That two became four. And twenty and a hundred, and a thousand, a million ... Each one he took, remade as himself, he gifted. They in turn gifted those they took, re-made. Some perished, it was true, discovered and destroyed. But always enough remained of the – the *race* he had founded. Their numbers swelled. The fountain overflowed. It covered and consumed; the Flood. They drained the human world, sucked it dry, laid it out to rest, and beheld it return – as they had. As *They*. At last, beyond their kind, there were no others. A world all vampire, all hunter, with nothing left to prey upon.

Then began the bestial time. They seized the beasts and despoiled them. But the beasts did not satisfy. And even so, they beasts became as they were. Here and there, a freak chance, one human remaining, found, overwhelmed, lost. The blood in their own veins, second-hand, could kill. Despite this they rent each other, or fell upon each other in grief, the cannibalism of panic and anguish. For even everlasting life could not survive without its sustenance. Blood was not only food and drink, the succour of the flesh. It was that mysterious spiritual thing, that occult bonding, that brought life, and sustained it. No vampire could survive without it. Not only did they starve, their souls starved. Both starvations were agonising and terrible, and slowly, as if with nails driven through organs, joints and brains, by reason of their nature, they died.

She had not needed to tell him, really, of the awful crying that had risen in the streets – Bucharest, London, New York, Paris, Moscow; across golden lands and green, and white and grey. The howling of the damned.

The sorrow in him now was a void of silence. He was not sure that he cared that Berenice had come to him at the ending of the world, or if he were glad, or if it only made him more afraid. Love is dying, he told himself, causer of this.

'I'm touched you are here,' he said. He turned to the doorway. 'I shall call Ygore for you. Amusing, is it not? Something so rough and ready. But I promised him in the beginning I would make him one of us. He's too stupid to grasp that to be one of us, now ...'

She said softly. 'Don't call him. Please, I want no more than those things you also have. You spoke of the inevitable.'

'But did you guess what I must mean?'

'Yes.'

'Are you certain, Berenice? The sun brings a death of unspeakable horror. It may seem to last a million years of hurting. Those flaming white and yellow hells of pain that writers have described so ably. The other death, of famine, is scarcely less appalling, and besides, prolonged.'

'I must eventually experience one, or the other. There's no escape. Is there?'

'None,' he said, compassionate, almost tender.

She smiled a little. 'The first time I went to you, not understanding, I thought it meant death – total death. I was in error. Perhaps this other death too – But no, I do see. Yes, I do.'

'The Bible has it,' he said, strangely. 'The Third Horseman, who is famine, and the Fourth, who is death.'

Far away, through the hollow ribs of the castle, Ygore's grisly imbecile laugh dully resounded. Between the velvet drapes of the window, there was another sour red glaze beginning on the sky – not yet dawn, but fire, somewhere.

Berenice had unfastened the ribbon from her throat. The two small marks, like tiny leaden stars, put the Count in mind of a branding, less upon her neck than across his forehead.

Though, unlike Cain, he was not to be the first murderer. But the last.

Presently he took her hand.

Down in the depths of the castle, Ygore too fell silent. Intuitive as he was, he grasped fully that the time had come when he might end his own masquerade. Unlucky from birth, he had been maltreated by his fellow men. It had taken the vampire overlord to rescue him – a whim, maybe, some blind jest … But it had saved Ygore's neck, and perhaps his strong and intelligent mind. True, he had acted that he was the fool and peculiarity the Count naively always thought him. And also he had let the Count, and his guests, make free of his, Ygore's blood. A small price for the much nicer life he had led at the castle. Besides, the Count had taught him to read, and so opened up for Ygore a world far better and more beautiful than any, among the ignorance of his times, he could probably ever otherwise have known. For all this then, he blessed the Count. And now, the Count must die, and vilely, as were all his people.

Ygore could do nothing to save them. He had done all he could. Even to letting them enjoy their mockery at his expense. A great actor, Ygore. And – so full yet, so full of life.

He did not know what would become of him now. Indeed he dreaded the sunrise, his true and kindly heart aching and cringing in advance of the cries he would soon hear from above. He would bury their ash at least, with due respect. And then –

Crouched like a sad and humpbacked crow, Ygore foresaw his lonely future. As the Count had become the Last Murderer, Ygore knew the Laws of Life had other aims. His system, boosted by the many vampiric onslaughts it had endured yet not been finished by, would give him at the very least longevity. Perhaps therefore, when the shadow had fallen and had passed, one mostly human man might emerge from the rubble of all things, upon the surface of the blackened and broken world.

As the sun began to split the edges of the horizon with thinnest gold, Ygore stood, and braced himself against a pillar of stone. He was already weeping, but he did not stop his ears. The last thanks he owed his unthinking master was endurance in the face of another's pain. He had obligingly acted the idiot for centuries. Now he would be himself.

MIRROR, MIRROR

In the early winter a vampire began to call at our house. What made it so terrible was that my mother, who was wise and lovely and perfect, was infatuated with her. Inside a week she was calling the vampire 'Miriam', and they would sit overcast afternoons face to face, on the long backless couch, which caused them to lean together like two dark tulips in a vase.

Both wore black, my mother because she was still in mourning for my father, though he had died five years before. The vampire because, presumably, she favoured sombreness, just as she liked the night and the winter days when the sun was hidden in a cloud. Miriam the vampire's dresses were long, with tight boned waists and flounces. She wore black hats with veils fixed to her hair with an enormous ruby pin. When she came in the house she would draw out the pin and take off the hat. She would then play with the pin as if with a red berry or a drop of frozen blood. She was eccentric, and did not put up her hair as my mother did. Miriam's hair hung to her waist like the black cloud that kept the sun in. She was extremely beautiful, in an awful way, her face so white and smooth without a single line, so it was like the face of a child turned to marble. Her eyes were black and rather dull but large enough they must be called beautiful too. Her lips were the pale pink of a faded sugared almond kept in the dark.

All the children on the block knew that Miriam was a vampire. The moment we saw her we knew. The way she came from nowhere as soon as the sun was obscured, and vanished again if it chanced to escape. The way she walked in her black clothes and now and then looked at us with soft hatred, as if we were flowers she would uproot. Adults passed Miriam often with a second look, but without an inkling of what she was. We were aware, sadly, we too would move eventually into that realm, where we would be half-blind and half-deaf. It was the fee that must be paid for losing our half-dumbness. So soon as we had learned to speak fully, to control language, our other senses would be mutilated.

But for now, we saw the vampire and we recognised her. We understood it was only a question of time. And then, as in a horrible game, it was my gate she approached, and our narrow patterned steps she ascended. On my mother's door she knocked, and my mother fell in love with her at once and let her in.

I have no idea what excuse Miriam made for coming to the house. Perhaps that she was looking for some lost relative. It did not matter really. Within minutes, seconds, she had won. And I, returning from play, found her there on the long couch, her hat beside her, the pin twirling in her fingers, and her other hand uplifting a smoking cigarette in a long holder of bone.

My mother introduced her by some foreign name I could not assimilate and have forgotten. In any case soon it was 'Miriam'.

Soon, too, I came to know the particular grey afternoons, like dusks, when I would enter the house and find my lovely mother in the thrall of the vampire, on the long couch, with the long windows and long ruched blinds behind them.

'Look, here's Miriam.'

And the table would be piled with dainty cakes and jugs of homemade lemonade, and the matte lacquer teapot, none of which Miriam, of course, could ever be persuaded to sample, although my mother would beg her: 'You're so slight, Miriam. And with the winter coming … I must try to fatten you up a little, darling.'

When Miriam's leaden eyes would go over me, there would come the soft flicker of hatred once again. How easy I would be to pluck. When Miriam gazed at my mother her look was quite unreadable and dense. Yet in it my mother seemed to find irresistible magic. My mother had once stared into my eyes like that, but no more.

There was another reason too why the vampire had come to our house, beyond my mother's loving and marvellous nature.

Just as she must avoid the sun, and all holy things, sacred wine and bread, the cross, Miriam must avoid a looking-glass. And in our house there was none. The night my father had died of pneumonia, my mother had veiled all the mirrors, and later she had sent them away like wicked servants who had stood by and coldly watched her husband's final struggle and defeat. In rather the same way, maybe, she had locked up a drawer in the bureau that contained all his treasures, things I did not know about, as if no-one must be permitted to look.

For Miriam, naturally, a house without mirrors, which would refuse to reflect her and so would give her away, was a wonderful piece of luck. How had she known? But then, everything about her was mysterious and foul. Where for example did she come from and return to out of the twilight? Probably a graveyard, but none of us had dared to follow. The very swish of her skirt warned us we must not.

'Oh, Miriam,' said my mother adoringly, 'do try a little of this raspberry cake. I baked it just this morning.'

But Miriam did not touch the cake, only smoking her pale cigarettes in the ivory holder, and fiddling with the strange fruit of the ruby pin.

How long would it be before she could delay no more, before the exquisite foreplay could no longer be drawn out, and she pulled my mother into her rustling embrace and pierced my mother's human neck, and drank her blood?

Every night, when I kissed my mother goodbye before the journey into sleep, I examined her throat closely. Once she had scratched herself with a little brooch she sometimes wore, and my heart stopped. But it was not the mark of teeth.

I had never tried to *tell* her the truth, for I knew infallibly that despite her wisdom, because of the blindness and deafness of her adult state, she either would not hear or could not grasp what I would say. And if she found that I was Miriam's enemy, she might keep us apart. Probably my presence in the room, or the possibility of my arrival there, were part of the reason Miriam had held off from her deadly kiss.

In the monosyllables of our dumbness and lack of language, I conferred with other children. What could I do?

'If only there were a mirror,' said Dorothy.

Then Dorothy hung her head and made her confession. 'The vampire came to our house once. I saw her in the hall. There's granny's old green mirror there like a pond. And my mother saw in it. I couldn't see in the mirror, only my mother did, but she blinked, two or three times, as if something had got into her eyes. And then she said to the vampire, "No, I can't help you." And she shut the door.'

Dorothy and I realised that Dorothy's mother, being partly blind, did not comprehend what she had glimpsed – Miriam's invisibility in a reflecting surface. But nevertheless some preserving instinct had been activated.

It seemed to me that, since my mother was special, she, seeing or not seeing Miriam in a mirror, would know the truth fully. For my mother had beheld a fairy woman once in the park when she was all of 17. She had told me solemnly about the tinsel antennae and the tiny wings. So she had more sight left than most adults. It was only that Miriam had put a spell on her.

How then to bring Miriam to a mirror and to let my mother see?

In a way it might be easy, for when Miriam was in the house, my mother paid me scarcely any attention. I could have eaten all the cakes on the table.

Then again, Miriam was subtly conscious of me, as one would be of an animal one did not like prowling in the room.

Dorothy ran up to me in her big old garden. It was a sunny wintry morning, but by two o'clock the cloud in the east would have swallowed up the sun, turning it from gold to smothered silver.

In Dorothy's hand, a misty foretaste of that silver sun.

'My shell mirror,' said Dorothy. 'It's all I've got.'

We considered the mirror, staring down into each of our faces, puzzled to see ourselves so different from what we knew we were.

'There's a little loop,' I said.

'Yes, I hang it on the wall. Then when I sit my doll on the chest, she can watch her face.'

Dorothy and her doll were making a sacrifice for my sake, and I took the mirror carefully. It was the size of a small pumpkin, and the shells that decorated its edge hardly hid any of the surface. Yet it was light too, and would hang from the loop.

I took it home quickly. My mother was busy in the kitchen, sifting flour and stoning summer damsons, sensing of course that darkness was coming, and so, Miriam.

I wandered about the room where Miriam would sit, looking for a spot to set the mirror. Normally Miriam would surely detect such a thing at once, but I sensed that she was by now so involved with my mother, the clean scent of her, cologne and brushed hair, my mother's delicate skin with the tiny fairy antennae lines about the mouth and eyes, that Miriam's vampire cleverness was slightly dimmed. If I could only find a place that she avoided, perhaps she would not realise.

Ultimately it was simple. The area of the room that Miriam intuitively did not care for was, not unnaturally, the two long windows. She would seat herself on the backless couch, turned away from them, and would not look in that direction even if my mother went through this part of the room. My mother also had taken to pampering Miriam's aversion. When she guessed that Miriam would be coming, my mother let down the ruched yellow blinds, and today, already, they were in place.

Going upstairs I took a large safety pin from my mother's pottery bowl. Returning with it below, I stood on a chair and attached the loop of the mirror to the yellow ruched blind of the second window. Something useful occurred. The reflected yellow folds of the blind shone into the mirror, like a buttery sun into a pond. It was not easy to see. I got down, crossed the room and stood in my usual position, just beyond the table where the cakes and tea were laid. It seemed to me that Miriam, sitting on the right of the couch as she always did, would now be reflected from the back into the mirror. Except there would be nothing to show.

As the sun moved low over the sky and the cloud rose after it like a bank of fog, the light died from the windows and the mirror too turned dull.

A glorious smell of baking drifted from the kitchen. But I felt sick with hope and rage.

At two o'clock, as the cakes were lifted from the oven, cloud absorbed the sun and all down the block grey dusk breathed out into the day. The sun was pale at first as a lemon, and then it melted entirely. And as I glared out from my bedroom window, I saw the black figure of the vampire walking up the street. About her slender ankles her black skirts bounded like little dogs, and in her hat the red pin smouldered like a coal.

I ran downstairs, and as I stationed myself behind the table, our front door was knocked upon.

My mother came, washed and powdered and sweet, with combs in her hair.

'Oh, Miriam,' she sighed. 'Oh, Miriam. How good to see you.'

The vampire glided into the room as she had so often done, and as so often over me her dead eyes glimmered, and with her colourless tongue she licked her lip, thinking, I suppose, of when she could pull me up and throw me on the compost. How aggravating for her that I was always here, always about. How she would have liked to cut off my head and be done with me. Her hatred was so vast, so cushiony, she could not catch sight of mine, nor of my excitement.

She drew out the ruby pin and let fall her ghastly hat. She lit a cigarette in the bone holder. But she did not sit down.

I would not let my eyes go to the blind. Not yet. She must not have a hint. I squinted instead at her black buckled shoes and her nasty flounced yipping dog of a skirt.

My mother entered with golden cakes and the steaming teapot. Patting them on the table, she added the frosted decanter of sherry.

'Something to warm you, Miriam?'

But Miriam gently shook her head. What could warm her, after all, but one thing only?

'It seems so long since I saw you, darling,' said my mother, and she sat down on the long couch, to the left. I would not glance at the mirror on the blind. I stared at Miriam's ruby pin spinning in one set of her fingers, and the other set with the smoking bone of the cigarette holder.

She gazed at my mother, and seduced, Miriam also sat.

Then I looked straight up into the mirror.

What I saw was so ludicrous, so terrifying, that it produced a spontaneous and unforeseen reaction.

I had forgotten, or never thought, that while Miriam would not be caught in any reflective surface, her clothes were still corporeal.

And so I beheld a corseted black dress sat upright on the couch, straight as a rod, and in the air there flashed a turning jewel, and then, floating some four inches free of the black cuff, an ivory holder and a cigarette, which borne higher up into the headless space where the collar of the dress ended, sparkled with sudden life, and out of nothing came a gush of smoke like a cloud.

Never before or since have I known the sensation, but at that instant my blood ran cold. Cold as liquid ice beneath a river at midnight.

And I screamed.

From the corner of vision I noticed my mother's head jerk up. What Miriam did I could not see, but in the looking-glass her clothing did not shift.

My mother spoke to me sharply, but I was beyond response. My eyes were wide and fixed, glued to the image in the mirror, the headless dress of the invisible smoking woman.

And then my mother was beside me. I felt her kneeling, staring into my face. I wanted to shriek that she must turn round, look there, *there* – but no further noise would come out of me and I could not seem to move.

My mother stood up abruptly.

'How foolish children are,' she said, quietly.

These terrible words loosened all my limbs, and I flopped down on the floor. I was able to look about now, and saw my mother go over to the bureau. She was unlocking the drawer with my father's treasures in it.

'But then,' said my mother, slipping in her hand and taking something out, 'here's a thing I'd like to show you, darling.'

From my mother's hand depended a golden crucifix that shone and burned brighter than either the coal of the ruby or the cigarette.

The vampire started up. She snatched on her hat and drove the pin into it, as it seemed right through her skull.

'Oh, must you be going? What a shame.'

My mother saw Miriam to the door. Miriam opened and slipped round it like a puff of smoke, already perhaps vanishing.

My mother shut the door. She held the crucifix in her hand, and slowly her gaze settled on me.

'Silly child, not to have told me. Did you think I wouldn't believe you?'

I stammered something.

'Or did you only suddenly see?' asked my mother.

'The mirror!' I cried.

'What mirror?' inquired my mother.

I babbled that surely she must understand, she must have seen into the mirror on the blind – though how? – for why else had she fathomed what Miriam was?

'Oh, yes,' said my mother calmly, 'of course I saw. Her dress without anyone in it. But not in a mirror.' I gaped at her miraculousness. She smiled, and said, her voice trembling slightly, 'I saw the reflection in your eyes.'

NUNC DIMITTIS

The Nunc Dimittis *is the traditional Gospel Canticle of Night Prayer (Compline).
It begins:* Nunc dimittis servum tuum, Domine, secundum verbum tuum in pace. *(Now you are releasing your servant, Master, according to your word in peace. – Luke 2:29)*

The Vampire was old, and no longer beautiful. In common with all living things, she had aged, though very slowly, like the tall trees in the park. Slender and gaunt and leafless, they stood out there, beyond the long windows, rain-dashed in the grey morning. While she sat in her high-backed chair in that corner of the room where the curtains of thick yellow lace and the wine-coloured blinds kept every drop of daylight out. In the glimmer of the ornate oil lamp, she had been reading. The lamp came from a Russian palace. The book had once graced the library of a corrupt pope named, in his temporal existence, Rodrigo Borgia. Now the Vampire's dry hands had fallen upon the page. She sat in her black lace dress that was one hundred and eighty years of age, far younger than she herself, and looked at the old man, streaked by the shine of distant windows.

'You say you are tired, Vassu. I know how it is. To be so tired, and unable to rest. It is a terrible thing.'

'But, Princess,' said the old man quietly, 'it is more than this. I am dying.'

The Vampire stirred a little. The pale leaves of her hands rustled on

227

the page. She stared with an almost childlike wonder.

'Dying? Can this be? You are sure?'

The old man, very clean and neat in his dark clothing, nodded humbly.

'Yes, Princess.'

'Oh, Vassu,' she said, 'are you glad?'

He seemed a little embarrassed. Finally he said:

'Forgive me, Princess, but I am very glad. Yes, very glad.'

'I understand.'

'Only,' he said, 'I am troubled for your sake.'

'No, no,' said the Vampire, with the fragile perfect courtesy of her class and kind. 'No, it must not concern you. You have been a good servant. Far better than I might ever have hoped for. I am thankful, Vassu, for all your care of me. I shall miss you. But you have earned ...' She hesitated, then said, 'You have more than earned your peace.'

'But you,' he said.

'I shall do very well. My requirements are small, now. The days when I was a huntress are gone, and the nights. Do you remember, Vassu?'

'I remember, Princess.'

'When I was so hungry, and so relentless. And so lovely. My white face in a thousand ballroom mirrors. My silk slippers stained with dew. And my lovers waking in the cold morning, where I had left them. But now, I do not sleep, I am seldom hungry. I never lust. I never love. These are the comforts of old age. There is only one comfort that is denied to me. And who knows. One day, I too ...'

She smiled at him. Her teeth were beautiful, but almost even now, the exquisite points of the canines quite worn away. 'Leave me when you must,' she said. 'I shall mourn you. I shall envy you. But I ask nothing more, my good and noble friend.'

The old man bowed his head.

'I have,' he said, 'a few days, a handful of nights. There is something I wish to try to do in this time. I will try to find one who may take my place.'

The Vampire stared at him again, now astonished. 'But Vassu, my irreplaceable help – it is no longer possible.'

'Yes. If I am swift.'

'The world is not as it was,' she said, with a grave and dreadful wisdom.

He lifted his head. More gravely, he answered:

'The world is as it has always been, Princess. Only our perceptions of it have grown more acute. Our knowledge less bearable.'

She nodded.

'Yes, this must be so. How could the world have changed so terribly?

It must be we who have changed.'

He trimmed the lamp before he left her.

Outside, the rain dripped steadily from the trees.

The city, in the rain, was not unlike a forest. But the old man, who had been in many forests and many cities, had no special feeling for it. His feelings, his senses, were primed to other things.

Nevertheless, he was conscious of his bizarre and anachronistic effect, like that of a figure in some surrealist painting, walking the streets in clothes of a bygone era, aware he did not blend with his surroundings, nor render them homage of any kind. Yet even when, as sometimes happened, a gang of children or youths jeered and called after him the foul names he was familiar with in twenty languages, he neither cringed nor cared. He had no concern for such things. He had been so many places, seen so many sights; cities that burned or fell in ruin, the young who grew old, as he had, and who died, as now, at last, he too would die. This thought of death soothed him, comforted him, and brought with it a great sadness, a strange jealousy. He did not want to leave her. Of course he did not. The idea of her vulnerability in this harsh world, not new in its cruelty but ancient, though freshly recognised – it horrified him. This was the sadness. And the jealousy … that, because he must try to find another to take his place. And that other would come to be for her, as he had been.

The memories rose and sank in his brain like waking dreams all the time he moved about the streets. As he climbed the steps of museums and underpasses, he remembered other steps in other lands, of marble and fine stone. And looking out from high balconies, the city reduced to a map, he recollected the towers of cathedrals, the star swept points of mountains. And then at last, as if turning over the pages of a book backwards, he reached the beginning.

There she stood, between two tall white graves, the chateau grounds behind her, everything silvered in the dusk before the dawn. She wore a ball gown, and a long white cloak. And even then, her hair was dressed in the fashion of a century ago; dark hair, like black flowers.

He had known for a year before that he would serve her. The moment he had heard them talk of her in the town. They were not afraid of her, but in awe. She did not prey upon her own people, as some of her line had done.

When he could get up, he went to her. He had kneeled, and stammered something; he was only 16, and she not much older. But she had simply looked at him quietly and said: 'I know. You are welcome.' The words had been in a language they seldom spoke together now. Yet always, when he recalled that meeting, she said them in that tongue, and with the same gentle inflection.

All about, in the small café where he had paused to sit and drink coffee, vague shapes came and went. Of no interest to him, no use to her. Throughout the morning, there had been nothing to alert him. He would know. He would know, as he had known it of himself.

He rose, and left the café, and the waking dream walked with him. A lean black car slid by, and he recaptured a carriage carving through white snow –

A step brushed the pavement, perhaps twenty feet behind him. The old man did not hesitate. He stepped on, and into an alleyway that ran between the high buildings. The steps followed him; he could not hear them all, only one in seven, or eight. A little wire of tension began to draw taut within him, but he gave no sign. Water trickled along the brickwork beside him, and the noise of the city was lost.

Abruptly, a hand was on the back of his neck, a capable hand, warm and sure, not harming him yet, almost the touch of a lover.

'That's right, old man. Keep still. I'm not going to hurt you, not if you do what I say.'

He stood, the warm and vital hand on his neck, and waited.

'All right,' said the voice, which was masculine and young and with some other elusive quality to it. 'Now let me have your wallet.'

The old man spoke in a faltering tone, very foreign, very fearful. 'I have – no wallet.'

The hand changed its nature, gripped him, bit.

'Don't lie. I can hurt you. I don't want to, but I can. Give me whatever money you have.'

'Yes,' he faltered, 'yes – yes –'

And slipped from the sure and merciless grip like water, spinning, gripping in turn, flinging away – there was a whirl of movement.

The old man's attacker slammed against the wet grey wall and rolled down it. He lay on the rainy debris of the alley floor, and stared up, too surprised to look surprised.

This had happened many times before. Several had supposed the old man an easy mark, but he had all the steely power of what he was. Even now, even dying, he was terrible in his strength. And yet, though it had happened often, now it was different. The tension had not gone away.

Swiftly, deliberately, the old man studied the young one.

Something struck home instantly. Even sprawled, the adversary was peculiarly graceful, the grace of enormous physical coordination. The touch of the hand, also, impervious and certain – there was strength here, too. And now the eyes. Yes, the eyes were steady, intelligent, and with a curious lambency, an innocence –

'Get up,' the old man said. He had waited upon an aristocrat. He had become one himself, and sounded it. 'Up. I will not hit you again.'

The young man grinned, aware of the irony. The humour flitted through his eyes. In the dull light of the alley, they were the colour of leopards – not the eyes of leopards, but their *pelts*.

'Yes, and you could, couldn't you, Granddad.'

'My name,' said the old man, 'is Vasyelu Gorin. I am the father to none, and my non-existent sons and daughters have no children. And you?'

'My name,' said the young man, 'is Snake.'

The old man nodded. He did not really care about names, either.

'Get up, Snake. You attempted to rob me, because you are poor, having no work, and no wish for work. I will buy you food, now.'

The young man continued to lie, as if at ease, on the ground.

'Why?'

'Because I want something from you.'

'What? You're right. I'll do almost anything, if you pay me enough. So you can tell me.'

The old man looked at the young man called Snake, and knew that all he said was a fact. Knew that here was one who had stolen and whored, and stolen again when the slack bodies slept, both male and female, exhausted by the sexual vampirism he had practiced on them, drawing their misguided souls out through their pores as later he would draw the notes from purse and pocket. Yes, a vampire. Maybe a murderer, too. Very probably a murderer.

'If you will do anything,' said the old man, 'I need not tell you beforehand. You will do it anyway.'

'Almost anything, is what I said.'

'Advise me then,' said Vasyelu Gorin, the servant of the Vampire, 'what you will not do. I shall then refrain from asking it of you.'

The young man laughed. In one fluid movement he came to his feet. When the old man walked on, he followed.

Testing him, the old man took Snake to an expensive restaurant, far up the white hills of the city, where the glass geography nearly scratched the sky. Ignoring the mud on his dilapidated leather jacket, Snake became a flawless image of decorum, became what is always ultimately respected, one who does not care. The old man, who also did not care, appreciated this act, but knew it was nothing more. Snake had learned how to be a prince. But he was a gigolo with a closet full of skins to put on. Now and then the speckled leopard eyes, searching, wary, would give him away.

After the good food and the excellent wine, the cognac, the cigarettes taken from the silver box – Snake had stolen three, but, stylishly overt, had left them sticking like porcupine quills from his breast pocket – they went out again into the rain.

The dark was gathering, and Snake solicitously took the old man's arm. Vasyelu Gorin dislodged him, offended by the cheapness of the gesture after the acceptable one with the cigarettes.

'Don't you like me anymore?' said Snake. 'I can go now, if you want. But you might pay for my wasted time.'

'Stop that,' said Vasyelu Gorin. 'Come along.'

Smiling, Snake came with him. They walked, between the glowing pyramids of stores, through shadowy tunnels, over the wet paving. When the thoroughfares folded away and the meadows of the great gardens began, Snake grew tense. The landscape was less familiar to him, obviously. This part of the forest was unknown.

Trees hung down from the air to the sides of the road.

'I could kill you here,' said Snake. 'Take your money, and run.'

'You could try,'' said the old man, but he was becoming weary. He was no longer certain, and yet, he was sufficiently certain that his jealousy had assumed a tinge of hatred. If the young man were stupid enough to set on him, how simple it would be to break the columnar neck, like pale amber, between his fleshless hands. But then, she would know. She would know he had found for her, and destroyed the finding. And she would be generous, and he would leave her, aware he had failed her, too.

When the huge gates appeared, Snake made no comment. He seemed, by then, to anticipate them. The old man went into the park, moving quickly now, in order to outdistance his own feelings. Snake loped at his side.

Three windows were alight, high in the house. Her windows. And as they came to the stair that led up, under its skeins of ivy, into the porch, her pencil-thin shadow passed over the lights above like smoke, or a ghost.

'I thought you lived alone,' said Snake. 'I thought you were lonely.'

The old man did not answer anymore. He went up the stair and opened the door. Snake came in behind him, and stood quite still, until Vasyelu Gorin had found the lamp in the niche by the door, and lit it. Unnatural stained glass flared in the door panels, and the window-niches either side, owls and lotuses and far-off temples, scrolled and luminous, oddly aloof.

Vasyelu began to walk toward the inner stair.

'Just a minute,' said Snake. Vasyelu halted, saying nothing. 'I'd just like to know,' said Snake, 'how many of your friends are here, and just what your friends are figuring to do, and how I fit into their plans.'

The old man sighed.

'There is one woman in the room above. I am taking you to see her. She is a princess. Her name is Darejan Draculas.' He began to ascend the stair.

Left in the dark, the visitor said softly:

'What?'

'You think you have heard the name. You are correct. But it is another branch.'

He heard only the first step as it touched the carpeted stair. With a bound the creature was upon him, the lamp was lifted from his hand. Snake danced behind it, glittering and unreal.

'Dracula,' he said.

'Draculas. Another branch.'

'A vampire.'

'Do you believe in such things?' said the old man. 'You should, living as you do, preying as you do.'

'I never,' said Snake, 'pray.'

'Prey,' said the old man. 'Prey upon. You cannot even speak your own language. Give me the lamp, or shall I take it? The stair is steep. You may be damaged, this time. Which will not be good for any of your trades.'

Snake made a little bow, and returned the lamp.

They continued up the carpeted hill of stair, and reached a landing and so a passage, and so her door.

The appurtenances of the house, even glimpsed in the erratic fleeting light of the lamp, were very gracious. The old man was used to them, but Snake, perhaps, took note. Then again, like the size and importance of the park gates, the young thief might well have anticipated such elegance.

And there was no neglect, no dust, no air of decay, or, more tritely, of the grave. Women arrived regularly from the city to clean, under Vasyelu Gorin's stern command; flowers were even arranged in the salon for those occasions when the Princess came downstairs. Which was rarely, now. How tired she had grown. Not aged, but bored by life. The old man sighed again, and knocked upon her door.

Her response was given softly. Vasyelu Gorin saw, from the tail of his eye, the young man's reaction, his ears almost pricked, like a cats.

'Wait here,' Vasyelu said, and went into the room, shutting the door, leaving the other outside it in the dark.

The windows that had shone bright outside were black within. The candles burned, red and white as carnations.

The Vampire was seated before her little harpsichord. She had probably been playing it, its song so quiet it was seldom audible beyond her door. Long ago, nonetheless, he would have heard it. Long ago –

'Princess,' he said, 'I have brought someone with me.'

He had not been sure what she would do, or say, confronted by the actuality. She might even remonstrate, grow angry, though he had not often seen her angry. But he saw now she had guessed, in some tangible way, that he would not return alone, and she had been preparing herself. As she rose to her feet, he beheld the red satin dress, the jewelled silver crucifix at her throat, the trickle of silver from her ears. On the thin hands, the great rings throbbed their sable colours. Her hair, which had never lost its blackness, abbreviated at her shoulders and waved in a fashion of only twenty years before, framed the starved bones of her face with a savage luxuriance. She was magnificent. Gaunt, elderly, her beauty lost, her heart dulled, yet – magnificent, wondrous.

He stared at her humbly, ready to weep because, for the half of one half moment, he had doubted.

'Yes,' she said. She gave him the briefest smile, like a swift caress. 'Then I will see him, Vassu.'

Snake was seated cross-legged a short distance along the passage. He had discovered, in the dark, a slender Chinese vase of the *yang ts'ai* palette, and held it between his hands, his chin resting on the brim.

'Shall I break this?' he asked.

Vasyelu ignored the remark. He indicated the opened door.

'You may go in now.'

'May I? How excited you're making me.'

Snake flowed upright. Still holding the vase, he went through into the Vampire's apartment. The old man came into the room after him, placing his black-garbed body, like a shadow, by the door, which he left now standing wide. The old man watched Snake.

Circling slightly, perhaps unconsciously, he had approached a third of the chamber's length toward the woman. Seeing him from the back, Vasyelu Gorin was able to observe all the play of tautening muscles along the spine, like those of something readying itself to spring, or to escape. Yet, not seeing the face, the eyes, was unsatisfactory. The old man shifted his position, edged shadowlike along the room's perimeter, until he had gained a better vantage.

'Good evening,' the Vampire said to Snake. 'Would you care to put down the vase? Or, if you prefer, smash it. Indecision can be distressing.'

'Perhaps I'd prefer to keep the vase.'

'Oh, then do so, by all means. But I suggest you allow Vasyelu to wrap it up for you, before you go. Or someone may rob you on the street.'

Snake pivoted, lightly, like a dancer, and put the vase on a side table. Turning again, he smiled at her.

'There are so many valuable things here. What shall I take? What about the silver cross you're wearing?'

The Vampire also smiled.

'An heirloom. I am rather fond of it. I do not recommend you should try to take that.'

Snake's eyes enlarged. He was naive, amazed.

'But I thought, if I did what you wanted, if I made you happy – I could have whatever I liked. Wasn't that the bargain?'

'And how would you propose to make me happy?'

Snake went close to her; he prowled about her, very slowly. Disgusted, fascinated, the old man watched him. Snake stood behind her, leaning against her, his breath stirring the filaments of her hair. He slipped his left hand along her shoulder, sliding from the red satin to the dry uncoloured skin of her throat. Vasyelu remembered the touch of the hand, electric, and so sensitive, the fingers of an artist or a surgeon.

The Vampire never changed. She said:

'No. You will not make me happy, my child.'

'Oh,' Snake said into her ear. 'You can't be certain. If you like, if you really like, I'll let you drink my blood.'

The Vampire laughed. It was frightening. Something dormant yet intensely powerful seemed to come alive in her as she did so, like flame from a finished coal. The sound, the appalling life, shook the young man away from her. And for an instant, the old man saw fear in the leopard yellow eyes, a fear as intrinsic to the being of Snake as to cause fear was intrinsic to the being of the Vampire. And, still blazing with her power, she turned on him.

'What do you think I am?' she said, 'some senile hag greedy to rub her scaly flesh against your smoothness; some hag you can, being yourself without sanity or fastidiousness, corrupt with the phantoms, the leftovers of pleasure, and then murder, tearing the gems from her fingers with your teeth? Or I am a perverted hag, wanting to lick up your youth with your juices. Am I that? Come now,' she said, her fire lowering itself, crackling with its amusement, with everything she held in check, her voice a long, long pin, skewering what she spoke to against the farther wall. 'Come now. How can I be such a fiend, and wear the crucifix on my breast? My ancient, withered, fallen, empty breast. Come now. What's in a name?'

As the pin of her voice came out of him, the young man pushed himself away from the wall. For an instant there was an air of panic about him. He was accustomed to the characteristics of the world. Old men creeping through rainy alleys could not strike mighty blows with their iron hands. Women were moths that burnt, but did not burn, tones of tinsel and pleading, not razor blades.

Snake shuddered all over. And then his panic went away. Instinctively, he told something from the aura of the room itself. Living as he did, generally he had come to trust his instincts.

He slunk back to the woman, not close, this time, no nearer than two yards.

'Your man over there,' he said, 'he took me to a fancy restaurant. He got me drunk. I say things when I'm drunk I shouldn't say. You see? I'm a lout. I shouldn't be here in your nice house. I don't know how to talk to people like you. To a lady. You see? But I haven't any money. None. Ask him. I explained it all. I'll do anything for money. And the way I talk. Some of them like it. You see? It makes me sound dangerous. They like that. But it's just an act.' Fawning on her, bending on her the groundless glory of his eyes, he had also retreated, was almost at the door.

The Vampire made no move. Like a marvellous waxwork she dominated the room, red and white and black, and the old man was only a shadow in a corner.

Snake darted about and bolted. In the blind lightlessness, he skimmed the passage, leaped out in space upon the stairs, touched, leaped, touched, reached the open area beyond. Some glint of starshine revealed the stained-glass panes in the door. As it crashed open, he knew quite well that he had been let go. Then it slammed behind him and he pelted through ivy and down the outer steps, and across the hollow plain of tall wet trees.

So much, infallibly, his instincts had told him. Strangely, even as he came out of the gates upon the vacant road, and raced toward the heart of the city, they did not tell him he was free.

'Do you recollect,' said the Vampire, 'you asked me, at the very beginning, about the crucifix.'

'I do recollect, Princess. It seemed odd to me, then. I did not understand, of course.'

'And you,' she said. 'How would you have it, after –' She waited. She said, 'After you leave me.'

He rejoiced that his death would cause her a momentary pain. He could not help that, now. He had seen the fire wake in her, flash and scald in her, as it had not done for half a century, ignited by the presence of the thief, the gigolo, the parasite.

'He,' said the old man, 'is young and strong, and can dig some pit for me.'

'And no ceremony?' She had overlooked his petulance, of course, and her tact made him ashamed.

'Just to lie quiet will be enough,' he said, 'but thank you, Princess, for your care. I do not suppose it will matter. Either there is nothing, or there is something so different I shall be astonished by it.'

'Ah, my friend. Then you do not imagine yourself damned?'

'No,' he said. 'No, no.' And all at once there was passion in his voice, one last fire of his own to offer her. 'In the life you gave me, I was blessed.'

She closed her eyes, and Vasyelu Gorin perceived he had wounded her with his love. And, no longer peevishly, but in the way of a lover, he was glad.

The next day, a little before three in the afternoon, Snake returned.

A wind was blowing, and seemed to have blown him to the door in a scurry of old brown leaves. His hair was also blown, and bright, his face wind-slapped to a ridiculous freshness. His eyes, however, were heavy, encircled, dulled. The eyes showed, as did nothing else about him, that he had spent the night, the forenoon, engaged in his second line of commerce. They might have drawn thick curtains and blown out the lights, but that would not have helped him. The senses of Snake were doubly acute in the dark, and he could see in the dark, like a lynx.

'Yes?' said the old man, looking at him blankly, as if at a tradesman.

'Yes,' said Snake, and came by him into the house.

Vasyelu did not stop him. Of course not. He allowed the young man, and all his blown gleamingness and his wretched roué eyes to stroll across to the doors of the salon, and walk through. Vasyelu followed.

The blinds, a sombre ivory colour, were down, and the lamps had been lit; on a polished table hothouse flowers foamed from a jade bowl. A second door stood open on the small library, the soft glow of the lamps trembling over gold-worked spines, up and up, a torrent of static, priceless books.

Snake went into and around the library, and came out.

'I didn't take anything.'

'Can you even read?' snapped Vasyelu Gorin, remembering when he could not, a woodcutter's fifth son, an oaf and a sot, drinking his way or sleeping his way through a life without windows or vistas, a mere blackness of error and unrecognised boredom. Long ago. In that little town cobbled together under the forest. And the chateau with its starry lights, the carriages on the road, shining, the dark trees either side. And bowing in answer to a question, lifting a silver comfit box from a pocket as easily as he had lifted a coin the day before

Snake sat down, leaning back relaxedly in the chair. He was not relaxed, the old man knew. What was he telling himself? That there was money here, eccentricity to be battened upon. That he could take her, the old woman, one way or another. There were always excuses that one could make to oneself.

When the Vampire entered the room, Snake, practiced, a gigolo, came to his feet. And the Vampire was amused by him, gently now. She wore a bone-white frock that had been sent from Paris last year. She had never worn it before. Pinned at the neck was a black velvet rose with a single drop of dew shivering on a single petal: a pearl that had come from the crown jewels of a czar. Her tact, her peerless tact. *Naturally*, the pearl was saying, *this is why you have come back. Naturally. There is nothing to fear.*

Vasyelu Gorin left them. He returned later with the decanters and glasses. The cold supper had been laid out by people from the city who handled such things, pâté and lobster and chicken, lemon slices cut like flowers, orange slices like suns, tomatoes that were anemones, oceans of green lettuce, and cold, glittering ice. He decanted the wines. He arranged the silver coffee service, the boxes of different cigarettes. The winter night had settled by then against the house, and, roused by the brilliantly lighted rooms, a moth was dashing itself between the candles and the coloured fruits. The old man caught it in a crystal goblet, took it away, let it go into the darkness. For a hundred years and more, he had never killed anything.

Sometimes, he heard them laugh. The young man's laughter was at first too eloquent, too beautiful, too unreal. But then, it became ragged, boisterous; it became genuine.

The wind blew stonily. Vasyelu Gorin imagined the frail moth beating its wings against the huge wings of the wind, falling spent to the ground. It would be good to rest.

In the last half hour before dawn, she came quietly from the salon, and up the stair. The old man knew she had seen him as he waited in the shadows. That she did not look at him or call to him was her attempt to spare him this sudden sheen that was upon her, its direct and pitiless glare. So he glimpsed it obliquely, no more. Her straight pale figure ascending, slim and limpid as a girl's. Her eyes were young, full of a primal refinding, full of utter newness.

In the salon, Snake slept under his jacket on the long white couch, its brocaded cushions beneath his cheek. Would he, on waking, carefully examine his throat in a mirror?

The old man watched the young man sleeping. She had taught Vasyelu Gorin how to speak five languages, and how to read three others. She had allowed him to discover music, and art, history and the stars; profundity, mercy. He had found the closed tomb of life opened out on every side into unbelievable, inexpressible landscapes. And yet, and yet. The journey must have its end. Worn out with ecstasy and experience, too tired any more to laugh with joy. To rest was everything. To be still. Only she could continue, for only she could be eternally reborn. For Vasyelu, once had been enough.

He left the young man sleeping. Five hours later, Snake was noiselessly gone. He had taken all the cigarettes, but nothing else.

Snake sold the cigarettes quickly. At one of the cafés he sometimes frequented, he met with those who, sensing some change in his fortunes, urged him to boast. Snake did not, remaining irritatingly reticent, vague. It was another patron. An old man who liked to give him things. Where did the old man live? Oh, a fine apartment, the north side of the city.

Some of the day, he walked.

A hunter, he distrusted the open veldt of daylight. There was too little cover, and equally too great cover for the things he stalked. In the afternoon, he sat in the gardens of a museum. Students came and went, seriously alone, or in groups riotously. Snake observed them. They were scarcely younger than he himself, yet to him, another species. Now and then a girl, catching his eye, might smile, or make an attempt to linger, to interest him. Snake did not respond. With the economic contempt of what he had become, he dismissed all such sexual encounters. Their allure, their youth, these were commodities valueless in others. They would not pay him.

The old woman, however, he did not dismiss. How old was she? Sixty, perhaps – no, much older. Ninety was more likely. And yet, her face, her neck, her hands were curiously smooth, unlined. At times, she might have been only fifty. And the dyed hair, which should have made her seem raddled, somehow enhanced the illusion of a young woman.

Yes, she fascinated him. Probably she had been an actress. Foreign, theatrical – rich. If she was prepared to keep him, thinking him mistakenly her pet cat, then he was willing, for a while. He could steal from her when she began to cloy and he decided to leave.

Yet, something in the uncomplexity of these thoughts disturbed him. The first time he had run away, he was unsure now from what. Not the vampire name, certainly, a stage name – *Draculas* – what else? But from something – some awareness of fate for which idea his vocabulary had no word, and no explanation. Driven once away, driven thereafter to return, since it was foolish not to. And she had known how to treat him. Gracefully, graciously. She would be honourable, for her kind always were.

Used to spending money for what they wanted, they did not balk at buying people, too. They had never forgotten flesh, also, had a price, since their roots were firmly locked in an era when there had been slaves.

But. But he would not, he told himself, go there tonight. No. It would be good she should not be able to rely on him. He might go tomorrow, or the next day, but not tonight.

The turning world lifted away from the sun, through a winter sunset, into darkness. Snake was glad to see the ending of the light, and false light instead spring up from the apartment blocks, the cafés.

He moved out onto the wide pavement of a street, and a man came and took his arm on the right side, another starting to walk by him on the left.

'Yes, this is the one, the one who calls himself Snake'

'Are you?' the man who walked beside him asked.

'Of course it is,' said the first man, squeezing his arm. 'Didn't we have an exact description? Isn't he just the way he was described?'

'And the right place, too,' agreed the other man, who did not hold him. 'The right area'

The men wore neat nondescript clothing. Their faces were sallow and smiling, and fixed. This was a routine with which both were familiar. Snake did not know them, but he knew the touch, the accent, the smiling fixture of their masks. He had tensed. Now he let the tension melt away, so they should see and feel it had gone.

'What do you want?'

The man who held his arm only smiled.

The other man said, 'Just to earn our living.'

'Doing what?'

On either side the lighted street went by. Ahead, at the street's corner, a vacant lot opened where a broken wall lunged away into the shadows.

'It seems you upset someone,' said the man who only walked. 'Upset them badly.'

'I upset a lot of people,' Snake said.

'I'm sure you do. But some of them won't stand for it.'

'Who was this? Perhaps I should see them.'

'No. They don't want that. They don't want you to see anybody.' The black turn was a few feet away.

'Perhaps I can put it right.'

'No. That's what we've been paid to do.'

'But if I don't know –' said Snake, and lurched against the man who held his arm, ramming his fist into the soft belly. The man let go of him and fell. Snake ran. He ran past the lot, into the brilliant glare of another street beyond, and was almost laughing when the thrown knife caught him in the back.

The lights turned over. Something hard and cold struck his chest, his face. Snake realised it was the pavement. There was a dim blurred noise, coming and going, perhaps a crowd gathering. Someone stood on his ribs and pulled the knife out of him and the pain began.

'Is that it?' a choked voice asked some way above him: the man he had punched in the stomach.

'It'll do nicely.'

A new voice shouted. A car swam to the kerb and pulled up raucously. The car door slammed, and footsteps went over the cement. Behind him, Snake heard the two men walking briskly away.

Snake began to get up, and was surprised to find he was unable to.

'What happened?' someone asked, high, high above.

'I don't know.'

A woman said softly, 'Look, there's blood –'

Snake took no notice. After a moment he tried again to get up, and succeeded in getting to his knees. He had been hurt, that was all. He could feel the pain, no longer sharp, blurred, like the noise he could hear, coming and going. He opened his eyes. The light had faded, then came back in a long wave, then faded again. There seemed to he only five or six people stood around him. As he rose, the nearer shapes backed away.

'He shouldn't move,' someone said urgently.

A hand touched his shoulder, fluttered off, like an insect.

The light faded into black, and the noise swept in like a tide, filling his ears, dazing him. Something supported him, and he shook it from him – a wall –

'Come back, son,' a man called. The lights burned up again, reminiscent of a cinema. He would be all right in a moment. He walked away from the small crowd, not looking at them. Respectfully, in awe, they let him go, and noted his blood trailing behind him along the pavement.

The French clock chimed sweetly in the salon; it was seven. Beyond the window, the park was black. It had begun to rain again.

The old man had been watching from the downstairs window for rather more than an hour. Sometimes, he would step restlessly away, circle the room, straighten a picture, pick up a petal discarded by the dying flowers. Then go back to the window, looking out at the trees, the rain and the night.

Less than a minute after the chiming of the clock, a piece of the static darkness came away and began to move, very slowly, toward the house.

Vasyelu Gorin went out into the hall. As he did so, he glanced toward the stairway. The lamp at the stair head was alight, and she stood there in its rays, her hands hanging loosely at her sides, elegant as if weightless, her head raised.

'Princess?'

'Yes, I know. Please hurry, Vassu. I think there is scarcely any margin left.'

The old man opened the door quickly. He sprang down the steps as lightly as a boy of 18. The black rain swept against his face, redolent of a thousand memories, and he ran through an orchard in Burgundy, across a hillside in Tuscany, along the path of a wild garden near St Petersburg that was St Petersburg no more, until he reached the body of a young man lying over the roots of a tree.

The old man bent down, and an eye opened palely in the dark and looked at him.

'Knifed me,' said Snake. 'Crawled all this way.'

Vasyelu Gorin leaned in the rain to the grass of France, Italy and Russia, and lifted Snake in his arms. The body lolled, heavy, not helping him. But it did not matter. How strong he was, he might marvel at it, as he stood, holding the young man across his breast, and turning, ran back toward the house.

'I don't know,' Snake muttered, 'don't know who sent them. Plenty would like to – How bad is it? I didn't think it was so bad.'

The ivy drifted across Snake's face and he closed his eyes.

As Vasyelu entered the hall, the Vampire was already on the lowest stair. Vasyelu carried the dying man across to her, and laid him at her feet. Then Vasyelu turned to leave.

'Wait,' she said.

'No, Princess. This is a private thing. Between the two of you, as once it was between us. I do not want to see it, Princess. I do not want to see it with another.'

She looked at him, for a moment like a child, sorry to have distressed him, unwilling to give in. Then she nodded. 'Go then, my dear.'

He went away at once. So he did not witness it as she left the stair, and knelt beside Snake on the Turkish carpet newly coloured with blood. Yet, it seemed to him he heard the rustle her dress made, like thin crisp paper, and the whisper of the tiny dagger parting her flesh, and then the long still sigh.

He walked down through the house, into the clean and frigid modern kitchen full of electricity. There he sat, and remembered the forest above the town, the torches as the yelling aristocrats hunted him for his theft of the comfit box, the blows when they caught up with him. He remembered, with a painless unoppressed refinding, what it was like to begin to die in such a way, the confused anger, the coming and going of tangible things, long pulses of being alternating with deep valleys of nonbeing. And then the agonised impossible crawl, fingers in the earth itself, pulling him forward, legs sometimes able to assist, sometimes failing, passengers that must be dragged with the rest. In the graveyard at the edge of the estate, he ceased to move. He could go no farther. The soil was cold, and the white tombs, curious petrified vegetation over his head, seemed to suck the black sky into themselves, so they darkened, and the sky grew pale.

But as the sky was drained of its blood, the foretaste of day began to possess it. In less than an hour, the sun would rise.

He had heard her name, and known he would eventually come to serve her. The way in which he had known, both for himself and for the young man called Snake, had been in a presage of violent death.

All the while, searching through the city, there had been no-one with that stigma upon them, that mark. Until, in the alley, the warm hand gripped his neck, until he looked into the leopard-coloured eyes. Then Vasyelu saw the mark, smelled the scent of it like singed bone.

How Snake, crippled by a mortal wound, bleeding and semi-aware, had brought himself such a distance, through the long streets hard as nails, through the mossy garden-land of the rich, through the colossal gates, over the watery, night-tuned plain, so far, dying, the old man did not require to ask, or to be puzzled by. He, too, had done such a thing, more than two centuries ago. And there she had found him, between the tall white graves. When he could focus his vision again, he had looked and seen her, the most beautiful thing he ever set eyes upon. She had given him her blood. He had drunk the blood of Darejan Draculas, a princess, a vampire. Unique elixir, it had saved him. All wounds had healed. Death had dropped from him like a torn skin, and everything he had been – scavenger, thief, brawler, drunkard, and, for a certain number of coins, *whore* – each of these things had crumbled away. Standing up, he had trodden on them, left them behind. He had gone to her, and kneeled down as, a short while before, she had kneeled by him, cradling him, giving him the life of her silver veins.

And this, all this, was now for the other. Even her blood, it seemed, did not bestow immortality, only longevity, at last coming to a stop for Vasyelu Gorin. And so, many, many decades from this night, the other, too, would come to the same hiatus. Snake, too, would remember the waking moment, conscious another now endured the stupefied thrill of it, and all that would begin thereafter.

Finally, with a sort of guiltiness, the old man left the hygienic kitchen and went back toward the glow of the upper floor, stealing out into the shadow at the light's edge.

He understood that she would sense him there, untroubled by his presence – had she not been prepared to let him remain?

It was done.

Her dress was spread like an open rose, the young man lying against her, his eyes wide, gazing up at her. And she would be the most beautiful thing that he had ever seen. All about, invisible, the shed skins of his life, husks he would presently scuff uncaringly underfoot. And she?

The Vampire's head inclined toward Snake. The dark hair fell softly. Her face, powdered by the lampshine, was young, was full of vitality, serene vivacity, loveliness. Everything had come back to her. She was reborn.

Perhaps it was only an illusion.

The old man bowed his head, there in the shadows. The jealousy, the regret were gone. In the end, his life with her had become only another skin that he must cast. He would have the peace that she might never have, and be glad of it. The young man would serve her, and she would be huntress once more, and dancer, a bright phantom gliding over the ballroom of the city, this city and others, and all the worlds of land and soul between.

Vasyelu Gorin stirred on the platform of his existence. He would depart now, or very soon; already he heard the murmur of the approaching train. It would be simple, this time, not like the other time at all. To go willingly, everything achieved, in order. Knowing she was safe.

There was even a faint colour in her cheeks, a blooming. Or maybe, that was just a trick of the lamp.

The old man waited until they had risen to their feet, and walked together quietly into the salon, before he came from the shadows and began to climb the stairs, hearing the silence, their silence, like that of new lovers.

At the head of the stair, beyond the lamp, the dark was gentle, soft as the Vampire's hair. Vasyelu walked forward into the dark without misgiving, tenderly.

How he had loved her.

LA VAMPIRESSE

Going up in the elevator, he felt a wave of depression so intense at what he was about to do, that he almost rushed out at another floor. But then what would he see? The eerie elongate building was frosted with a dry desert cold. On the ground floor he had already encountered strange sliding, creeping or slipping shades. He had glimpsed creatures – things – he didn't want to be at large among. And anyway, there was the man with him in the lift, 'helping' him to reach the proper place.

'How is she today?' he had asked, when they first got in.

'As always.'

'Ah.'

And that was all.

Ornamental, the elevator had fretted screens of delicately-wrought white metal. Its internal light was soft, but not warm, and when the cage finally rattled to a halt, and the screens parted, a cold blast hit him from an open window.

'Is that safe?'

'What?' asked the man.

'That window – surely –'

'That's fine. See the grille?'

He looked and saw the grille. And in any case, now they were in the heart of a desert night. The sunset had been sucked under, sucked up like red blood, in the minute or so of the elevator's ascent. Stars glittered out in the black sky, undimmed even by the lights of this immense, automated mansion. Soon a

245

moon would rise.

'Thanks,' he said humbly, to the attendant. Should he tip him? Perhaps not. The man was already undoing a door and it seemed *he* should go through – go through alone. And now, after the depression, for a moment he was afraid.

'Am I okay in there?' He tried to sound flippant.

The attendant smiled suddenly, contemptuous as a wolf. 'Sure. It's all right, you know. She's sated.'

'She is?'

'Yes. Quite.'

'Sated.'

'Yes.'

'How?' he heard himself ask. The ghoulish word hung there in the slightly-warmed cold air.

The attendant said, 'Best not to ask, mister.'

'No ...'

'Best not to ask,' the man repeated, as fools or the nervous or the indomitable often did.

But this time, he resisted, himself, doing so.

And then he was through the door, which – as it seemed with its own laughter – shut fast and closed him in.

The first thing he saw in the great wide room was the Christmas tree. It was that blue-green variety, about two metres tall, and growing in a stone pot. He knew of the tree, had indeed seen pictures of it. Probably not the same tree, but the *same* type of tree, and decorated approximately in the same way, for it was hung with long pearl necklaces.

The room was luxurious. Thickly carpeted, with deep chairs upholstered in what looked like velvet, or leather. The drapes were looped back from two tall windows, in one of which the moon was now coming up from the desert.

In fact, this whole room was very like the other room, the room he had seen photographs of. Not absolutely, he supposed, but enough.

He looked around carefully. On a gallery up a stair were book-stacks lined with volumes of calf and silk, gilded. A globe stood up there on a table, and down here, one long decanter filled with dark fluid, and two crystal goblets.

'It isn't blood.'

He snapped around so fast a muscle twanged at the top of his neck.

Christ. She had risen up silent as the moon rose, out of that chair in the corner, in the half light beyond the lamps, a shadow.

'No, truly, not blood. Alcohol. I keep it for my guests.'

He knew what to do. And if he hadn't known, he had had it droned into him by everyone he had had to deal with, lawyers, his own office, and inevitably, the people here. So he bowed to her, the short military bow of a culture and a world long over. But not, of course, for her.

'Madame Chaikassia.'

'Ah,' she said. 'At last. One who knows how to say my name.'

Naturally he knew. He had known from the day he saw her in an interview on TV. Rather as he had seen the actress Bette Davis in an interview years before, and she had been asked how her first name was pronounced. So that he therefore knew it was *not* pronounced, as most persons now did, in the French way, Bett, but – for he had heard the actress herself reply – as Betty. And in the same way he knew the female being before him now did not pronounce her name as so many did, Ché Kasee-ah, but Ch'high-kazya.

She did not ask who *he* was. They would have told her, when they said he would be coming. After all, without her permission, he would never have been allowed into this room. And all the way here, if the truth were known, he had been sweating, thinking she would, after his journey of two thousand miles and more, suddenly change her mind.

'Help yourself,' she said idly, 'to a drink.'

So he thanked her, and went and poured himself one. To his surprise, when he sipped it, it was a decent malt whisky. Despite her words, he had expected anything but alcohol. Yet obviously, they knew *she* would never drink *this*.

When she beckoned to him, he sat down facing her, where she had once more sat down. The side lamps cast the mildest glow, but behind her the harsh white neon of moon was coming up with incredible rapidity. It would shine into his face, not hers.

In the soft, flattering light, he studied her.

Even under these lamps, she looked old. He had been prepared for that. No-one knew her exact age, or those who did kept quiet. But twenty, twenty-five years ago, when he had seen her in that interview, or more recently in little remaining clips of film, she had looked only a glamorous thirty, forty. Now he would have said she was well into her sixties. She looked like that. Except, of course, she was still glamorous, and still she had her wonderful mask of bones, on which the flesh stayed pinned, not by surgery, but by that random good luck that chance sometimes handed out, just now and then, to the chosen few.

In fact, she was still beautiful, and he had a feeling that even when she looked seventy, eighty, one hundred, she would even then keep those two things, the glamour and the beauty.

Although again, probably she wouldn't live that long, not now. Now she was in captivity, and ruined.

She lost a little more each day, they had told him that. A little more.

But you'd never know.

Her hair was long as in the old pictures and just as lustrous and thick, though fine silver wires of the best kind of grey silked through it. She wore a minimum of make-up, eye-shadow and false lashes. No powder he could detect. And though her lips were a startling scarlet, it was a softer scarlet, to suit the aging of her face.

Her body, like her throat, was long and slender. She wore one of those long black gowns, just close enough in fit he had seen, in her rising and sitting, her figure looked, at least when clothed, like that of a woman half her apparent age.

And she had on high heels – black velvet pumps on slender tapering pins. She had surrendered very little, that way.

As for her hands, always the big giveaway, she wore mittens of thin black lace, and her nails were long and painted dull gold.

'Well,' she said. 'What do you wish to know?'

'Whatever you're kind enough to tell me.'

'There is so much.'

'Yes.'

'Time,' she said. She shrugged.

'We have some time.'

'I mean, my time. Such a great amount. Like the snows and the forests. Like the mountains I saw from the beginning of my life. And always in moonlight or the light of the stars. So many nights. Centuries, and all in the dark. '

She had hypnotised him. He felt it. He didn't struggle. But she said, 'Don't be nervous,' as if he had stuttered or flinched or drawn back. 'You know, don't you, you are perfectly safe with me tonight?'

'Yes, Madame Chaikassia.'

'That's good. Not everyone is able to relax.'

'I know,' he said, 'that you've given your word. And you never break your word.'

She smiled then. She had beautiful teeth, but they were all caps. Thank God, he thought, with a rare compassion, she had not needed new teeth until such excellent dentistry had become available.

He could remember the little headline in a scurrilous magazine: *False Fangs for a Vampire.*

'Do you know my story?' she asked, not coyly, but with dignity.

Surely it would be impossible not to respond to this pride and self-control? At least, for him.

'Something of it. But only from the movies, and the book.'

'Oh, my book.' She was dismissive. Any authorial arrogance had left her, or else she had never had any. 'I did not write everything I should have done. Or they would not let me. Always there are these restraints.'

'Yes,' he said.

She said, 'It must surprise you to find me here.'

He waited, careful.

She sighed. She said, 'As the world shrinks, I have been taken like an exotic animal and put into this zoo – this menagerie. And I have allowed it, for there was nothing else I could do. I am the last of my kind. A unique exhibit. And of course, they feed me.'

At the vulgar flick of her last words, he found, to his slight dismay, the hair crawled on his scalp. Then curiosity, his stock-in-trade, made him say, 'Can I ask you, Madame, in the realm of food, on what do they –?'

'On what do you *think?*'

She leaned forward. Her black eyes, that had no aging mark on them beyond a faint reddening at their corners, burned into his. And he felt, and was glad to feel, an electric weakening in his spine.

If only I could give you what you need.

He heard the line in his head, as he had heard and read it on several occasions. But he kept the sense not to say it.

She had given her word, La Vampiresse, that she would not harm him. But there was one story, if real or false he hadn't been able to find out. One journalistic interviewer had teasingly gone too far with her, and left this place in an ambulance.

So he only waited, letting the recorder tick unheard in his pocket – they had said, she didn't object to such machines, provided she didn't have to see or hear them.

And she leaned back after a moment and said, 'They bring me what I must have. It is taken quite legally. And only from the willing, and the healthy.'

He risked it. 'Blood, madame.'

'*Blood*, monsieur. But I will tell you something. They must, by law, disguise what it is.'

'How is that possible?'

'They add a little juice, some little meat extract or other. This is required by the government. Astonishing, their hypocrisy, would you not say?'

'I'd say so, yes.'

'For everyone knows what I am, and what I must have, to live. But in order to protect the sensibility of a few, they perpetrate a travesty. However,' she folded her hands, her rings dark as her eyes, 'I can taste what it really is, under its camouflage. And it does what it must. As you see. I am still alive.'

He had been an adolescent when he saw her first, and that was on film. He was not the only one whose earliest sexual fantasies had been lit up all through by La Vampiresse.

But also, romantically, he had fallen in love with her world, recreated so earnestly on the screen. A country and landscape of forests, mountains, spired cities on frozen rivers, of winter palaces and sleighs and wolves, and of darkness, always that, where the full moon was the only sun. Russia, or some component of Russia, but a Russia vanished far away, where the aristocrats spoke French and the slavery of serfdom persisted.

As he grew up, found fleshly women that, for all their faults, were actually embraceable, actually penetrable, he lost the dreams of blood and moonlight. And with them, perhaps strangely, or not, lost to the romance of *place*. So that when, all these years after, he had been looking again at the film, or at those bits of it that had been – aptly – dug up, he was amused. At himself, for ever liking these scenarios at all. At the scenarios themselves, their naivety and censored charms. Oh yes, the imagination, in those days, sexual and otherwise, had had to work overtime. And from doing it, the imagination had grown muscular and strong. So that in memory after, you saw what you had *not* been shown, the fondling behind the smoky drape, that closed boudoir door, or even the rending among that hustle of far-off feeding wolves …

Altogether, he was sorry the romance had died for him with his youth. What was more, though they had only been, to begin with, such images, a recreation, coming here he grew rather afraid she too, La Vampiresse herself, would also disappoint. Worse, that she would horrify him, with scorn or pity or disgust.

But now, sat facing her, he had to admit he was nearly aroused. Oh, not in any erotic way. Better than that – *imaginatively*. Those strong imagination-muscles hadn't after all wasted completely away. For here and now he was filling in once more the hidden or obscured vision. So that under her age, still, he could make out what she had been and was, in her own manner.

And when she spoke of her food, the blood, he didn't want to smile behind his hand or gag at the thing she had told him. He felt a kind of wild rejoicing. Despite the fact she was here in this building in the desert, despite her growing old and – nearly – tame, she had remained *Chaikassia*. Everything else had gone, or was in retreat. Not that.

Because of this, he was finding it easy to talk to her, and would find it easy to perform the interview. And he wondered if others had found this too. He even wondered if that had been the problem for the one who left under the care of paramedics – it had been, for him, *too* easy.

At the nineteenth hour, when the moon was at the top of the first window and crossing to the top of the second, someone came in to check on them.

They had been talking about two and a half hours.

Verbally, they had crossed vast tracts of land, lingered in crypts and on high towers, seen armies gleam and sink, and sunrise slit the edge of air like a knife. And she had been, through memory, a child, a girl, a woman.

She had spoken of much of her life, even of her childhood, of which, until now, he had known little. A vampire's childhood, unrevealed in her book, or in any other medium. He had even been able to glimpse her own adolescence, where she stood for him, frosted like the finest glass with candleshine and ghostly falling snow.

As the door was knocked on, this contemporary and unforgivable door, in such an old-fashioned and fake way, Chaikassia threw back her head and laughed.

'They must come in. To see if I have attacked you.'

He knew quite well that there were three concealed cameras in the room, perhaps for her protection as much as his. He suspected she knew about these cameras too.

But he said, 'They see, surely, you would never do that.'

She glanced playfully at him. 'But I might after all be tempted.'

He said, 'You're flattering me.'

'Yes,' she said. 'But also I am telling you a fact. But again, I have given my word, and you are safe.'

Then a uniformed man and woman were in the room. Both gave a little brief bow to La Vampiresse. Then the man came over and handed her a beaker like a little silver thimble on a silver tray.

'Oh,' she said, 'is it time for this, now?'

'Yes, madame.'

She glanced at him again. 'Did you know, they make me also swallow such drugs?'

'I knew something about it.'

'Here is the proof. For my health, they say. Do you not?' she added to the man. *He* smiled and stood waiting. Chaikassia tipped the contents of the silver thimble into her mouth. Her throat moved smoothly, used to this. 'But really, it is to subdue me,' she murmured softly. And then, more softly, almost lovingly, 'As if it ever could.'

The uniformed woman had come over and stood by his chair. She said to him politely, 'Do you wish for coffee, sir, hot tea, or a soft drink?'

'No, thank you.'

'I must remind you, sir, that your three hours are nearly through.'

'Yes, I'm keeping count.'

When they had gone out again, Chaikassia stood up.

'Three hours,' she murmured. 'Have we talked so long?'

'We have twenty-four minutes left.'

'Twenty-four. So exact. Ah, monsieur, what a captain you would have made.'

He too had got up, courteous, in the old style. He saw now, taken aback for a moment, that even in her high heels she was shorter than he. He had gained the impression, entering, approaching, she was about a tenth of a metre taller, for he wasn't tall.

She had always seemed tall to him, as well. Perhaps she had shrunk a little. Despite their best efforts – the diet she now lived on … like the loss of her own teeth.

'What else shall I tell you?' she asked.

'Anything, madame. Everything you wish to.'

So she began again one of her vivid rambling anecdotes. Only now and then did he require to lead her with a question, or comment. Of all the things she had already told him, many he recognised from the other material. Yet others had proved changeable, or quite fresh, like the childhood scenes, different and new. He was aware, they alone might make a book. The tape chugged on over his heart, a full four hours of it, to be on the safe side, its clever receptor catching every nuance, even when, for a moment, she might turn her head. And he marvelled at her coherence. So much and all so perfectly rendered. If she repeated herself, he barely noticed. It didn't matter. This was a reality more real than anything else, surely? More impactful and apposite than any tragedy that was human.

'Look at the moon,' she suddenly said. 'How arid and cold and old she is tonight.' Her voice altered. 'Have they told you? I'm always better, when the moon's up. When it's full. I wonder why the hell that is? Crazy, isn't it?'

And something in him stumbled, as it seemed something had done in her. For not only the pattern of her speech had altered, the faint accent wiped away, but as she looked back at him her face was fallen and stricken. And from her eyes ran out two thin shining tears. Lost tears, all alone.

Made dumb, he stood there, seeing her oldness and her shrunkenness. Then he heard his voice come from him, and for a second was afraid of what it would say.

'Madame Chaikassia, how you must miss your freedom. It must be so intense, the lonely sorrow of all these hundreds of years you have lived – and you are the last of your kind. You must feel the moon is your only friend at last, the only thing that can comprehend you.'

And then her face was smoothing over, the strength of imagination working its power upon her. The trite banality of his words, like some splash of bad dialogue from the worst of the scripts, but able to change her, give her back her courage and her centre. So that again she rose, towering over him, her eyes wiser than a thousand nights, older than a million moons.

'You are a poet, monsieur. And you are perceptive. Come to the window. Do you see – the bars are of finest steel, otherwise, they think, my captors, I will escape them. But they have forgotten – oh, shall I tell you my secret?'

They leaned together by the cold glass, observing the slender bars.

She said, 'Unlike most of my kind, I am able to make myself visible, monsieur, in mirrors – have they ever told you? Oh, yes, an old trick. How else was I able for so long to deceive your race and live among you? But there is, through this, a reverse ability. I can pass through glass. Through *this* glass, through these *bars*. I do go out, therefore, into the vastness of the night.

But I am then invisible. I see you believe me.'

'Yes, Madame Chaikassia. Many of us have long thought this was what you must be doing.'

She leaned back from him, triumphant, and laughed sharply again. He caught the faint antiseptic tang of the drug on her breath, the drug they gave her to 'subdue' her.

'I fly by night. And though I return then to this prison-cage – one night, one night when I am ready – believe me, *I shall be gone forever.*'

Her eyes glittered back the stars.

He knew what to do. He took her hand, and brushed the air above it with his lips.

'I'm so glad, so very glad, madame, you are no longer shut in. I salute your intrepid spirit, and your freedom.'

'You will tell no-one.' Not a plea, an order. (Yes, she had now forgotten the cameras.)

'I *swear* I will tell no-one.'

'Nor when you print your story-piece about me.'

'Nor even then. Of *course* not then.'

Flirtatiously she said, 'You are afraid I will kill you otherwise?'

'Madame,' he said, 'you could kill me, I'm well aware, at any instant. But you've given your word and will not. Now I have given *my* word, and your secret is secure with me, to my grave.'

He found his eyes had filled, as hers had, with tears. This would embarrass him later, but at the time it had been, maybe, necessary.

She saw his emotion. Still smiling, she turned from him and walked away across the room, and up the steps to her gallery of books. She did this with the sublime indifference of her superior state, dismissing him, now and utterly, for all her unfathomable length of time, in which he had been only one tiny dot.

So he went to the door and pressed the button, but it opened at once, because the cameras had shown the interview was over.

A copy of the piece he wrote – less story or interview than article – would be sent to her, apparently. She had stipulated this as part of the deal.

And so had he. He had made sure, too, the copy she received, which would be only one of three, one for her, one for himself, and one for the archive, was exactly and precisely right. Which meant that it stayed faithful to the flawless lie she was now living.

He didn't want her or intend her ever to see the real article, the commissioned one. Nobody wanted her to see that. But that one was the one the public would see. Christ, he would cut his throat if she ever saw *that* one – well, perhaps not go so far as cutting his throat … But he had made absolutely certain. The truth was the truth, but he'd never grasped why truth always had to be used to hurt someone. To her, life had done enough. And death would do the rest.

So in his version of the article that Chaikassia would later receive and glance over in her great room, in the tall building in the cold, moon-bled desert, an article complete with a most beautiful photograph of her, taken some twenty years before, she would see, if she looked, only what she might expect from one devoted, loyal and bound by her magical spell. But that was not what the rest of them would read, marvelling and sneering, or simply turned to stone by fear at the tricks destiny or God could play.

But the real article would anyway make little stir. It wasn't even going to be very lucrative for him, since the travel expenses had been so high. And it was of interest only to certain cliques and cults and elderly admirers, and to himself, of course, which was why he had agreed to write it, provided he could interview her, by which he had meant meet her, look at her, be with her those three hours.

The photograph used in the real article was chosen by his editor. It was very cruel. It showed her as she had become – not even, he thought, as she had appeared to *him*. But perhaps some of them, with imaginative muscles, would still see something in it of who she was, had been. Was, *was*. This phantom of his adolescence, who would now be the haunting of his dying middle-age.

Who remembers Pella Blai?

She was once said to be one of the most beautiful women in the world, or at least, on TV. She had the eponymous role in that fantasy series of the previous century, *La Vampiresse*.

The storylines of the series were gorgeous if slender. It was all about a (seemingly – somewhat) Russian vampire, located (somewhere) between the Caucasus and Siberia, though God knows where. A winter country around 18-something, of moonlit gardens and gravestones, and wolf-scrambled forest. And here she flew by night under the moon, gliding at first light down into her coffin, as any vampire must.

Though never at the top of the tree (not even her famous pearl-hung Christmas Tree at Bel Delores), Pella enjoyed much success, and most of us forty years and up know the name. But then the whole ethos of this kind of romantic celluloid vampirism slunk from prominence.

What she did with her between-years remains something of a mystery. And even the lady herself never now talks of them. But there is one very good reason for that.

Diagnosed in her fifties with Alzheimer's disease, Pella lives out her final years in a luxurious private clinic somewhere south of the northern USA. It is a clinic for the rich and damned, a salutary lesson for any visitor of what fate may bring. But in the case of Pella Blai, there is one extraordinary factor.

For the strangest thing has happened. Another blow of fate – but whether savage or benign, who dare say? For Pella Blai's disintegrating brain has by now wholly convinced her that she is not herself at all, but the heroine she played all those years back on TV, on screen, and about whom she wrote her own novel: the one true vampire left alive on Earth.

Her only memories then, and perhaps continually reinvented, concern the role she acted and has now come to live, Chaikassia, the eternal vampire. (And please note, that is pronounced Ch'high-kazya.)

Bizarrely, inside this framework, she is pretty damn near perfectly coherent. It is only, they tell you, when she comes out of it, and just now and then she does, that she grows confused, distressed, forgetful and enraged. When she is Chaikassia, and that takes up around ninety percent of her time – she's word-perfect. No-one seems to know why that is. But having spoken some while to her, I can confirm the fact.

Chaikassia's wants and wishes too, are all those of a vampire – let me add, a graceful and well-bred vampire. And to this end, the amenable if expensive clinic permits her to sleep in some sort of box through the day. While at mealtimes she is served 'blood' – which is actually a concoction of fruit juice, bouillon and vitamins – the only nourishment she will knowingly take. They can even leave a decanter of malt whisky in her room. She never touches it – what decent vampire would? 'For guests' she tells you, with her Russian aristocrat's grace, learnt in her earliest youth in a winter palace of the mind – *her* mind. Which is all so very unlike the real Pella Blai, the hard-drinking daughter of an immigrant family dragged up somewhere in lower London, England.

Frankly, having met her only last month, I venture to say there is nothing left of that real Pella at all. Instead I talked with a being who can make herself *appear* in mirrors to deceive us all, and who passes at will out through the bars of her nocturnal windows. A being too who never takes your blood if she has promised not to, but who once, with one of the fake books from her gallery, broke the nose of a reporter who offended her.

And this being lives in a high white tower in the middle of a moon-leached desert, as far away from the rest of us as it is possible to get. And, until the last of her mind sets in oblivion and night, and finally lets her free forever, I swear to you she is, without any doubt – La Vampiresse.

SCARABESQUE:
THE GIRL WHO BROKE
DRACULA

Friday is the Day of Freya (the Nordic Venus): the Day of Love.

The girl in the night:

It was summer, the sun just gone, the sky Lycra blue. So far not a streetlamp lit, not a star. But the girl carried midnight with her. It made up her long hair, her long dress, the long boots she wore. It filled and surrounded her eyes, and sprinkled from her ears in tiny shiny drops. At one shoulder only was a silken scarlet slash, left by some descending sun much older than the orb recently fallen behind the high street. That ancient sunset had also splashed her lips and nails. And a bone-white moonlight her skin.

She moved in her own darkness, personal to her as all fantasy, yet externalised into armour and a mask.

Some of the late shoppers up by Sainsbury's certainly stared at her, in disapproval and contempt, envy … lust. Not only at and of her body, but of her insulting ability to be alive. She was slender and young. She looked beautiful, and strange.

'Fucking goth,' said someone.

She heard the voice, the girl, but she was in her armour, sealed in safe

257

as any knight – or night.

She walked through the tree-hung alley to the station, and met only a cat, also coal-black and white of face. They exchanged a momentary greeting, and like sentries on some castle wall, passed on.

No-one was in the booking hall, the ticket office shut. But the night-girl had her ticket.

She stood on the platform and waited for the train.

Already she could smell, over the treey scent of the suburbs, the hot-cinder pheromones of London.

Her name was Ruby Sin.

Behind her, in a one-room flat of the dilapidated house across Woolworth's car park, she had left lying the body of her schizophrenic other half. That was a girl of the day and the working week, with short, mouse-brown hair and nervous pale eyes. She was called Sue Wyatt.

Ruby Sin had to kill Sue Wyatt every Friday evening. First in a bath with salts of cedar, frankincense and myrrh. Then with black clothing and red and black costume jewels, and a long black wig. Next smothering her in black and white and red make-up and nail polish. All through the murder, poor Sue Wyatt stared in horror and fear – but at the end her eyes were shut behind jet-black contacts. Dead, dead, left behind on the floor like a shed toenail clipping.

A man on the train reminded Ruby Sin of Sue Wyatt's father. She had seen him before once or twice, travelling up to town behind his newspaper. He wore an expensive middle-aged suit and strongly smelled of cologne and aftershave. But of course, it could never have been Sue's father – *he* would, at this hour or earlier, have been travelling the other way, out to Guildford.

Nevertheless, she never liked to see him there.

He got out at Waterloo, as always.

It was dark by now, after ten, and London opened like the well-lit basement area of a huge department store, whose upper floors were coloured neons and an unreal, darkly milky sky.

Ruby Sin walked obliquely westward, toward the pub known as the Vixen, on Carder Street.

Here in the metropolis, very few turned to gaze at her – a herd of hoodies once, and later a guy who sailed by on a skateboard, and flicked her sleeve in apparent approval of her looks.

The pub was packed, standing room only by now. Music throbbed and tangled, while yellow light slid over the pub's skeletons in metal, and posters strafed with painted blood.

Big young men, bare-shouldered in black leather, allowed Ruby Sin to squeeze her way up to the bar. She gestured for her drink, the usual sour red wine, in sign language. Then she pressed her way into a corner. She slotted herself between the heat-palpitating tables and the shouting patrons. She lifted her head into the smoke and music. The band being played was Lash. She knew the words, so she did not need to hear them.

The first sips of wine, the percussion's thud, these enabled Ruby Sin to continue inward and upward on her journey of self-release.

She appeared cool and static, but her brain was growing by the moment lighter. It was beginning to fill with the dream that every night pathetic Sue Wyatt also indulged, lying on the flat mattress opposite Woolworth's.

This was, nearly, a Cinderella dream, of going out into the night disguised as Ruby Sin. In excited terror, almost nauseous with it, heart pounding and missing beats, Sue Wyatt then saw behind her closed eyes and all over the inside of her body a dark male Being who walked between the crowds, as a full-fed black leopard sometimes walks between the restless passivity of feeding deer.

But to Sue Wyatt in the dream, 'Who are you?' said the leopard, and she must answer. So she (who anyway, in these fantasies under the sheet, was already re-possessed by Ruby Sin and so dead again) appropriately said, 'Ruby Sin.' 'And I,' he said, 'am Darkness.'

There was never sex in these fantasies. There was only a fearful prolonged hiatus, and dialogue like a slow, fencing duel, during which she was always about to fall and he about to catch and seize her. She knew he would then obliterate her. But it would be an orgasm of the spirit, not the genitals.

Besides, it can never happen. Never does.

Finally every night she (or Sue) collapsed asleep from exhaustion. And sometimes then really she dreamed of him, though still she never saw his face.

Stood in the Vixen on Friday, waiting, also like Cinderella – but in reverse – for midnight, Ruby Sin burned slowly up like a black candle. For she believed, if only on Fridays, that one night he *would* come out of the lacy, metallic, leathery, rubber crowd, out of the reds and blacks and silvers, the knives and spikes of steel and hair.

One night. In the end.

She was only 24, after all. She had been waiting ten years. Which of course had lasted forever. But any Friday, the first forever might finish. And then the next wonderful Forever would begin.

'Hi, babe,' said a young man. His jet-black mane was streaked with blue. She had never seen him before, or she had and he had been different. But she had seen others who might have been his clones. 'Want to get us both a drink?' he asked her, crisping the note temptingly before her eyes.

Sue Wyatt, who had to serve customers by daylight, when her vampire other-self slept in a shadow-coffin of the psyche, would have been polite.

Oh, no, thanks, Sue Wyatt would apologetically have replied.

But Ruby Sin coldly turned her head away.

'Fuck yourself then,' said the blue-streaked goth. He spoke mildly. More a formality. Fifty years ago he would have said substantially the same: *Please* yourself then, he would have said.

Ruby Sin however did please only, did fuck only, herself.

She sipped her second wine, which had to last. Soon it would be midnight, and the club would open.

As always, it had occurred to her that the night-stalking leopard might be there, not here.

Ten years of waiting. Since she was 14.

Her family, the Wyatt family, had lived – perhaps still did – in a nice cul-de-sac near the river. Lots of greenery, trees and lawns, a semi with white walls and pseudo Tudor accoutrements.

Oliver Wyatt worked in the city, at one of those mysterious male jobs that were quite lucrative. And Sue's mother, Jane, was the manageress of a small smart dress shop. The income was good. They wanted for nothing – three bathrooms, a well-stocked fridge and freezer, closets of clothes, cabinets of videos and even a few shelves of books. There were also two cars, his a silver Merc, and Jane's a blue Vauxhall Nova: her 'little runaround.' There were holidays in Italy or the Lake District.

Sue went to a good school as well. She was supposedly quite 'bright,' if only she would 'concentrate.'

An only child, Sue wandered through her childhood fairly happily, admiring her parents, accepting them as the alpha male and female. Because she was amiable, impressed and reasonably obedient, they were adequately satisfied with her, though a little disappointed by her lack of looks.

Once she was past 11, Sue saw less darkly through the optic glass.

The view of both her parents and herself altered. She knew she was plain, skinny, unpromising, and that her mother was a bit over-made-up and a bit shrill, her father stuffy and quite prim.

It was the day after her fourteenth birthday that Sue looked into her mirror. Something in the amber setting of sunlight caught her face. It showed – not exactly beauty – but a *possibility*. She stood marvelling, until the light moved on and left her there, marooned and ugly again.

Two weeks later she found out about *Dracula*.

Somehow, like much else, he and his kind had passed her by.

She had if anything been scared of the idea of vampires – afraid of an enduring image, fostered in her by a male cousin when she was six, of the insectile undead crawling up the brickwork of the wall toward her, in the hardly tomb-black luminescence of the Guildford night.

Now everything had changed. Insidiously at first. Next by advancing wild leaps. She had begun to menstruate the year before. Perhaps it was hormones, mostly. She never thought of this, and never would, because the clever little informative books Jane had given her child to read seemed to have nothing whatever to do with the physical, let alone the mental, life of Sue Wyatt.

At midnight the club across from Carder Street opened its doors.

The club's name, written in purplish-blue light, was The Family Axe.

Two girls, about twenty, were in front of Ruby Sin in the queue that waited to get in. One was all in shimmering white, with a necklace of glass blood drops. The other wore black male clothing from the Victorian era, sequined, and with a boned external corset. Sometimes they glanced back at Ruby Sin with their long eyes.

The darker one said to her at last, as the line trod forward again, 'I've seen you here before.'

Ruby Sin said nothing.

The girl in white commented, 'She don't talk.'

'Don't you?' asked the girl dressed like a combination Liberace-Byron-Frank N Furter.

Ruby Sin barely heard them. Her own black eyes had skimmed the slowly moving crowd. Although *He* was nowhere in view, as once or twice before she *sensed* Him. He was here, somewhere here, in the essence of the loud daylit night, the polluted overcast of swarthy milk. This did not mean, of course, that she would *see* Him.

The black- and white-clothed girls leaned their heads together and murmured.

Up by the doors, the bouncers, Chick and Zara, were checking customers before admitting them. To enter here you must be properly attired in one of the many goth fashions, reasonably sober, and not in any way off your skull.

Even at this instant, Chick was shaking his cropped head at two guys in yuppie gear, plainly high on some powder. Chick was built like a human ox, his arms trying to burst the sleeves of his parachute-silk-effect jacket, his thighs straining the seams of his black jeans. But the yuppies were just too far gone to give up; one even playfully wagged a finger at Chick. 'What yer gonna do, pussy-pie?'

Chick moved, but before he could take hold of them, Zara had both guys by the arms. She swiftly manhandled them out of the line and down the street, turning them as she did so to face away from the club. She must have said something too. One of the yuppies stared at her, greenishly.

Then they both scuttled off.

Zara came back flipping the tail of her severely tied-back hair. She was half South American, thin as whipcord and about as strong.

Ruby Sin had no trouble in gaining admittance. Nor did the two girls in front of her.

Inside the dark-bright foyer, another female bouncer, blonde Chloe, felt the girls over, investigated any pockets and purses. From Ruby Sin's little beaded bag came a stick of mascara; two crayons, for lips and eyes; a Kleenex; some money; and a door key to the flat by the car park.

The second male bouncer, Barry, had found some pills on the tall goth male with blue-streamered hair.

'They're fuckin' Nurofen!'

'Expecting a bad headache, are you?'

Beyond the foyer the music was beginning in fractalled shards of sound: the Damned. A huge dark space rose and rose, splintered with light that pinpointed or swirled or blinked.

Ruby Sin moved into the space, and the sound and the light undid the lid of her brain, so her spirit could fly right up, and look about, clear-sighted as a hawk, from the tower-top of her body. The beating heart of the song remade her flesh. She was all part of it now, the night. Safely locked in, yet her soul flying free, connected to her only by a hair-fine silver chain.

Even as Ruby Sin stood at the ground-floor bar, pulsing in the music pulse, under the hanging festoons of swords, axes, scimitars, ordering one double vodka with Cherry-Red, her soul was fluttering up to the gallery that overhung the dance floor.

Her soul perched there on the rail, and that was when Ruby Sin, at the bar, felt *something* – some *one* – *touch* her ...

The most intimate of touches.

Not to breast or groin, but stroking over the fibre of her psychic life.

Her head jerked up, the crimsoned glass in her grip.

And before she could turn to see, the girl in black from the queue set her hand (physical, only that) lightly on Ruby Sin's shoulder.

'Hey, don't be startled. Or do you like to be startled, little no-talk bunny, eh?'

Chloe looked down her blunt nose at the dance area beyond the inner doors.

'That guy,' she said, 'is up on the gallery.'

'What guy?' Barry was still busy disposing of the 'Nurofen' abstracted from the blue-haired goth. 'Don't he know,' mused Barry, 'that he can get all this in *there* – and *only* in there?'

'E, you mean? Is that what they are?'

'I don't even know what these tabs are – Christ, maybe they *are* painkillers ...'

'He's just up there,' said Chloe.

'What are you on about?'

'The guy what came in earlier – the one who came in before we opened. Hank let him in before he went off – said this guy knows Frank Collins.'

Barry patted his pocket, where the initials of the security firm were emblazoned. FRC, for Frank Roland Collins. 'Well, if Collins said okay, it's okay.'

'Don't like him,' said Chloe. 'Don't like the guy. Something. Trouble.'

Barry too squinted through the doors. In the fractured lights he took a moment to locate the man Chloe was bothered about.

Tall, all in black, as most of them were. Long black hair, a flood of it, like a woman's ... pale face leaded in by probably mascaraed black eyes and eyebrows.

Chloe, squat as a tank with muscles, still maintained an active imagination, apparently. But even so, Barry went out of the front doors to check with Zara and Chick. Just in case.

Sue read the book first. She found it dense and almost difficult, to begin with. Then the vampiric sequences of Stoker's rogue masterpiece of transmogrified sex, began to quicken her. Why had she *wanted* to read it in the first place? Someone must have said something. Ten years after, recalling everything else, neither Sue nor Ruby Sin could remember.

Almost a month later she realised – or heard – about the film. Not the earlier versions of *Dracula*, but something more contemporary.

'Dad, there's this video I want to see.'

Oliver Wyatt had peered at her with impatient indulgence over some report he was studying. 'What did you say?'

'There's a movie – a film I'd like to watch, Dad.'

'Well, tell your mother.'

'I did. She won't let me.'

'Why not?' Absently now.

'She said it's too old for me. But it isn't. I've read the book.'

'A schoolbook, is it?'

Sue had not, then, learned properly to lie to her parents. Had never thought she had to.

'No.'

'What's it called?'

Sue told him.

His look. A look initially of surprise, then scornful amusement. And then of sombre disapproval.

'No, Sue. That's not one for you.'

She had tried to argue.

Oliver lost his temper, threw down his papers and got up, looming there in his study like a big tanned pig in a suit. 'You will not argue with me. I've told you, it's inappropriate. Besides being utter rubbish. I suggest you go and get on with your homework, Sue. That's where you need to concentrate your energies, believe me, or you're going to amount to nothing. Is that what you want?'

Cowed, distressed – for even by then, she still bowed to parental authority perforce, and to the unknown ambiguous future, during which she must become 'adult' and 'responsible' – Sue Wyatt lowered her head and slunk away.

In her room, with its Jane-chosen floral prints and curtains, and frilled-over bed, among the ancient toys that could no longer help her, she got out her maths homework. The questions might have been written in French – another subject she never managed, either, to grasp. She cried. Then she went and looked in her mirror.

She saw a young, ugly girl, with tear-reddened eyes.

She was (feebly?) angry with herself, and with all the rest of them.

That night she woke up at some vague hour of morning with one of the sharp cramps her periods caused when starting. Fumbling to the bathroom, and then for aspirin in the bedside drawer, Sue rehearsed other means to acquire a forbidden film.

'I told you. This one don't talk.'

'Course she will. With me. Won't you, bunny?'

Ruby Sin looked at the girl in white, the girl in masculine black.

Through her transcendental Friday-night equilibrium, a worm of panic began to ooze. (The unknown touch on her soul – muddled now, fading away …)

What did they want, these girls?

At school … Sue had been bullied. Oh, rarely a physical assault – or, if one occurred, no more than a pinch, a slap, someone spitting into her eye: That's for *this* … This is for *that* … They could frighten her so easily with threats and name-calling, insults and subtle promises, blows were largely redundant.

She had always been bullied. At the infants' school, eight years old, Sue, crying with horror at the thought of more terror in the morning, had reduced Jane to running her to school in the bright blue car. Then marching into the head's office – Jane marched, Sue, like a convict, marched.

'This can't go on, Mr Mayberry.'

'But it's nothing, Mrs Wyatt. She has to toughen up a bit. Has the child any marks on her? No? Well, then.'

And presently thereafter, in the so-called playground: 'You went to see Fartberries, didn't you?' Slap, pinch, etc.

Sue had only, briefly, ever had one friend, a colourless studious bore called Clare, that nobody ever bothered to bully because she was too limp.

This now, however *this*, under the fractal lights and the beat of drums, of all things reminded Ruby Sin of Sue Wyatt's childhood coercion. She realised the two girls had cornered her, in just that same way, and were now driving her back along a wall, people obligingly making room for them to pass.

Ruby Sin turned abruptly, and walked off across the dance floor.

The white and black girls, one frowning, one smiling, went after her.

'Look, she don't dance neither.'

'Yes, she will.'

Black Sequins seized Ruby Sin's wrist and forced her arm awkwardly upward in a dancer's movement.

'You need to loosen up.'

Arm dropped again, Ruby Sin watched her tormentors as they circled round her like two young wolves.

She was suddenly truly afraid. As if, despite everything, she were Sue stood here.

Real life, always less lovely, less wanted, more terrible than fantasy, had hunted for and found her. Unforgivably *here*.

Why should she have thought herself exempt? It had happened before. Happened most definitely on that night ten years ago – that first Dracula night.

Now they were leading her, despite her resistance, off the dance floor, between the bolts of synthetic lighting, the writhing and swaying figures, the blade-edged shadows of things that did not look possible, and were not.

Ruby Sin gripped her glass. They were in an alcove, just off the floor, out of the lights.

Sequins was leaning forward, kissing Ruby Sin's neck, while the girl in white held Ruby Sin's arms, casually, ready to be firm.

'Want to be a donor tonight, little vampire bunny?'

Even in the half dark, Ruby Sin saw the glint of metal and glass. It was a syringe ejecting from a plastic wrap.

'In my bootstrap – clever, yes? But see, still quite clean.'

Too fast for the girl in white, who had thought the victim quiescent, even complacent, Ruby Sin's right hand sprang forward. Vodka and Cherry-Red splashed into Sequins' face and eyes. The syringe fell. Someone trod on it with a splintering crunch. The girl in white screamed, like an actress in a horror movie of the 1960s. Perhaps she was practiced.

The scream was violent enough that it reached the nearest dancers seen over the music and the beat. Heads turned, eager or disdainful.

Ruby Sin and the girl in white struggled, and Ruby Sin's enamel nails opened three long clawings across the screamer's cheek, so now she *shrieked*.

Up on his rostrum the deejay swayed, lethargic, noting nothing, lost in ear-protected sound. But the bar staff had glimpsed the fracas, and a button was pressed.

Out in the foyer a fiery light erupted like freshest blood.

'Here we go,' said Barry, and shouldered through the doors.

There had been a large ceramic bowl on the Wyatt hall table, both bowl and table carefully dusted by the cleaning woman. In the bowl lay most of the family plastic, aside, naturally, from credit cards.

Sue flipped through the cards for library and various memberships, until she found the one for Epic Videos.

Wearing her Saturday non-school clothes and shoes, her face powdered as her parents now permitted, she entered the store one evening when she was supposedly meeting the long-discarded Clare for a walk.

At first Sue failed to find the movie. Then she did find it on a special display. The pictures on the box alone filled her with an incoherent, nearly panicky excitement.

But she kept her (fake) cool quite well. The rude younger man, who never bothered with anyone, was at the till, as Sue had hoped. He didn't bat an eyelid at her choice, nor her mother's card. Though when she paid cash, he short-changed her, which Sue discovered only later.

It scarcely mattered. She had the film, hidden in her bag. It was hers for three whole nights.

The best thing of all had happened, too.

Jane and Oliver were going up to town tomorrow. It was a Friday, and they were intending to shop, as Jane insisted, for Christmas presents. But really it was only October, and they would be visiting some gallery they had been invited to, perhaps having lunch, and later decidedly having dinner somewhere expensive.

'We won't be back until after 1am, I shouldn't think,' Jane had said. 'We're taking your father's car, so he can't drink, but never mind,' spangled Jane, who – not allowed to drive Oliver's Merc – could drink herself silly and no doubt would.

(There had been other giggly nights like that. Sue had overheard them; she would have had to have been deaf not to. Oliver staying a while downstairs to catch up via the whiskey decanter. Then noises in the bedroom along the corridor. Sue knew what they were doing. All those bizarre little educative books had informed her – without understanding, of course. It wasn't that the sounds of the Wyatts in full rut scared Sue. They simply appalled her, that was all.)

But she had no thought of any of that. She smiled and wished her mother and father a lovely day and evening, quite warmly promised she would spend at least two and a half hours on her homework, and would be in bed by 10 pm.

She was, better late than never, learning how to lie.

Ruby Sin found she had been taken prisoner again. These arms felt inhumanly hard and irresistible. The breasted chest her spine was pressed to was almost as hard.

Chloe said, with icy menace, 'Relax. Good. That's it.'

But not letting go.

Then they were out in the foyer.

Zara had the black sequins girl by one arm only, and Barry stood over the assemblage glowering, while the girl in white-no-longer dripped incarnadine on him.

Barry proclaimed, 'You're all going out. Okay? And you're all barred. *No* trouble. It'll hurt you more than us.'

'That bitch started it –' (Sequins.)

'Too bad.'

The inner doors behind them moved. 'Stop,' someone said. It was a command.

Barry looked sidelong.

Everyone had turned. Even Ruby Sin (hung on the cross of Chloe), her slender muscles splitting at the tug of Chloe's tank-top torso.

Ruby Sin ... she *saw* ...

Her eyes dropped shut like those of a doll. For a second she sagged, and only Chloe's Rottweiler frame held her.

But then Ruby Sin's eyes flew wider than wide. A blind woman given sight, she stared. For He was there. *He* had come here.

He spoke again, in a tonelessly musical voice. 'Let her go.'

Barry lunged.

Barry was good, but somehow *not* so good, not tonight. The tall, black-haired man was neither floored nor in custody, and somehow Barry was down on one knee.

Only for a second. But it counted.

'No,' said the young man with long black hair, to Barry, to all of them. 'Don't. None of you would like it.'

Chloe said, 'It's him, off the gallery. Says he knows Frank Collins. I told you.'

'I do,' said the young man. 'Why don't you call him? Say, *Anduin*.'

'What?'

'A-N-D-U-I-N. Me. I think you'd better. You might not want to make Frank angry.'

Chick was there. 'I'll do it. Anduin, you say?'

'Yes.' He stood by the doors, and behind him the light went on exploding, and the dark haemorrhaging over all.

'It's all right,' he said softly, looking into her eyes.

Ruby Sin found she was shaking. Chloe had lessened her hold.

The sequined and shimmer-white girls quarrelled. Tears and blood rolled down the scratched face.

Sue would have been distressed by what she had done in self-defence – for, once or twice, in self-defence, she had done things. Ruby Sin, however, was sinless.

Chick had gone out on the pavement, away from some of the noise. He was talking on his mobile. Then listening. Then: 'What? He's who? Okay, Mr Collins. Sure, Mr Collins. Right.'

Chick re-entered and looked at Zara. Nodded.

Zara took hold of both the girl in black and the girl in white and seemed to lift both of them off their feet. They were slung out of the front doors of the club. They huddled like orphans under the blue glare of The Family Axe, hissing and calling: It was *her* … was *her* …

But the club doors shut again, and Chick and Barry stood in front of the man who had named himself Anduin, and Chloe still kept her grip on Ruby Sin.

Until through the blaze of music there was the abrupt undercurrent of a car screeching around a corner and drawing up outside.

'Jesus, 's him,' said Chick.

The night parted, then with a rush the doors. A big man, in heavy and gym-honed middle age, pushed through, two others at his back.

His head was covered with short thick hair and his eyes by an a-physical lens like vitreous.

He glanced at the bouncers, then directly at the young man in black.

Frank Roland Collins said something in another language, which could have been Russian. This took his crew by surprise, but not the young man, who answered in two or three unknown, alien words.

Frank turned to Chick.

'Didn't know I had any foreign, did ya?'

'No, Mr Collins.'

'One word I want ya ter learn.'

'Yes, Mr Collins?'

'All of yer. *Scarabae*. He, this gentlemen, is one of the Scarabae. Right?'

They nodded. He made each of them, bemusedly, repeat the name. Then Frank walked over to the young man, who, Frank alone was aware, might well be much, much older than Frank himself. 'My apologies, Anduin.'

'Accepted. But tell your woman to let go of mine.'

'Clo,' said Frank, 'do as the gentleman says.'

Chloe let Ruby Sin go.

Ruby Sin put out her hand on the air, to catch something to steady herself. But the air was empty. Then she discovered that the black-clad shape, the black *eyes* of Anduin, now held her up.

'Did you both want to go back inside, Anduin?' asked Frank Roland Collins politely.

'No.'

'I hope you'll forgive my people. Forgive 'em, eh, they know not what they fuckin' do.'

'We're leaving,' said Anduin.

He walked across to Ruby Sin, and Chick hurried to open a door.

'Come back anytime,' said Frank. 'Free admission. Drinks on the house.'

'Thank you,' said Anduin.

When the doors had closed behind him and the girl with long black hair, Frank drew the pewter brandy flask out of his jacket. Normally he never did that, not during a night when he was patrolling his clubs.

'Jesus Christ,' he said to Chick. 'One more go like that, I'll need me fuckin' heart pills.'

'Who was he?'

'You don't wanna know. Just remember that name.'

'Scarab-bye.'

'Scarab-*bee*. Scarabae. Just fuckin' remember.'

She had scratched one of the bullies in the playground. About a quarter inch above the eyes – there had been quite a scene, Jane summoned to the school, and so on. It was all apparently Sue's fault. Somehow, if she had felt she must, she should have defended herself in some more honourable, even more feminine way.

'She may have to be suspended, Mrs Wyatt. We can't have this sort of thing. The other girl could have lost an eye.'

Sue had felt fear and awful remorse (which Jane's subsequent lecture fuelled). But also a weird, secret delight. It was that year she was 14.

And the bully failed to attack Sue again. It was the last time any of them bullied her, although she still had no friends.

Later, of course, there had been greater crimes, the last one of which (and the one that ten years after, still continued) was when Sue Wyatt started to blackmail her father.

'My family is an old one.'

They were walking through the London streets. It was late, after 2 am. Ruby Sin could not be sure how long they had walked, nor which direction they had taken, took.

The sky stayed milky, and the neons painted rainbow colours on the upper storeys of the city. Here, there were few people on the streets. But they had come into a district where the street lamps were pale gold, rather than Martian orange, and the shadows lay violet on dry paving. All the night was vampiric now.

They walked side by side, not particularly fast, and now and then he spoke to her in his low, extraordinary voice.

Not once had he asked her what she wanted, or told her what he might want. Only at one point, there was an off-license, curiously still open, lit yet deserted, and going in he took a bottle of wine from one of the shelves and left a twenty-pound note lying on the counter. No-one came to remonstrate, or to accept the money. No alarm sounded either as he entered or as he left with the bottle.

He undid the foil cap and drew out the cork, somehow, with his white teeth. How strong they must be. But naturally they would be.

'My father,' Anduin said, once he had passed her the wine and she had drunk some, 'rides with a gang of bikers. He looks younger than he did. Or perhaps he's older again, or he's doing something else. He has always refused to credit that I exist, as if that could unmake me. My mother was Spanish-Hungarian. Where she is I've no idea either. But I'm hardly alone. There is the Family. My Family,' he added, 'is very old.'

'Yes,' whispered Ruby Sin. She held out the bottle to him and he drank.

His family was old as history. Older.

'What do you think?' he asked her gently, as they turned down a long and winding alley under high blank walls. She said nothing. He said, 'I mean, what do you think I am?'

Ruby Sin stopped. She had to. Her heart was leaping and choking her. She could not anyway have said his name – not even that other name, which must be a modern lie, a camouflage. *Scarabae*.

But he turned to her now and, for the first time, touched her, putting his hands on her upper arms. It was like warm electricity. And it burnt straight through her sleeves, her skin and flesh and bones, and touched her soul, just as it somehow had on the gallery at the club.

'You don't know me, but you think you do, don't you? And you're not afraid,' he said.

He was not like any other ever imagined, let alone seen. His face was perfect, like a carving, and the eyes were made of real jewels, black as obsidian.

As in all her fantasies, Ruby Sin should now play with him the verbal fencing game of her dreams.

But nor would these words come.

She said, 'This isn't my hair. It's a wig. My hair is brown. Short. And … it's contacts, the colour of my eyes.'

'Ah, darling,' said Anduin. He drew her to him and held her close, folding her in against the contoured strength of his alien, supernatural and astonishing, *real* body. 'Don't you think I can guess all that? You only look like my kind. Your kind is different.'

'Then –'

'It's you,' he said, his mouth against her temple. 'I am interested in *you*. Tell me what you're called.'

She shuddered. 'Sue.'

He laughed, and she felt the laugh move through his chest, and through her breasts, as he held her.

'No,' he said. 'Your true name.'

Ruby Sin thought. She knew he did not mean her invented name. Then she remembered what was written on her birth certificate, which she had stolen, even if it were hers, from her mother's box file, nine years ago.

'Susanna.'

'Beautiful,' said Anduin. 'That's a Hebrew name. Do you know what it means?' She shook her head against him. Something like the warm, delicious sleep of snow-death was stealing over her. 'It means *the lily*. Susanna the Lily. Come on,' he softly said. 'It isn't far now.'

Sue's parents had left for their jaunt to town just after eight o'clock that Friday morning. They would have been off a little earlier, but Oliver's car had acted up, and there was a small row. They left in a flurry, Oliver scowling and Jane huffy. 'Do that homework!' was the parting shot, as the Merc slid away like a shark up the cul-de-sac, and out into the land of adult pleasures.

But Sue went into the house. As she had a free period this morning, and it was not a day for the cleaning woman, Sue was supposed to do the washing up before she left for school.

Instead she ran upstairs and drew the video of *Dracula* out from under her bed. Going down again to the spacious cream and maroon sitting-room, she set up the TV and pulled the heavy drapes.

Before she sat down to watch her fantasy world brought to life, she poured herself a stiff Fino sherry. She had got into the habit of sometimes sneaking one before school in any case. Now it wasn't fear that drove her to it, only an extreme excitement that made her mouth arid, her palms damp.

Sherry swallowed; she started the film.

What unrolled before her was a magic carpet. Lush, erotic, full of terrors, lamped by beauty and desire, spiritually *appetising*, and so intense that this alone might have persuaded her forever to some elevated and unusual form of yearning. It woke her fully from the dismal torpor of a pallid existence. It tore her open to show her the passion and cruelty, the creation and artistry that might just be there in her own self.

She was at an age of turnings. Beginnings.

The influence could well have been wonderfully good.

After she had played the movie through, some (well-trained) part of her thought she must now behave rationally. Sue wandered out, dazed, into the kitchen. She saw the stacks of last night's fouled plates and glasses. And stared at them, unrecognising, like a being from another world.

Anyway, it was now too late to clear up any of this mess; she would have to do it this evening, before her homework, when she got back from school.

So then she thought of school. A couple of hours of dull geography, badly taught, and lunch in the noisy friendless dining room. Then a double period of maths – incomprehensible horror, presided over by sarcastic Mr Brenn.

This, her world. Not flame, peacock eyes, perverse delirium, tragic galvanic love. Solely this … crap.

She moved to the phone like a robot. When someone answered, she spoke into it like a robot, too, pre-programmed and clever, and with a London accent.

'Hallo, this is Mrs Wyatt's cleaning lady. I'm afraid Sue's been ever so sick. She won't be in, very sorry. Mrs Wyatt? No, dear, I'm afraid she's off to town. Doctor? Oh, he's been. Says it's a bit of tummy trouble, that's all. You know what they're like at that age.'

It was a fair impersonation, even if Sue's voice was a little too high for Jane's cleaning woman. The accent was exact. (Sue had heard Jane scornfully mimic the cleaner very often.)

After she put the phone down, still in a sort of trance, Sue made herself a piece of toast. Then she had another sherry and put the film on again.

She watched it through altogether five times. The intervals between the shows were brief – enough to allow her to pee, to eat more toast, to pour two more sherries. Somehow the sherry combined with the movie, in a way Sue did not analyse.

The more she watched the film, the more she felt herself changing. She knew that she was *becoming* part of it. She knew also that, by the sorceress process of reiteration, she was making it come to life.

She wanted nothing else. Even if – yes, even if it meant her death.

But then it did not mean death. The vampiric kiss meant, evidently, immortality. Yet really, she could not think beyond that embrace of fire, that thrashing whirlpool of scarlet –

It was after 9 pm, the film once more just ended, when the other idea came to her, swimmingly.

Again then like a robot, Sue got up and left the sitting-room, and unstumblingly glided her newly coordinated way up the cold (she had forgotten to revive the central heating), dark house. Not a light burned, only the blue post-video screen of the TV downstairs.

There was suddenly something tremendous about being alone here, in this masonry tower that no longer had anything fake, let alone fake Tudor, about it.

There was nothing worthwhile, nothing art nouveau or Victorian, available to her here. But nevertheless, there were adult things – things to do with erotic mysteries. Intuitively, infallibly, she sought them.

In her parents' vast bedroom, Sue opened her mother's forbidden drawers. Here lay the black silk kimono, the black silk uplift bras and narrow black lace panties with their red ribbons, the expensive perfumes and costly make-up. And, on a perch inside the wardrobe, the long black wig that Jane sometimes put on, either for a party, or to entertain Oliver in bed. It had clips, the wig, to fasten it securely into Jane's short-cut hair.

The 14-year-old Sue had no compunction now. She drew the curtain, put on the lights about the mirror.

A miracle had happened, as she had known it must.

Sue Wyatt was already mostly gone.

Her name now must be Mina, or Lucy.

Her clear white skin, large eyes that were full of the shadows …

She had watched her mother make up several times, though never being allowed herself to use more than powder. As for the lingerie, Sue knew how to put on underclothes. And if these were generally a little too big for her, there were also some that had been deliberately purchased that were too small for her mother.

Sipping the last of her fourth sherry, Sue-Mina-Lucy stripped.

She ignored her body in the harsh light until she had reclad it in black lace, red ribbon and balconied wire, and draped over it the short black kimono, which on her almost reached to her ankles.

Then she dressed her face – the first time ever – in the fruits of the tree of carnal knowledge.

These were the accoutrements of Jane's excursions and rutting nights. Sue did not even consider that her mother might well be putting them on *herself*, much later, when she and Oliver came home.

Sue managed her face quite well. In fact, very well. Her eyes were shaded with dark grey and the lashes inches thick in black, her face white, lips carmine. She did her nails, too, perhaps not quite so skilfully, but the effect was, in the mirror, not bad. Lastly she drew on and pinned the black wig, over and into her own mousy hair.

There then she stood. A contemporary Mina-Lucy. Truly. Finally.

Gorgeous, and sexual, ripe as the moon for one searing scarlet cloud …

Mina-Lucy turned out the lights again and went along to her own bedroom, by the flicking gleam of two of her mother's aromatherapy candles.

Mina-Lucy shut her bedroom door, set the candles at the bedside, and, going to the window, flung it open on the still, frosty, garden-darkened night.

Despite any streetlights, once she lay back on her bed, Guildford became Transylvania.

Her head spun a little. She smelled, over the perfume, the cold and the freshness of chilled autumn trees and the river-dark forest, freezing falls. She shivered and did not mind it. Her ears roared, as if the cataract poured there – it did; her waiting blood.

She anticipated Him.

She knew He must come to her.

Her own intensity would lure Him to her.

Up the wall, up the brickwork, an insect, a bat, graceful and crawling, young again in hopes of the feast she would be for Him …

Up and up – scaling the wall of her body … His hands on her … His mouth closing, savage and ecstatic, on her throat …

Of all that she anticipated, what came was not any element of it.

What came was sleep.

Drained by excitement and desire, drunk on Fino sherry, the candles, and her mother's lavishly sprayed scent, Sueminalucy fell miles down into a sleep of undeath.

She woke again just before 11.30 to scalding light and her father's furious voice shouting in the doorway: 'What in God's name do you think you're doing?'

The building was condemned. Like all the others in the street.

Briars and nettles stood up like ornamental iron railings.

Anduin pushed wide a piece of boarding that had looked immovable, and courteously held it for her, like an open door.

He must live in a squat of some kind – as she had once tried to do, in her case rather unsuccessfully.

But even a squat … surely there would by now be some lights visible?

None showed anywhere, except for a pair of street lamps, one at either end of the row of tall, dead houses.

'Appearances,' he said, 'deceptive.'

She nodded mutely. Did not care.

As they crossed the garden, summer smells of garbage, sweating grass, the fragrance of night trees. Something rustled, and two tiny pins of eyes flashed garnet.

'It's only rats,' he said.

There was a boarded door that was also opened. Then, in blackness, an uncarpeted staircase in surprisingly good repair.

They climbed, up and up.

He undid the last door, not with keys, but by pushing a button in the frame. Another eye flashed, not a rat's: technology.

'It knows my fingerprint,' said Anduin.

And they walked through into a suite of rooms at the top of the derelict house.

Hanging lamps bloomed on, soft honey colours and rose, through white and indigo glass. The ceilings lifted high, and their 1800s plasterwork of cherubs and fruit had been renewed and gilded. A huge fireplace, marble, was empty but for a terracotta pitcher that looked like something from an epic Roman film.

There was a long window – full of daylight. Of course not. It must be illuminated from behind. The opaque glass had no picture, but a complex pattern, the red of blood, the blue of moons that make wishes come true.

He was moving toward her with two goblets of greyish crystal in his hands, full of the wine he had taken or bought on their journey here.

'What a lovely face you have,' he said. 'Lovely Susanna who is a lily.'

Something broke inside her. It was like eggshell porcelain breaking at a single quiet sigh.

'Please don't,' she said. She started to cry. She felt the tears like burning cotton pulled from her eyes, loosening the waterproof mascara. 'Don't fuck me,' she pleaded, weeping.

He removed her wineglass and put down his own. He drew her, lightly, without threat, onto a couch with a high carved back. He held her hands. 'Why not?'

'Please – no. Just … please … just drink my blood. I know you will, you can – I want it so much. But not … not to have sex.' And incredibly, unknowingly, in the words of some clichéd Victorian heroine, now given frightful veracity: 'Anything but that.'

He had filled the doorway, as stabbing light filled her bedroom and all the house – it had been set on fire.

He bellowed.

'The place is a tip – you haven't done a stroke, have you, haven't done the washing up – you are a parasite, Sue. Worthless. Your poor mother breaking her ankle like that – I've had to leave her in the bloody hospital – and then the ruddy traffic – and now this, this shambles. You know you've destroyed that video, don't you, which anyway you shouldn't have been watching? It's an 18, Sue, for adults only. You've broken the law.

And something's happened, the damn thing's got itself all wound round itself – snapped when I pulled it out – and all that washing up, just left there, stinking. Do you expect your mother to do it? Christ almighty, she'll be on crutches for six bloody weeks.

You need to buck your ideas up, girl. And look at you. What in Christ are you up to – is that your mother's bra you've got on?'

Made moronic by shock and terror, Sue sat up to face this ranting being, supposedly her father.

She felt as sick now as she had lied she was to the school.

'Sluts dress like that,' said Oliver Wyatt. His voice, however, had become less strident. He looked at her, long and hard. 'Prostitutes,' he added.

Then he came over to the bed and slapped her, once, across the face.

This stunned her. She cried, but far away. He pushed her backward, and when she felt the bra, like tape and ankles, break across her breasts, she thought it was only one more part of the punishment.

As indeed it was.

'Filthy little cunt,' he panted, his sweat and spit dribbling down her face and neck, 'this is what filthy little cunt bitches get –'

The pain was like thunder. He split her. Like an evil lightning.

When he left the room, still thickly raging, muttering, her bed was steeped in the blood of her ripped virginity. But there had been little menstrual accidents in the past. Even when she now threw up all over the carpet, vomit reeking of sherry and shame. Even that could be blamed on one more bad period.

Downstairs she heard far off the furious resentful crashing as he washed up the plates.

'I thought it could only happen once,' she said, in the elegant rooms above the derelict house. 'But after a week, he did it to me again. First of all he said it served me right; it was to teach me a lesson. But then he came into the bedroom when Mum was asleep from the painkillers for her ankle. He said, *I didn't tell her you broke the tape or left the washing up. So don't you tell her about this. Don't tell your mother; she'll be angry with you.*'

'Fathers often have a bad record among the Scarabae. How long did this go on?'

'Another year. Then I heard ... a girl at school told a teacher her father was abusing her. The whole school got to hear about it. And I saw it wasn't meant to happen. And her father had said just what Dad had said, *Don't tell.* So when he came in again, I said to him, *You'd better stop now, or I'll tell Mum, and you'll go to prison.* He said, *She won't believe you. They'll put you in a madhouse.* I said, *You have a big purple birthmark on your willy. How could I know unless I've seen it?* He said – incredibly, as if he forgot, and pompously, the way he always spoke – *I'd never let any daughter of mine see me unclothed.* And I said, *Yes, exactly.*'

'Clever Susanna the Lily,' said Anduin.

She said, 'I ran away soon after. By then he'd had to pay me to keep quiet. He was scared of scandal, and the police. And Mum.' Ruby Sin breathed in and breathed out. She said, on no breath at all, 'He had to pay for the video, too. *Coppola's Dracula.* The one I broke.'

'Lie back,' Anduin said. 'I'm not my father. Or yours. My kind – you know us. Yes, we're vampires. And I think this was agreed between us, you and I, many centuries ago. Do you trust me?'

'Only you.'

Sueminalucy lies deep on cushions. Through the dim gold of the lamps, He bends above her. He is shadow and He is light. A solar midnight, the dark of the sun.

Scaling the impossible wall ...

He strokes her breasts, kisses them, sweetly. He makes love to her, which no-one has ever done, or been allowed to do. At last, he cups her centre strongly in one hand and lowers his mouth to her throat.

The bite is agonising. Marvellous. What she has dreamed of.

As he draws her blood into his mouth, she comes in long, full, pouring waves of joy, crying aloud, and does not recall any other such cries ever, nor realises that anyone else has ever known this paroxysm, since the beginning of the world.

'Sleep now,' he says.

She is tired ... or perhaps he has put something into her wine.

But this time she can slumber fulfilled. What she has always longed for has occurred. The real virginity is taken at last. Now her immortality can commence, her life as Ruby Sin. Or Susanna.

She woke up in the prepaid taxi with strangely obscured number plates, which was carrying her 'home' to the flat facing Woolworth's (and quite near the bank, where, once every month, she could access fifty pounds, courtesy of Oliver Wyatt).

She was drowsy and disorientated, but not unhappy or ill. Someone had put a clean dressing on her neck. And wound over it a priceless piece of black-and-red Chinese silk, dating from around 1760.

In the flat, though, she sobbed till hours after sunrise, keeping the noise down to avoid other tenants coming to complain.

At about 9 am, memory of the past, she called in sick.

'Well, Miss Wyatt, this really is most awkward. It is *Saturday*, you know. Our busiest day.'

But Susanna did not bother with that, and a few weeks later anyway, she sacked herself, and moved farther into London, telling Oliver, by e-mail straight to his laptop via a booth, that she would now need one hundred and fifty a month.

Oliver apparently thought he had no sure way to reach her, only she could reach him – or Jane. He could have bluffed it out by now. But he paid up.

How then does she spend her Friday nights? Susanna, in garments of darkness and blood, still prepares herself, and travels to the heart of the metropolis. She walks, walks the byways of the city, up and down, round and about. She has no time now to visit clubs or pubs. Only once did she visit The Family Axe, but the bouncers were different ones, and besides would not say anything about a man called Anduin, let alone Scarabae, or Dracula.

She is looking for the street of derelict houses she was at first too entranced, later too sleepy, too satiated, to identify. She should have asked the taxi driver that night. Yet he had seemed rather unusual, rather silent. It might have been no use.

So far (two years now), neither Susanna nor even Ruby Sin has found a clue.

Anduin has therefore returned into her dreams and fantasies, where, like before, his face is fading from her inner eye. But then, he was a demon lover, and he and his mansion have vanished from the Earth. As they normally do.

VERMILIA

He wrote: 'She is a vampire. Now I know. I thought I was alone.'

He felt the inevitable amalgam. Shock and excitement, jealous resentment, unease.

He would never have said *The city is mine.* How could it be? There must be several others, like himself. But he had never met one, here. Not here. And, otherwise, none for half a century.

They kept to themselves. Like certain of the big cats, they did not live easily together, the vampires. They *drew* together for sex, sometimes even for love. Then parted. Eventually.

And if one was *sensed*, then generally, they would be avoided – by their own kind.

But now, now he wondered if he had wanted …? The one who said no man was an island, was quite wrong. Every man is, every woman is, both prey and predator. *Alone.*

And she was an island lit by gorgeous lamps, smooth and lustrous in her approach, her hidden depths and heights alive with unknown temptations.

Of course. She was a vampire.

Flirtatiously he wrote: 'What now?'

The first time he saw her, was across a crowded bar. It was just after sunset, vampire dawn. She had that fresh look a vampire had, waking to the prospect of a pleasant 'day'. Obviously, there were others who had it, too –

certain night-workers who enjoyed their jobs. But vampires *loved* their employment. Most of them. The stories of guilt and angst were generally spurious – or poetic.

She moved about the bar, sometimes sitting, crossing and uncrossing her long pale legs in their sheaths of silk. She had black hair with a hint of red, and a bright red dress with a hint of blue, sleeveless and body-clinging, the sort that only a woman with a perfect figure could wear. And her figure was perfect.

The face was something else again – sly and secretive, with elusive eyes. The mouth crayoned the colour of the dress. For this vermilion colour, he coined a name for her almost at once: Vermilia.

She would be pleased, he later thought, once he had seen her at work. Vampires tended to obscure their true names, at least from each other. The invented name he would offer her, like a first gift.

Why she had initially caught his attention he was not so sure. Possibly vampiric telepathy, empathy … For there were other attractive women in the bar, even with perfect forms, and faces that were actually beautiful, if only in the synthetic contemporary manner.

Naturally, she did not look like that. She would have appeared as well in a sweeping Renaissance gown, or corseted crinoline.

From involuntary observation, he began to watch her.

It was soon apparent she was there to secure company. But, she was selective. She would speak to men, engage their interest – even allowing a couple to buy her a drink – but then she would drift away. Not for a moment did he take her for a hooker. She was not – *businesslike*. You could see, she liked what she was doing. For her, it was *foreplay*.

That night, himself, he had no rush. He had taken rich sustenance for three consecutive nights, draining his source with civilised slow thoroughness. She had died, happily, in the hour before sunrise. Tonight, then, was a leisurely reconnoitre, no more. He would not need blood again for 72 hours at least.

He felt nothing for his prey, or very little. He was seldom rough or cruel – there was seldom any need. To seduce, to entrance, was second nature to his kind. Was he thinking Vermilia might be a worthy successor to the last dish? Probably not. After someone so lovely as the last young woman who had died, he would have preferred a very different type, perhaps even ugly. You did not want always the same flavour.

Besides, he soon began to realise about Vermilia.

She was drinking red wine. It was a human myth that vampires could not eat, or imbibe any fluid save one. They did not need to, certainly, but they could. He himself disliked alcohol, and drank mineral water, but that was his personal taste. He understood also she did not favour red wine because it reminded her of blood. What else was ever like blood?

Finally, she was with a boy, stood right up to the bar now, across from him as he watched her. For a second even, her eyes slid over his face. Did she see him?

Sense him, as he had begun to sense her? Maybe not. She was intent on her prey.

The boy – he *was* a boy, though probably forty years of age, arrested in some odd gauche slim adolescence of human immaturity – was fascinated at once. He bought her another wine. Then another.

'Yes,' he wrote, 'right then I did truly suspect. I was sure she was not a professional. Therefore, and in any case, why fasten on this oddball character, plainly not rich, not handsome, and not wise?' A new flavour?

They were there for about twenty minutes more. He even caught phrases from their conversation. 'You do? Wow.' And she, 'Let me show you. Would you like that?' They were not talking about sex. It was a building, the building where she lived. Some old-style architecture, that had been used in a movie, she said. He did not catch the name of the director or actors in the movie. Conceivably she made it up. He was almost sure by then.

When they left the bar, he left also, sidling out into the hot night, to follow them unseen.

The city was black, jewelled but not lit up by its coruscating terraces of lights. Humanity idled by, skimpily clad, drinking beers and snorting drugs from cones of paper. Police cars shrilled through the canyons, rock music thumped.

They reached the famous building. It rose high above, and did look extremely gothic, with some sort of gargoyles leaning out from the fortieth floor.

The foyer was open to anyone, at least to any vampire, dim and shadowed, with carven girls holding up pots of fern, and the doorman watching a TV. Either he waved to Vermilia, or thought he waved to some other woman he knew to reside there. To *him*, the doorman said, not turning, 'Hot night, Mr Engel.'

'It is.'

Vermilia did not turn either. She was showing her boy the statues and the cornice, and summoning an elevator.

He got in with them. Vermilia did not glance. The boy looked slightly embarrassed, then forgot, the way a vampire could always make a human forget.

They got off at the fifty-first floor. He rode up to 52. When he came back down the stairs, they were still outside her apartment.

The corridor was dimmer even than the foyer. The doors were wide-spaced and no-one was there. He stood like an invisible shadow by the stair door, and looked.

'Oh – I forgot my key. Or I lost it.'

'Maybe I can pry it open with this –' The credit card twiddled in boyish old fingers.

'Honey,' said Vermilia.

It occurred to him she did not live here at all, liked the chancy stuff of doing it right now, in the corridor.

She had her arms round the boy's neck. The boy kissed her, sloppily, the way you would expect. Then she put her face into his neck.

He gave a little squeal.

'Ssh,' she said softly. 'It's sexy. You'll like it.' Then a pause, and then, 'Don't you like it?'

'Ye-aah, I guess …'

It did not last long.

As she pulled away, a vermilion thread was on her chin. It might only have been smeared lipstick.

The boy breathed fast. He turned to try to open the door.

She said, 'Oh, leave that. Let's go out. I'd rather go out.'

'But I thought maybe –'

She was already by the elevator again.

The boy shambled after her, pressing a surprised handkerchief to his bleeding neck. 'Hey – you drew blood –'

'Sorry, honey.'

The elevator came.

He knew she would lose the boy somewhere in the crowds.

He let her go.

He went back to his living space, and wrote about it in the book he kept. He wrote, 'She did not relish his blood. She took only a little. Must then have gone looking for someone else.'

And then, flirtatiously again, 'What now?'

But he knew. He would go after her. As no-one else could, he could find her. Hunt her down. Oh, Vermilia …

He had never thought of them much as victims, the ones he took. Some he even allowed to recover, and forget him. The best, he drained over three, four, five nights, at the end eking it out. There was no other pleasure in the world like it.

Sex, the closest, was anaemic beside it. He would never have tried to describe the delight, the power and the glory. There were no words in any language, or from any time.

The night after he saw Vermilia in the bar, he took a girl off the sidewalk near the park. Perhaps it was Vermilia's fault, in some incoherent way. He did not control himself, and drained the girl, among the trees. Her passage from slight surprise to thrill to ecstasy to delirium and oblivion, was encompassed in two hours. Because he had been incautious, he had then to obscure her death, to cut her throat – almost bloodless – and roll her down the 3 am slope into the kids' wading pool. One more puzzle for all those whirling car-bound cops.

The next night he began the hunt.

He was very perplexed not to find her at once, Vermilia.

But the reason he did not was very stupid. He had never thought she would return instantly to the bar, and do exactly the same there as before.

When she left with her new beau, a muscled moron, he let her have him. Did not even bother to go in the building with them – the same building.

Presently, about half an hour after, the moron came plunging out, looking both smug and unnerved.

He went up to him. 'Say, are you okay, son?'

'Sure, sure – some weird babe.'

'You gotta be careful.'

'Yeah, old man, I guess you do.'

He knew the moron, who had surgical dressing now on his thick neck, saw him as some cobwebby, bent old guy, leaning on a cane.

The moron swaggered off, proud of his youth. She must have let him have some sex, in payment. Perhaps the blood had been good; he looked strong. But it was not always that way; sometimes the puny ones had the nicest taste.

He went in, and the doorman, watching TV, called out, 'Mind the floor, Mr Korowitcz. Woman spilled the wash bucket, still damp.'

The elevator took him up to 51, and he walked along to her door. Presumably it *was* her door. Of course, she might have taken the stairs, as he had, last time. But why would she? Unless she had seen him – there was always that.

He tried the door.

He was thinking, she might assume it was the moron back, angry maybe, or just wanting another helping.

Or she merely might not answer.

Then the door opened.

She looked right up at him in a cool still amazement that made him aware she had, somehow, not sensed him at all, not properly *seen* him, until that moment.

Later, writing, he wrote: 'Should I have been more careful? *I*? I was innocent after all, worse than the "boy" in the bar. How could I guess?'

She said, 'Who are *you*?'

'A ... kindred spirit.'

'Really?'

She looked glad enough to have him there. But that was usual. To the one he focused on, he was everything, a prince among men. With his own kind, it was not quite the same. Even so. He was all her conquests had not been, and more. What struck him was that she did not seem at all wary. No, she was inviting – if not exactly yielding.

'May I come in?'

She laughed. 'I see. I have to ask you over the threshold.'

'I think you know better than that.'

'Do I?'

'We,' he said, peremptorily, 'decide. Asked or not.'

'My.' She pivoted. 'Come on *in*, then.'

As he passed her, she ran her hand lightly along his arm. Even through the summer jacket, he felt the *life* of her.

The apartment was in keeping with its grand façade and foyer, and just as dimly lit. What startled him was its total ambience of cliché. Velvet draperies hung, and tall white candles burned, dark perfumes wafted, Byzantine chant murmured, stained glass obscured the windows. There were no mirrors he could see. This room was exactly what *humans* expected a vampire's apartment to be. Yes, even to the skull on the real marble mantle, the ancient dusty books, and the chess-set in ivory and ebony stood ornately to one side.

He had never come across, on the rare occasions that he met them, any vampire who lived like this, and he himself did not. His room was inexpensive and plain, without curios. Without, really, anything.

She had a piano too.

Now she walked over to it, and ran her fingers over the keys – clashing with the chanting. He could tell from the way she did that, too, she could not play the thing at all. Show then. Just for show.

'Like a drink?' she said. 'Or am I being forward?' And she snapped her teeth.

He smiled. Grimly. Her vulgarity – he would have preferred to leave. But something – herself, obviously – held him there.

A drink … She was perverse, kinky, a freak. Vampires did sometimes like such games together. He too had done so, long, long ago. Acting prey-predator, drinking each other's blood. It could be amusing, as a novelty. But that was all it was. She, though, he could tell from some infinitesimal quivering in her, found the idea a turn-on.

Was it just possible she did not believe he was what he was – one of her own kind?

He walked over to the sofa and sat down, sinking miles deep. She moved about him, round the room, prowling like a cat, and now, to his disgust, lit some sort of incense She must be very young. She looked about 25 – maybe less than a hundred, then. For vampires, though immortal, did age, in their own way. No sags or wrinkles, but something in the line of the bones, the way they *were*.

'But tell me about yourself,' she coyly said.

And she came and sat down beside him, leaning back a little, displaying herself, her eyes gleaming now, yet still elusive – *reflective*, like the mirrors she did not have.

'Nothing to tell,' he said. 'You know that. Our lives are all very much the same.'

'Why are you here?' she asked.

He looked at her. Why was he?

'You,' he said.

'I've put my spell on you. I did that the other night, didn't I? Across the bar. I thought, my oh my.'

'Did you?'

'Yes. I bet you spied on me with Puddie.'

'With *whom*?'

'Puddle. That guy.'

'Which one?'

She smiled, and her teeth glinted. He could see their sharpness. She was not being careful. Of course, with him, that would be a futile precaution.

'You know what I do. And I know what you do,' she said. 'Come on, let's do it.'

'You want that with me?'

'You bet I do. Oh yes. So much.'

He did not want to drink from her. Later, he wrote, 'I wanted nothing less than her blood. That was my fatal mistake. But she had – as she said so naively, foiling me further, cast a spell on me of some sort. And for me, Vermilia was the first of my kind for all that time.'

He lay back, almost bored. 'Ladies first.'

'Oh, how sweet. Yes, then.'

As she leaned over him, he had – he afterwards told himself – a premonition. But he was too indolent to heed it.

She smelled wonderful too, new scents; fresh-baked bread and fresh-cut melon, and this perfume, and the incense smoke that had caught in her hair.

Her bite was clumsy. She hurt him and he swore.

Why put up with this? He was thinking, he would give her one minute.

He wrote, 'Suddenly something happened to me. Unprepared – how could I be otherwise? – I was flooded, overwhelmed. The – no other word is legitimate – *rapture*.'

He did not, writing, compare it at all to sex. But again, probably, that was the nearest comparable thing. The tingling, surging, racing – and presently, the pleasure- gallop exploded as if it hit some crystal ceiling of the brain – a kind of orgasm. He blacked out.

When he came to, which, that first time, was only a few seconds later, she was sat back, looking at him, licking her lips.

'Sorry I hurt you,' she said. 'I need them sharpened again. The teeth, I mean. But my little Chinese guy, who does it for me – he's off someplace. He's a great dentist , too.'

He was thinking, *Is that what they feel, when I –?* Dizzy and wondering, when she put her hand up to her lips. She slipped the two eye-teeth out of her mouth. They were removable caps. Her own teeth – were blunt, ordinary.

'Did you like that, honey?' she asked, needlessly. 'I'll make some coffee.'

While she was gone, somehow he found the strength to get up, and get out of the apartment.

In the elevator, he almost passed out a second time.

As he wandered across the foyer, the doorman said, 'You don't look too good, Mr O'Connor.'

He thought doubtless he did not.

Having no intention of going back, the next night he hunted among the bars many blocks away from the gothic building.

He took three women, and each time found he had killed them, which was a nuisance, in the matter of disposal. The last one he did not bother to hide, leaving her among the trash cans in an alley. Despite the excess of blood, he felt enervated, and depressed.

The following night he overslept, waking two hours before midnight. This was not unheard of for a vampire. But it was rare.

Vermilia.

He found himself in some nightclub, sipping a mineral water that cost seven dollars, saying her name in his head – the name he had given her.

He kept thinking about what had happened to him, with her. He was pretty sure he had also dreamed of it.

Again, vampires did dream. But not much.

He wrote, 'I am like some little virgin bride after her first night. I infuriate myself.'

He discovered that now, when he took the blood from his prey, he did not enjoy it so much. At first, desperate for the blood, he had not noticed.

Did he, then, want the blood of Vermilia? Somehow, that thought revolted him. Almost made him, in fact, retch. Why was that? The blood of another vampire could not properly nourish. But it was not repulsive, or poisonous –

He thought of her leaning to him, and piercing his throat with the peculiar caps she needed because somehow her teeth had grown deformed and useless. He thought of the rhythm beginning, and his head went round.

He bought a bottle of Jack Daniels. Drank some. Threw up.

The next night, he threw up the blood he had taken from his prey. Twice.

He lay in the dark of his bare room, cursing her.

What was it? What had happened to him? A human might have feared some disease, but he, a vampire, was immune to such diseases. And she, a vampire, would not carry any disease.

The *next* night, he went to the gothic building. And in the foyer the TV-doorman turned morosely and said, 'Hey, bud, who the hell are you?'

He stood there, made stupid. Never before had he been seen like this, when he had not meant to be.

He mumbled, 'Number 51. The lady.'

'Oh, who's that?'

Who indeed?

'She knows me.'

'Okay, bud. No funny stuff. Get outa here.'

He walked out, and there was Vermilia, like in the best movie, dawdling toward him up the street. She wore black tonight, but her mouth was still the proper colour.

'Honey!' she cried. She ran and hugged him. 'You look beat.'

They walked by the doorman, who now seemed to see neither of them.

In the elevator she jabbered about some idiotic thing, he did not grasp what she said. Why was he here – with her?

In the apartment, she lit the candles, the incense.

He stood coughing and trembling.

'Like a beer?'

'I'd like you to do what you did last time.'

'Oh sure. But let's get in the mood.'

He fell down on the sofa. She caressed him. He writhed with need and dragged her mouth to his neck. 'Do it. For God's sake –'

She did it.

It was the same as before. Ecstasy, racing, explosion. Out.

This time he was unconscious for an hour. She said so anyway, shaking him. 'Come on. You always fall asleep. If you weren't so beautiful ... I need my bed. I have to be at work in the mornings.'

New stupefaction hit him only as he reeled towards the elevator. *Mornings?*

Three more times he went to her. Between, he was able to take a little blood, here and there. It was no longer easy to do this. Partly because he did not properly want it, and besides sometimes got sick when he had taken it. Also partly because his ability to seduce seemed strangely less. In the past, he had needed only to look, perhaps to touch or speak. That was enough. Even at the moment of impact, if there was a struggle, his great strength could subdue at once, but, more likely he could still them with a brushing of his lips, a whisper.

Now some of the prey got cold feet. Some fought with him.

And he did not have the energy to pursue these ones. And anyway, he knew, he was losing it. Losing it all.

He thought he had said to her, the third time, 'What have you done to me, what *are* you?'

And she had said, 'I'm a vampire, honey. Just like you. Only you just like to play it one way, don't you?

But that's fine by me. I like it best this way. Sometimes.'

More than the terrifying pleasure, it was something else that brought him back, and back. The spell. But what *was* the spell?

'How old are you?' he said.

'You're no gentleman,' she said. Then she said, 'Oh, hundreds of years, of course.' She lied. He knew she lied.

It was worse than that. She was losing interest in him. She had by now told the doorman to let him up, but when he was with her, now, she said, 'You might do something for *me*.'

What was she talking about? Exhausted he closed his eyes. Exhausted, he begged her to do what she did.

That time, when he came around, he knew she was killing him.

It had to stop.

But he was hooked.

'Okay,' she said. 'Come tomorrow. I may have a friend here. You'll like her.'

'Will you -?'

'Yes. Go on now. It's so late. You were asleep *four* hours and I couldn't wake you.'

'You have work in the morning,' he drearily remarked.

'Sure do. My stinking job.'

'But the sun,' he said.

'Oh, get out of here,' she said, laughing and impatient.

Outside – he leaned on her door and then he began to see. Swimming down in the nauseated elevator, he saw more.

The doorman glared. 'Hey, you on drugs or something, mister?'

He got to his bare room, and lay down.

Tomorrow night. He would go. He could not help himself. No-one could help him. But he thought now he understood. And tomorrow, before he left, he would write it in his book. In case, in the future, to some other this same thing might happen, as well it might.

As well it might.

'This is Raven,' she said.

Raven had long black hair and a face made up white as a clown's. At the corner of her mouth she had painted a ruby drop, but her lipstick was black.

'My,' said Raven, and she curtseyed to him, leering. But Raven was the same as Vermilia – the same kind and species.

Tonight it was to be different, Vermilia said. They would take off all their clothes. They took them off.

He stared at their bodies, Vermilia's perfect, Raven's not, both irrelevant.

In turn they ogled him.

Then they all lay down on the wide sofa. The girls drank wine, and tongued him, and all he could smell was hair and flesh and perfume and wine, and all he wanted was for them to have his blood, and he knew this time would be the last, and he cursed himself and them and the world and all his hundreds of years that had not saved him. Consumed with fear, he shook with desire.

'He likes to be the subserve,' said Vermilia. He hated her accent. Hated her. 'Go on, Rave, he'll like it.'

Raven picked up his wrist. She sank in her teeth, also caps, he supposed. The pain was horrible. He wished he could kill her. Then, it began, even so, began –

And Vermilia's lips were on his neck, and then the bite, sharper, better – her dentist must be back in town.

Like an express train, a locomotive of fire, the surge rose up in him. He forgot he would die. Forgot he had been alive.

The fireworks erupted through gold to red and white, and to vermilion.

As his brain and heart burst, he screamed for joy.

Leaving him, Raven and Vermilia, whose true name was Sheila – but who called herself, on such nights, Flamea, which he had never bothered to learn – turned to each other.

When they were through, they got up.

'He sleeps for hours.'

'He's great-looking. But what a drag.'

They left him, and went to get some chocolate cake.

While they were in the kitchen, since he had died and was a vampire, he disintegrated quickly and completely to the finest white dust, which presently blew off through the air, coating the apartment lightly, and making Sheila-Flamea sneeze for days.

Some human myths of vampires were true.

When the girls came back, they commented on his absence, and that he had rudely got up and gone.

'But look, he left his clothes.'

They raised their brows, and shrugged.

Earlier, he had written in his book:

'I know now. She is no vampire. She is a human. A woman playing at being a vampire. This is how she has her fun. Pretending she is our kind. Acting it out.

'But why it should do *this* to me, I have no notion. Perhaps it is only me, but such a scenario may affect others of my kind in the same fashion, and to them I leave this warning.

'We have taken the blood of humans all these millennia. Now, unknowing, they are prepared to take ours – by accident, thinking we are the same as they – or not recognising us – or not thinking there is any difference between us and them. And when they do take our blood – *this* may be the result. I have no answer as to why. I have no resistance to it. Perhaps it has evolved, this power, naturally. Like some virus or germ. Perhaps this is now their *natural* means of protecting themselves against us.'

His last lines were these:

'Her kind have always killed my kind. That used to be with stakes and garlic, honed swords, sunlight and fire. Now, is it this way? Her kind kills my kind with … kindness.'

VHONE

I love my Vhone. Of course, I loved all my other phones too. When they got superseded, I even said a quick goodbye to them as I threw them in the waste-chute. And then each new one became my one True Love. Till the next one.

They all do fantastically useful things now, don't they? I mean, obviously, you can make calls on them, and send messages or actual gifts, and your phone just puts in the order through BuyBuddy (You pay the same way – s'eazy) and your account gets charged. And they turn off or on the lights, the heating, the cooling, or run a bath with essences, or – anything – in your apartment, however far away you are right then. And they can take pix or make movies when you want, and play you music you want, and order you a meal or a drink for you at a grazery, or it's delivered, anything from a steak to a Tasty, a hot Chocolaffo to a stem of white champagne. And they can give you entry to the latest game-course, or let you read something – if you have time to read anything, or show you anything or tell you anything about anything or anywhere in the whole wide world or even in outer space. And naturally a Vhone does all that too. Perfectly.

But the Vhone can do so much more.

I couldn't quite believe the claims when I first saw the ad on my homm-comm.

Then one of my Part Time Friends showed me her Vhone. And first of all it was so chick-chiquette. Glossy black, with that single glowing golden eye – that blinks at you, or gazes at you. And its soft musical voice that can sound like any sleb you want it to – my Vhone has the voice of Claska Krak – dark as dark velvet. And *then* my PTF showed me another thing the Vhone will do. I couldn't believe this right off. 'What – do they *hire* someone?' I stupidly asked. 'But isn't that *illegal*?' 'Oh,' she said, 'don't be stupe. It's not *real*. It just – *seems* so. I mean, like completely real.' 'Yes,' I said, dazed. 'Go on,' she said. 'Buy one. You can afford it after your labour increment. Sure, I'd get a bite of commission, but it's not that. I just think it's *made* for *you*.'

And I thought about this a while, and then I put through the call to *V-V-V-(Ph)One dot star*. And next morning, there was my Vhone. Mine.

I didn't quite have the courage until the fourth night after I got the Vhone.

I think I was a bit scared of being disappointed.

A bit scared, anyway.

PTF had shown me an edited recreation on her own Vhone. But such things can be faked or edited in – I'd believed, but not hard enough. Then, I did it, sent the signal. Trust me, it costs. But as they say, the best things in life are never free.

When they acknowledged the order and lit up the delivery time, which was 23 space mean time (with a prelim of 22-30), the golden eye turned a deep, deep indigo-blue.

I got ready, but mostly they do it. And at 22.23 presc, the sort of cloud stuff came and I found myself, like that girl in the story – Kinda-Bella is it? – in this designer dream-dress and shoes and jewellery, and my hair with extra hair in, and wonderful make-up. And the room had changed, like in the advert it does, and the bed was huge and white and gold, and this chandel-light floated, and champagne was poured. And then through a door that usually isn't there, he came toward me.

Oh and he was – well, maybe a bit like Claska Krak – but, impossibly, even better – oh, I never, not even on a mile-screen – never saw anyone so absol. And he came to me, and smiled into my eyes, and handed me a silvery glass of the champagne, and spoke things to me I won't put here, and kissed me, and kissed me, and never, never in my life – never till then – and we went to the bed, to the fantastic bed the Vhone had made, just as it had made him, only right then I forgot, and even remembering I forget he wasn't really *real* – only – he was, he was – oh, he was.

When I came to I cried. I cried for ten whole minutes, and then I called up five of my PTFriends and let them see the edit-versh, and I said, You've just got to have a Vhone.

And now I am in love with my Vhone, and whenever I can afford to, I order up him. And oh. And oh.

So there you are. Why not you get one too, or two, so maybe you can loan one to another PTF at the special loan-a-lot rate?

Just one more thing. I almost forgot. How you recharge a Vhone. It's unique! And, in its own way, it's such fun, too. You'll love it, honestly.

It's best to do it every second day, if you can. It lets you know anyway if it's low, one soft little blink every three secs.

But I do it when I go to sleep. A lot of my PTs do too. You take it to lie down with you, and it rests against your neck, and then – and this is so special, so sweet – you *feed* it – you feed it from your own blood – and there's *nothing to pay*, you see, nothing. Isn't that special? And it's so gentle and soft. Soft as a little soft conjure-kitten. But you can hear it softly sipping and sipping till it's just nice and full and fully working order again. And then I sleep, and maybe it sleeps. I'll tell you a secret, only I don't think I'm alone in this! To me, well, it's really like a little soft temporary baby. I love it so, and I stroke it as it feeds/recharges. And sometimes – don't tell – I sing to it, just like they used to, back Then. Lulla-lulla-lulla – sleep pretty Vhone, and don't you cry, and I will sing a lullabye ... I love my Vhone.

I love my Vhone.

REAL AND VIRE

How tired she looks, the grey drab little female, sat there squashed among the other exhausted home-going commuters. But she was lucky to have got a seat. She knows it. The ones who must stand, they know it too. And hanging there, each by an arm, from the agonising torture straps that ribbon down from the transport's ceiling – like the filaments of some evil insect – whenever possible, at any lurch of the rumbling vehicle, they stagger and 'accidentally' step on her toes, or kick her narrow little bruised feet in their shoddy footwear, as too the hapless feet of all who have been able to sit. They are, everyone, poor, these travellers – these commuters – obviously, or they would not be in this situation. Low-paid workers, putting in 12 to 16 hours per day or night (or both), six or seven days a week. It is 8 pm now, or 20 by the new compulsory clocks. The transport will reach the last station, at which the downtrodden grey female must alight, around 9 pm, provided there are no more delays or power-failures. But even now a judder goes through the vehicle. It sighs ponderously. So, it seems to say, this human rubbish thinks it is tired? What about myself, the transport? Running all day, all night, *all* days, *all* seasons – sod them. The only rest *I* get *is* when I break down. As the carriages jerk and jumble to another halt, the hanging or squash-sat commuters variously curse or moan. One man even begins to cry, but quickly stubs out his tears like the butts of the recently banned and illegal cigarettes no-one may smoke anymore, though they were filled by carrot-fibre. Just as no-one may drink anything stronger than the heavily disinfected water. Coffee, tea, alcohol have been prohibited for years; recently all sweet drinks, including fruit juice, have become criminal and unavailable. 'Food' of course consists of fake bread spread with an oil-derivative that is oil-less, *invented* meat, *new* vegetables that have neither texture nor flavour. Such is life in the world now.

The transport is definitely stalled again. The grey drab woman makes no complaint, however. She goes on staring vaguely into nothingness. How old is she? Perhaps fifty … fifty-seven? A non-unusual face, thin and dry as the slice of a modern loaf. Eyes empty.

And yet, behind the eyes, one must expect (as no doubt behind the empty opaque eyes of so many of these poor human remnants) is the dream of eventually getting home. Not, that is, a dream of home itself, which for the woman, as for so many of the rest, comprises a room slightly larger than a cupboard, with a separate shared kitchen-cubicle and lavatoriet down the passage. But *in* the room, in the home, will be the wonderful god who can and does save all mankind: a Computer. They – she? – will stagger in, perhaps cram down their throats some mouthful of gormless and unappetising permitted 'food', then activate the Machine of Delight. In this dire day and desperate age, what human being does not resort to that *other* world – the world of Virtual Reality, or 'Vire', as popular abbreviation now has it. Vire, where you can do *anything*, be *anything*, eat banquets, get drunk, fornicate, love and laugh and sing and *live*. That's where home is then, for 99 percent of the populace of these purgatories of contemporary civilisation. The *alternate* world of dreams-that-come-true, haven from hell, the only, yet perfect rescue from Real Life.

Surely, surely, she too must be longing now for that?

And yes … she *is* thinking of her Computer, of course she is. Of the importance of switching over from one existence to another. Reality to Virtuality. Real to Vire to Real to – She has held off so long, feeling guilty. She has refused to do it, resisted. But now, she *must* give in. This has gone on too long.

Skipping then a scene or two more of the beached transport, its slow, wallowing revival, the 11 (23) o'clock station, the grey woman's lonely trudge through nearly unlit streets policed by seeing electric eyes, the opening of a low door, a narrow stair, another lower door, the manifestation of a great golden square of light and potential. Is there the tap-tap of keys, like a piano played in silence? Or did that already occur, before …?

And then – the transformation.

One moment here – then there. (As there, then here.) In-out, out-of in-to. Away, away.

Away.

She is flying, high up, under a sky of midnight black so strung with stars – platinum, green, topaz – it seems light as day to her. But then, inevitably, she has not seen or experienced an actual day for some three hundred years.

Behind her, on its crag, the huge stone mansion, by starlight like a marvellous model cut from blackest granite and lit with tall, dim, blue windows. Below, before, the tumble of the jet-stone forests, their topmost spires star-polished to silver. There, just beneath, the familiar tarn, a piece of mirror that reflects her shadow somewhat, but as no looking-glass on Earth now ever can. But that scarcely matters. She remembers well her beauty, her dark red hair, the moon whiteness of her flawless flesh. Her mouth is red and succulent as edible cinnabar, and set with teeth both peerless and workmanlike.

She swoops down, the tree-tips harmlessly brushing her mostly-invulnerable form, a caress of sharp urgent fingers – but is to come.

And here, miles from her mountain fortress, she sees the villages lying now, updated with concrete and steel and netted electric masts – yet, this way, still littered like pretty pebbles along the banks of the wide river. And next the town appears, also enhanced, but the hedge of its raised needles of church towers remain – at these she only smiles. Crosses will never hurt her; all that is a lie. As for the stake through her beautiful hungry vampire heart, that has been tried, once or twice. It never took. She healed and rose up, laughing, throwing off the soil of her burial like an annoying quilt …

And there now too, directly opening from among the trees beyond the town, she recognises the glade where, some nights ago, she noted a young man standing. He is a poet, who leaves his father's wealthy town house to come out and stargaze. And noticing him then, his handsome face and fine body, she had alighted quietly, and so walked toward him, soft as a gazelle through the pines. And he had not believed his eyes, asking her if she were an angel, or his muse. The opium product he had indulged in earlier had apparently added to his perceptions. But she nodded serenely. Of course, what else. She was and is his angel *and* his muse.

She had done little that first time. A kiss, a sip (the opium was not unpleasant), no more, leaving desire to grow in worth with waiting. And she knows now, while she has liked the gap of waiting, *he* has been frantically yearning – yes, see how pale he is. His eyes so dark and deep – They will take her reflection too, that she alone can see, if inadequately.

'My love – my soul –' he whispers, as she glides down now to the fragrant balsamic ground. He is not alarmed that she can levitate or fly – what else, for an angel?

She slides her slender ivory hands about his neck, holding the strong and glorious vessel of it, a wine cup so charmingly fashioned for her lips to drink at, and at last to drain.

Within a few minutes, no explanation asked or offered, they lie among the clawed roots of the trees. He caresses her very ably and deliciously, then loses all will and becomes an arc of blind singing lust beneath her. Her bite is honed as a serpent's. Through the crystal straw of his vein she sucks out the crimson elixir.

The taste of it –! There is nothing in a million years or worlds, not spice, nor honey, nor wine, to match the flavour and kick of sheer human blood. It is, this drink, the Water of Immortality, red as sunset, clear as diamond. You cannot ever get enough. Until, obviously, all is consumed. She has learned this every time, yet curiously, on each occasion, seems also to forget. The ecstasy of greed and fulfilment is followed always and instantly, by a strange second surge, a sickening emotion – not regret, not sorrow, but a peculiar lowering and heaviness, dullness. She lets him fall back, dead naturally as death itself, a tasty thing now ruined and useless.

For a while after she has left her victim, the beautiful vampire wanders the lighter woodland that opens beyond the pines. On some clear nights she will fly again as far as the coast, and stare across the acres of wave-pleated water, to the unknown and exotic, if undesired, countries that lie there unseen. Why should she bother with them? All places, however dissimilar, are alike to her. She is impervious and absolute. She may do as she pleases. Every door opens to her. And the delirious joy of blood is followed always by the surging out-drawn tide of weight and dreariness.

Long before the pink and hideous dawn has even hinted, she rises up again and soars toward the mountain crag and the mansion that will shelter her in its vaults. Long before she needs to sleep, she will pretend to.

Her house is full of treasures and astonishments – man-size dolls that dance and sing, clockwork birds that twitter and flitter, books seeming old almost as the planet, experiments and games she has invented and played with and let alone. There are also the most ancient puzzles and most current inventions ever devised to amuse and comfort the mind and heart and soul.

In the great chair of gilded bronze and yew she sits a short while. She is considering. But it is too soon. She must not even contemplate – not yet – not *yet* –

She is *day*-dreaming, the beautiful vampire.

Of a stalled train packed with graceless, desperate and exhausted people – or at least the facsimiles of such a train and such people. A mindless and thankless, hard and ill-paid job of work. Of rising at four on mornings still black with night, or grey as ash with night's crushed dog-ends. Of horrible cramped journeys, disgusting food, a room small as a closet, a lavatory-closet (she never, as herself, requires such an essential) smaller almost than the lavatory it holds. Dark pitiless streets with sneaking police-eyes, stinking drains, the ugliness and unimportance of the skinny old-before-its-time face – hers – that she can always see in any mirror. Dreaming of the one she can become, the ash-grey, drab little female working six to 18 o'clock, or to 24 pm if she can get it. A life that is real, solid, dramatic in its awfulness, significant in its despair. Real – but *not* real, of course. For her luxurious and supernatural life here, in the castle, or out hunting the forests for human blood, that – *this* – is the Real World. And how it burdens her, bores her even to death – if she, a vampire, could ever in fact die. Thank God, who of course cannot hurt her either, for human genius that has invented the Computer, and set within it such wonderful miracles as the portal to a second, truer, *better* Fantasy life – the world of Virtual Reality: Vire.

And how she longs now for Vire, even though she has only been back in reality here for part of one night. She must control herself. She must say No. She did before – and then gave in. And so prior to this night, she had remained to revel in the grey glory of the Vire hell-world one whole *month*. Therefore now she must *not* return there after so short a stay in reality.

When the sun rises she will go down to the vaults and step elegantly into her sumptuous coffin, lay her noble head, her fox-red, red hair, her lovely face upon the linen pillow, and sleep. She will not instead, as she has, seal the upper room to blackness, and stay *there*, awake, asleep, in Vire with the Computer … Sleeping in the coffin, if only she might dream truly of the Vire world. But vampires, as she knows too well, never dream.

She has closed and locked up the Computer. The golden gateway of the screen is void. She is an addict and must resist. Tomorrow evening, maybe, she will contact the System, and cancel her membership in the Vire … or maybe …

How tired she looks, the drab female, stood rocking and leaning there, hanging on to the torturer-insect's filament strap dangled from the transport ceiling. Then the transport jumps again, and once more everyone missteps. A man treads heavily on her toe.

A squeak of genuine pain. A sigh. Sheer bliss.

THE BEAUTIFUL BITING MACHINE

When the two suns go down and it starts to get dark, the Nightfair wakes up, a beast with a thousand bright eyes.

Five miles long, four miles wide, the valley is full of lights, noises, musics, between the tall and echoing hills.

This world's a pleasure planet. It has many and various attractions. The Nightfair is only one. Here there are spinning wheels of yellow sparks against the dusk, and glimmering neon ghost towers ringing with screams, and carousels that maybe come alive. Not everyone cares for these, or the candy awnings, the peppermint arenas, the cries of fortune-tellers in glass cages, the crashing of prearranged safe vehicular accidents, the soaring space-flights that never leave the ground. Those that don't care for them don't come. But for those that do, there are the cuisine and superstition and popular art, the sex and syntax and the sin of twenty worlds, to be sampled for a night, or a week of nights. (Who could tolerate more?)

So visit the Valley of Lights. Hurry, hurry, don't be slow or sly or shy.

Welcome to the Nightfair.

This gentlevyrainian's gotta slight complaint.'

'Tell him to see a doctor.'

'Don't cheek me, Beldek.'

'No, Mr Qire. What seems to be the trouble, sir?'

Beldek and Qire looked through the one-way window at the gentleman from Vyraini. Like all Vyrainians, he was humanoid, greenish, fretful. Vyraini did not esteem the human race, but was patronisingly intrigued by it and its culture. Anything human, where possible, should be experienced, explored. Now this Vyrainian had come to Qire's pavilion at the Nightfair, and was not quite satisfied, had a slight complaint.

'Go and talk to it – him,' said Qire.

'*Me*, sir?'

'You. You speak their lingo. You speak half the damn gurglings of half the damn galaxy, don't you, Beldek? You lazy son-of-a-ghex.'

'If you say so, Mr Qire.'

Beldek opened the long window and stepped through. The other side of the window it looked like a door, glamorous with enamel paint and stained glass. Beldek bowed to the gentlevyrainian with his hands to his face, which was the correct form of greeting from an outworlder. The Vyrainian stood impassive, ears folded.

'*Fo ogch m'mr bnn?*' Beldek inquired courteously.

The Vyrainian seemed gratified, lifted its ears and broke into staccato Vyrainese.

The glottal conversation continued for two and a half minutes. After which, feeling Qire's beady little eyes on him through the one-way door-window, Beldek leisurely set the computer for a twenty percent refund.

The Vyrainian took its cash, and offered Beldek the salute used when bidding farewell to an inferior but valuable alien. Not all Earthmen knew exactly what the salute implied (a rough translation was: I will let you lick my feet another time, O wise one). Beldek, who did, smiled pleasantly.

The whaal-ivory screens of the outer doors closed on the Vyrainian's exit.

Beldek turned as Qire came storming from the inner office. Qire was a bulging, broad-faced type, the little eyes somewhat slanting, the mane of golden hair an implant. His clothes, though gaudy, were the best – real silk shirt, whaal-leather sandals. A ruby in his neck-chain.

'Why d'yah do that?'

'What, Mr Qire, sir?'

'Refund the bastard his money.'

'Twenty percent. The amount he agreed would compensate for the slight complaint.'

'What was wrong with her?'

Beldek said, ultra-apologetically, fawningly, 'A little something I told you about, that clicks –'

'Why the Garbundian Hell didn't you, for Christ's sake, get it fixed?'

'I have tried, Mr Qire,' said Beldek humbly. 'I truly have.'

Qire glowered.

'I should put you out on your butt. Why don't I?'

'I'm useful?' Beldek, attempting humbly to be helpful, now.

'Like urx-faron you are. All right. Give me the receipts. I'm going over to Next Valley. I'll be here again five-day week. Chakki'll be by in three days.'

Beldek keyed the computer for the cash receipts, tore them off when they came, and presented them to Qire. Qire riffled through them, glancing for mistakes. 'Okay, Beldek. I want to hear from Chakki that *she's* back in good order, you savvy?'

'Oh yes, Mr Qire, *sir*.'

Qire swore. At the whaal-ivory doors he turned for one last snarl.

'I've got other concerns on this planet, Beldek. If Malvanda packs up, it's no great loss to me. You're the one'll suffer. Back to hoofing the space-lanes with your card tricks and your dipscop seventh-rate jaar. You get me?'

'To the heart, sir,' said Beldek. 'And all the way up *yours*, Mr Qire.'

Qire cursed him and slammed out.

The doors, ever serene, whispered shut in his wake.

Beldek leaned on the ornamental counter, keying the computer, which he had long ago rigged, to count the amount he had creamed off Qire's takings for the last five-day period. Qire, of course, guessed he did this. It was an inevitable perk of the job. All told, Qire seemed to value disliking Beldek. Value the hypertensive rage that came to the boil whenever Beldek's cool clear eyes met his with such angelic sweetness above the long, smiling mouth that said: Yes, Mr Qire, *sir*. Most of the human portion of the Valley of Lights knew about Qire's hatred of his employee Beldek, the drifter from the space-lanes. Beldek who could speak half the languages of the galaxy, and could charm rain from a desert sky, if he wanted. Usually he didn't want. Beldek, whose un-implanted long thick lank brass-coloured hair hung on his shoulders and over his high wide forehead. Lean as a sculpture and tall, from birth on some unspecified lower-gravity world. Pale and pale-eyed. Something about him: more than the rumoured past, card-sharp, kept creature of male, female, humanoid ... tales of a man murdered out among the stars ... More than the fact of working for Qire, in attendance on one of the weirdest novelties of the Nightfair. Be careful of Beldek.

The pavilion stood on a rise. A quarter of a mile below, a bowl of dizzy fires, the Arena of Arson, flashed and flared. Back a way, one of the great wheels whirled gold against the black sky. But the crimson pavilion was clouded round with Sirrian cedars. Far-off lamps winked on their branches; the apex of the pavilion, a diadem of rose-red glass lit subtly from within, just pierced, with a wicked symbolism of many carnal things, from the upper boughs. Once among the trees, the rest of the Fair seemed siphoned off. You came to the kiosk with the ivory doors. You went in, read something, signed something, paid something, and were let through another door, this one of black Sinoese lacquer. And then the Fair was very far away indeed. For then you were in the Mansion of Malvanda. And she was there with you ...

A faint bell chimed on the console. Beldek killed the read-out and looked urbanely at the door-screens. Another customer.

The doors opened.

A new-worlder stepped through. He was alone. Most of them came alone, the same as most were men, or rather, most were male. A mixture of human and some genetically-adhesive other-race, the new-worlder was fresh-skinned, grinning, handsome, and without whites to his eyes.

'Say,' he said.

'Good-evening, gentlenewman. You wish to visit Malvanda's Mansion?'

'Su-ure,' said the new-worlder.

'Take a seat, please.'

Grinning, the new-worlder rippled onto a couch. Double-jointed, too. That should offer Malvanda a challenge.

Beldek came around the counter and extended a small steel wafer.

'You understand, this entertainment being of the kind it is, you must first –'

'Sign a disclaimer? Yes, su-ure.' The new-worlder was already excited, a little drunk or otherwise stimulated. That had usually happened too, before they got themselves to these doors.

The newman accepted the wafer, which hummed, and spoke to him, telling him of possible dangers involved in what he was about to experience. As it droned on, the newman grinned and nodded, nodded and grinned, and sometimes his all-blue eyes went to Beldek, and he grinned wider, as if they were in a conspiracy. When the machine finished, the new-worlder was already up at the counter, his six fingers out for the disclaimer and stylus. He signed with a flourish. He paid the fee in one large bill, and shiftily counted his change from habit, not really concentrating.

'What now?'

'Now you meet the lady.'

'Say,' said the newman.

Beldek fed the disclaimer into the computer. The back of the kiosk murmured and rose, revealing the black lacquer door. The new-worlder tensed. There was sudden sweat on his face and he licked his lips. Then the door opened, inward.

Standing well back by the counter, Beldek got a glimpse of sombre plush, sulky, wine-smoked light, the vague shimmer of draperies in a smooth wind scented with camellias and sorrow-flowers, the floral things of drugged funerals. He had seen the poisonously-alluring aperture, that throbbing carnelian camellia vulva of doorway, many thousands of times. The new-worlder had not. Mindlessly, helplessly, he went forward, as if mesmerised, and poured over the threshold. A heavy curtain fell. The door swung shut. The ultimate orifice had closed upon him.

Beldek moved around behind the counter and touched the voyeur-button. He watched for less than a minute, his face matte as fresh linen, ironed young and expressionless. Then he cut off the circuit.

Such a device, mostly unknown to clients, was necessary by law, which did not call it a voyeur-button. Persons who underwent such events as Malvanda had to be monitored and easy of access should an emergency occur. Twice, before Beldek joined the show, a client had died in there. Because the disclaimers were in order, and medical aid was rushed to the spot, Qire was covered and no action resulted. The newman, however, had registered healthy on the wafer. Beldek had told at a glance he was strong. There was no need to watch.

Qire sometimes came around just to do that. There was a more private extension of the voyeur-button in the cubicle off the inner office. Qire had not invented Malvanda's Mansion, only sponsored the design and then bought the product. But he liked it. He liked to watch. Sometimes, Qire brought a friend with him.

Beldek went into the inner office and dropped crystals in his ears that would play him an hour of wild thin music, a concerto for Celestina and starsteel.

He did not need to watch Malvanda.

He knew what happened.

When the hour was up, Beldek tidied the office, and reset the computer. The panels dimmed one by one as the lamps softened in the kiosk and the carnal peak on the roof went out. The new-worlder was the last customer of the night. In thirty minutes, dawn would start to seep across the eastern hills.

As Beldek was revamping the computer program for tomorrow night, the black lacquer door shifted open behind him. He heard the newman emerge, stumbling a little on his double joints.

The hiccupping footsteps got all the way to the whaal-ivory doors before the voice said, 'Say.' The voice had changed. It was husky, demoralised. 'Say.'

Reluctantly, abrasively polite, Beldek turned. He levelled a wordless query at the sagging male by the kiosk doors. The newman's eyes were muddy, looking sightless. He seemed to go on trying to communicate.

'Yes, sir?'

'Nothing,' said the new-worlder. 'Just – nothing.' The doors opened and like a husk he almost blew into the diluting darkness, and away through the dregs and embers of the Fair.

Whatever else, the click in the mechanism obviously hadn't spoiled it for him at all.

By day, the Nightfair goes to ground. Some of the big architectures and marts sink down literally into the bedrock. Others close up like clams. Coming over the hills too early, you get a view of acres of bare earth, burned-looking, as if after some disaster. Here and there the robot cleaning-machines wander, in a snowstorm of rinds, wrappers, drugstick butts, lost tinsels. Places that stand, naked to the two eyes of heaven, the pair of dog-suns, have a look of peeled potatoes, indecent and vulnerable.

Awnings of durable wait like rags, dipped flags, for the glow and glitter of neon night.

The peoples of the Nightfair are wolves, foxes, coomors, they sleep by day in their burrows, or their nests up in the scaffolded phantom towers, among the peaceful wrecks of sky-buses, their wry lemon dreams filling the air with acids.

In the last of the afternoon there begins to be some movement, furtive, rats on a golden hill of rubbish littered with tin-can calliopes.

'Beldek, is that you, you ghexy guy?'

Qire's runner, Chakki, having used his key to the whaal-ivory doors, peered about the office.

'Who else did you hope to find?'

Beldek was tinkering with a small box of wires and three or four laser-battery tools. He did not turn round. Chakki now and then dropped by, never when expected, checking up for Mr Qire, or just nosing. Scrawny and pretty, Chakki was a being of instinct rather than thought or compunction, an alley cat that runs in, steals a chicken dinner, pees in a corner, and, soulless physical ghost, is gone.

'What ya doing, lovely Beldek?'

'Trying to repair a click.'

'My ... Malvanda clicketh. Yeah, I heard about it. Better now?'

'We shall see.'

'You going in to give it her?'

Beldek walked past him toward the back wall of the kiosk, which was going up to reveal the door of Sinoese lacquer.

'You lucky buck. Bet she bends ya.'

'So long, Chakki.'

The lacquer door started to open. Chakki stared tiptoe over Beldek's shoulder into camellia, carnelian, lilies-go-roses, funereal virgo unintacta.

'Let's have a piece, Bel?'

'If you can afford it. Come back tonight with the other clientele.'

'Go swiff yourself, Bell*rung*.'

The curtain fell. The door had closed.

Beyond the door, no matter the time of day or season, it was always midnight in Indian Summer.

Around the great oval room there were long windows that seemed to give onto a hot perfumed night, mobile only with the choruses of crickets. There were lush gardens out there, under the multiplicity of stars, the best constellations of ten planets, and beyond the gardens, hills, the backs of black lions lying down. Now and then a moth or two fluttered like bright flakes of tissue past the open glass. They never came in. It might distract the customer.

The roof apparently was also of glass, ribbed into vanes, like the ceiling of a conservatory. You saw the stars through it, and soon a huge white moon would come over, too big to be true.

There were carpets on the walls. Draperies hung down, plum velvets, transparencies with embroidery and sequins, dividing the room like segments of a dream. Everything bathed in the aromatic smoke of a church of incense candles. The other scent was flowers. They bloomed out of the bodies of marble animals grouped around little oases of water thick with sinuous snake-fish. Red-black flowers, albino flowers, flowers stained between red and white and black, grey flowers, fever and blush flowers, bushes of pale, sighing faints.

The marble stair went up to shadows, and reflected in the polished floor. If you looked in the floor at the reflection, presently something moved, upside down, a figure in fluid. Then you looked up again at the stair. And saw Malvanda, out of the shadows, coming down.

Malvanda was tall and 22 years old, slim but not slender, her shoulders wide for elegance, her hips wide as if to balance panniers, her waist to be spanned by a man's hands, her breasts high and firm and full to fill them, spill them. Malvanda's skin was as white as the sorrow-flowers, with just that vague almost-colourless flush, at the temples, ear-lobes, hollow of the throat, insteps, wrists … that the sorrow-flowers had at the edges of their petals. She was platinum blonde. Flaxen hair without a trace of gold or yellow, hair that is white, like moonlight blanching metal. Her eyebrows were just two shades darker, but her lashes were like tarnished brass and her eyes were like untarnished brass. Wolf-colour eyes, large; glowing now, fixed on him.

A small movement of her head shifted the coils of platinum hair away over her shoulder. The column of her throat went down and down into the crimson dress. The V of the neckline ended just under her breasts. She smiled a little, just a very little. Her lips were a softer crimson than the gown. Rose mouth. She began to come toward him, and her hand stole from her side, moving out to him ahead of her, as if it couldn't wait to make contact.

Beldek walked up to her, and, as the smooth hand floated to his arm, he guided her fingers away. He ran his own hand in under the heavy silk hair to the base of her skull and touched.

Switched off, Malvanda stood quite still, her lips slightly parted, her eyes dreaming, brazen, swimming with late afternoon veldt.

Beldek ran his thumb around her throat and jabbed into the hollow. He pressed the second disc under her right ear, and the third under her left index fingernail, deactivating the safety. There had to be a suitably obtuse series of pressures, to avoid random deactivation by a client, when caressing her. Beldek knelt at Malvanda's feet. He raised the hem of her gown and drew one flawless foot onto his knee. He gripped under the instep, and drew out the power-booster from the panel.

Then he got up and went around, undoing the cling-zip on the back of her gown. The keyboard opened where her lower spine should be. He compared it to the box of wires he had brought in, then, selecting one of the fine plumbing needles, he began to work on her.

After four and a half minutes he found the fault that might be responsible for the unfortunate click that had offended the aesthetic values of the Vyrainian. Two levers, the size of whiskers, had unaligned and were rubbing together. Looking through the magnifier, he eased them away and put in a drop of stabiliser. That area of the board could be overheating, so causing the levers' unwanted expansion together. He would need to check it again in a couple of days.

Having closed the panel and sealed her dress, he replaced the power-booster in her foot. The gauge in her board had showed nearly full, so it was time to empty the sac before reactivating.

Very gently, Beldek parted her beautiful carmine lips, and reached in, past the beautiful teeth, to the narrow tube of throat.

The sac was not too easy to come at, of course. When Qire took him on, the first two things he had wanted to see were Beldek's hands. Articulate and long-fingered, they had passed the test.

Beldek was half-way through disposing of the sac's contents when he heard a noise behind him.

The moon was coming up over the glass ceiling, augmenting the candle-and-lamplight. Not that he really needed it to see Chakki, transfixed there, against the curtain with his mouth open and his eyes bulging.

Before coming in, Beldek always cut off the voyeur-button, both on the console and in the office cubicle. At such times as this, the computer would only release the black lacquer door to Beldek. Somehow, Chakki had found a way either to fool the computer or to force the door.

'What the Garbundian Hop-Hell are you doing, Beldek?' said Chakki, all agog.

'Emptying the sac,' said Beldek. 'As you saw.'

'Yeah but –' Chakki burst into a wild laugh. 'Holla, man. You're kinkier than I ever thought.'

Chakki, unable to spy in the usual way, had obviously badly wanted to see Beldek in operation with Malvanda. Chakki had always, blatantly, imagined Beldek liked to get free what the patrons paid for. If he'd managed an entry one minute earlier, or one minute later, it need not have mattered.

'Kinkier than you thought? Of course I am, Chakki.' Beldek resettled the sac in Malvanda's mouth, and let it go down the throat, always an easier manoeuvre this, than retraction. He keyed on the relays. Malvanda did not move just yet. She took a moment to warm up after deactivation. 'I suppose I'll have to bribe you, now, Chakki. Won't I?'

Chakki giggled. He looked nervous. In a second he would start to back away.

'How about,' said Beldek, 'a free ride with Malvanda?' Then he sprinted, faster than any alley cat, straight through the candlelamp moonlight. He caught Chakki like a lover. 'How about that?' he asked, and Chakki shivered against him, scared now, but not quite able to make up his mind to run.

Beldek led him firmly, kindly stroking him a little, to the centre of the floor where Malvanda had been left standing.

As they got near, her eyelids flickered.

'She's something,' said Chakki. 'Maybe I could come round tonight.'

'Busy tonight. Do it now. You always wanted to. Have fun.'

Chakki's shiver grew up into a shudder. He glanced toward the curtained door. Then Malvanda woke up.

Beldek moved aside. Malvanda's hand went to Chakki's face, sensuous and sure.

She was taller than Qire's runner. Beldek's height. Her mouth parted naturally now, the wonderful strange smile, inviting, certain. Just showing the tips of the teeth.

This time, Beldek *would* watch.

Chakki wriggled, still afraid. But the drugs in the candles were affecting him by now, and the water-lily touches, on the neck, the chest, slipping, lingering. He put out one hand, careful, into her neckline, and found a breast. Half-frightened, aroused, wanting approval, he looked at Beldek. 'She feels *real*.'

'She's meant to, Chakki.'

'Hey, I never really saw what you –'

'That's okay, Chakki. Enjoy.'

Malvanda's strawberry tongue ran over Chakki's lips. Her left arm held him like a loved child, her right hand moved like a small trusting animal seeking shelter, and discovered it, there in Chakki's groin, and played and tickled, and burrowed, and coiled.

They were on the couch now. Chakki with his clothes off, with handfuls of Malvanda's gown clenched in his fists, his nose between her breasts, was writhing and squeaking. Malvanda bent her head to do the thing they paid for, and the thing Chakki had not paid for. The true thrill, the perverse unique titillation that Malvanda offered. Her platinum hair fell over them, obscuring. But Beldek knew what went on under the wave of hair. Chakki was coming, noisily and completely, the way most of them did.

Beldek walked quickly across to the couch. He tapped Malvanda on the right shoulder, just once.

He had had the maintenance of her a long while. He had been able to innovate a little. A very little. Enough. Provision for a Chakki day.

Chakki was subsiding. Then struggling.

'Beldek,' he said, 'she's still – ah – Christ – Beldek!'

His arms flailed and his legs, as naked and puny. Chakki tried to push Malvanda away. But Malvanda was strong as only a machine could be. She held him down, pinned beneath her, her marmoreal body oblivious to the kicks and scratches that did not even mar its surface, as she went on doing what Beldek had just told her to go on doing.

Ignoring the screams, which gradually became more frenzied and more hopeless, Beldek walked out of Malvanda's Mansion.

The marks where the door had been forced were not bad but quite plain. A paint job would see to it. Chakki would have planned to do that before Qire got back. Now Qire would have to see them.

Beldek shut the door and Chakki's last wailing thinning shrieks were gone.

Just before suns' set, Beldek called Qire on the interphone. He broke the news mildly. Qire's runner had got through the Mansion door when Beldek was in the bathroom. Entering the Mansion to check Malvanda, Beldek found Chakki. He had died of haemorrhage and shock, the way the two others had. There was, obviously, no disclaimer. What did Quire want him to do?'

He could hear the boss-man sweating all along the cable from Next Valley.

'You called anyone else, Beldek?'

'No.'

'The pol?'

'Not yet.'

He listened to Qire bubbling over, over there. The two prior deaths in Qire's pavilion made things awkward, despite all the cover on the world. This third death, minus cover, could look like shoddy goods. And Chakki was a private matter. Beldek had known what Qire would do.

'All right. Don't call 'em. You listening, Beldek?'

'Oh yes, Mr Qire. Most attentively.'

'Don't scad me, Beldek. I'm gonna give you a number. You call *that*. Someone'll come see to things. Okay?'

'Anything you say, Mr Qire.'

'And keep your mouth shut.'

'Yes, *sir*.'

Qire gave him the number and he used it. The voice at the other end was mechanised. He said to it the brace of phrases Qire had briefed him with, and then there were noises, and the line went blind.

The suns were stubbed out and the wild flame wheels began to turn on the sky of Indian ink, and the coloured arsons shot across the arena bowl below, and the carousels practised their siren-songs and got them perfect.

Someone came and tried to breach the darkened pavilion.

Beldek went out and stood on the lawn.

Two Pheshines stared from their steamy eyes, lashing their tails in the grass.

'*Dena mi ess, condlu ess, sollu ess. Dibbit?*'

Beldek had told them, in Phesh, the show was closed. The gentlephesh did *dibbit*, and went off spitting to each other.

The nondescript carry-van drew up an hour later. Men walked into the kiosk and presently into the Mansion. They walked out with a big plastic bag and took it away.

Beldek had already cleaned up, before they came.

Not much later, Beldek lit the pavilion and opened for business, but no-one else stopped by that night.

Beldek sat up in the tall echoing hills, watching the dawn borning and the Nightfair slink to ground.

Malvanda, had she been real, would not have been able to do this. Sunlight was anathema to Malvanda's kind. Sunlight and mirrors and garlic-flowers, and thorns, and crucifixes and holy wafers, and running water. It just went to show.

Beldek leaned back on the still-cool slate, looking down the four by five miles of the valley.

Gorgeous Malvanda, Terran turn-on, Phesh *tasha-mi*, Venusian wet dream; Angel of Orgasm, kiss of death. Malvanda, the Beautiful Biting Machine. Malvanda the robot vampire.

He didn't know her whole history. How some sick-minded talent had thought her up and put her together. Her place of origin was a mystery. But what she did. He knew that. A connoisseur's sexual *desideratum*. The actual bite was controlled to a hair's breadth by her keyboard. The teeth went in, naturally. She sucked out blood. That's what they paid for, was it not? Money's worth. Blood money. Only a little, of course. More would be dangerous. And the teeth left built-in coagulant behind them, zippering up the flesh all nice. Unimpaired, the client staggers forth, only a bit woozy. A bite woozy.

Some of them even came back, days, months, years later, for another turn.

It was harmless, unless you were sick, had some weakness …

Or unless Beldek tapped Malvanda's right shoulder that particular way he had when she was with Chakki. Then another key snapped down its command through her wires and circuits. And Malvanda kept on biting, biting and sucking, like a bloody vacuum cleaner. Till all the blood was in Malvanda's throat sac and spilling over and on the floor and everywhere. But Beldek had cleaned that away, and bathed her, and changed her gown, before Qire's goonfriends arrived with their big plastic bag.

It had been fairly uncomplex to tidy his mistake, this time. But he must beware of mistakes from now on. Tomorrow, today, Beldek would work something out to make the Mansion door impregnable.

Even so, Beldek didn't really mind too much. It had been a bonus, all that blood. Better than just the contents of the sac, which Chakki had, unfortunately for Chakki, seen Beldek drinking earlier.

Beldek sunned himself on the hills for several hours. He never browned in sunshine, but he liked it, it was good for him. His hair, the tone of Malvanda's eyes, gleamed and began playfully to curl.

When he strolled back through the valley, the Fair was in its somnolent jackal-and-bone midday phase. Qire's buggy was at the entry to the pavilion. Qire was inside, in the Mansion, pawing Malvanda over, and the furnishings, making sure everything had been left as the customers would wish to find it.

Beldek followed him in.

'I should throw you out on your butt,' said Qire.

'Throw me,' said Beldek. 'I'll have some interesting stories to tell.'

Qire glared.

'Don't think you can make anything outa what happened. It was your, for Christ's sake, negligence.'

They both knew Qire would never fire him. Beldek was too handy at the job. And knew too much. And would be too difficult to dispose of.

Presently they went into the office and Qire handed Beldek a sheaf of large notes. 'Any noise,' said Qire, 'something might happen you might not be happy about. And fix that damn door. *She* seems okay. She damaged at all?'

'No. Still what your pamphlets say. The Night- Blooming Bella Donna of Eternal Gothic Fantasy.'

When Qire had gone, Beldek listened to symphonies on music crystals in the office.

It had always rather fascinated him, the way in which vampires, a myth no-one any longer believed, had become inextricably and dependently connected with sex. Actually, vampirism had nothing to do with sex. Beldek could have told them that. Just as it had nothing to do with sunlight or mirrors or crosses. It was simply and solely (though not soully) about basic nourishment.

Later, he set the program for the night. He had a premonition there would be a lot of custom. Somehow, without anyone knowing about it in any logical way, some enticing whiff of velvet morbidity would be blowing around the pavilion, luring them in like flies. The sac would have to be emptied many times tonight, in Beldek's own special way, which was not the way the instruction manual advocated.

Just before it got dark and he lit up the lights to match the exploding ignition of the Fair, Beldek looked in on Malvanda. She had been returned to her shadowy alcove above the marble stair, and was waiting there for the first client to come in and gaspingly watch her descend. Beldek climbed the steps and brushed her platinum hair, and refilled the perfumery glands behind her ears.

He cared nothing for the sentient races that were his prey. But for the beautiful biting machine, he felt a certain malign affection. Why not? After a century or so of insecure monotonous, and frequently inadequate hit-and-miss hunting, which left little space for other pursuits, the Nightfair had provided Beldek the softest option on twenty worlds. Now Malvanda saw to everything. She paid his bills. She kept him fed.

BEYOND THE SUN

Imagine a night that lasts for one whole year – or longer. Think what you could achieve in a year-long night –

That was what the recruiting flyer said, and their promise wasn't a lie. While of course, when the sun finally constantly rises, you're far away already. Even, if you play the roster carefully, straight into your next long nighttime.

Heth once said, in one of his more lucid moments, 'It's like a chessboard, isn't it, where the white squares don't come on until you've won.'

But I guess I've already won, me, and my kind. Present perfect, and the future beautifully dark. It's only the past that can't be improved. Because, I suppose, the more symmetrically faultless our lives become, the more dangerously unwieldy grow the things that already happened, and the memories that *can't* be made to fit.

We look at Anka in the mirror, Heth and I. He seems happy, satiated. I, Anka, look – what word? *Satisfied?* Heth's one of my two Blood-Donors aboard this ship. He loves to give of himself and blissfully comes, over and over (a pleasant possibility bred into him), as I draw my meal from his smooth veins. His blood tastes good, as ever. And he's a good-looking guy. The best wine, in a charming champagne flute.

'That was great,' he murmurs, sleepy now. He will need a full nine hours' slumber, but that's only sensible.

'Thank you, darling,' say I. 'What would I do without you?'

'Starve?' he dreamily asks. Oh, a snippy moment then.

One can never tell with Heth. Amber skin and ice-blond hair, blue, blue eyes, the colour of the sort of morning sky I haven't seen, except on DV-dex, for almost 200 years.

Corvyra, my other Bee-Dee, isn't at all like him. Sex doesn't come into the equation. We use a slender crystal tube fixed in her alabaster arm. Her hair is a much darker blue than Heth's eyes – more just post-dusk – my sort of time. She has a cat's green eyes. She tastes of fresh oranges; breakfast in a wonderful hotel. We talk about clothes and books and politics as I leisurely drink her. She requires only an hour's rest after sessions. But it all works out okay, or so it appears, for all of us. We've been together on seven trips now, eight and a half years, we three. And the ship, too, of course, the *Mirandusa*. What a lot of numbers. One more: Simlon 12. The new sun.

It's not even born yet. And I, the sun-hater, the one whose tribe carry the pure *gene* of sun-hatred, I'm the creator who will wake this sun, as I always do.

Once, only God woke suns – with a word or a breath or a sigh.

I, and my kind, do it with a building program and a finger on a button. The last, while we watch (and cower) in protected darkness.

And Anka said, *Let there be light.*

Or, the button says it.

After topping up from Heth, I go out to do my space-walking, and then to check Planet 3, down below. Unlike the still unborn sun, the individual worlds of this system-in-waiting don't have names yet. Though Corvyra has nicknamed them Champion (1), Cuddles (2 – the planet that may not take) and Fatgirl (3). Fatgirl, fairly obviously, is the largest, and reads as the most Earth-type and lush specimen. There are other little chunks and balls and slivers circling about. Not to mention the pair of handsome moons already mecho-chemically lit. They have a duration of 300-400 Earth years, after which, if wanted, they and the others can be set up, and/or rekindled. But Simlon, like every sun that gets started, will last for millennia. The general consensus has it that these solarities will all exceed the span of the original Earth sun, which by now, as we know, is fading fast.

Outside the airlock I drift free, pause and gaze about me. Beautiful. Can you ever tire of such a sight? The limitless heaven of space, deepest black, or luminously translucent with galactic swarms or holo-gas clouds, the inflammatory litter of distant stars – other *suns*, natural or man-and-machine created.

After a while I drift on, around the bulk of *Mirandusa*. She's in good shape, just a minor repair finishing up on her left-frontal hull. I assess the outer work-machines. One is corroding slightly, so I send it back in and tap Main Comp for a replacement.

Far off something glitters as it dives through airlessness like a flung knife. Some meteor. You often see them. A little eye blinks in the ship's side, registering that the passer-by is harmless.

Before I joined the Space Corps I worked in various nocturnal jobs – night-gardens, aviation; I had, back then, another motive to govern my life. Afterwards ... space opened its glamorous arms to me instead. And here I am.

Time to go down now to Planet 3.

It's much easier, as they found out all those centuries ago, for my kind to do this. We don't need jet-boosters, or separate navigation, or suits of any sort, beyond the minimum of sensible protection. We don't need oxygen. We can levitate – or 'fly', as the earliest of our detractors described it. And since we can negate gravity for ourselves, we can also personally institute it. To lift away, select and use the correct direction, and once there anchor without fuss, is that very same thing they caught us doing back on Earth in the Dark Ages, when we took off like bats across the sky, or walked upside-down from castle towers to the ground. As for the oxygen, when they were wont to find us in our graves and coffins, we didn't breathe then – we 'lay like the dead'. Our sort *only* breathe to take nourishment from oxygenated air, just as we *drink* oxygen from the clarity of human blood. But we can shut off respiration without difficulty, or ill-effect. Especially when supplied by a rich diet. We do need the power of a ship, however. No-one wants to walk or fly that kind of distance. Anyhow, we can't travel faster than light. Despite the stories.

But you know all this.

Or not, I suppose. There's still a lot of ignorance about us. More no doubt since so many of us became employed by the Space Corps, and left Earth behind forever, to make our lives in endlessly long and lovely sleepless Night.

The basement apartment on Czechoslovus Street was half a mile down, remnant of an old bomb-shelter from the '20s. In summer, it grew boiling hot. The stone walls ran with pale green water, like exquisite sweat.

He looked up, when the young woman entered.

And she stopped, and stared back at him with enlarged dark eyes. She was scared, scared to *death*. She knew what he was, this – man? Did you call a male Vampire a *man*? Perhaps once. And since the RUSA Alliance of '35, such a variety of mixed ethnic types ... They said he was part Rus, part German, part Canad-François.

He was called Taras. No second name was to be used.

There was one window, a fake with softly grey-lighted glass. In this austere if silvery glow she took in his black hair and lens-dark eyes. He had wonderful musician's hands, and a slightly crooked nose.

'It was kind of you to visit,' he said. 'Anka – do I have your name correctly?'

'Yes.' Her voice sounded thin to her own ears.

'Please sit down, the red chair's quite comfortable. Or do you prefer the green chair? Some of my guests ...' he hesitated.

She said, brazen with nerves, 'They don't like the red chair because it's the colour of blood.'

'It isn't, nevertheless,' he flatly answered. 'Have you ever seen blood? I mean *looked* at it? There's no colour on Earth quite like it, Anka. But please, I don't mean to make you uncomfortable. Would you like a drink?'

'Water,' she said.

'Water.' He lowered his eyes and smiled slightly. 'You all want water.' He added with a strange and unsuitable urbanity, 'As if you can wash your insides clean of what I'll do. As if it will stain. It won't, Anka. I swear it.'

Anka sat in the red chair. She crossed her legs so the short skirt – short was the fashion that summer – rode up. He glanced, no more. 'I'll have a geneva then, thank you.'

Then he laughed. This was a fantastic laugh, like that of a very young man. But he was, she had been told, about 190 years of age. He looked barely forty. Lean and strong, elegant. Yet ... old too, in there behind the polarised dark of his eyes.

It was part of her Citizen Service, to be here. Others took up assistant teaching or nursing, or police work, or training-and-enactment in the Military Corps. But those options all entailed one full year stint. While to do *this*, help maintain the Vampire population – who were turning out to be so useful – was only a matter of three months with, if properly performed, a guaranteed financial increment.

Anka had not been afraid. She had believed this work was straightforward. By then no Vampire would harm you, for if such a thing occurred, they were subject to the force of a computerised and infallible law, equally paramount and non-negotiable. Any trespass would result in what was known as Expungement.

Why then this terror that assailed her the moment she was shown the image of Taras on a screen? And why too had she not backed out? There were always three choices of client. Why was she here? She was just 19.

He brought her the geneva and she drank it in a gulp. He sat down again, facing her.

'Well,' she said briskly. 'Let's get on.'

He cleared his throat. 'Anka, I don't want you if you're frightened.'

'Oh, aren't any of your – *visitors* ever nervous?'

'Yes, but there's a difference between uncertainty and terror.'

'I'm not terrified.'

'Thank you,' he said, rising, 'for calling. Don't worry, I'll be tactful with the agency. Nothing to concern you.'

She too flung up from her chair. 'No! I'm not going anywhere.' Her heart raced, she felt her face scald with passion – was it anger or panic? She heard herself cry in a wild pleading voice, 'Don't send me away –'

And then he laughed once more, a laugh quite unlike the first, soft and dark and very low. 'My God,' said Taras, 'you're in love with me. I didn't know I could still do that.'

'What?' But her mind was caught up on his use of the term 'God', now generally obsolete. Her mind could not get past the odd 'God' word. And so she began to feel what the rest of her was really saying. Anka wilted, now white as the electra-light inside the silver window.

And Taras came to her and took her in his arms and held her gently, inescapably, pressed the length of his body, and through the blackness of his shirt she felt the slow steady immortal thunder of his own almighty heart.

'My love,' he said into her hair, against her lips as he kissed them, 'I don't deserve such a beautiful gift, after so many years. My love,' he said. 'My Anka.'

While he drank directly from her neck, she started only vaguely at the initial deflowering sting. She was already falling down and down through the illimitable haven of *him*, of Taras. As if through the star-streamed heaven of space. Never so lost, never so found. Safe in abandon. Like death. Better even than sex (even the glorious sex they two would also partner in), this psychic orgasm of consensual surrender.

There's a painting you can see in the Venezi-Gifford Gallery, New Kroy, or else reproduced here and there in various art books or dealers' on-screen catalogues. It's called *Planting Out the Sheaves*, and is a cute enough take on old Earth-west farming techniques, as applied to the 'seeding' of about-to-be-solar-system planets. (I hope that's helpful, and not patronising, to suggest it might assist you to get some idea of how I work out here, how it looks, vertically levitate-flying across the wide open plains and soaring mountainsides, attended by my flock of clever machines. Some of the little robots and autohands are well-reproduced in this painting, particularly the tiny drivers that prepare the ground ahead and below. The male figure on the canvas, the painted Vampire overseer-farmer, of course, is romanticised to an ultimate degree. He looks like a cross between some gorgeous Earth Pre-Raphaelite saint and one of their 21st Century superheroes, and his golden hair flows behind him as he strides the midnight airlessness, mysteriously lit by chemo-mech moons.)

I travel usually about three metres above the surface. Sometimes I go up a bit higher, or dip down, more closely to inspect what the machines are doing. Occasionally I call them off one area, or send them to another they've missed. Robotics isn't perfect, even now. Perhaps a good thing, or would any of us have a job out here at all? Probably. There's still enough human life in most of our genes to assess terrain and feasibility with – as they now call it – psycho-voyance. (Human intuition, I believe that means.)

Planet 3 is vast. The cliffs and mountains are colossal, evidence of thinned atmosphere even in the era of the first sun. Waterless seabeds, and the gigantic arteries of dead rivers, fissure its surface. The moons softly shine on all this; when they vanish to the planet's far side, the stars render light. But I can see in total darkness.

Planet 2 (Corvyra's Cuddles) is far less featured than 3 (Fatgirl). And Planet 1 (Champion) is mostly a defunct ocean. But oh, we'll change all that. I've already seen to it there are myriad atoms and organisms peri-dormantly at work on Planet 1. Even Cuddles has a chance.

Inevitably, since building, I've checked the sun, too, during the months we've been here. An unlit solar-disc is no problem for my kind. And when that alters, *Mirandusa*, and all of us, Vampire, Bee-Dees, robot crew, Main Comp, will be stood way off. Down in her jet-black chamber, like a nice cosy tomb, Anka will only watch her viewer. And what will I see? A vacant lot, where suddenly a gargantuan explosion happens: it is impressively spectacular, aqua, emerald, scarlet. And then, behind the display, a tiny fiery yellow dot is burning through, the eye of Things to Come …

And that's the new sun alight.

One question is often asked, despite the images freely available. *Until ignition, what does a solarity – a constructed sun – look like?*

Picture a huge spider's web spun from black sapphire, with sapphire rods, lobes and weird antennae poking out of it. It hangs there, this exquisite mechanised chemecular skeleton, immobile, to all intents and purposes quiescent, purposeless. Till I press that magic button.

Maybe you see a psychological analogy … The seemingly moribund solar disc, the solarity Simlon 12. Inert – then galvanised awake, on fire, radiating and incinerous, *alive*. But no. That isn't like Vampiric life.

Do you know what it's like? Like memories that don't fit anymore, that won't lie still. Like old love that is dead and mummified to corundum, but never can die because, after however many million centuries of forgetting, a moment's recollected whisper or touch will raise it from the grave, and bring it back to searing, quenchless flame.

We have a communal evening on the ship later. I say evening, since the time-pieces aboard mark solar planet time in the 'human' crew areas. Corvyra and Heth eat steaks and green apples from the store, and drink white champagne. I eat and drink my synth versions of those items, all of which carry my essential nutrient, even in the alcohol.

After, we watch an old movie, I forget what it was. C and H pay little attention either, necking like a couple of kids. (I don't mind this. Why should I? I can have sex with Heth whenever I think I'll enjoy it.) When they go off together to combine, machines neatly tidy the room.

Back in my cabin I update my work-journal and send it off to the receptors at New Kroy.

I sit looking out of the port, watching the three planets infinitesimally turn, and the moons setting over their shoulders. My kind can see that sort of motion, just as we do the circling hands on an old clock.

And if there's no sunrise to hide from, we never need sleep. Sleep is only our massive all-over shut-down in the face of an untenable foe – sunlight. So out here in Endless Night, we have a lot of extra time. Just what humans constantly say they crave.

But *that* much time needs to get filled.

That much time.

You think you'll never have enough. But then, you do.

She had been his only constant 'partner' for a year, when they decided that he would 'turn' her. Anka had known for several months that this was what she wanted most.

Taras then spoke very seriously to her, with an intense and almost paternal manner he sometimes assumed – which, by then, made her insanely and amusedly happy. She knew she could change him back into a 35-year-old boy in seconds, into a sort of pantherine demiurge even. But she listened very carefully.

'No,' Anka said. 'I don't want to become what *you* are, for any of those reasons – longevity, strength – the power of levitating – God knows –' (By then too she had caught his habit of profaning 'God'.) 'I'd probably get vertigo – *no*, don't interrupt me, Taras. I heard you out. But I *know* these things, and you know I don't give a *fuck* –' (also an obsolete obscenity, but it had made him smile) '– I want to be what you are because of what I feel about you, for you – I want to live as you do. I want to – to –'

'To *be* me?' he asked her quietly. 'The absolute in possession?'

'No, no. *Surely* you must understand?'

She was only 20, and her eyes had filled with tears. Of course, it had been she who had instigated the conversation. He said to her, a decade afterward, that *he* could not have presumed. At the time he said, now, gravely, 'You realise that I shall need other partners for blood? As indeed, sweetheart, will you.'

'Yes, naturally I know that too.'

'Will it offend you? Hurt you?'

'No,' she said firmly. 'So long as we stay lovers. More importantly, so long as we still have *this.*'

At which he lowered his eyes, that nearly feminine response he sometimes gave her. 'My kind, *our* kind if you join us, live a great while. Maybe not forever, but for centuries. And we do age a little, too. You're 20, Anka. Perhaps in 150 years you'll appear to be 30, 35. But inside, my love, you'll have the experience and the *passions* of a woman far older. Will you still want me? Don't forget, I'll grow older too, and in both those same ways.'

But at this she laughed. 'Does that mean you agree, then? Yes?'

The City Corps was pleased as well. They generally let such liaisons as hers with Taras continue well over term, in the hopes of a human deciding to 'turn'. Vampires, now collated as they had been for some 27 years into the mortal Life-Way, were proving virtually hourly of more value, their practical scope and physical talents far exceeding those of the best of mankind. So, there was no difficulty, and indeed a legal civil ceremony took place, reminding Anka of an old-fashioned marriage, and followed by a party.

Nor was she afraid of what had come to be called D & R (Death and Resurrection). She fell asleep inside the fortress circle of his arms, and woke into the dawn of dark without a solitary regret.

Tonight, that is *ship*'s-night, I alone look at Anka in the mirror.

I know her pretty well after all this time, that dark-eyed, youngish woman of 212. So why look? Because, it sometimes seems to me, on these long nights amid the Endless Night, that I have an actual look of *him.* Of Taras. I dyed my hair black once, to enhance this illusion. That was about 17 years after we parted. But strangely – or logically perhaps – to me I seemed *less* like him, then. They say too, don't they, people (even un-people?) who stay connected, come to resemble each other. Even people who don't live together, as he and I never did. Yet are close, in *some* way together, a great while.

Down the corridors of the *Mirandusa* the other lovers are making their love. Different, we know, from the mere ecstatic delights of really good sex, the sort I get with Heth, and he with me. I'm fond of them, my Bee-Dees; it's more than sustenance. We three have grown together too, I suppose, over the eight and a half years we've shared this peripatetic life. I remember once, one of the hull shields malfunctioned during a meteor storm. We worked with the machines, Corvyra, Heth and I, and got the thing patched up and saved our skins. And when it was all over, the three of us ran together, thoughtless as water-drops on a pane, there in the control room, under the Main Comp's big blue benign maternal eye, and held each other close. Only for a moment. But it marks out that hour for Corvyra and Heth, for me, too. We are our own type of family. I never had one before I knew them. And with Taras, evidently, with him – 'God' knows what unnamable entity we two formed. But those uncountable hours were marked indelibly. And it lasted. It lasted all of 71 years. This cabin, mine, is the only room that ever sees me cry now. I'll cry tonight.

Chasing the moons over the saucer-rim of a world, Planet 1, the Champion. The exhilaration of it – to fly – yes, fly. I'm flying – skimming the wide lake of black space with its shimmers and shallow skerries of rippling particles, gaseous flumes – down to the sunless seabed, with canyons deep as any philosopher's abyss, and all of it now a fallow field that, with the coming of great Light, may – will – must blossom, bloom and grow. In a quadrennium, less, a fast-built home for humans, as they range forever outward through the stars.

But from here the stars aren't suns. They're friendly sprigs of neon hung in the night sky. And over there the big moon at full, and the smaller crescent that the planet's shadow makes, even though the lunar fire is inside.

Where I've set down I stand, though my personally-engendered gravity already means I could run over the surface. I'll be careful anyway, not to disturb the plantings.

Because I don't breathe, there's no waver to the vistas of space or landmass.

Despite the lack of breath, or air, a faint esoteric scent comes to me. The odour of an ancient past. The planet's. My own.

I walk the world.

And through my mind my life spills, like a phantom of the planet's ocean. My days, my years. And so I come again to Taras, and begin with and am *with* Taras, and at last, as it has to, the tide reaches its height, and brings to me that ultimate month we were together, when he told me we should part.

It wasn't, he said, so tenderly and kindly, that he had ceased to love me, nor, he said, did he think I had yet grown tired of him. There was no other he wanted, or thought that *I* did. But this had been enough, he said. What, *what* did that mean? – I cried to him. Enough? *Enough?* But he only repeated, in his wonderful dark voice, the same litany. We must leave each other and go our separate ways. We must do it before our union, our love – if I preferred that name – was stale. What we had had, still had, must never be spoiled by becoming *less*.

I raged and begged. I mocked him. He said no more. I didn't believe he had not found another he liked better than me. Much farther on, knowing him as I had, I *did* believe, however. There had been no replacement. Which made what happened worse. By the month's finish I reckoned he had come around. I had arranged quite ordinarily to see him the next day, to which he seemed to agree. But when I went to his apartment, he was gone. It's unachievable, to trace our kind, as you may be aware, if they legally refuse it. He did, it seems, so refuse. I never saw him, my Vampire lover, ever again. Except, you'll guess, in my mind, the high tide of memory, by such and similar means.

If he lives still, or is dead, I don't, I never shall, know.

And now –

Anka discovered the cave in the ravine wall almost inadvertently; her thoughts had been otherwise engaged. A warped black stalagmite pillar guarded the entrance.

Inside, lightglow arrested and astonished her.

With enormous care, she moved forward. The roof of the cave was quite high, and then the sides of it opened out. A sheer black chamber, bright at the centre with a chem-burner ... reddish light.

There were other things in the cave, which plainly was being used as a sort of living-room. A rock – a *chair?* – on one side of the burner. (How had it been brought here?) A second chair waited back in the shadows. Moisture gleamed on the walls, but the scent in the cave was wholesome and quite dry.

He stood behind the light. A tall silhouette.

Having no breath to catch, her ribs involuntarily convulse as she catches it. Vacuum, for a split second, sucks at Anka's lungs. She begins to double over, though already her Vampire stamina has corrected the silly physical mistake. And then from dark through light to dark he springs toward her, grips her – inexorable, gentle – in a hold that paralyses with its *knownness*.

'How can you be here?' she mutters into the shoulder of his coat. 'Have I gone mad?'

She can speak without breath. She has needed to.

'Oh, my love,' he says, in such a tired, sad, *gladdened* voice. 'We – our kind – can go anywhere, do anything – didn't I teach you that?'

Then she's herself again, the older wiser Anka he warned her of and promised, in the time before he left her. She straightens and stares up into his face. The face of Taras.

He is real, sentient. *He* is older. Now his hair is iced silver, his face everywhere finely lined. He looks ... like a beautiful, hale, thin, indomitable man, perhaps 65, 67. His teeth – what else? – are flawless. His black eyes clear as space itself inside a lens. And he has not let her go.

He says, 'We'll drink geneva. Then.'

'Then,' she answers. 'Then.'

Their entity formed, body to body, mouth to mouth, there could be, and was, no margin or necessity for any explanation or debate, no other element but this love, this truth, vaster than a world, more infinite than time. Life after death.

I cry my heart out, as I was aware I should. They leave me to myself, my Blood-Donors. My work is in-date, the program on target. They've learnt, after a few hours I'll be back to normal. This has happened before.

I loved him so much, Taras. I'll always love him like that. A dead coal in my guts that flares up like an igniting sun, just as Simlon will, in seven more months.

No-one can be blamed for their dreams. Particularly not us, the *Vampire* kind. Out here, in perpetual darkness where we never need to sleep ... *our* dreams take on a specialised waking form. We *hear* them approach, like footsteps, but can't hold them off. Conveyed by an *awake* consciousness, they have a potency, a *realness* as vital – more – than reality itself. Our dreams come *true*. While they last. And when they're done, what's left – is cobwebs. Dust.

Tonight we were lovers again, Taras and Anka. And I was alive as never otherwise I shall be, even if my body lasts forever.

This dream visits me quite often. I dread it. I welcome it. I pray to God it will come back.

But now, on and on, I shed my tears.

In Endless Night, the ghost of lost love shines so brightly it fades the stars. Such fire – is *beyond* the sun.

ON REFLECTION
THE EPILOGUE

You could not, now, really tell one horizon from the other. As you could not really tell the past from the future. The Earth … Centuries have passed. Then more than centuries. The sun, some while back, did the most extraordinary and vulgar thing, rather like an ill-treated and resultantly appalling child determined to ruin the adults' party. It had burnt and gnawed the Earth's globe, and then gone hysterically nova – but an *aborted* nova. It was, and is, something rare, this, hardly documented. A vast detonation that did not, contrary to expectation, destroy the immediate planets, and that inflicted true arson only on one, the Earth again, and that not by any means entire.

Aeonids after, when the sun was tiny if still vaguely alight, like a flickering and dim red electric bulb from a long lost era, the Earth planet remained, although it was not, and is not, naturally, as ever it had been, but 'Fried to a crisp' someone has said, using fashionably inexplicable historic jargon.

The other remaining orbs of the solar system that had survived (Mercury and Neptune were long gone due to other, antique cosmic disasters) had had by then, for enormous ages, their own individual and created man-made suns.

Nobody any more needed the light of the actual solar disc. So let it be a red bulb till it flickered out. 'Granny' some of them named it, a little unconvincingly, since by now human grannies of many hundred years are normally glamorous and sprightly.

A story soon rose though, like a ghostly moth from the cupboards of travellers' tales, the yarns of astronauts and other space-voyagers.

One such man, going down to take a closer look at the scorched and ended Earth had, while wandering across the sands that had covered all its surface, stumbled – or rather the boot of his astrosuit had – on a piece of what, on inspection, seemed to be an ancient mirror. 'Something the Victorian English might have made,' he was later said to have said. 'Or, could have been older – old as the Pyramids of Eg².' He had peered into it, too, but been unable to catch any sort of reflection under the dull sun-ray, and through the immutably polarised visor of his suit. This man was part of a three-man expedition. That night, back in their shuttle, the *Corkillus*, something very weird happened. Or so the visitors declared. During the depth of the sun-gone night, the astrosuit the man who had found the mirror had worn – had got up, by itself, and started to blunder about the small vessel.

It seemed to be searching for something. The mirror fragment? Perhaps for that: it transpired the man who had found it had after all mislaid it again before re-entering the shuttle.

Finally the suit was crashing against the airlock, making strange grunting sounds. It seemed, the travellers said later, as if it 'needed to go outside'! And well, what else, eventually they opened up the doors and let it free. Off it blundered, on two suit-feet, over the surface of the extinct world. Luckily the ship carried spare suits.

Inside half an hour, the suit had vanished from all view; even the mechanical optics of the shuttle failed to find it. Next morning, the three men and their shuttle took off for Mars, their home base.

Some believed the story, when told. Most did not believe it. Once science fiction became true, as the famous Professor Gullgren once phrased it, the best course was to disbelieve almost every word.

Now, if one stands upon the carapace of any of the surviving planets, Mars, Jupiter, Vulcan, Venus, Orcar (each lit by their own private artificial sun), a view is still feasible of the deceased mother globe, dead Earth, though from these far-off worlds she is small, a single dull overweight star. (In one era she seemed bigger – was bigger? – and shone blue: her seas. No longer. Today she is faded tawny or grey: the sand.)

When sand burns it makes glass. That is how glass was made, in the archaeological past. And the sands of Earth have burned and re-burned, and fused by now. The partial nova saw to that. The idea that anyone located a mirror there, ever, springs rather foolishly one surmises from this fact.

---

² Egypt.

328

Although, of course, if the covering of the entire Earth is, at last, a mirror, then we – even from this vast distance – will be reflected in it. There was a superstition at one time. Vampires did not reflect in mirrors. (You will have heard of vampires? If not, please see the Iconic Reference on warp-page 00I0XY.) Or, otherwise, the vampire legend implied that certain mirrors were themselves vampires, and thus to reflect there – en-vampirised any person or thing so to do.

Peculiar, the ideas and notions of bygone days. And of now. The Earth's ever-changing face has become a mirror? But there is nothing to fear. Not anymore. Since truth has become fiction.

And fiction – truth.

ABOUT THE AUTHOR

Tanith Lee was born in North London (UK) in 1947. Because her parents were professional dancers (ballroom, Latin American) and had to live where the work was, she attended a number of truly terrible schools, and didn't learn to read – she is also dyslexic – until almost age 8. And then only because her father taught her. This opened the world of books to Lee, and by 9 she was writing. After much better education at a grammar school, Lee went on to work in a library. This was followed by various other jobs – shop assistant, waitress, clerk – plus a year at art college when she was 25-26. In 1974 this mosaic ended when DAW Books of America, under the leadership of Donald A Wollheim, bought and published Lee's The Birthgrave, and thereafter 26 of her novels and collections.

Since then Lee has written around 90 books, and approaching 300 short stories. 4 of her radio plays have been broadcast by the BBC; she also wrote 2 episodes ('Sarcophagus' and 'Sand') for the TV series Blake's 7. Some of her stories regularly get read on Radio 7.

Lee writes in many styles in and across many genres, including Horror, SF and Fantasy, Historical, Detective, Contemporary-Psychological, Children and Young Adult. Her preoccupation, though, is always people.

In 1992 she married the writer-artist-photographer John Kaiine, her companion since 1987. They live on the Sussex Weald, near the sea, in a house full of books and plants, with two black and white overlords called cats.

COPYRIGHT DETAILS

OTHER TELOS TITLES

GRAHAM MASTERTON
RULES OF DUEL
THE DJINN

SAM STONE

THE JINX CHRONICLES
1: JINX TOWN
2: JINX MAGIC (Autumn 2015)
3: JINX BOUND (Autumn 2016)

KAT LIGHTFOOT MYSTERIES
1: ZOMBIES AT TIFFANY'S
2: KAT ON A HOT TIN AIRSHIP
3: WHAT'S DEAD PUSSYKAT
4: KAT OF GREEN TENTACLES (Autumn 2015)

THE DARKNESS WITHIN: FINAL CUT
ZOMBIES IN NEW YORK AND OTHER BLOODY JOTTINGS

RAVEN DANE
ABSINTHE & ARSENIC
DEATH'S DARK WINGS

KING OF ALL THE DEAD by STEVE LOCKLEY & PAUL LEWIS

THE HUMAN ABSTRACT by GEORGE MANN

BREATHE by CHRISTOPHER FOWLER
The Office meets *Night of the Living Dead*.

HOUDINI'S LAST ILLUSION by STEVE SAVILE

ALICE'S JOURNEY BEYOND THE MOON by R J CARTER

APPROACHING OMEGA by ERIC BROWN

VALLEY OF LIGHTS by STEPHEN GALLAGHER

PRETTY YOUNG THINGS by DOMINIC MCDONAGH

A MANHATTAN GHOST STORY by T M WRIGHT

FORCE MAJEURE by DANIEL O'MAHONY

BLACK TIDE by DEL STONE JR

DOCTOR TRIPPS: KAIJU COCKTAIL by KIT COX

SPECTRE by STEPHEN LAWS

CAPTAINS STUPENDOUS by RHYS HUGHES

HEALTH AND SPIRIT

CELTIC SPELLS by ALLISON BELDON-SMITH and MARY BAKER
A year in the life of a Modern Welsh Witch
This attractively-presented book, illustrated with full-colour photographs
throughout, celebrates the beauty of the Welsh countryside, and the
pleasure of life and nature in balance. The spells and meditations
contained within are designed to be simple to carry out and will enrich
your thinking and appreciation of nature, of friends, of love and of life.

ROMANTIC ENCOUNTERS

JULIETTE BENZONI
1: CATHERINE: ONE LOVE IS ENOUGH
2: CATHERINE
3: BELLE CATHERINE
4: CATHERINE: HER GREAT JOURNEY
5: CATHERINE: A TIME FOR LOVE
6: A TRAP FOR CATHERINE
7: CATHERINE: THE LADY OF MONTSALVY

HELEN MCCABE
A GARDEN FAIR
HIGHWAY TO FEAR
HOSTAGE TO LOVE
IN SEARCH OF LOVE
LOVE IN HIDING
THE HOUSE ON THE MOUNTAIN
THE PRICE OF LOVE
WHEN LOVE RIDES OUT

EROTICA

AWAKENING JESSICA by ATHENA MICHAELS

BYTE ME by ROBERTA STEELE

CRIME

PRISCILLA MASTERS
WINDING UP THE SERPENT
CATCH THE FALLEN SPARROW
A WREATH FOR MY SISTER
AND NONE SHALL SLEEP
SCARING CROWS
EMBROIDERING SHROUDS

MIKE RIPLEY
JUST ANOTHER ANGEL
ANGEL TOUCH
ANGEL HUNT
ANGEL ON THE INSIDE
ANGEL CONFIDENTIAL
ANGEL CITY
ANGELS IN ARMS
FAMILY OF ANGELS
BOOTLEGGED ANGEL
THAT ANGEL LOOK
LIGHTS, CAMERA, ANGEL
ANGEL UNDERGROUND

ANDREW PUCKETT
BLOODHOUND
DESOLATION POINT
SHADOWS BEHIND A SCREEN

ANDREW HOOK
THE IMMORTALISTS
CHURCH OF WIRE

TONY RICHARDS
THE DESERT KEEPS ITS DEAD

OTHER CRIME
THE LONG, BIG KISS GOODBYE
by SCOTT MONTGOMERY

EVGENY GRIDDNEFF
A STINK IN THE TALE

HANK JANSON
TORMENT
WOMEN HATE TILL DEATH
SOME LOOK BETTER DEAD
SKIRTS BRING ME SORROW
WHEN DAMES GET TOUGH
ACCUSED
KILLER
FRAILS CAN BE SO TOUGH
BROADS DON'T SCARE EASY
KILL HER IF YOU CAN
LILIES FOR MY LOVELY
BLONDE ON THE SPOT
THIS WOMAN IS DEATH
THE LADY HAS A SCAR

NON-FICTION
THE TRIALS OF HANK JANSON
by STEVE HOLLAND

TELOS PUBLISHING
Email: orders@telos.co.uk
Web: www.telos.co.uk

To order copies of any Telos books, please visit our website where there are
full details of all titles and facilities for worldwide credit card online
ordering, as well as occasional special offers.

Made in the USA
Charleston, SC
28 March 2015